A Novel

The
LAST
LETTER

KATHLEEN SHOOP

shoop@kshoop.com
Kshoop.com

Cover design: Monica Gurevich/Julie Metz Ltd.
Cover photo © fotosearch

ISBN: 1456347209
ISBN-13: 9781456347208
Library of Congress Control Number: 2010916960

To Bill

Chapter 1

1905
Des Moines, Iowa

Katherine rubbed the second knuckle of her pinky finger—the spot where it had been amputated nearly two decades before. The scarred wound pulsed with each heartbeat as her mind flashed through the events that led to its removal. Was it possible for an infection to form inside an old sore?

Don't think about it. Just do your work.

She snatched the clump of metal from the stone saucer and scrubbed the iron pot as though issuing it punishment. She caught her forefinger on blackened beans. *Damn.* She sucked on the nail. With her free hand she yanked the plug from the soapstone sink then opened the back door. Hot, thick wind brushed her cheeks and forced her eyes closed as she yanked the rope that made the dinner bell clang.

With a jerk of her hip she booted the door closed and wiped her hands on the gravy-splattered apron that draped her body. A crash came from the front of the house. A ball through the window? Another wrestling match over the last "up" at bat? She dashed toward the foyer to see what her children were up to.

1

She tripped over the edge of the carpet and caught her balance, gaping at the sight. There on the floor was her husband, Aleksey, kneeling over her sister Yale. A shattered flow-blue vase lay scattered around them.

Yale burped sending a burst of gin-scented breath upward.

Katherine recoiled as the odor hit her nose. "She's *drunk*? Take her to my mother's!"

Aleksey looked up, his face strained. "Just help…"

She couldn't handle Yale. Not right then. She turned and headed back toward the kitchen. Their mother would have to rescue Yale this time. As though being scolded from afar, her missing finger throbbed again, like a knife scraping at the marrow deep inside her bones the pain forced her to stop. Her mother hadn't been there when she lost the finger. Her mother was never where she was supposed to be.

Katherine looked over her shoulder at the pair on the floor and clutched her hand against her chest. Yale gurgled, growing pale grey. Aleksey hoisted her and carried her to the couch.

She looked down at her smarting hand, against her heart, and clarity took over. It wasn't Yale's fault she was fragile. She'd been born that way. *She's your sister. Do something.* She puffed out her cheeks with air and then released it. Her anger receded taking the throbbing pulse in her hand with it.

She grabbed a pot of hydrangeas from a side-table and ran out the front door, shook the billowy, blue flowers out of the pot sending coal-black dirt splashing over the wood planks.

Back in the house she slid onto the couch, Yale's head in her lap, pot perched on the floor to catch the vomit. Aleksey paced in front of the women.

"She was at Sweeny's. *Alone.* Men, tossing her back and forth like a billiard ball. I barely…"

Katherine covered her mouth. She had enough of her mother's failures. "I knew this kind of thing would happen. And, now—"

"She's your *sister* and I know you love them even if you say you don't care. Your mother's *dying*. We have to help them." Aleksey's jaw tensed. Katherine bit the inside of her cheek, struck by his rare disapproval of her.

"You can't ignore this one more minute," Aleksey said, "*seventeen* years is long enough to forgive."

Without warning, Yale bucked forward and vomited, spackling Katherine with booze-scented chunks before passing out again. Tears gathered in her eyes. Hand quivering, she swiped a chunk from her chin with the back of her hand then smoothed Yale's black hair off her pale, clammy forehead.

She gulped and gritted her teeth. "If Mother can't take care of Yale, then it's time for the institution." The words were sour in Katherine's mouth, yet she couldn't stop them from forming, from hanging in the air, the spitefulness making Aleksey break her gaze.

Aleksey pulled the pot from between Katherine's feet and held it near Yale as she started to gag again. "Yale can stay here. They both can."

Katherine rocked Yale, not wanting to let her go, but knowing she had to hold her mother accountable. She was the *mother* after all. She shook her head and slid Yale off her lap, patting her head as she stood.

Aleksey rolled Yale to her side as she heaved into the pot. "I'll call Mother," she said heading toward the stairs.

"I recall a time," Aleksey said as he held Yale like she was one of his own, "when you called your mother, Mama, and the word swelled with adoration."

Katherine turned from the bottom step, her posture straight and sure, like she was headed to dinner and a play rather than to scrape someone's vomit from her skin. She gripped the banister trying to channel the mish-mash of emotion into the wood rather than feel it.

"I don't recall that. Calling her Mama, feeling warmth in the word. I don't recall it a bit." And with that she trudged upstairs to peel off the rancid clothes and to stifle the rotten feelings that always materialized upon the sight of her family, drunk or not.

Chapter 2

1887
Dakota Territory

"**M**ama?"

Jeanie jumped at her daughter's thin voice. Katherine lay below her in tall sinuous grasses that bent with the wind, covering and uncovering her with each shifting gust.

"I'm hot and tired and when will Father be back?" Katherine rose up on her elbows. "I understand complaining is like an ice-pick in your ear, but I'm plum hot and plum parched and tired of waiting." She jerked a blade of grass from the ground and bit on it.

Jeanie nodded and rubbed her belly. She was pregnant but hadn't told anyone. Cramps pulled inside her pelvis. Would she lose this one? Nervous, she grabbed for the fat pearls that used to decorate her neck and smacked her tongue off the roof of her arid mouth.

She hacked up a clump of phlegm, turned her back to Katherine and spit it into the air. A sudden blast of air blew the green mucus back, landing on her skirt. Hands spread up to the sky, she stared at the ugly splotch marveling at how quickly her life had transformed. She would never have believed it possible before the scandal hit her own family.

With clenched teeth she wrenched a corner of her petticoat from under the skirt to wipe away the lumpy secretion. Her thoughts tripped over each other. Jeanie would not let doubt linger, mix with fear and paralyze her. She would be sure the family re-grew their fortune, that they reclaimed their contentment, their name, their everything. If only Frank were more reliable. Damn Frank was never where he was supposed to be.

Arms wrapped across her body, Jeanie tapped her silk-shoed foot. They should head for water, but she didn't think that was prudent. She'd heard people could lose direction quickly in such expansive land. That frightened her, not being in control, but she also thought perhaps the people who ended up wandering the prairie lost were simply not that smart or were careless. Slowly, as she ran her fingers down the front of her swelling throat, each scratchy swallow symbolized the wagonload of errors Jeanie had made and she started to understand that intelligence and survival did not always walk together.

Damn him. Five hours. They'd waited long enough for Frank. She pushed away the rising tears that grew from thinking of the mess her father and darling husband had made for them. Be brave.

They needed to take action or they'd prune from the inside out.

"Let's head for water." Jeanie clasped Katherine's hand and pulled her to standing. *We can do this*, Jeanie thought. Frank had tied red sashes around taller bushes that were scattered in the direction of the well. Katherine wiggled free of her mother's grasp and raced—as much as a girl could dart through grasses that whapped at her chest—over the land.

"Stay close!" Jeanie stopped and pulled her foot off the ground. She sucked back her breath as her slim-heeled shoes dug into her ankles. Katherine looked up from ahead, waving a bunch of purple prairie crocus over her head at Jeanie.

Jeanie turned to see how far they'd moved from the wagon. She could only see the tip of the white canvas that arched over it. She looked back in the direction of the well, of Katherine. The wind stilled. The sudden hush was heavy. The absence of Katherine's lavender bonnet sent blood flashing through her veins.

"Katherine?" *She must be pulling more flowers,* Jeanie thought and rose to her tiptoes. "Katherine?"

Jeanie looked back at the wagon.

"Katherine!" Jeanie stomped some of the grass hoping the depressed sections would somehow stick out amidst the chunky high grass when they needed to return.

"Katherine!" Jeanie's voice cracked. She cleared her throat and shouted again. No answer. She shivered then clenched her skirt and hiked it up, thundering in the direction of Katherine.

KatherineKatherineKatherineKatherine! Bolting through the grasses, the wind swelled, it pushed Jeanie back as she pressed forward, turning her shouts back at her, filling her ears with her own words as she strained to hear a reply.

Jeanie stopped as though slamming into a wall, swallowing loud breaths hoping the silence would allow Katherine's voice to hit her ears. Nothing. She ran again, right out of her luxurious, city-shoes, while cursing the mass of skirts and crinoline that swallowed her legs. Her feet slammed over the dirt.

The grasses tangled around her ankles, tripping her. Jeanie scrambled back to her feet and took three steps before taking one right off the edge of the earth. She plummeted into water. A pond. Jeanie stood and spit out foamy, beer-colored water. At least she could touch bottom.

"Katthhh-errrrr—ine!" She slogged through the waist deep water, her attention nowhere and everywhere at once. The sounds of splashing and choking finally made Jeanie focus on one area of the pond. She shot around a bend in the bank to see Katherine's face go under the water taking what little wind Jeanie had left in her lungs away.

Katherine shot back up. "Mama, Mama!" She dropped back under.

Jeanie lunged and groped for Katherine as the bottom of the pond fell away. Jeanie treaded water, the skirts strangling her efforts to be efficient. A bit further! The bottom must be shallow or Katherine couldn't have bounced up as she had.

But the bottom didn't rise up and Jeanie choked on grainy water. She burst forward on her stomach, taking an arm-stroke, her feet scrounging for the bottom. Her face sunk under the surface.

We're going to die, Jeanie thought. Frank would never find them. Her boys!

Bubbles appeared in front of Jeanie and she reached through the murky water for Katherine. Finally, hands grabbed back, gripping Jeanie's. She could feel every precious finger threaded through hers. Jeanie jerked Katherine into her body, lumbered toward the bank then shoved the floppy girl up onto it. Katherine lay on the grass, hacking and inhaling so deep that she folded over, gagging. Jeanie squirmed out and pulled Katherine across her lap, thumping her back until there was nothing left but empty heaves.

Silent tears camouflaged by stale, pond water warmed Jeanie's cheeks. Her hand shook as she pushed Katherine's matted hair away from her eyes, rocking her.

"We'll be fine, Katherine. We'll build a life and start over and be happy. We will. Believe it deep inside your very young bones."

Katherine snuffled then blew her nose in her filthy, sodden skirt. Her voice squeaked. "Oh, Mama." Katherine burrowed into Jeanie's chest and curled into a ball in her lap.

Jeanie wiped Katherine's mouth with the edge of her skirt, streaking mud across her cheek. She used her thumb to clean away the muck. Her daughter in need was all that kept Jeanie from rolling into a ball herself.

"My, my. We'll be fine," Jeanie said. And as her heart fell back into its normal rhythms heavy exhaustion braced her. "We'll enjoy the sunshine all the more if we've had a few shadows first. Right?

That's right." Jeanie knew those words sounded ridiculous in light of all they'd been through, but still they dribbled out of her mouth, as though simply discussing a broken bit of Limoges.

Katherine nodded into her mother's chest. Jeanie shuddered, a leaden tumor of dread swelled in her gut. She wouldn't let it settle there.

"Shush, shush, little one," Jeanie kissed her cheeks. If Katherine and she lived through that they could live through anything. The pond event, as it came to be in Jeanie's mind, was evidence they'd paid a price and would be free to accept all the treasures the prairie offered from that point forward.

"Are you crying Mama?"

Jeanie forced a smile then looked into Katherine's upturned face. "We're *not* crying people." Her fingers quivered as she tucked the stiff chestnut tendrils into Katherine's bonnet. "Besides there's nothing to cry about."

Katherine gripped her mother tighter. "I knew you'd save us, Mama. Even in Des Moines, I knew that no matter what, *you* could save us."

Jeanie hugged Katherine close hiding the splintered confidence she knew must be creased into her face. What did Katherine know? She *couldn't* know the details of their disgrace. She must have simply picked up on the weightiness of their leaving the family home for this—this nothingness.

Jeanie squeezed her eyes shut, trying to find the strength inside her. She would not fake her self-assurance. She believed that kind of thing lived inside a person's skin, never really leaving, even if it did weaken from time to time. Yes, Jeanie told herself, she was the same person she had been three weeks before. Losing everything she owned didn't mean she had to lose herself.

Jeanie stood at the edge of the pond and inventoried her most recent losses: impractical shoes she shouldn't have been wearing anyway; silver chatelaine that held her pen, paper, and watch; pride. Well, no, she was determined to salvage her self-respect. She clutched her waist with both hands, considering their options, then pulled Katherine to her feet.

"This standing pond water will poison us. We'll continue to the well."

Katherine patted her mother's back then bent over to pluck some prairie grass from the ground.

The wooly sunrays seemed to lower onto their heads rather than move further away, settling into the west. Their dresses dried crisp—the pond-water debris acted as a starch—while the skirts underneath remained moist and mealy.

Jeanie wiggled her toes. They burned inside the holey stockings.

"Our new home will have a spring house, right Mama? Icy, fresh spring water?"

"I'm afraid, no, little lamb."

"Oh *gaaaa-loshes*," Katherine said.

Jeanie slung her arm around Katherine. "Let me think for a moment, Darling."

The endless land looked the same though not familiar, appearing perfectly flat, though housing hidden rises in land and gaping holes that were obvious only after it was too late. All Jeanie could remember was running straight to the spot that ended up being a pond. Her heart thudded hard again reminding her she had no control of her existence.

A sob rumbled inside Jeanie, wracking her body, forcing an obnoxious, weak moan to ooze from her clenched lips. *Toughen up*. She pushed her shoulders down as her throat swelled around another rising sob.

Katherine pushed a piece of grass upward, offering it to Jeanie to chew on. "You said you came around a bend, Mama."

Jeanie closed her fingers over the blade of grass and wiped her mouth with the back of her hand. "We'll curve back around to get to the point where we can head straight back toward the wagon. Then we'll know where the well is from there."

They held hands, traipsed around the edge of the pond and rose up a gentle hill. From there, they could see a tree. Just one. Tall, yet knobby, as though surrendering to death a bit. But, even in its contorted form, Jeanie could see its vibrant green foliage and white blooms.

Katherine pointed. "I forgot the world had trees."

"Yes."

"I'm thirsty Mama."

"Don't feel out of spirits. We'll find the well. Better to ignore the thirst until then." Jeanie wished she could take her own advice but she'd felt parched since she first perched atop the wagon seat three days before.

Katherine squeezed Jeanie's hand three times saying "I love you" with the gesture. Jeanie squeezed back to say the same then looked away from the tree into nothingness.

They hugged the edge of the pond, following the bends back to the spot where Jeanie's foot caught the cusp of the pond, tearing out some earth. Facing directly east, they headed back to where Jeanie thought the wagon sat.

"Get on my shoulders," Jeanie said.

They faced each other with Jeanie's wrists crossed, hands joined. Jeanie bent her knees and exploded upward swinging Katherine around her back. Katherine wiggled into a comfortable place on Jeanie's shoulders and fastened her ankles around Jeanie's chest.

"You all right, Mama?"

"My yes, Sweet Pea. All is well." She was going to make all of that true. "Peel your eyes for the wagon." Jeanie plodded, feeling Katherine's weight quickly, thinking of the baby inside.

"Yes, Mama." Katherine hummed a tune.

"Concentrate on the looking," Jeanie said.

"The humming helps me look."

"Well, then," Jeanie said through heavy breaths. "Keep those eyes wide as a prairie night."

"Wide as a what?" Katherine said.

"A prairie night," Jeanie said. Katherine's legs stiffened and she pulled hard around Jeanie's neck.

Jeanie halted, absorbing Katherine's tension.

"What's wrong? What do you see?" Jeanie looked upward at Katherine's face above her. She squeezed Katherine's thigh to get her attention. Were they about to step into a snake pit, be trampled by a herd of cows?

"What is it?"

"A man," Katherine said.

"Who?" Ridiculous question in light of them not knowing a soul in Dakota.

Katherine's legs kicked—she gripped Jeanie's bonnet making its ties nearly choke her.

Jeanie's heart began its clunking patterns again. "Where?"

Katherine didn't respond so Jeanie swung her from her shoulders and tucked her behind her skirts. Jeanie glanced about the ground for something sharp or big. There was nothing that could be used as a weapon against a small rodent let alone a man.

Katherine clenched Jeanie so tight that the two nearly flew off their feet. Steadied, Jeanie couldn't see anyone coming toward them. Her bare feet pulsed with pain making her feel more vulnerable. Katherine must be hallucinating, the thirst taking its toll on her.

Jeanie spun in place, craning for the sight of a man, the sound of feet, but a windblast made anything that might emit noise, soundless.

For a moment Jeanie was tempted to burrow into the grasses, hide there, play dead, anything to avoid the man, if there was a man. A new burst of sweat gathered at her hairline and dripped down the sides of her face. Katherine's fingers delved into the loosened stays of Jeanie's corset.

"Who's there?" Jeanie yelled into the wind. She shuddered. She could feel someone watching them. She whirled again, Katherine whipped around with her.

"*Who's there?*" Jeanie shouted. This time her words tore through the air, the winds momentarily still.

"It's Howard Templeton! Jeanie Arthur? That you?" A full, gruff voice came from behind. Jeanie and Katherine twisted around a final time. Jeanie's body relaxed. If he knew her name it must be a good sign. She tensed again, maybe not. Maybe he tortured Frank and the boys and…she wouldn't think about it. This Templeton sported a pristine black hat. His ropy limbs were strong though not bulky, not threatening in any setting other than that of the naked prairie.

Jeanie shaded her eyes and looked into his six feet two inches, meeting his gaze. A crooked grin pulled his mouth a centimeter away from being a smirk.

"Mrs. Arthur, I presume? There. That's more proper, isn't it? Don't be nervous."

"It was the wind," Jeanie said. You scared me blind, she wanted to say, but wouldn't. "I couldn't pinpoint…well, no matter." She wasn't accustomed to making her own introductions. It felt rude to say, *who are you?* So, she said nothing.

Templeton removed his hat and bent at the waist, lifting his eyes. Was he flirting with this dramatic bow? She grabbed for absent pearls then smoothed the front of her dress before pulling Katherine into her side.

He straightened, replaced his hat. "I met your husband, Frank, on his way to stake a claim."

Jeanie flinched. Where *was* Frank?

Templeton jammed one of his mitts toward Jeanie, offering a handshake. She stepped backward while still offering her hand in return.

He clasped her hand inside both of his. They were remarkably soft for a man ferreting out a home on the prairie. He held the handclasp and their gaze. Jeanie looked away glimpsing their joined hands. She cleared her throat and wormed her hand out of his.

She wished there had been a manual pertaining to the etiquette of meeting on the prairie. Etiquette *should* have traveled anywhere one went, but she could feel, standing there embarrassed in so many ways, how unreliable everything she had learned about life would be in that setting. Jeanie ran the freed hand over her bonnet, straightening it then smoothing the front of her pond-mucked skirt.

Templeton shifted his weight, and drew Jeanie's attention back. "I advised your Frank to jump a claim. To take up in the Henderson's place. That family never proved up and rather than you starting from scratch, I figured you might as well start from something. Besides, I miss having a direct neighbor. Darlington Township might have well over a hundred homesteads settled, but it's really the few closest to you, the ones you form cooperatives with, that matter."

Jeanie swallowed hard. She eyed his canteen and had to hold her hand back to keep from rudely snatching it right off his body. "Well, I'm not keen on jumping a claim, Mr. Templeton. I'll have to consult my own inclination before we put pen to paper on that."

She bit the inside of her mouth, regretting she'd lost her manners, her mind. "I'm sorry. My manners. It's a pleasure to meet you. This is my daughter Katherine."

Katherine smiled. "Pleased to make your acquaintance."

Templeton shook her hand then folded his arms across his chest.

"You, Katherine, are the picture of your father. Prettier though, of course, with your mother's darker coloring, I see."

Katherine reddened, peered upward from under her bonnet then darted away, leaping and spinning.

"Stay close!" Jeanie said.

"So what bit you with good old prairie fever?" Templeton asked.

14

Jeanie looked around as though something drew her attention. She hadn't considered what her response to that query would be. Her heart burst at the chest wall. Templeton's quiet patience, his steadfast gaze heightened Jeanie's discomfort.

"Circumstances."

"I know all about circumstances," Howard said.

"I don't mean to be ill-mannered, but…" Jeanie eyed the canteen Templeton had slung across his body.

He rubbed his chin then slid the strap over his head. "Frank sent me with some water, figured you'd need it, that I'd be the best person to find you."

"Water, thank you, my yes." Jeanie licked her lips.

He handed it to Jeanie. Her hands shook, nearly dropping it as she unclasped the catch. She would give her daughter the first drink.

"Katherine! Water!"

Katherine skipped toward them. She took the canteen, shoulders hunched, eyes wide as they had been on Christmas morning.

"Watch, don't dribble." Jeanie held her hands up under the canteen. She forced her gaze away, knowing she must look crazed, staring at Katherine's throat swallowing, barely able to wait her turn.

Katherine stopped drinking and sighed, eyes closed, content. She held the canteen to her mother.

Jeanie threw her head back, water drenching her insides. The liquid engorged every cell of her shriveled body. She took it from her lips and offered it back to Katherine.

"You finish up," Jeanie said, cupping Katherine's chin, lifting it to get a good look into her now glistening eyes.

"There's got to be plenty back at the wagon now, right, Mr. Templeton?" Jeanie said.

He didn't reply. He squatted down, squinting at Jeanie's bare feet.

"You're not going another inch with naked feet and phalanges. What a great word, I haven't had use for since, well, never mind that," Templeton said.

Katherine's eyes widened.

"I'll thank you to find your manners, Mr. Templeton," Jeanie said stepping back.

"Don't be harebrained, Mrs. Arthur. Allow me to wrap your feet so they're protected should you step on a rattler, or into a gopher hole. I'll be as doctorly as possible." Templeton stood and unbuttoned his shirt.

Jeanie waved her hands back and forth. "No, now, no, now please don't do..." But before she could arrange her words to match her thoughts, Templeton ripped his shirt into strips and helped Jeanie to the ground. He turned her left foot back and forth. Jeanie's eyes flew wide open, her mouth gaping.

Katherine sighed with her entire body. "Sure am glad we stumbled upon Mr. Templeton. My mama wasn't trying to be disagreeable. She's just proper is all."

"Katherine Margaret Arthur." Jeanie snatched for her daughter's arm, but she leapt away, humming, cart-wheeling. Jeanie's face flamed.

Templeton's deep laugh shook his whole body. He began to wrap her foot. "These feet look to have been damaged by more than a simple run across the land."

Jeanie bit the inside of her cheek. She wouldn't confide her utter stupidity to a stranger.

"Let me guess," Templeton said. "I'd say you had a little trouble parting with your city shoes? Perhaps? The way your feet are lacerated below the ankles, as though stiff shoes meant for decoration more than work had their way with you?"

"Stay close Katherine!" Jeanie shouted to avoid admitting that in fact, she'd kept three pairs of delicate, pretty shoes and only traded one for a pair of black clodhoppers. The clodhoppers that bounced out of the back of the wagon just beyond their stop in Yankton.

Jeanie flinched as Templeton bandaged the other foot.

"Did I hurt you?"

Jeanie covered her mouth then recovered her poise. "No. Let's finish this production and get moving." It was then Jeanie realized she was shoeless—and not temporarily speaking. She wouldn't be able to sausage her swollen feet into the pretty shoes and she had nothing utilitarian in reserve. Frank was a miracle worker with wood, but wooden shoes? That wasn't an option.

Templeton whistled. "Nice you have such a grand family to cheer you while you make your home on the prairie. Times like this I wish I had the same. No wife, no children to speak of."

"You're *unmarried*?" Jeanie smoldered at the thought that not only a strange man handled her feet, her naked toes, but one who was batching-it! A scandal in the eyes of many. Thankfully, there were no prying eyes to add this outrage to her hobbled reputation.

Templeton snickered repeatedly as he moved with a doctor's detachment. The feel of hands so gently, though firmly, caring for her, nearly put Jeanie in a trance. She couldn't remember the last time someone had done such a thing for her.

"There. Good as new. Until we get you to the wagon, anyway. I assume you have another pair of boots there."

"Well, I uh, I…" She told herself to find her composure, that she was one step away from a reputation as an adventuress or an imbecile if she didn't put forth the picture of a respectable woman.

"Had a shoe mishap?"

"It could be characterized that way." Jeanie wanted to die. How stupid could she have been?

She turned one foot back and forth and then the other before having no choice but to look at Templeton and thank him for his assistance. Blood seeped through bandages and she nodded knowing he had been right. She'd have been wrought with infection and open to the bone if he hadn't wrapped her.

"Thank you Mr. Templeton. I thank you sincerely." Jeanie put her hand over her heart.

He pulled Jeanie to her feet.

"My pleasure." Templeton gave another shallow bow then tied an extra shred of his white shirt to a small cobwebby bush to use as a landmark, to show Jeanie and Katherine how the prairie land could work against even the most knowledgeable pioneer.

Jeanie knew she'd been careless that day, but she certainly didn't need white ties all over the prairie to keep her from getting lost again. She'd be more vigilant next time.

Move on, Jeanie. No time for moping. Jeanie drew back and lifted her skirts. She stepped onto the fresh bandages then snapped her foot back in pain. She held her breath and pressed forward ignoring the pain.

"It's *this* way," Templeton said. "You're turned around."

Jeanie halted. Her face warmed further than the heat and anxiety had already flushed it. "I suppose I've made some dire errors today, Mr. Templeton."

"I suppose we all do at first, Mrs. Arthur."

Jeanie puckered her lips in front of unspoken embarrassment. When was the last time she'd faced a string of endless failures? Never. She wondered if that could be possible, or if she was just making such a fact up in her mind.

"This way, my sweet!" Jeanie pushed her shoulders back, tugged her skirts against her legs and took off in the correct direction, Katherine beside her with Templeton just behind, gently guiding them back to Jeanie's family, back to the life she didn't think she could actually live with, but would not survive without.

Chapter 3

1905
Des Moines, Iowa

In the three days since Yale had stumbled drunk into Katherine and Aleksey's home, the couple had made the decision that their Edwardian home, even with four children, allowed more than enough space to care for both the cancer-stricken Jeanie and Yale, who was slow. There wasn't much to do in the way of transporting her sister and mother's belongings into Katherine's home for other than two trunks and some hanging clothes; they did not own a single item that needed to be moved.

It wasn't Katherine's decision to have them come. She resisted with all her might but Aleksey, had for the first time in their marriage, asserted the type of overbearing male dominance so many men reveled in regularly. He told Katherine she had no choice but to let Jeanie and Yale live with them. It was Katherine's duty to nurse her mother back to life or onward to death and it was her job to comfort and house her struggling sister.

Katherine stood in their doorway and watched Aleksey help Jeanie, one awkward step after another, up the front steps and across the porch. Katherine may not have remembered any warmth toward her mother, any sweet, shared moments or precious mother/daughter secrets, but she felt them from time to time, inside her skin, down in her soul, coursing through her body. Below the surface of her conscious mind was the memory of a woman she once adored. Normally when that flash of love for her mother shot through Katherine, she pushed it away, and let the resentment, the gritty hate that seemed to be layered like bricks, weigh on the goodness, squashing it out.

But now, with her mother being ushered into her home for Katherine to tend until she took her final breath, she let the shot of warm feelings sit a bit; saturate her mind, hoping the sensation would allow her to cope.

As Aleksey and Jeanie entered the front room, Katherine watched Jeanie's gaze fall over the carved-legged mohair davenport, velvet chair, and an oil painting done by Katherine herself. The thick Oriental rug drew Jeanie's attention, then when Katherine pushed the button, the diamond-like chandelier jumped to life, drawing Jeanie's gaze before she settled it back on Katherine's painting, one she'd done when they lived on the prairie.

Jeanie's once graceful posture was hunched over an ugly black cane as her hand opened and closed around the handle as though the action soothed her. Jeanie's brown hair, pulled tight into a bun, was thin, sprouting out of the severe style. The frail woman straightened, stared at the painting then brushed the front of her dress before falling hunched over her cane again.

Katherine told herself to find the love she wanted to feel. She took Jeanie's elbow and helped her to the couch, hoping it didn't smell like the old hound that often curled on one corner.

Aleksey kissed Jeanie's cheek and took her cane, supporting that side as they shuffled to the davenport. Acid rose up inside Katherine and blossomed into full envy at the warmth Aleksey showed Jeanie—the fact that he could touch her without looking as though his skin would combust on contact, as Katherine felt hers would.

Katherine gritted her teeth as she and Aleksey turned Jeanie and settled her onto the davenport. She sighed and squinted at

Aleksey. She loved him more than anyone except their own children, but this may be too much.

"I'll get that sweet tea you made, Katherine." Aleksey headed toward the hall.

Katherine couldn't have guessed exactly what her mother was thinking, but the puckered lips and narrowed brows didn't look positive. "Well," Jeanie said. "You're a little late with your spring cleaning, but the place is respectable all the same. I can see you purchase things that last." Jeanie smoothed her dress over her knees then smiled at Katherine.

"I know you mean that as a joke, Mother, but I don't appreciate it."

Jeanie scowled and Katherine flinched, waiting for hard words in return. Her mother opened her mouth and closed it then stared toward the painting with reed straight posture.

The pounding of the ice pick as Aleksey split the ice into cold slivers mimicked Katherine's heartbeat. She took a deep breath. How could a person feel so uncomfortable with the very person who gave her life? She prayed for Aleksey to speed it up in the kitchen as time moved like a fly in honey for the two in the front parlor.

With a startling jerk, Jeanie grasped Katherine's hand. She jumped in her seat, so surprised that her mother actually touched her. She stared at their hands then at her mother's profile. Jeanie gazed at the moody landscape Katherine had created on that awful day so long ago.

"You were such a beautiful artist," Jeanie said. "I remember when you did that one."

Prickly heat leapt between their hands, making Katherine sweat with anxiety. Jeanie caught her confused expression then squeezed her daughter's hand three distinct times. I love you. Each unspoken word was hidden in the three contractions of Jeanie's grip. Katherine nearly choked on swelling anger as she fought the burst of tears that threatened to fall.

With her free hand, Jeanie brushed some hair back from Katherine's face. Katherine, still as marble, wanting her mother to stop touching her, cleared her throat, feeling like she might pass out.

"Oh, I know," Jeanie said. "So very serious you are. I was once that way...I...well. I'm sorry, Katherine. I shouldn't have...I *should* have told you everything years ago, but..." Jeanie's gaze went back to the painting. "I want to explain."

Katherine nodded once but angled her shoulders away, trying to put as much space between them as possible. Katherine couldn't go down *that* old prairie path again. It was too late for explanations. She would have sprinted out the door, but her legs were numb. The only energy in her body seemed to exist inside the space between her and her mother's intertwined fingers. *Hurry Aleksey.* Katherine closed her eyes. Aleksey returned with a tray and tea, ice cubes clinking in the tall glasses.

He set the tray on the table in front of the women. Katherine silently begged him to notice her blood had rushed to her feet, that he should hoist her over his shoulder and take her away from this woman who, in merely touching Katherine, made her unable to render useful thought, to move, to live.

Trust Aleksey, Katherine told herself. She told herself to hope, to believe that something would be gained from this operation— from what Katherine saw as self-inflicted torture.

But, with Aleksey standing there, handing out tea, acting as though it were perfectly normal that Jeanie was there, with Yale asleep upstairs, Katherine decided she might never speak to Aleksey again.

Chapter 4

1887
Dakota Territory

Jeanie, Katherine, and Templeton crested a hill and stopped. Jeanie was eager to get to their wagon but relieved to give her smarting feet a break. She lifted one foot then the other, grimacing, as Templeton discussed their trek up to that point. He motioned back in the direction they had come, where he had tied a piece of his shirt to a bush, saying that even though the path to the crest upon which they stood had risen slightly and slowly, that Jeanie should always be aware of how deceptive the prairie land could be.

She turned in place, taking it in, seeing that on that sloping land the world seemed to open up but also it hid things. The fat, blue sky stretched in every direction without a landmark to mar a bit of it. Like the tie on that bush. It was gone, as though it never existed. Jeanie shook her head. So, it wasn't just that she and Katherine had been irresponsible in getting lost earlier, it *was* tricky land.

Templeton walked Jeanie and Katherine twenty yards further over the slope. And as though a magician had lifted a curtain, there appeared, one hundred and fifty yards east, a small frame home and the Arthur's wagon sitting near a crooked barn. Even from that distance, Jeanie could make out Frank, their eleven-year-old son James, and Katherine's twin brother Tommy fiddling with the wagon wheel.

The three of them walked east as though searching for something lost in the grass. Frank swaggered; his wiry body bore his unconscious confidence. But, he tapped the side of his leg—the one outward sign that something was bothering him. His movements were like a set of fingerprints. Jeanie could pick him out of a thousand other men if they were all in shadow, she was sure.

Katherine tore away from Jeanie and Templeton, galloping, twirling around to wave at Jeanie before breaking into full sprint to greet her father and brothers. Tommy glanced up at his approaching sister then carried on with his play—walking a few yards before throwing himself to the ground, shot, by some evil intruder.

And her James. Jeanie's first born. He lagged behind, but leapt into the air as Katherine raced by him and slapped his backside, making her fall into giggles that carried over the land. James had perfected a subtle, bellow of brooding, never quick to laugh or lash out. Each of them unique though together they formed a mass of love and pride, each one inhabiting a chamber of Jeanie's heart. If one were to disappear it would surely kill her instantly.

Templeton pointed west, past Jeanie's nose. "If Katherine fell into the pond I think you're describing, you must have seen that tree."

Jeanie nodded toward the crooked one she'd seen earlier.

"That's the bee tree. It's actually part of the Henderson's, no, *your* homestead, now. You can't see the tree from everywhere, but it's an anchor of sorts. Then there's another anchor just over there, at the far end of the Hunt's property, a cluster of six or seven trees."

Jeanie rose to her toes to look.

"Your bee tree and the Hunt's cluster are the most obvious landmarks between the five closest homesteads in Darlington Township. Gifts, sprouting from the land to guide and direct us."

Hoots of joy from Frank and the children startled Jeanie. She looked back at the family. They ran into the sun, past the sinking yolk, their bodies exploded blaze yellow, each outlined in black to mark where one golden body ended and another began.

Jeanie looked at Templeton and realized for the first time since he'd disrobed to wrap her feet that he was not properly dressed, that it would be shameful to someone with a suspicious mind.

"Uh, well...Mr. Templeton, I'll be..." Jeanie had no words. She shook her head, ignored the scorching pain in her feet and limped toward the wagon. "I'm going now, Mr. Templeton. My family awaits!" Jeanie's words had barely sailed out on prairie winds before she decided to ignore her screaming feet and whipped her body into a full-out run.

☯

Jeanie tore across the land. Her children caught sight of her and sprinted toward her. When they reached each other, they collapsed in a massive hug. Jeanie pulled each of their faces to hers, kissing their dirty cheeks, eyes, hands, clutching them, kneading their arms, making sure each was actually alive.

"No more of that wandering," Jeanie's mouth was taut, her gasping breaths making her words choppy. "We have to stick together...we have to..."

Tommy yanked on Jeanie's sleeve. "Can we have lamb chops tonight? And pancakes for breakfast. With Vermont maple syrup, like we love?"

Jeanie squinted down at him. "Now, Tommy, my, my, we discussed this matter repeatedly. You're a ten-year-old young man, capable of grasping..." Jeanie turned to be sure Templeton was out of earshot, "...our circumstances."

"Ahhhh, but…"

Jeanie knelt in front of him. Anger sprouted from the fatigue and thirst that lingered, but she wouldn't raise her voice. "Now Thomas Hart Arthur. We will have syrup yet again and I'm sure lamb will grace our table before long, but I am ordering you not to whine. We are in these dire straits for now, but only now. And I want this to be our last conversation on the matter."

She squeezed Tommy's arms and looked into James' and Katherine's faces to be sure they understood as well. "This station, our current position, these circumstances are not *who* we are—they are simply *where* we are right now."

She gave Tommy's arms one final squeeze then rose, determined that the conversation, the self-pity, and whining was at its end for no one wanted to mope and wail and bleat more than she. But, no one knew better than she that such acts would get them nowhere.

Frank came up behind Jeanie.

"All's all right, right?" he said.

Jeanie felt the joy at reconnecting with her children diminished by the arrival of Frank. Realizing, admitting that, even in her own mind, shamed her. She had been angry he had taken so long to get water, that he put them in the position of nearly drowning. But, beyond the relief that she needed him to survive, she felt jarred by the notion that the love and romance she once held for him, seemed fully dissolved.

Frank pulled Jeanie into his chest. She went stiff in his arms, unable to soften into his embrace. The scent of sweat, and homemade soap filled her nose. The familiarity was comforting and that reassured her in the face of her general distaste for him. Maybe they could recapture the love that had once beguiled them both.

She remembered the water. "Frank, my Lord, the water." She spoke into his shoulder, weakened with the thought of what had nearly happened. "Where did you go? Katherine. I lost her and we fell into a pond, we nearly died. When I stop and think—" Jeanie felt the calmness she'd forced upon herself disappear now that she was safe.

Frank gripped Jeanie's shoulders and shook her as he looked directly into her face. "You look fine to me, Jeanie Arthur. Just peachy."

The fear Jeanie had felt and ignored earlier finally settled in heavy, making her legs buckle. Frank caught her and she began to hyperventilate. Her shoulders heaved while she looked around to be sure the children weren't watching them. "I'm scared. I don't like the feeling. I've never felt this before, this—"

"Doesn't matter, we're fine, ignore it." Frank pulled her into his body and hugged her so hard that her breath had no choice but to slow. She realized she didn't want his reassurance. *He* was the one who left them in the position to be in danger.

Jeanie sniffled then pushed away. Templeton approached from the west. Jeanie's feet stung with every heartbeat that rushed her blood past the lesions. And, there was shirtless Templeton. Frank's face creased with what Jeanie knew must be confusion.

Jeanie lifted the hem of her skirts.

"My shoes. Mr. Templeton, he used his shirt…such a gentleman, this Templeton. We'll have to go back to Yankton, to get some suitable footwear." She turned back to Frank.

Frank glanced at Jeanie's feet then waved her off, walking away, leaving her with Templeton. "You'll make do. You're the 'Quintessential Housewife' after all."

Jeanie's mouth gaped.

"You're what?" Templeton said.

Frank turned back, hands spread to the sky like a preacher. "She's the *real* 'Quintessential Housewife', Templeton, the author? Didn't she tell you?" Frank dropped his hands and continued to walk away.

"Well, I'll be. Really?" Templeton cocked his head at Jeanie, rubbing his chin while the creases in at the corners of his eyes winked. "The Moore sisters will be crazed when they hear that. They're always hovering over your articles, making me bring copies back from Yankton every time I go. Oh, they'll eat this up."

"It's nothing." Jeanie stared at the ground then at her feet. She despised Frank's actions. That with his unconcern for her feet he demonstrated that he was as miserable as her husband as she was his wife. The difference being that she never embarrassed him in front of others. She took their vows to heart, even if the very uttering of them twelve years before had created the very noose that now sat poised around her neck.

Jeanie straightened. She wouldn't share an intimate moment of shocked reality with another man.

Templeton looked from Jeanie's feet to Frank who was headed toward the wagon. She shifted her weight. He was enough a gentlemen not to make eye contact or to comment on what he'd seen. Frank had never been a simple man to understand and he was even more complicated to explain to others.

"What exactly is the Quintessential Housewife? I've never read anything, I'm sorry to say, just brought the articles for the ladies over yonder," Templeton said.

Jeanie bit the inside of her cheek. Frank's mocking tone didn't get past Templeton. "It's well, a series of books and home-keeping columns I wrote in Des Moines. I was…well, no matter. I'm done with that now."

She covered her mouth and fought back the embarrassment she felt even though Templeton had no idea the depth of it. Damn Frank for bringing that up. She did not want to explore their past.

"Frank!" Templeton shouted over the wind. "It'll be dark soon. You'll all have to stay for dinner and sleep. I caught three jackrabbits just this morning."

Frank trudged back toward them.

Templeton stretched and yawned. "Why don't Frank, the boys and I head to the well and you ladies strike up a meal? Everything you might need is in the house, in plain site."

"Well, no—"

"She'd be obliged to cook up some dinner." Frank talked over Jeanie. "There's not a homemaker alive who can stand in *her* kitchen. And she's got the books to prove it." Frank stalked away.

"My feet...Frank?" Jeanie said.

Templeton started to walk away with Frank then turned back, pulling Frank's arm as he did. "Your wife's feet, Frank..." Frank pulled his arm out of Templeton's grasp and lumbered on.

"Uh, well, Jeanie, Mrs. Arthur, I mean..." Templeton tossed his head in the direction of the slender, whitewashed house. "You don't have shoes? Mrs. Henderson—from the homestead you're jumping—she left a pair behind. At least I think they're hers. Check under my bedstead...they're somewhere in there."

Templeton lifted his hand to Frank as if to call him back, but Frank was shrinking in the distance, not listening or caring that Jeanie had bleeding feet and no shoes.

"Oh, and Mrs. Arthur," Templeton said for the first time not making eye contact.

"I'm much obliged to sample your cooking as Frank said I'd be in for dandy-good eatings. That's a real treat, that is. I appreciate it." And he followed Frank's path to the well.

Jeanie's lips quivered. She couldn't swallow. How could she confess to Templeton that yes, she could run a home, but that home was typically outfitted with a staff of six and a kitchen the size of his entire house?

It wasn't until right that moment that she realized she should admit that same fact to Frank. But, Frank's mocking tone returned to Jeanie's thoughts and it was instantly clear. Frank was well aware of her limitations and it looked as though he would enjoy seeing her run into them as they tried to make a home on the empty prairie land.

Well, she would show him. If he was so willing to enjoy her humiliation, she wouldn't allow him the opportunity. Jeanie scrunched her face. "Dandy eatings. I'll show you both dandy-good eatings. If it's the last thing I do."

Hands on hips, Jeanie climbed the two steps leading to Templeton's worn porch. She kicked a stone across the boards, into a hole at the far end, and then bounced a little, testing its strength. Not too bad. If the Henderson homestead—the claim the Arthurs were jumping—was like this, Jeanie could make it livable. She imagined her family resting in the shade of the porch roof, rocking in chairs, the children playing jacks and checkers on the wood floor. Yes, this just might work for Jeanie.

Templeton's house was one floor, about 14x20. He'd built it sideways so the length of it promised more than it delivered in size, but the faded indigo door burst against the white wash and green grasses with the same awe that a human being floating among the clouds would inspire.

Jeanie threw open the door, ready to tackle dinner in clean quarters as opposed to the outdoors as she'd cooked in the last few nights. Sunlight flooded through the doorway and lit up the dusty space. Jeanie stepped inside, her bare feet lifting dirt, leaving prints as she circled the room. Did Templeton ever clean?

A bedstead stood in the far corner, a cook-stove in the fireplace and a squatty square table served as a spot to take his meals. Three stacks of books stood near the bed and one towered under the only rectangle window. Jeanie couldn't help but smile at what took up most of the space. In the middle of the rat-trap stood a grand piano.

She plunked a few keys then swiped her finger along the top of it, revealing a path of glossy black paint under the blanket of dust. The sound made her throw her head back with ironic laughter. This beautiful, enormous thing, here amidst dirty nothingness.

Her feet burned. The shoes. She got on all fours in front of Templeton's bedstead and began pulling things out. Mismatched men's shoes, hats, billiard balls, sheet music, a tin cup, and a Spode platter, crusted with either burnt beans or rancid meat. She finally dislodged a pair of boots from under the far corner of the bedstead. The shoes were a size too big, but given the state of her feet, she thought that might be better.

Clodhoppers. Ugly, wicked-looking things. Heavy scars creased the leather and curled the toes upward, telling Jeanie stories she didn't want to hear. And though she didn't know the details of the events, the shoes proclaimed that the woman who'd owned them before lived hard.

She slipped the shoes over her reddened feet and said a prayer to a God she wasn't sure she knew, that her feet wouldn't grow infected. She stood up and lifted her skirt, turning her foot side to side before letting her skirts drop over the ghastly sight. She begged herself not to allow self-pity a home inside her heart. If she went there, there'd be no way to get back. Yet, the dismay at her station. It was there.

Katherine came into the house with a bucket of water, forcing Jeanie away from the enticing self-pity.

"Don't touch a thing, Katherine," Jeanie said. They had work to do, cleaning things up before they set to the real work.

"It doesn't seem as though there's anything to make dirty or break, Mama."

"This place is filthy. Poor Templeton is batching-it. We can't expect a man to do everything around the house. He's got crops to sow and bring in."

"Hmm," Katherine said.

"This is a prime example of why a woman's place in the world is firmly..." Jeanie took the bucket from Katherine and shrugged, unable to finish the nonsense she once so happily dispensed to any-one who would listen.

"Well, we women," Katherine said, standing rod straight, imitating her mother's stance and pursed lips, "are having a day of it. This home expressing exactly why women are obliged to tend the homes of men." Katherine swooped her hand outward as though putting the house on display. "There are no more pressing circumstances for a woman in the home, than in an uncivilized place like this," Katherine said.

Jeanie playfully pulled a section of Katherine's hair making them both giggle.

Jeanie would have told Katherine she rethought her position on women's rights, but one—she wasn't sure she had, and two—she didn't have time to discuss such things anymore.

"We better get to dinner," Jeanie said.

They scoured the house for food and cooking tools.

Not that there was much space to search. Templeton's home consisted of one large room. Off to the left, in the back, there was an alcove. Jeanie, limping again, went to it and peered inside the space. "Well, sweet heaven and hell," Jeanie said.

Templeton's urine sat in a ceramic chamber pot, nearly filling it up. She sandwiched the sides of the pot between her palms, picked it up, trying not to wrap her fingers around the rim, while trying not to slosh any liquid from the vessel. "Mercy heavens, damn and hell." Jeanie whispered the curses.

Katherine's head whipped toward Jeanie.

"You didn't hear that, Sweet Pea," Jeanie said. Once they'd scrubbed down the cook-stove and washed their hands as best they could, trying to limit the wasted water, they worked fast, though not prettily. Out behind the house, they set up for preparing dinner—something Jeanie had never done herself. Not like this.

Jeanie wanted to cry at what she was doing. "We're not crying people. There's no room for self-pity. We're not crying people." Jeanie repeated the mantra to herself as she clenched her jaw and used a dull knife to skin the jackrabbits. The ripping sound as she separated the rabbit's coat from his muscle and fat made her skin prickly, chilling her. The sweet and sour odor of blood filled her nose and seemed to settle in her mouth as though she were eating the creature raw.

Jeanie's eyes watered and she gagged, turning to throw up her empty stomach.

"I can do this, Mama," Katherine rubbed her mother's back and took the knife from Jeanie's hand. Jeanie straightened.

"Nonsense, my Sweet Pea. No." Jeanie took the knife back. She held her breath and started to skin the second animal. Gagging again, she finally let Katherine finish the dirty work while she chopped the carrots and onions she'd found in a storage space above the bedstead.

Jeanie wanted to make Katherine stop, tell her that she just needed to settle her stomach, that she was pregnant and that must be getting the best of her. But she hadn't told Frank of the baby yet, and though Jeanie couldn't admit she was only partly capable of taking a meal from beginning to end, that splattering blood from one end of the back of the house to the other was something she'd never done, Katherine already knew it and Jeanie was sure she'd keep her secret. They were mother and daughter after all and Jeanie had never felt so fortunate to be able to say that.

Jeanie concocted a stew that only partly thickened. Nothing was available to make biscuits or cakes, so Jeanie hoped the company itself would do. It certainly wasn't a dandy-good supper. That much Jeanie knew.

She and Katherine spread some raggedy linens, loosely described as such, on the floor and used the small table to set the stew to be served to everyone. Jeanie sent Katherine out to gather everyone into the house.

Frank appeared in the doorway first. "Here. Water. Templeton's working with the boys. Apparently he's a whiz with the weather indications and even had a post with the Army until three years ago. James has taken an interest in predicting the weather."

"Predicting the weather?"

"I know," Frank said. "What good is something like that? Doesn't matter much what the weather might or might not be in the future, just what it is at the time you're wondering. I mean since there's no way to know what's going to happen." He tapped his leg, causing Jeanie to worry, knowing he was insecure about something—perhaps it was that James was taking an interest in another man's hobby—no matter what made him feel insecure it never lead to anything good for Jeanie. But, it was only their recent losses that made it such a problem that he may be an unstable man.

"What Frank?" She threw her hands up to the sky. "What in damn hell is the matter?"

Frank bit down so hard Jeanie could feel it in her bones across the room. She dropped her hands as though burdened with sacks of rocks.

"Nothing, Jeanie. Nothing you could help me with." And he left the room, shouting to the others that dinner was ready.

The meal was a disaster. The man Jeanie was beginning to think of as "sweet Templeton," had gobbled up three steaming bowls of the disastrous, somehow bitter, stew while her own family barely managed one slurp. The children and Frank were still operating with visions of one-inch steak, buttery biscuits, thick mashed potatoes, sweet peas, and towering chocolate cake in their minds and on their taste buds, and not yet hungry enough to eat rancid stew.

She knew Templeton was only being kind as he sopped up every last drop with his finger at the end, saying "dandy-good eats" every three minutes, acting as though it tasted scrumptious not just edible. Not that it was any of that.

All night Templeton passed back and forth by the bedstead where he allowed the Arthurs to sleep that night. He groaned as his bowels emptied repeatedly, slopping into one bowl and then another he'd dug out of God knew where. The children gagged at the sound and odor and Jeanie spent the night kicking the children under the covers so they wouldn't humiliate a man for emptying his body of the poison their mother had fed him.

Waking the next morning, Jeanie was relieved to see Templeton had cleared the pots and acted as though nothing out of the ordinary had occurred during the night.

She couldn't look him in the eye, even as he searched out her gaze, and even went so far as to reassure her that she would make a fine prairie wife.

"You're clearly too smart to be anything but a blazing success," Templeton had said tipping his hat to her. Jeanie hadn't known how to respond, so she just let the heavy failure she'd felt turn steely, inside her, inspiring her to be a better person, wife than she'd clearly been when she'd had a army of servants and cooks to assist her in being the Quintessential Housewife as she'd come to be known in Des Moines.

The Arthurs left Templeton's home about nine a.m. Frank seemed back in good spirits. In the wagon, he was taken by his peppy, happy personality. He rambled like a train roaring down the track, ticking off the list of things they needed to do in order to claim the Henderson's homestead as theirs. Two trips to Yankton. One to file papers, one to pick up the wood he'd agreed to work into furniture for some men they'd met when they stopped over there.

"You all right?" Frank put his hand on her back as she curved forward, head on knees. Gripped by cramps so tight, Jeanie would have sworn she was in labor or miscarrying, she couldn't even speak. She nodded into her lap then sat back up hoping that stretching her body would release the tension inside her womb. She'd desperately wanted more children, but considering the extensive work ahead of them, perhaps if nature stole her baby as it had the others since Tommy and Katherine were born, they'd be better off.

"You eat some rabbit stew for breakfast?" Frank chuckled. "Man that Templeton's not too bright, is he? Slurping down that stew as though the old cooks in Des Moines had actually done the work. It must feel good, though, to finally put all that advice you've doled out over the years to use, right?"

Jeanie couldn't respond as she bent into the pain tearing at her insides.

"I'm joshing; just poking fun...you know after all, we need to laugh a little, right?"

Jeanie groaned, trying to keep it quiet so the kids in the back wouldn't hear. She forced herself to straighten reducing some of the pain.

Frank clicked his tongue and slowed the horses. She stared into the great land, which looked much the same as Templeton's had, except over the night, tinges of brown had taken the tips of the grasses muting the contrast of jade grass joining the cobalt sky.

"Keep going." Jeanie rubbed her belly.

"We're officially, here. On our very own homestead. Our very own land, the place where dreams live."

Without waiting for responses from anyone, Frank hopped from the wagon, dragged water and the horses' feed bags out from the back of the wagon and signaled the kids to get out, unbridle the horses, and tie them to the railing that stood near a three-walled structure that could be used as a door-less barn.

Jeanie stood and waited for a fresh wave of cramping. Nothing came and as quickly as the pains had gripped her, they were gone, leaving her wondering if they were as bad as her memory said they were.

She couldn't be sure how far along she was, but it was early—due sometime after Christmas, she guessed. Most women might not have realized such a subtle change in their body, such a quickening in their womb long before she would actually feel her baby stretch and kick. But, Jeanie's body worked like a fine clock and any missed tick like her painful, monthly visitor, was noticed as clearly as a clock missing every other second.

Jeanie braced herself to hop out of the wagon. As she began to disembark, the toe of the too-large boot brushed the wooden side, making her trip.

"Whoa." Frank caught Jeanie as she fell flat out from above.

He set her down and she smoothed her skirts. *Damn, ugly shoes.* She lifted her skirts staring at the beastly shoes, the toes curling upward, further searing the family's bad turn into Jeanie's mind.

Frank lifted his arms and dropped his head back, face upward at the sun, grinning. "Home. We're home and it feels magnificent."

Jeanie shook her head. "There's nothing here. There's that barely a barn over there but..."

Frank pointed into the empty expanse. "See that bank of trees there, below there, a little ways, take a look," Frank said. He pulled her hand and they craned their necks peering around the wagon. "Templeton told me those are olive trees—straight from Russia. The Zurchenko's—their homestead starts on the north end of ours—brought them straight from Russia when they set up here three years ago."

His excitement was baffling. Jeanie couldn't make sense of her strange husband, whose oddball tendencies had been so nicely camouflaged by their former, privileged existence. Without thinking, for no good reason Jeanie blurted out her news.

"I'm pregnant."

He stared at her and scratched his head. Jeanie could see the children over Frank's shoulder, leaping, chasing prairie chickens, laughing, yelling, their voices cutting holes through the grown-up's conversation.

"Frank?"

"Hey kids! Water those damn horses!"

Jeanie grabbed his arm. "Don't be so harsh with them. They've a lot to adjust to."

"Ready to see our new home, our path to unimagined riches?" Frank hopped up and pulled Jeanie to her feet.

"Did you hear me? I'm pregnant."

"Don't make me be mean to you, Jeanie. Things are hard enough right now."

"Don't make me deal with your black moods, then. How about that?" Jeanie said. She bit her lip, afraid of the anger pushing words out of her mouth, thoughts she'd always kept inside, sentiments that couldn't be snatched back once free and embedded in his mind.

He crossed his arms and sighed. "I'm always thrilled to hear you're pregnant, Jeanie."

They stared at each other. Jeanie crossed her arms back at him, trying to soothe her anger. "But, you don't think this baby will live, so it doesn't matter?"

"I didn't say that."

James stepped into their locked gaze, breaking it. "I think it might rain. Templeton said—"

"Well, old Templeton's something else, now isn't he?" Frank said. Spit flew from his lips as he turned his black mood on James. "How about we let old Mama set up house, James, my boy. She's pregnant, you know."

"I thought so. You looked tired, Mama," James said. "Like the last two times." James stepped into Jeanie and she hugged him into her side and kissed his forehead. She didn't know what she would do without him.

"The house? Frank? You're right. We need to set up. Take me to my home."

Frank stomped his foot. But didn't go anywhere.

Jeanie could ignore Frank's meanness if it meant turning his ire away from her James and focusing her energy on life and death—setting up house.

"Frank? The house? Which way?" Jeanie held her hands open to the sky.

She couldn't see anything but the skeletal tree she'd seen the day before, the bank of olive trees slightly below them, the make-shift barn, and the red fabric they'd tied to a single wooden stake in the ground that marked the way to the well in the distance.

"We're here." Frank grinned and stomped again.

Jeanie jerked her head in one direction then the other, peering into the distance in every direction. "I'm *sure*," Jeanie said, "Templeton indicated the Henderson's homesteaded for three years and I don't see hide nor hair of a pretty white frame house like his. I mean, those falling down sod walls over there were clearly just a place to tie the animals against the wind. The Hendersons *can't* have lived inside that. I can smell animal from here, they couldn't have...even a dirty frame house would be easy to clean up and make ready for our—"

"You're right. They did tie their horses over there." Frank slung his arm around Jeanie's shoulder with a jolt. He stomped his foot again. "You're *standing* on it," Frank said.

"Standing on what?" Jeanie stamped her foot back at Frank.

He grabbed her hand and yanked her so hard that she stopped forming thoughts or words. He guided her down the shallow bank and around the front of where they had been standing above. There, dug into the hill was a hole with a door.

"No," she said. She knew what she was staring at, but she wouldn't accept it. She would *not* live there.

A wooden plank door clearly marked the space as a home. But she couldn't get her mind to make sense of what that meant. She'd heard of dugouts, a step down from building a sod home, but she never entertained the chance they might inhabit one.

It looked like and essentially was a giant mud-ball into which someone had carved a hole. Spiky grass—not even the soft, pretty stuff that waved in the wind, grew from the top of the hill. Above the front door, marching across the top like soldiers, the Hendersons had created a foyer, of sod bricks, and nailed to the bricks was a sign painted with what looked like tar. "Help Yourself to Hell—the Hendersons. 1885-1887!"

Frank couldn't be serious. Jeanie grabbed her skirts and dug into the material to steady herself, to stave off her inclination to tumble to the ground and melt into the earth at hearing such news.

"We can't live here," Jeanie said. "Like animals. You're mocking me again? We're a lot of things, but animals, we're not," she said. Her voice rose to a childish squeal. She hated him with her whole body, the blood rushing through her, carrying poisonous distaste. Clearly he felt the same to do this to her, to suggest she ought to live inside the edges of the earth.

"Just for a while," Frank said. "Why should we waste energy building a new home when we need to dig into the land, plant some corn? It'll afford us the chance to save time and money and you'll be back in silk, in no time, fast. In the end it'll be worth it."

Jeanie paced back and forth. "Darling. This is a *shack* burrowed out of earth to suit *maybe* one person. One. The kids' tree house in Des Moines held more luxuries than this. This rat-trap. Not to be ungrateful considering the state of our lives, but this is utterly unacceptable."

"Your sense of entitlement is showing," Frank tore a piece of grass from the ground and chomped on it.

"Two, darling Frank, there's something wrong with jumping a claim, not paying someone for their trouble. My greediness got the best of me when Templeton entertained us in his home. I allowed my mind to wander to material comforts that will come later rather than using the time to deal with particular things we need now."

Jeanie splayed her fingers in front of her, feeling all of her tension center in the tips. "I'll just put away the notions that came alive in that twelve-hour time period and get back to where we started—building a 20x24 free standing soddie until we turn enough profit on corn, your carpentry...and I'll sew! Someone around here must need curtains or dresses..."

She turned around, palms upward as though an entire neighborhood would drop down around them, full of people needing the services of a woman with expert sewing skills.

She couldn't do this. She balled her fists around her skirt again, so hard she could feel each nail through the fabric digging into palm, but she wouldn't look Frank in the eye. "Please. I'm begging you. And until a month ago, I think you know I went twenty-seven years of life never begging anything. *Please*. Don't make me beg you."

Frank took her chin between his thumb and finger. One corner of his mouth climbed higher than the other as though he might see things her way or that he was about to burst out laughing. Laffin' was the way he always said the word.

"You," Frank said. He unlatched her fingers from around her skirts and held her balled fists in his hands. "You could turn a heap of mud into a showcase any old day."

A month ago, she might have agreed.

"That's really not the point." She flinched and stared past him, out over the land. Was Frank pulling a kernel of sincerity from the depths of artificiality trying to make it seem like the biggest truth in the world? For that moment, she wanted to believe that truth. What choice did she have? What choice had she ever had?

Right then, she realized like no other time in her life that they were stuck together and as much as they disliked each other, their life on that prairie teetered on the cusp of death and they would have to work as one just to get by.

"Come on. You'll see." Frank nudged her toward the opening of the dugout. He pushed the wooden door—its hinges screeched.

Jeanie looked back to see the kids standing behind her, their faces appearing shocked at the sight of their new home.

"Just stay there," Jeanie said. She didn't want the kids to see the place until she was sure they were staying there. She held a morsel of hope that she could talk Frank out of this nightmare.

She stepped inside and covered her mouth and nose as her eyes adjusted to the darkness. It was bigger than she imagined and filthier. Templeton's home appeared to be kept by a staff of eleven compared to the dugout.

The musty, peppery earth filled her nose, pricking each sense to life, choking her on the reality of what they'd done in going there. She swallowed bile and cleared her throat. So her father swindled half of Des Moines out of their money? So Frank had stupidly, inadvertently helped her father do it? They were so shamed that lighting out for the prairie was a better choice? This filth was what Jeanie's pride had gotten her. And now it was too late.

The evacuated family—the Hendersons—had attempted to whitewash one wall—they'd tried to build a layer of sod brick walls on the inside to give it a more finished look.

"There's nothing like earthen bricks to cheer things," Jeanie said under her breath. She touched the dirt rectangles where white flecks of paint clung to the occasional sprig of old grass that sprouted like thin hair on an ancient bald man. They must have run out of paint or energy and then tacked up their wagon sheet on the remaining walls.

Though she didn't see any, it was clear that rodents had long since burrowed into the structure, eating through the canvas, leaving ragged holes as evidence of their unlawful entry.

"Well, at least we brought the extra wagon cover," she said. "We can start fresh with that if we can't lay our hands on whitewash." She cleared her throat again to push away the suffocating anxiety. She had to find a way to make this work.

Frank stepped behind Jeanie and looked over her shoulder at the wall in front of them. "I wanted to start off in Yankton, too. To build a frame house, to work in the bank, there with Jeremiah." He turned her around to look out a window and she was too stunned to stop him from manipulating her like she were a puppet.

"But after what your father did at his bank. To those people. They wouldn't hire me." Jeanie pushed away and brushed past him.

"I don't think he was alone in his stupidity." She picked at a crispy layer of dirt that shrouded the glass panes of the window.

"Moving forward is the only choice. We can do this, Jeanie. This is our life and as you scribble in that book of yours or mend dresses, and someday build another home, you'll be proud of what develops. You'll be proud. You'll be proud of me. Think of what we'll leave our children. Their children."

Jeanie pulled up a section of her dress and covered her finger to scrape harder at the dirt on the window. She couldn't will herself to fawn over his plan, to make him feel useful and faultless. She knew she should do that, for all their sakes, but at that moment nothing helpful came to her.

She walked to the far back of the dugout. Hanging on the wall was a dinner plate sized wreath with dried berries and flowers woven into it.

"See," Frank said reaching up to touch it. "The prior lady of the home was just as inclined to make this a fairy-tale abode as you. She even decorated it."

Jeanie slapped his hand away from the thing, plucked it off the wall, and shook it at Frank. Her stomach shuddered at the sight of it, spurring a fresh cycle of frustration and anger through her.

"Why're you breathing like that?" Frank stood in front of her, his face pulled in worried furrows.

"*This* is not a home, Frank. It's a hole in the crust of the earth. And this...this...thing is not...it's a wreath made of *hair*, Frank. The hair of the Henderson's—the family, who according to their welcome sign outside, apparently walked arm and arm with Lucifer himself. And I will not live with this beastly hair thing as though it's a gesture of hospitality from the Women's Convention of Darlington Township." And, she could not imagine having to share such a small grotesque space with a person she disliked so much.

Frank looked as though he'd sucked lemons as she shook the hairy thing under his nose. Then he pushed his hand through his hair, its yellow fullness flopped back over his brow.

"It's filthy in here. I'm not saying we need a frame home, but it would be much more tolerable to make a home with fresh sod—clean sod."

"Any way you break up the sod, it'll still be dirt, Jeanie. The dugout is just temporary, to get us through one crop, one winter."

Jeanie tramped from the dugout flinging open the door so hard it flew from its rusty hinges. She barreled into the openness, past the children. Tommy chased after her.

"Mama? Can we go back? I like to play cowboys and Indians, but I don't think I like living like one. I want pancakes and steak and…"

Jeanie heaved the hair-wreath as far as she could, hoping Tommy would leave her alone for just five minutes. He hung back and Katherine took his place, running to keep pace with Jeanie's angry strides.

Katherine grabbed for her hand and once their fingers were threaded, Jeanie felt small shards of anger fall away, her pace slowed, her heartbeat measured. She and Katherine grasped each other's hands so hard Jeanie could feel Katherine's tiny bones in her grip. She stopped walking and closed her eyes, chin dropping to her chest. She looked up to see Frank tapping his leg.

Jeanie smoothed the front of her grubby dress then turned to Katherine, speaking loud enough that Frank would be able to hear. "I can see we have no choice in the matter. We've come this far and there's no point in whining over it. But just so we're clear, I'm not happy and this place is a shanty. And I won't pretend it's anything but that." She turned to Frank. "But I won't whine about it either."

He nodded, lip sticking out like a pouting child. She'd won nothing, but felt as though she was superior in saying she deemed the place a disgrace. And standing there, watching the husband she'd shamed in front of his daughter, it occurred to her that these elements—their disgruntlement with one another, her quickness to criticize, was not new. But recognizing it was.

And, at that time, though she realized what she was doing was cruel, she was too broken to act above. So, she left things, her cutting words as they were, lingering there, ready to be wielded again when desperation came and took her over.

"Okay, Jeanie, it's a deal. Let's just make it through one winter and I'll carry the wood for a new home on my back from Yankton if I have to. Just one winter." Frank clapped his hands before rubbing them together with the enthusiasm that was clearly bubbling inside him but was inaccessible to Jeanie.

Jeanie nodded, knowing there was no other choice for them. "I think I just need to clean up. A bath would shed some joyful light on this abode. I'm just not accustomed to carrying as much dirt on my person as the earth carries on itself. If you could bring me some water for bathing. I think I'll be fine."

"Well *all right*," Frank said. "Let's get things together. I'll get the water and let you get to fixing up the...well, our home, and I'll take the kids to show them exactly where everyone's property is so they can get around unattended."

"Mama?" James said, "Is that all right? I can stay and help unload." He looked at his father then back at Jeanie. She knew how much James wanted their family to be content.

"My, my, no. You go on. I can handle the unloading."

"But the baby," James said. Katherine latched onto Jeanie's waist.

"Listen James, darling. If this baby is meant to be born, it'll be born while I work, not while I lay about like a wealthy maiden from the South of France. I think I've learned *that much* over the course of the last few pregnancies, wouldn't you say?"

James pursed his lips and shoved his hands deep inside his pockets before nodding. "Okay, Mama, okay."

He walked off behind Frank while Jeanie unlatched Katherine from her body and sent her behind the men with a tap on her bottom. Jeanie forced her words to be light, to cheer her family even if the sentiments wouldn't do the same for her. Tommy had already passed by Frank, clearly loving the chance to explore.

Maybe if they discovered that one of them belonged in a place like that prairie dugout, it would be enough for Jeanie to survive. If she could just get Tommy to forget about his damn pancakes, maybe then they'd be all right. And, as Frank's body disappeared from Jeanie's sight and his voice from her ears Jeanie exhaled for the first time in what felt like hours.

Chapter 5

And as per Frank's suggestion, he took the children over the plains, educating them on where their homestead butted up to others, to come to know the land with the intimacy that they'd known each nook of their home in Des Moines. Jeanie hoped he remembered to walk off the acreage for corn and a vegetable garden that might yield food fairly fast.

Jeanie's sole responsibility at that moment was to set up house. The heat of the day pulsed down in great waves, nearly in unison with surges of cramping that gripped Jeanie's middle. Thick gusts of wind burst occasionally filling her ears, taking away the sharpness of the heat momentarily. No matter the force or frequency of wind, the heat caused her clothes to soak into her skin as though part of her body's makeup.

All of this sweat and odor convinced her the attempt to wear crinoline skirts into the west was at best naïve. She hauled up the hem of her white dress and latched it between her teeth, wrangled her hands behind her waist and undid the strings of the crinoline. She pushed it down her legs and stepped out of it then dropped the cotton from her teeth. The skirt collapsed around her legs with a heavy whoosh. She wiped the powdery dirt from her mouth with the back of her hand and said a short prayer to the God she didn't really believe in that jumping a person's claim wasn't a step in the direction of the decimation of their dreams.

Jeanie looked around the space and saw nothing and most importantly, no one. She hauled up her skirts and pushed her pantaloons down letting the breeze cool her legs. Even knowing in her head how hot the air was, lifting her skirts lowered her temperature by ten degrees at least. After a short time she pulled up her pantaloons and stretched.

The cramping had lessened and in the absence of that grip she felt nearly wonderful, physically. She'd suffered countless miscarriages and two babies who were born dead since the twins were born and though accustomed to the notion that her pregnancy might not last, the thought that it might not still carried a shock. Luckily, she had the great expanse of building a home from nothing to draw her attention the minute the cramps subsided enough to forget what they might mean.

Jeanie stood atop their dugout shading her gaze from the elephantine sun. Even through the bonnet, it crisped her scalp like flour in a skillet. Since the children were with Frank, it gave her a chance to concentrate on her work without wondering if someone was getting swallowed into the great vastness.

God, it was vacuous, filled with a lot of nothing. *Why would someone happily, willfully go there*, Jeanie thought. Surely, everyone who did, had a tale of woe like hers, surely no one chose to live there. Even in the obvious beauty of the open land, Jeanie's emptiness, the sadness in losing everything, felt appropriate for land like that.

Frank, she thought, *take care of the children. Please don't fade away, forget where you are, what is at stake.* Jeanie sipped water sparingly from her blue tin cup and headed toward the wagon to begin the business of setting up house. She'd done it once before—at the barely ripe age of fifteen. Though even at that age, married so young, she functioned like a woman twice as old, knowing exactly what to purchase and where to place it and who to hire to carry out her wishes.

Twelve years later, she couldn't rattle away the image of herself, standing in front of her home, awaiting her furnishings, primly attired, hat tilted just so and dress pinching her waist where it was fashionable that year. She cracked a smile at the thought. Perhaps she had been trying too hard to prove—screaming out with her actions—she was not a child though her age only whispered she wasn't.

But, the truth was like a beating. Looking back she saw, nearly every achievement was the fruit of dumb luck—being born into a family that had every luxury and wouldn't allow her brainless elopement to ruin her standing in the community.

She recalled her father's response to the elopement. It wasn't to shun her as she feared. He pretended he orchestrated the whole shebang himself. Jeanie's mind spun the images—the parade of wagons that stopped in front of the mansion, the way each groaned with fine furnishings. The wedding gifts—twelve china and silver place settings, silken bed coverings, a velvet lounge and their family jewel, a smallish carved piano, along with other household items—symbolized something lovely in its use and also in its meaning. To Jeanie, having all those things meant life intended good things for her and Frank.

And, for over a decade, that was exactly the way things went. That very day she and Frank moved into their graceful home, her father and his best friend, Mr. Tumulty, watched as she gave orders, smoothed over discrepancies, and kindly orchestrated the mass of furnishings into an inviting home. She impressed Mr. Tumulty, owner of the *Des Moines Register,* so much so that he offered her a chance to write a homemaking column. Jeanie's opinions read like controlled tornados with powerful bursts of words that made her readers feel simultaneously chastised and capable of everything Jeanie said a fine housewife should accomplish.

But that time had passed for Jeanie. There on the prairie, she chortled at her hubris. She scoffed at how she had sauntered through life unknowingly walking a tightrope that until she fell from it, she'd been unaware her life had been strung on a single tenuous thread.

She told herself to get to work. Jeanie hiked up her skirt, tied it into a knot with her pantaloons exposed for all the prairie to see and hopped into the wagon. She spit at her black boots, their ugliness. In the back of the wagon she wedged her feet in between her mama's faded, though still crimson trunk, and surveyed the spare cargo.

Jeanie tried to unload the wagon, but for the first time since *it* happened, she allowed herself to recall every wretched inch of the events that occurred two weeks past.

Nausea gripped her as images of the residents of Des Moines popped into her mind. Elizabeth wearing Jeanie's sapphire necklace. The calm, but chilling anger in Mr. Kaplan's eyes. Lawyers and policemen roping off her home, claiming and proving that Jeanie and Frank owned nothing they thought they had.

A fly buzzed at Jeanie's ear. She smacked it away. She shuddered, fully realizing she could never afford to entertain memories of her past again. There was no time to sit and mourn anything. If you weren't moving on the prairie, you weren't surviving.

She had to accept that. Her father sure had moved on. He killed himself and left Jeanie and Frank to take the consequences for all his misdeeds. Kaplan had followed Jeanie and Frank to the Renaults, attempting to explain his part in the looting. His voice was gentle in submitting to Jeanie that her father's opium habit had been his undoing.

Opium? Jeanie scoured her mind for evidence of such a thing. She'd never seen her father stumble, sleep during the day, inarticulate. If he died from opium it must have been a one-time instance Jeanie had thought. Kaplan had read those silent thoughts and assured her that some opium eaters indulged for years with no one knowing the better, before it took control and made the user lose his soul and heart, to cause him to hurt those around him.

Then, she did remember. Her father, dashing into her water closet to freshen up, emerging as though, well, as though spurred by an outside energy, ready to clobber the world. Her father's gaze cloudy, his mind slow as he processed the world around him. Jeanie had always attributed it to him being a thinker—lost in the world of his own mind. How stupidly her own mind worked to allow such things to happen right in her own midst. And Frank, he had gone along with things, with her father.

Luckily Frank hadn't been industrious enough to mastermind any portion of the downfall, but still the facts were there. Frank had participated in the family's misdeeds by allowing her father to continue his stealing, suggesting empty investments, building useless air castles out of baseless dreams. Frank was always happy to entertain such thoughts while his hand was in someone else's pocket. She hadn't fully realized that until that ugly day Mr. Kaplan stopped by to explain.

Jeanie began to feel dizzy. She collapsed onto the trunk in between her legs. Her thoughts crashed through the defenses that had allowed her to ignore, to overlook to forget. Sitting there, face in hands, a scent rose from her boots, sour and foreign. She gagged at the thought that the beaten shoes held the sweat and stink of another woman. A woman who'd run screaming from the prairie.

Jeanie sat disoriented by the odor of the shoes, the stench somehow conjuring the very person who'd once worn them. She bent over her knees willing the nausea away. She could feel the woman's dampened spirit and smell her failure. In having to wear that woman's shoes, Jeanie was wearing another woman's catastrophe. Head in hands, crying at the thought she might give rise and shape to a stranger's demise simply by wearing her shoes, bringing the failure to bear in her own life, Jeanie thought she might not be able to carry on.

Sweat pulsed in concert with Jeanie's heart. She pushed her sleeves up and gripped the sides of the wagon. Invisible particles of dirt rose from the plains, and adhered to her skin instantly as though the filth seeped from her skin rather than settling in from the air. She shuddered, crippled by self-pity, heaving tears, grunts and sobs that echoed in the wagon and she figured, carried over the land.

Jeanie threw her arms out to the universe then clawed at her own skin, the pain seemed separate from her mind. She stomped her feet like a child, digging her heels into the wood floor of the wagon with all the strength she could muster.

She could see herself critically, having a temper-tantrum like a spoiled ninny, but was unable to stop. She was surprised at the force of what she had kept inside, almost without her knowing. And by the end of her fit, she'd taken fun in wailing as obnoxiously as possible—screaming out like an animal.

This gave way to laughter. And her mind, satisfied at having won out over her lacerated heart, knew that none of the incidents in Des Moines mattered. A flash of her father came—he'd taken money from good people, promised to hold it in his bank and somehow not fulfilled that.

That was his sin, not hers. No. She wouldn't think of him anymore. She'd detached from him already and this final burst of emotion broke the clasp to the things that had once defined their lives. The fit was the last indulgence she'd allow herself. For she had much work to do.

There was Frank. She would deal with him. And, she would never let her children suffer as she had. Coming to know her father was not the man she thought was worse than everything they lost. Jeanie would protect her children from that fate if it was the last thing she managed in her dreary new life.

Jeanie nodded and blew her nose into her skirt. She could survive and do it well. This would be better—creating a life with the things they could do best—his carpentry skills, her writing, a garden, corn, eventually livestock. She began to feel her burden lift. They had the ability to create something rather than just take things and shift them around an enormous house until achieving the appropriate look.

This prairie life would be better. It would *mean* something. They were the artists of their existence and in that endeavor, Jeanie plumped up, feeling optimism rush back in. Like she had felt when she bought a new flow-blue vase, when she wrote books that enticed people to recite her sentences back to her. Once they'd created a home, a life, from the ground up, no one could take it from them. And she would begin again, her writing, her life as it was. Only better.

Determined, Jeanie began to empty the wagon, laying its contents outside the dugout. She scampered down the tongue of the wagon, carrying clothing, a set of tin dinnerware and inexpensive silverware, mismatched tea cups and their chamber pot—the only remaining relative of their Blue Italian china. She dragged one of two pine hope chests into the dugout that Frank had taken out of the wagon earlier.

The first chest held the makings of optimism. Her fabric, silver scissors and thimbles, darning egg, paper, pens, some of Frank's tools, and the letters Frank and she'd written in the year of their engagement—the things she didn't part with to raise the funds to make this trip. It also held four tin plates, saucers, and three more cups, the skillet, a coffee pot, and a cook pot.

Next she yanked the faded green trunk that was filled to bursting with books—the books no one in Des Moines saw as valuable, apparently. Jeanie lost her grip on it several times as she dragged it and it scraped down the back of her leg. Outside the dugout, she popped the lid and stared inside. She ran her hand over the leather tomes. Of all of Frank and her discussions about what to leave behind, what they didn't haggle over were the items that would lend their life a kernel of standing. Yes, they'd be plowing the earth and living inside it like prairie dogs, but from the innards of the earth would burst life as they remembered it.

Jeanie sat beside the trunk, running her fingers over the embossed title—*An American Family in Paris*—and stared at the opening of the dugout, its door standing off to the side. Chills crept through her body, raising the hair on her arms, turning the sweat she'd worked up frigid. What's the matter with a little dirt? Thousands of people started their homesteads with a dugout. It's only temporary. But the Hendersons...what happened...put the Hendersons out of your mind. Indians live in dugouts by design. Steel yourself, woman. Toughen-upToughen-upToughen-up.

Clearing her throat she stood, closed the chest, and dragged it into the dugout. For the first time she was in the dirty tunnel by herself. Her eyes adjusted to its darkness—like dusk in her home in Des Moines. The smell—grassy, but sweet and peppery—made her hold her breath. She forced a deeper breath and told herself that smelling a little of it at a time might actually suit her and perhaps she'd grow to crave the scent.

The coolness provided by the earth made her teeth chatter. She closed her eyes and the dugout's filth and life filled her. Life will be good again. I will love Frank again. She remembered their sappy love letters. She'd once been utter mush in his hands. She could be that in love again. She would make it so, make them happy, make them rich again.

"What a bunch of horseshit," Jeanie said out loud. "Horseshit. Horseshit. Horseshit. I hate my life. I hate my life. I hate my life." Jeanie wiped her hands on her skirts and went to the sole window in the shelter and lifted the gnarled, faded gingham curtain from the wooden slat that held it. It fell apart in her fingers.

The red fabric that hung from the ceiling near the back of the dugout met the same fate as the curtain. It offered privacy to whoever would be using the chamber pot or getting dressed. And, she imagined, for when Frank and she were in the frame of mind and body to engage in adult pursuits. She shook off the thought of being intimate so close to other living breathing people—children of all things—but she knew she'd heard the stories, that it was what homesteading required.

Inside the hovel she'd lost all sense of time as she'd not yet become accustomed to what the sun's movements over the home meant. But, hours must have passed as she fitted the window with snowy, percale curtains, tied back in a way that if she didn't look too close she might be fooled into thinking the view offered there was that of the rolling farms of Des Moines.

She'd replaced the red privacy curtain with white linen that billowed bright and clean, its hem barely brushed the dirt floor, but still instantly accepted the dusty molecules, browning the fresh fabric. If Jeanie looked at that in the right way, the dirt could be deemed a nice border lining the hem like grosgrain ribbon might. She'd decided to accept illusion over reality when it came to making their home.

"What a load of horseshit. I hate my life. I hate my life. I hate my life."

But she did admire her handy work. The way the simple curtains brought their own light into the dark space as well as any candle, oil lamp or electricity like they'd had in Des Moines. It's okay, she told herself. This was the place where she could marry prairie shanty squalor with society class then tell the world about it.

"Haute Hovel," Jeanie did a little jig, laughing at her joke, taken with the same force of hilarity that she'd been swept up in tears. "Yes, Haute Hovel. I can see the headlines now. 'All it takes to transform your pile of shit into Haute Hovel are a few of Mrs. Arthur's carefully placed designs.'"

She spun around the space then shook her head as she assessed the next job to tackle. If her old friends in Des Moines had swooned at the success of her writing and home-keeping prowess they would take to their graves over the unnamed, potential successes that lay right there in front of her. Written in the dirt.

The next right thing. That was it! Jeanie automatically reached for the lost chatelaine then rummaged through one trunk finding paper and a pen. Right there, inspiration burst from her pores with the filthy sweat. At that moment it didn't matter that Darlington Township may never be vibrant enough to support a newspaper or progressive enough to hire a woman writer. At that moment only the possibilities counted. With a glance at the notepaper, Jeanie's hand flew across it. "One never knows the intangible ways a home-maker can influence her family simply by being capable. There is power in wielding the matters of ordinary life as though a tool. At some point, every homemaker will feel its glory, but to get there one must *first* do the next, right thing. That's all life requires."

Jeanie tapped the paper with the pencil then dropped them into the book trunk. Yes, that was it. That was exactly what she needed to do. The next right thing.

Jeanie sighed deeply, still lost in the insane laughter that kept ripping through her. She stretched and touched the dirt ceiling. Dirt rained from above, tickling her scalp. She shuddered telling herself never to touch the filthy ceiling if she wanted to ever be clean at all. More dirt sprinkled over her scalp and shoulders. She looked up. Fine dirt filled her eyes and mouth. Chunks of earth fol-lowed as she squinted away, shaking her head, spitting and chok-ing. She swiped at her eyes, hacking with cough.

Hands on knees, Jeanie's coughs cleared her throat of its dirty film.

Positioned there, breathing heavy, something like a bundle of rope fell onto her back. She shot to standing and turned. Through tearing eyes she saw two snakes wrapped around each other as though trying to untangle themselves, but not able to do so. She hugged herself and backed toward the curtained off section of the room, fighting her dirt-filled eyes from closing. The frantic sound of their rattles was matched by her staccato breath.

The sight of them tangling themselves around each other, as confused as she was nearly made her pass out.

All at once they unleashed themselves from each other and coiled, staring at her, heads bobbing. Jeanie had no way of knowing where everyone was and when they'd be back to help her. All she knew was as frightened as she felt, there was no way she'd wait. She wiped her tearing eyes with the backs of her hands.

She reached below her and lifted the book-trunk lid and pulled out the one on the top, closest to her. She lobbed *A Midsummer's Night's Dream*. It landed in front of the pair, causing a swell of dirt that did not hide the snakes' offense at being confronted. Jeanie could not afford to be bitten. Though death would end her problems, she couldn't bear leaving her children behind. The snakes were peeved, hissing and rattling, but not scared.

Next, Jeanie pulled *An American Family in Paris* from the trunk. She swallowed and chucked it. The burst of dirt from its landing nearly on their faces followed by their angry hisses ignited a series of chills through her body. Third, her own book—a collection of her columns—*Living the Gracious Way*. It landed in front of the snakes causing them to bob and spit at her.

Jeanie needed a stick, something to coax them out. Inside the curtained off section was the broom. She grabbed it and held the bristle end first, trying to move them out, but they just wrapped themselves around the broom and headed upward toward her hands. With that, she tossed the broom to the side and dashed out, drowning in chilly fear. Outside under the naked sun, she shivered as the rays warmed her sweaty body.

"Hey mom, everyone's on the way!" Tommy's muffled voice came from above the dugout.

"Oh, Tommy!" Jeanie said. "Thank sweet heaven, you're back! You're safe! I'm just about—" Jeanie ran over the side of the dugout to its top toward her boy.

"We're going to have a party. Father says it'll be just like back home," Tommy said. He was only ten, but he was particularly incapable of using his manners or noticing when he should be asking a question instead of rattling off his own agenda.

When she reached the top, Tommy had already fled back into the grasses, hollering at no one and playing a solitary game of cowboys and Indians. Frank *must* be nearby. He couldn't have let Tommy just wander over the plains. She was eager to see all her children familiar with the land, too, but this was extreme. Where was he?

Jeanie moved slowly across the top of the dugout, kicking at the grass with the toe of her boot here, then the heel there, searching for a weakness in the sod where the snakes might have burrowed into what she was forced to think of as her roof. She couldn't see anything besides the very tip of the stovepipe.

It was covered with crosshatched metal fixture that allowed the smoke out, but should have kept critters from getting in. Jeanie bent over it, peering into it, wondering if snakes could make themselves the size of pencils to gain access through things like that. Clearly, there were holes somewhere. James came up behind her and put his arm around her shoulders. "What's the matter, Mama? You look spooked. You should sit."

Jeanie straightened and smiled at James' concern and cradled his cheek in her hand for a moment before adjusting his hat. She'd never been an overly affectionate mother. She hadn't realized that until the past few days, when she couldn't keep from touching her children, their faces, arms, hugging them, smelling them, causing them to draw back before submitting to the extra affection. It was as though losing so much of their lives illuminated the only things that were still there—the living, breathing human beings she should have been more drawn to in the first place.

"James. Get the second wagon sheet from the floorboards. And the hoe. That should do it," Jeanie said.

James' eyes widened then squinted. "What's going on, Mama?"

"Snakes. They have some of the rattler variety in the house or whatever that thing we're standing on is and as much as I attempt to support your father and all his endeavors, I will *not* share space with snakes. So, after I kill the two in the dugout, we're going to line the ceiling with the wagon sheet so they can't enter by way of dropping in like packages of explosives, scaring the life out of your mother."

"Mama, it's okay. It's—"

"Where's your father?"

"He's on his way. Said he'd help the Misses Lutie and Ruthie Moore with their chores so they can come to dinner. They don't have men folk with them. Except for Mr. Templeton. Apparently he's taken an interest in one of them, visiting sometimes, but neither show interest in him. Much as I could tell. They didn't even look at him. Or as Father said, they don't show interest in a man on account of them wanting to prove up their homesteads before getting married. So the land's in their names, not some man's."

Jeanie stopped looking for snakes. Surprised not only by James's unusual blathering, but by the content of his news. "Is that what your father reported to you? They want their own land?"

"I heard the report right from the sisters Moore themselves. And Miss Lutie is a divorcee."

"A divorcee? That can't be right."

"A divorcee, right."

"Stop saying that word. It's awful."

"Miss Lutie Moore didn't seem to think the word was awful. She near sang it out to the clouds, you know being a women's rights advocate and all."

Jeanie grabbed at her throat that was tensing as her eyes watered.

James stepped toward her and took her hand away from her throat. "Are you crying, Mama? What's the matter? You don't have to worry about Father helping the Moore women too often. They don't want help from us men for the most part. They're earnest about women's rights. Suffrage and all it entails."

Jeanie wiped her face with her sleeve. "I'm not crying. It's from the ceiling—the dirt—it fell into my eyes like salt from a shaker.

I must look a terrible mess. You go on and get that wagon sheet and hoe." She shooed him with her hand. James nodded and was down the hill and at the wagon, hauling out supplies so fast that until that moment she hadn't realized exactly how close he was to being a man.

"Women's rights advocates," she said. "Right here in Darlington Township. Imagine that."

"Ma? The snakes?"

"Oh, yes of course."

Tommy barreled over the top of the house, slamming into James.

"Cut it out, Tommy." James swatted at his brother's hat, knocking it off his head.

"Can I help with the snakes?" Tommy grinned, his expression full of interest.

"You're too young," James said heading down the side of the dugout.

"*Am not.*" Tommy threw his arms around himself, mouth twisting in irritation. "Am I, Mama?"

Jeanie took off Tommy's hat, smoothed his hair back and studied his face. She lifted his chin. "Don't go anywhere near that dugout door. Those snakes will kill you. Like the Shofeld boy last year. Remember that? The swelling, the death? Don't go near it."

Tommy shook his head and Jeanie smoothed his hair back again. She didn't want Tommy involved in the removal of snakes. Not because he would be frightened or any less capable than Jeanie herself, but Tommy moved like a tornado—plowing over this, plundering that, interested in the inner-workings of everything, so much so he preferred the insides of everything out.

James shared Tommy's curiosity for everything, but Jeanie couldn't risk either one being bitten. Even in a land where children had adult responsibilities at times, Jeanie had to protect her boys. Not that she wanted to do this duty herself. But she had as much to learn as the children about being self-sufficient. Lack of money and service people taught you that lesson fairly quick.

"You can both watch from across the way. Thank goodness Katherine's with your father. Be ready to move out of the way. This isn't a game."

"We have rattlesnake antidote, right? We wouldn't light out for the prairie without that, would we?"

Jeanie stopped and sealed that thought in her mind. *Be sure to find rattlesnake antidote. Where? Who knew?* She wanted to be back in her family home, safe from beasts, feeling cool breezes lift errant hairs off her neck, while she wrote at her fine mahogany desk, hearing the children's voices lift and fade through the open windows.

"We'll get some Tommy. We definitely will."

Jeanie stalked the door, taking a few practice swings with the hoe, cursing their situation, and her always missing-when-needed husband. Jeanie shivered despite the heat and wanted to run from the dugout and allow her nearly-a-man son James to stab and kill the rattlers, but she couldn't do that. Two weeks before she would have paid the help to do such things, but now, it was she who had to grow up and take control of their life whether she wanted to or not.

She took a deep breath and crept into the hovel, ears straining for the tell-tale rattle. Like a trained snakes-woman, if there were such a thing, Jeanie gritted her teeth and goaded the pair of snakes into a corner, then stabbed at them with cold, silent calculation Jeanie imagined only a person possessing great hate and a black, shallow soul could deliver. Somehow demure, ladylike Jeanie found that place inside her and made the most of it for the sake of her family.

Once the snakes were dead and their exposed innards shoveled out with the tainted dirt that had been sullied under the carcasses, Jeanie came to the conclusion that laying a rug on the dirt might not be ideal. If they were going to slay intruders on a regular basis, it wouldn't be long before a thick rug held the smells of death, defining the space as even more hellish than she cared to imagine.

Jeanie and the boys draped the ceiling with the spare wagon sheet, staking it into the dirt with a mallet and dowels that had been tucked into the floorboards of the wagon. Once that was finished, she commenced breathing again and for the first time in hours she remembered she was pregnant. A spark of fear that all this activity would surely end in another miscarriage was replaced with a calm grounded in the thought that the other miscarriages had come while she'd been ordered to bed. If this child was meant to be, he'd come amidst the birth of their new life and be the stronger for it.

A person didn't require a genius IQ to discern that the Arthurs would not be able to entertain their neighbors within the confines of their dugout. Jeanie knew—okay she was attempting to convince herself—it wouldn't take much for her to organize a system that would allow her to graciously accept guests, even the unexpected ones, but with that day being their first, she had nothing to offer the impending influx of visitors. Unless they each desired an embroidered handkerchief —not only did she have a store of them in one of the trunks, but she could stitch a spare design inside a few minutes.

She rotated around the center of the hovel, trying to decide what to do next. The stove top which sat near the back, with a stove pipe extending out of the top of the dugout, was charred underneath the layers of loose dirt she'd scraped off. She'd never seen something so primitive, not even her summer kitchen had such a filthy, small device. She wondered how they'd live with the beastly thing. She imagined the space either too hot or them suffocating on muck that surely would escape the thing when in use.

Jeanie stared at the bedstead the Henderson's left behind. The one the Arthurs would put to use. She shook her head. She could clean the bedstead up, recover it with fresh, plain cotton from her trunk and that would suffice. But its proximity to the rest of, well, the rest of everything, displeased her. The bedstead stood a mere six feet from the stove. A little behind it, was a similar bedstead, which all three children would share, until they moved out. And they would, Jeanie thought, they would be out of that hovel by spring.

Jeanie grew tired of staring at the contents of her new home and took some fresh air atop the house. Like a joke, it made her laugh that she stood on her roof, like a chimney sweep. She peered into the prairie, growing considerably irritated at Frank's decision to assist the sisters Moore with some household matter and to have decided to invite a pocket of Darlington Township for supper. He should have known better than to think even Jeanie could make that a pleasurable exercise in society.

Just before calling the children to her to put them to work after a day's exploration, heads began popping out of the earth's surface at the horizon. First an enormous man with legs like barrels—Jeanie could see that even from a distance. And with him, several only slightly smaller men, a little girl, and a woman carrying a small child.

That turned her blood on, Jeanie admitted, the sight of guests plodding toward her like an approaching army with her husband still nowhere in sight. She wanted to hide, and claim no admittance to supper and the shanty, but she'd never be able to gather the children in to participate in the ruse.

As the group got closer, it was entirely clear they were a family. They marched nearly in step, white blond hair flouncing under their hats and bonnets. When they reached her, Jeanie noticed their red skin blared like beets contrasting their eyes so greatly that she kept staring at each of them, questioning whether it were possible for eyes to be so definitely blue, but nearly transparent, the color of water, almost. They were not a smiley bunch—each wore an expression that bore what appeared to be the results of bouts of acid stomach or the onset of death.

"Mrs. Arthur," the man of the group announced as he held out his hand. His swallowed Jeanie's in what felt like sand paper, "I'm Nikolai Zurchenko. His voice was gentle, though its deep, accented tones boomed and reverberated easily. Jeanie nodded as each boy—Artem, Anton, Aleksey, and Adam introduced himself with grips that nearly buckled her knees. Little Anna, six years, and baby Anzhela, two years, stared at her from their parent's arms as though she'd threatened to kick them.

Finally, Greta broke into what Jeanie was sure was a smile, but only made her face grimmer. "Hello, Jeanie, pleasure to make your acquaintance. We've brought some things for supper, to get you started on the land." Greta shook her hand in both of hers. They were nearly as big as her husband's hands and just as rough. Greta was the largest woman Jeanie'd ever seen. Greta blocked the sun out as she overshadowed Jeanie's five-foot, seven-inch frame. She must have been at least six feet.

"Thank you so much for making the trek to see us," Jeanie said. "I'm afraid Frank is seeing to the Moore sisters and I've fallen behind in setting up house today, what with some snakes and, well, I'm sure I don't have to tell you," she said. Greta nodded along politely, but there was evidence that mucking about in the troubles of her day was not high on the list of the Zurchenko's wants and needs.

Nikolai stared at Jeanie, blank faced, but eyebrows raised at attention, as though Jeanie might offer heavy words of wisdom and portent of wonderful things to come. His expression didn't seem uninterested, but it offered no other signs to his thoughts either—whether Jeanie should stop yapping. The boys stood with board-straight backs, watching Jeanie with the same expressions as their father, ones that nearly made her giggle as she wondered what could possibly be careening around their minds, watching some prairie novice prattle on about snakes and things they've probably seen numerous times.

One of the boys handed Jeanie a hen. Another set one down near the wagon.

Jeanie stopped talking.

Greta turned sideways and swept her hand toward the hand wagon the boys had drug across the land. "Besides the hens, we've brought some potatoes—some ready for planting, watermelons—we've had a blessed crop that yields at least three ripes a week—some cakes, a bucket of water to get you started, and..."

Greta continued with the inventory and Jeanie grew twisted with a stew of gratitude, embarrassment, honor, and dismay that they were deemed so needy from so far a distance. She wondered what Frank had told everyone as he met them. Mostly, she couldn't take her eyes from the wagon, the watermelons the size of two of the Zurchenko men's heads, if they were set crown to crown. Jeanie wiped the corner of her mouth as she thought it was surely showing signs of dribbling saliva.

Jeanie swept her finger over the melon then knocked on it twice. She turned to see all of them staring, scowling. "Thank you all so much." Jeanie nearly bowed at them. She didn't know what to say except that her family couldn't accept all this. "Maybe once we're settled and bring in some—"

"Nonsense," Greta said. Baby Anzhela hung around her neck, legs latched around Greta's midsection like a monkey so that Greta didn't even need to touch her. She held her hands out to Jeanie, stretching around Anzhela, as though inviting her into their embrace.

Jeanie gave her hands to Greta but didn't step into any sort of clinch. Warmth coursed through Jeanie's body. Even when Greta's scowl broke into an even more severe grin, they instantly connected, with the suddenness that a room, blackened by night then suddenly taken by morning sun would do and they were, at once, old friends.

Greta squeezed Jeanie's hands. "We have many ways of helping one another and this is small compared to what will change hands among us in the future. These lands are...they're not for the…well, let's just say the prairie shows things that only will be endured by us, supporting each other. Our families."

Jeanie nodded, absorbed in Greta's liquid gaze. They released hands and Greta spun Anzhela around to her back where the little one peered over her mother's shoulder, squinting. Greta turned her attention to the wagon. Finally, Anzhela smiled at Jeanie, making her laugh at the little girl's chubby, delicate face—not at all Greta-like.

Off to the side, Nikolai barked orders—meaning he used about six words to get the boys moving as they spread out over the prairie doing only heaven knew what. Heavens, Jeanie thought, how that man could get a point across and conserve words at the same time.

Baby Anzhela rode on Greta's back and Anna held items from the wagon as Greta searched for something. Jeanie was still struck by them, unable to be mannerly or useful. Jeanie stared at Greta, her great size—she could be a man in a dress. She'd never seen a woman with so few charms. She didn't lack manners, but she didn't have delicacy about her—that coy womanly expression that most females used on each other as well as men, a means of manipulation, to present a certain image, to evoke a certain emotion or behavior in others. This woman simply was. And that was the greatest thing Jeanie'd ever seen in all her days.

Greta pulled Jeanie over to the line of trees that extended from the dugout. "These are Russian olive trees. They're not enormous, but I planted these here when we arrived with the Hendersons three years ago. They'll break the wind for you. You'd be surprised how much these can do in the dead of winter."

Jeanie clamped her hands in front of her at her waist, surprised that such still small trees could make a difference on this great plain. "And the bee tree? Mr. Templeton told me a little bit about it."

"Ah, the bee tree. You have the only one at present and I'd like to say we all make use of it in one way or another."

"The prospect of sweet honey does fill my mouth with water," Jeanie said.

"Being that it contributes to honey production, it makes the hard times a little sweeter. And it's the perfect landmark for those times when the boys go a little too far out on the prairie, or in the unusual case of guests finding their way to our property. But the inside of it is almost more valuable than the outside. There have been times when we were in need of roping one thing or another and I'd thought of having Nikolai chop it down and cut it open for its innards that make fine rope. But luckily, Nikolai is more level-headed than me. He understands the need to be particular as to what resources we take and those we leave."

"It's a bit surprising that such a scrawny tree can be so important. It's tall of course, but scrawny, indeed," Jeanie said.

Greta pulled the front of her bonnet out a bit to give her more shade as she stared at it. "The tree reminds me of us—we pioneers. Strong, resilient." She shrugged.

"It seems as though that's imperative for pioneers all right," Jeanie said.

Greta turned abruptly—so fast that Anzhela's legs nearly lost their grip on her mother. "Did you know that if a Bass wood tree is cut down, falls down, or burned or whatever might happen to one, it begins to sprout from itself—the seemingly dead trunk. One day it'll just start growing again." Her face was as animated, as animated as it could be, Jeanie guessed as it still managed to grow grim with the enthusiasm. Jeanie imagined how her mother would have dealt with Greta's lack of natural charms.

She could hear her saying "Dearest, Greta, you must sit in front of the mirror until you shape your scowl into a picture of peace and beauty. And if you can't muster a pretty expression while smiling, well, then develop an expression that doesn't make use of a smile." Jeanie's mother wouldn't have managed one minute on the prairie. For the first time, Jeanie wasn't merely glad her mother's life had ended before her father's for her sake, but Jeanie was glad for her own sake.

Jeanie shook off thoughts of her mother and let the inspiration of Greta's hopeful words sweep into her body. "I think the tree is magnificent. Ugly or not. It's as though its dream is to one day be the biggest, longest living tree on the prairie, the one that provides quiet useful service." Jeanie said only half joking.

"Dream? Well, dreams aren't much help out here, Jeanie. Dreams are sort of..." Greta swung baby Anzhela around front and began to poke at the bottom lid of her right eye, wiping dirt from the inside corners of it then the left with her thumbs. Anzhela finally squirmed and re-grasped onto her mother around the neck so she'd stop picking at her.

"Dreams are the only things that make me happy," Jeanie said. "The next step toward making the life I want. I couldn't live without dreams. The picture of myself living on our own property, in a white house, flower boxes, cutting gardens, luxury and writing. I'll write again and have something important to say. And the children. Having children who are educated and respectful. And, full of their own dreams. I don't remember a time in life when I didn't have a set of dreams for which I strived."

Greta grinned and shook her head. "You're smarter than that, Mrs. Frank Arthur. I don't mean to suppose and I know we haven't known one another but a minute, but on the prairie, there's a level of honesty not present in the civilized segments of the great United States. And I can say from this short minute of our acquaintance, that you are smarter than that."

Jeanie was about to tell her that intelligence and dreaming didn't exist as separate entities, but as Jeanie started to further engage Greta in this line of conversation, Frank, Templeton, and two women appeared atop the dugout, sitting astride two horses in an entirely inappropriate fashion. Templeton held a rope, making a leash of sorts, connected to a very full cow. Jeanie's gaze fell over Frank's legs that were nearly wrapped around one of the women who sat in front of him. The woman's skirts, though modestly lifted to accommodate the horse, were still lifted. Peeved by the sight of them, Jeanie wished the four slow-pokes and the horses would crash through the roof of the dugout making it impossible for the Arthurs to live inside it.

Chapter 6

1905
Des Moines, Iowa

Katherine's days changed once her mother and sister came to live with them. She and Aleksey still rose before dawn. She began the wash, made breakfast, and lured her family from warm beds with thick French toast and fluffy eggs while Aleksey shoveled the coal and lit the stove. He shuffled off to his law firm, as he always did. But, Katherine's afternoons were now spent consulting with Dr. Shoal about Jeanie's declining condition, Dr. Matthews regarding Yale's pending institutionalization, and Dr. Patterson regarding her own sanity.

Katherine forwent her weekly garden club meetings, quilting club meetings, and volunteer work at the library to make her mother as comfortable as possible. Katherine's actions—the way she brought her mother's food on a beautiful tray with silver utensils and a single flower in a vase, or turned her mother to gently remove and replace sheets—were serviceable and attentive. But, she could have been tending to a plant for as much warmth as she offered. She entered the guest room with a bundle of fresh sheets, towels and quilt.

"Did the blizzard take your tongue along with your pinky finger?" Jeanie said.

Katherine wanted to yank the sheet and dump her frail mother off the bed. Instead she pulled her linen bundle closer to her chest with one hand and with the other hand, she pulled the quilt from atop her mother.

"That's the rudest thing I've ever heard Mother. How could you? You know how that...I was only *ten* at the time. How *could* you?" Katherine squealed as though she were, indeed, ten again.

Jeanie shrugged, her hands clenched at her chest, face softened for the first time Katherine could ever remember. "I just wanted to hear your voice. See if there was a heart inside the shell of a person you've become."

Katherine pulled a corner of the quilt aside to remove it. Jeanie pulled it back.

Katherine felt secure in her kindness, the good works she did for anyone in need. And no one with half a brain to spare would think she was wrong for not doting on her selfish mother.

"I need to wash your linens. They smell sour. I know how much stink unsettles you."

Jeanie looked away, pulling the quilt under her chin.

"Mother, I don't want to wrestle it from your grasp. If you're cold, I'll put the fresh quilt over you right away," Katherine said. She yanked the bottom of the quilt up and exposed Jeanie's feet.

"Mother. What...why?" She pointed at Jeanie's feet. "Those wretched boots? Why on earth would you wear those horrible things?"

Jeanie turned on her side, refusing to speak.

"You hate those things. Let me take them off. They can't be comfortable. You're sick, you're...oh *please*, let me take those off of your feet." Katherine reached for the boots and Jeanie inched her feet to the other side of the bed, staring at the wall.

"Katherine. Let me die in peace. Unless you can forgive me. That's all I need from you. I know the rest will take care of itself, but I need to know that you understand I did my best."

"Of course I forgive you. I...I don't ever think about...yes, I forgot about it a long time ago."

Jeanie scoffed and shrugged, clearly not believing her daughter.

Katherine was stunned at her mother wearing the disgusting boots in bed, the black curled, scarred ones she'd once sworn never to wear past May 1888. Yet, there they were like miniature ghosts of their past, on Jeanie's feet, holes in the soles. But more than that, she was struck by Jeanie's request for forgiveness. She'd never wanted it before and though Katherine would say she forgave her mother, she wasn't sure she ever really could.

Jeanie pulled the quilt back over her feet. Katherine shook her head. What was the point of changing the quilt if Jeanie was going to house stinky black boots under it?

"So much happened, Katherine. You don't really understand, you were a child and I couldn't, I *wouldn't*...I was trying to protect you." Jeanie's voice was thin.

Katherine's mind spun. Was the woman insane? Protect her? She only protected herself.

"I know everything I need to know, Mother. You tried to be selfless to put us first, but in the end, you simply weren't equipped to do so. I thank you for the apology and you have my deepest forgiveness."

Jeanie lay there, stone still. "I once allowed a friend to die without my forgiveness. That selfish act of mine, it grips me still. It's an awful thing to do to a dying soul. Over the years I've realized she did her best at the time with what she had, her limitations. But, my heart was closed to her at the time..."

"Who?"

Jeanie's breath was her only reply.

"So you're doing *me* a favor by demanding my forgiveness? You stranded me with nothing. And while I know you need to unburden your heart and cleanse your soul because you are dying, Mama, I don't think I need to know any further details on the matter."

She covered her mouth wanting to trap the word Mama inside even though it had already escaped. She began to quake. It was as though birthing the words, having the conversation she did not want to have, made the meaning behind what was said and unsaid explode inside her, as though the earth separated and Katherine for the first time felt encompassed by true fear.

Her teeth chattered and she clutched the linen bundle tighter. She couldn't say what she felt at that moment, besides the oddest chill over her skin, but she knew she couldn't handle information or anything else her mother had to offer by way of assurance that she'd once loved her as a mother ought to.

"I did the best I could." Jeanie said

"It wasn't enough. I would never do that to my children. Never. I would die first."

"Finally. Truth. It's about time you uttered it," Jeanie said. "But, you don't know *my* truth. You don't know the half of it, Katherine."

"I know all that I need to."

"Well, I need to tell you what happened that year. What really happened."

"I want to give you that, Mother, a chance to repent, but whatever you have to say, I do not want to hear. I'll call a minister or Aleksey, since you're perfect bosom buddies these days. Anyone but me. Some things aren't meant to be shared between mother and daughter. That much I learned from you."

Jeanie shuddered as wind came through the open window. Katherine closed the window with one hand and wordlessly tucked the dirty quilt around every square inch of her mother's body.

She left the room with the bitter smell of death at her heels and the pitiful sound of her mother crying for her to come back, to please understand. She stood in the hallway, back against the closed door. She did want to understand, she did want to truly forgive her mother, she wanted her mother to experience earthly peace, but she didn't know if she could do that. No matter how much she might regret not forgiving her mother, as Jeanie suggested she would, she was too resentful to do more than act as though she forgave. And that, she hoped would be enough.

Chapter 7

1887
Dakota Territory

The sight of one's husband, intimately draped around another woman would be too much to take with no witnesses. But, for Jeanie to have Frank saunter into view, astride a horse and the woman sharing its back, with new neighbors watching? The sight buckled Jeanie's knees.

Greta grabbed Jeanie's arm, and kept her from crashing to the ground.

Jeanie felt her face bearing the crushed emotions that churned inside and she pulled away from Greta, smoothing her skirts then her hair. "I'm fine." Jeanie plastered a smile across her face and patted Greta's arm before striding toward the husband Jeanie wished, at that moment, wasn't hers.

As Jeanie neared the dugout, Frank dismounted the horse, helped the woman down, holding her wasp waist a little too long in Jeanie's opinion.

Frank dashed around the dugout, his blue eyes alive with something Jeanie couldn't identify.

"Oh, I love you my sweet Jeanie, my sweet friend, my love, my Jeanie. You look angry. I see behind that smile of yours." Frank led Jeanie away from the group, trying to soften her mood. "Please don't worry, lend me your worries and I'll take them far away into the prairie where they can be buried deep, so we can live in comfort and pleasantness. Please, don't buckle into the tensions of this new place. We'll grow to understand the land, to contemplate the beauties of its nature just as we did so many times in the dense action of Des Moines. We'll find that sort of feeling again. The freedom, the happiness. The everything we ever thought we wanted. It's all here for the taking. I can just feel it. Please, come meet Ruthie and Lutie Moore. I told them all about you. They can't wait to meet you."

Jeanie suddenly felt relieved. With the simple words "I told them all about you," Jeanie's anger fell away. She fell into Frank, letting him pet her. She felt dim-witted for letting cross feelings infiltrate her body and control its essence. Frank saw it from across the prairie, her discontent, and she was wrong for letting it show like that. It didn't matter that their life collapsed in Des Moines, that her father had buried himself beneath a mound of powdered morphine long before the coroner claimed him lifeless. None of it was any excuse for her falling into her own blackness, drug-free as it might have been.

She pushed Frank at the chest, then took his face in her hands, peppering him with kisses, not caring who saw or what it meant for society as it was becoming very clear, society as she knew it was not in their presence.

"Okay, I trust you, us, everything, this land. We can do this. I'm so sorry I've been disagreeable. We can make this work. I love you Frank Arthur. I love you like it was the first day we met." What she didn't say was that this trust she felt was artificial, forced, constructed from something that used to be there, like the life they used to know. But, at that point, all Jeanie had was the will to construct a new life, even if that meant forcing intangible aspects of it into being, hoping that the act of pretending might bring forth reality.

Jeanie and Frank turned toward the dugout and her normal energies returned. They headed to greet their guests in an appropriate manner, one that would be suitable in any civilized place.

Lutie Moore, the woman who Frank had ridden with, looked down from the dugout at Jeanie. She held a bucket, with water slushing over the sides. "Well, now, you must be the *famous*, pregnant Mrs. Arthur." She squealed like a child and squeezed her shoulders to her ears, face frozen into a smile of obnoxious glee.

Jeanie's hands flew to her waist. Her knees nearly buckled from the mortification that dripped over her like honey. Before Jeanie could respond, Lutie bounded down the side of the dugout and quite effectively skipped like a six-year-old. She placed the bucket at Jeanie's feet. "Pleased to meet you Mrs. Arthur. My sister Ruthie and I have both of your books and ten of your columns. The very chivalrous and debonair Howard Templeton is always kind enough to bring a copy of your column when he comes back from the city. You have a fine, fine husband and I can only say that I hope when the time comes, I can fetch a boy just like him."

Lutie stuck her hand out to shake Jeanie's. It was a tiny, smooth thing, with bones no larger than little Katherine's. Lutie's face, molded into a perfect oval, boasted wide-set eyes and lush lips like Jeanie'd only seen in *Harper's Bazaar*. Her slim waist seemed to only get smaller and smaller until it belled out as just the right juncture to make her appear as though an artist had drawn the essence of woman and Lutie came to life right off the paper.

Mostly, Lutie's youth and vibrance struck Jeanie, making her feel instantly dowdy and unworthy of her wiry, electrified husband. The word divorcee kept leaping to mind, making Jeanie immediately suspicious of the kind of woman who could possibly divorce and be so happy thereafter.

"My, my, my. A pleasure to meet you, Lutie. Call me Jeanie." If Jeanie had learned anything from her father and mother it was that a woman should never let anyone recognize her insecurity as it related to her looks or her husband's intentions. Such weaknesses, displayed for others was like blood in the water, calling all interested sharks to feed at the trough of one's husband.

"Oh, I will," Lutie said, "that's right pleasant of you. You just put me right to work as my sister Ruthie and I have sort of relaxed our conduct, not so much as to be scandalous, but in terms of keeping home. We've narrowed our work load to the nitty-gritty so to conserve time for music, song, and well, gardening and such. Your books are like home-keeping fantasy novels, fairytales that we can enjoy in print, but the chance of us bringing your words to life, are well, as slim as Cinderella herself riding over that plain there. But we are thrilled that you will be able to do just that. Imagine it. The great Jeanie Arthur, right here in Darlington Township. Our very own big-bug come to town to bestow us with great knowledge, eloquently bestowed, I'm sure."

Jeanie shifted her weight and shyly glanced at the others who were listening. In light of the current condition of her home and body, she couldn't have been more self-conscious of the mess it put her in to have written those books and to be held to their standard. Lutie didn't seem to notice the discomfort as she gushed on.

"And your Frank just about had a fit when he saw how we were mistreating our cows with improper milking technique. He said you were the fastest milk maid in Des Moines at one time," she rambled on.

"Well now, Jeanie," Greta said stepping into the conversation. "You didn't mention one bit of this—your skill as a milker. A writer of all things gracious, I know you said you dreamt of writing again, but I assumed it was letters you spoke of. Well, that's right wonderful seeing as Lutie and Ruthie neglect to milk at all half the time, why don't you, Lutie, offer Jeanie the cow in return for milk every few days?"

"Oh, no, we couldn't. We plan to buy livestock after we bring in the first crop or after Frank sells some of his furniture commissions," Jeanie said.

"Oh, why, Greta," Lutie said. "That's right intelligent of you, for an unread woman to come up with that. Well, okay, that'll give me a chance to see you Arthurs on a regular basis, and yes, well, yes. That's a great idea. How about we trade. Our cow for your home-keeping knowledge. We can be your apprentices." Lutie walked away, talking to herself, repeating those words, making a dead-line toward Ruthie.

"Greta, I can't accept that. It's not right."

"S'not right what's happening in that house of theirs. I call it the house of ill-repute."

Jeanie's jaw fell.

"No, no," Greta said. "There's not actually such devious acts taking place there, other than Lutie's blood-boiling flirtation, but they abuse their resources. Well *that's* a scandal if one were likely to see the world in that way. I have much less trouble with loose women than I do loose women with loose housekeeping."

Jeanie covered her mouth and chortled into her hand. "Greta, you're charming me right out of my blue mood. I have to thank you."

"And," Greta said, "Don't worry about Ruthie, she rules the roost over there—they'd be dead if not for her—but she's no more interested in milking than old Loopy Lutie."

Templeton made her way to Nikolai and the boys to help with what now she could see was plowing. Frank had disappeared into the dugout while the other men cleared space for the Arthur's garden. How could she let them do such back-breaking work while Frank entertained Darlington Township's ladies of leisure?

"Mrs. Arthur, uh, Jeanie?" The sister called Ruthie had come up on Jeanie without her noticing. Jeanie spun around.

"Jeanie, please. Call me that."

Ruthie bit her lower lip then sucked both into her mouth and clamped down, and averted her gaze. She seemed to nearly shake in Jeanie's presence. Her face was pock-marked, pudgy, without the planes that exposed just the right hills and valleys in a face, the contours that make one beautiful. Sprigs of Ruthie's hair jutted from under her bonnet like the grasses inside the dugout. Some were black and others were the color of the dirty foam that had gathered atop the pond that nearly swallowed Katherine and Jeanie whole the day before. It was wavy like Lutie's with none of the shine.

Ruthie finally looked Jeanie in the eye. "I know what you're thinking. What everyone does when they meet us. Are they really sisters? Well yes. Lutie's always been the lucky one right down to when, by pure happenstance, she escorted our mother to tend our sickly grandmother and in the interim, small-pox knocked back seventy-five percent of our town."

As Ruthie spoke her posture straightened and she trans-formed from a shy mouse into more of a Greta figure. Strong in her limitations.

Jeanie put her hand on Ruthie's arm. "I didn't think anything at all, Ruthie. I try not to put too many eggs in the attractiveness basket as I've found it guarantees nothing by way of happiness or honesty or loyalty."

Ruthie didn't say anything but instead whipped to her right and marched off toward Greta and Lutie as though Jeanie'd smacked her. Well, so far, Jeanie was one in three for finding an acquaintance that suited her. Perhaps the prairie would be even lonelier than she had guessed it could be.

Each time Jeanie tried to contribute to preparing the food, another neighbor arrived. The Hunts and their two sons Maxwell and Tobias were next. Mrs. Hunt was a minister of a Quaker Meeting and Mr. Hunt did his best to farm. That's how they intro-duced themselves and quickly they ran through where the monthly meetings would be held and all the ways they hoped to bring lit-eracy to the community while allowing each neighbor to find their inner light.

Jeanie didn't know anything about Quakers except that they were unlikely to cause problems and so she didn't give them much thought in terms of their religion. She was, however, mesmerized by the notion that it was Abby Hunt who was the minister. Not at all something she'd ever explored through her writing or thinking.

Frank had slipped into the conversation without Jeanie even realizing he was back from watering the horses or hiding in the dugout. "I like that notion, that Quakers hold as their guiding principle—finding the light within. Sort of how I make it my business to contemplate the beauties of nature. To really appreciate what beauty in that form means."

Jeanie had no idea where Frank had become informed of the principles of Quaker beliefs, but that wasn't the time to ask.

"Frank, darling," Jeanie said putting her hand on his back. "Won't you be a dear and bring in fresh water. I'd like some extra for the ladies as they may enjoy a fresh toilet before dinner." Those words, the manner in which she delivered them felt good, normal, as though she could bring a little of the past into their present and in the future, perhaps, they could create the kind of society that demanded proper behavior and allowed for enjoyment of culture.

"Sure," he said. His face drooped a bit, sorry definitely to be removed from the conversation. But compared to the Zurchenkos, none of them had done anything and that was humiliating to Jeanie. She didn't have time to work with Frank's limitations, push him to perform as he should have been innately inclined to do.

So, thanks to Ruthie, Greta and Abby Hunt, they enjoyed a rich dinner, conversation that revealed their little group as being slightly more intellectual than handy in nature and at that time Jeanie only gave that the label of interesting. It turned out Nikolai and Greta Zurchenko had only gone to school until sixth grade. And the current lot of Zurchenko children had barely attended at all. Ruthie had taught school for a year in Yankton before homesteading. Lutie had been promoted out of eighth grade, but showed no practical evidence of having done so. Ruthie had intimated that perhaps her parents thought Lutie had been secure in her beauty and standing, and hadn't pushed her to do much more than revel in her own splendor.

But, the flu took them and upon burial, the sisters discovered they were penniless. Lutie did the only thing she could imagine doing, and that was to get married, to attempt to bring some income to her and Ruthie. Greta discreetly told Jeanie that Lutie's divorce was solely her doing, that she couldn't stand being stifled by rules and a man's place in the home as superior to hers. She simply drew up papers with her husband's lawyer and walked out, requesting nothing.

Had it been a different grouping, different circumstance, Jeanie might have offered her experience—her father's death marked not only with typical grief, but laced with mind-numbing humiliation—as a means to bridging the enormous social gap, but Jeanie had never been the type to offer up weaknesses for conversational purposes. If she could pretend whatever was bad wasn't there, then so could those around her.

Jeanie enjoyed listening to the others anyway, shaping who each person was and was not in her mind. Frank, though, was blustery, gushing forth with all method of dreams and his latest in air castle construction as he suggested all manner of ways they might make quick money. Jeanie shuddered thinking that Greta would suppose Jeanie kept the same silly dreams tucked inside her as Frank did. But Jeanie'd never dreamed of something she couldn't achieve. She resisted the urge to tell Greta, she wasn't *that* kind of dreamer. She was practical in her wishes.

Sheep and cotton were two of Frank's latest areas of focus. He'd not yet researched each fully, but he pulled several stacks of literature from the bottom of the book trunk and shook the paper at everyone saying how the path to riches, though going through the township of Darlington, would not stop there.

Frank wielded his dreams as though he could spend them like cash—money to make people impressed. And this made Jeanie want to crawl into herself, made her grateful that get-togethers such as these would be limited by daily responsibilities. She wouldn't have to either book-end Frank's statements with impact softening verbal cotton, or shrink inside herself wishing she'd never met the man, then hating herself for not taking up residence inside each and every one of his very stately air castles.

"My dear Jeanie, here, disagrees with my plans, but that's all right. All it takes is one half of a couple to see the dream and grab it."

Jeanie felt attacked. "Now Frank, all I did was offer the information that flat prairie lands aren't conducive to..."

"Ah, that's my Jeanie," Frank's words bit her as his eyes narrowed and he shook his head. Jeanie drew back, unsure of what she'd done wrong. "Always has *all* the answers. Loves to offer them up for—"

Jeanie leaned across the table to get full view of Frank's face. "I don't have all the answers, darling Frank, I simply have ownership of all the *right* answers." The guests hooted with the exchange, thinking it was all in fun. But Jeanie knew better. She sat back straight, busying herself with arranging the plates in front of her, horrified at the exchange. The Arthurs weren't a screaming family, prone to dramatic histrionics. Jeanie understood, fully, that behind these simple, quietly delivered words were years of Frank's resentment of her, feelings she never cared to worry about in the past. She never had to. Her life had been stable and in that security, she could handle anything, even a man who'd been taken by a love/hate existence with his very own wife.

"My, my, my." Jeanie said at the sky, unaware she had spoken aloud until Greta nudged her with raised eyebrows and cocked head.

"Oh," Jeanie said. "It's nothing. Just...nothing." And she rose from the table to clear away the trash.

The sun perched high in the sky for so long that the guests waited past the reasonable time to leave. When the yellow sphere finally sunk into the horizon it sucked the light over the edge of the earth with it. It left them in split second shadows and blinding darkness that rendered the glow of kerosene lamps, candles and the fire practically useless.

They bumped around trying to arrange blankets and sleeping quarters near the dugout so everyone would be moderately comfortable. The children were thrilled to have guests for the night. The only thing that would drag them from a competitive game of jacks was Frank.

He bore no shortage of funny and ghostly tales to tell the children. His animated expression, happy eyes and warm affection toward everyone brought Jeanie a long lost twinge of love, near infatuation—the kind of sensation that had turned her heart toward him years before.

And, when Frank finished his last tale, a sort of fairy tale in which he used all the children's names and somehow had each child look like a hero in the story, Jeanie heard Lutie sigh. Jeanie studied the woman's fine profile and saw, in the moonlight, the look of love sparkling in her eyes as she watched Frank entertain them all.

Jeanie shook her head and crossed her arms.

"I'm well certain that someday I'll make the acquaintance of a man like Frank," Lutie said. "Musn't there be a Frank out there for each one of us, Jeanie? There must be, wouldn't you admit so?"

Jeanie didn't think Lutie really wanted a response but then Lutie turned to Jeanie, arching her eyebrows expectantly.

"I don't know, Lutie." Jeanie shrugged. A surge of disappointment reminded Jeanie that the Frank in front of her, the one charming the socks off everyone watching, was *not* the Frank she'd known the past few years. "I'm not sure you know a man's worth until after matrimony. It's then that the real man and woman are revealed to one another. And usually just to one another. Others will continue to tramp about the world harboring fantasies about each person and who they might really be inside their own skin, but really no one knows that husband except the wife."

"That sounds precious. How could a woman be married and not happy? Why marry if it's not the case that she will be?" Lutie said grinning, nearly licking her lips off.

"In the end, I believe it's a woman's own fault if she is not happy when she is married. I believe it to be the case. I'm happy and I make Frank happy because my love for him is true—"

Frank who must have been lurking yet again, inserted himself in the women's conversation, squatting in front of Lutie and Jeanie, knees spread apart in that way men always seemed to position themselves, emitting an odor of an unbathed man. Lutie either didn't notice it or the scent was love tonic to her olfactory system because she leaned toward Frank, mussing his hair before thanking him again for all his help.

"My Jeanie," Frank said, "She chases my dull worries and cares away and makes me forget there's trouble and sorrow in the world."

"There's trouble and sorrow in the world?" Lutie grabbed at her chest and fluttered her eyes at Frank.

"Well, not if you're lucky enough to call Jeanie Arthur your wife or mother."

Lutie shut her eyes and dropped her head back exposing her neck to the prairie. "Just three more winters and we'll prove up and I'll find a man like you, Frank Arthur," Lutie said to the sky. She looked back up and gazed directly at Frank and he back at her. Jeanie felt as though she'd entered a cocoon which had been constructed for the purposes of transforming Frank and Lutie from a larval stage of infatuation to full-fledged love.

Jeanie may have been a good wife but she was not stupid and she would not allow herself to be made to look dumb, not after looking right slow-headed in the case of her father and their family business. She stood then dragged Lutie to her feet. "Now Lutie Moore, I'm going to put you and your sister in your bed sacks. Two women homesteading as you are, need all the rest you can get I imagine. You're closest to the wagon, near all the children. I've arranged a toilet there with fresh rags and the most delicate of hand towels. The bed sacks came right out of my trunks, still pristine clean with the scent of lavender to assist you in your slumber. You shouldn't need anything in the night so you can be assured of good unbroken sleep away from the snoring men."

Jeanie pushed Lutie along, gripping her arms so tight that she expected Lutie to dig in her heels and ask her where Jeanie found the inclination to act as though her mother. That's what Jeanie would have done, but Jeanie harbored no rat-like tendencies and knew she'd never bat her lashes or any other of her assets at another woman's husband.

And so, when everyone was nestled into their sacks and only an occasional spark of children's laughter lit the quiet, Frank sat inside the dugout doorway, playing their song, Marie's song. He'd taken the tune and stretched it into a moody, dark version of the original upbeat version. It worried Jeanie that he'd taken to that version so heartily.

It nearly always signaled the beginning of one of his blue moods, but Jeanie told herself there was no time for him to indulge such states of mind for they were carving out his dream just as sure as this dugout carved out the hill.

"Good night, sweet friend," Frank said from the doorway, still sitting in the moonlight, "thy love ne'er alters till thy sweet life end."

"Good night, sweet friend," Jeanie said barely above a whisper. And she fell into a short, but heavy sleep. Jeanie set her internal clock for before dawn and was determined to offer their guests a breakfast as bloated with grace as sweetness. For, if there was anything Jeanie could do it was make a home and it was time she showed her new friends just what her strengths on this earth were.

Jeanie shot up to sitting, sweat drenched, breathing heavy. Jeanie's abdomen tightened with a cramp, making her think she'd be miscarrying by noon if her past was any indication. Her stomach released and she fell back on the pillow, then was struck by an image of Frank, a dream she'd had about him. That's what had wakened her as much as the cramps.

"I had that dream," she shook Frank's shoulder.

"Wha...the what? What dream?"

Jeanie whispered in his ear, feeling as though a normal conversational volume would carry out the door and into the ears of their sleeping guests. "The dream, where I know it's you, but I can't see your face and you're telling me you're leaving me...that dream."

"Ahhh, my Jeanie, that's just a dream. You know I could never leave you."

"But your face, my not being able to see it, that must mean something."

"You've been dreaming that since we were fifteen. I think it means nothing at all."

Jeanie was beginning to shake the odd, real feeling of abandonment that always accompanied the dream. "Okay, okay, There's breakfast to get anyway. I'll start things." Jeanie climbed over Frank to get out of bed then kissed his forehead.

"I'm making flapjacks," Jeanie said.

"That sounds superb," Frank said. Jeanie expected him to rise out of bed to help, to at least get water, but he rolled to his side and before Jeanie had even squatted over the chamber pot, she could hear him snoring.

Jeanie didn't have time to succumb to the twinge of disappointment that he would shirk his duties because as she emerged from behind the curtain to the chamber room, Aleksey Zurchenko and Katherine stood across the room, near the stove, with two water buckets, full to sloshing.

"Katherine? You went to the well?" Jeanie felt a surge of fear that after only one day on the prairie Katherine would be so brave as to go to the well by herself.

"I went with her, Ma'am. I woke to find her stepping over the rest of us slumbering kids and although she insisted I not go with her, she's a stubborn mule you know, I followed her and then escorted her back."

Jeanie was taken by a gust of laughter at Aleksey's characterization of Katherine. Katherine stood, making faces at Aleksey as he spoke.

"I think I can handle the retrieval of water from a silly old well, Mama. Aleksey didn't need to butt his way..."

"Language young lady," Jeanie said. "We aren't throwing all conventions of polite society under the wagon."

"Well, sometimes it's just better to make your point than wrap in pretty words that leave the listener confused and only hours later, do they determine what you really meant with your statement."

Jeanie scowled at Katherine. Clearly she was showing off for Aleksey and though Jeanie wanted to rap her on the back of the head for her sass, she didn't want to start down the road of defiance for defiance's sake.

"Well, darling, my sweet Katherine, if you're in such a strong state as to light out alone across the prairie, then you dump that water into the bucket and just head right back for more. Then have Aleksey show you how to milk the cow and how about you gather some more cow-chips. We're running low and we can't very well serve raw flapjacks to our guests."

"Well, that's just what I intended to do. Come on Aleksey, keep me company. Because you know, I already know very well how to milk a cow."

"Do you now?" Aleksey said.

"I fetched the old stone boat, Mrs. Arthur," Aleksey said.

"Stone boat?"

"We drag it 'cross the land, makes collecting cow-chips, corn cobs, even water a lot easier."

"My, my, my, a stone boat. Who would have thought."

Katherine blustered past Aleksey who followed her out like a puppy. Jeanie smiled at the sight, the idea that ten-year-old Katherine had such a hold on Aleksey and she was impressed by Aleksey's protective nature, something that was very similar to the way James treated his siblings.

Before starting breakfast, Jeanie poked her head outside to see if anyone else had risen. It was silent, with varying snores ripping through the peace. And James and Templeton were missing. Jeanie shook her head then stuffed away the rising fear that her children so quickly took to neighbors and the land that seemed so frightening to her.

She suspected they'd gone to the flag station Templeton had fashioned in order to collect information about the weather. James took an instant liking to the scientific processes involved in weather, trying to read it as though it were words needing to be decoded to unlock its secrets.

Jeanie drew a deep breath and headed to what she thought of as her dirty work. She used iron tongs to grip dried cow waste chunks, to lay them in the stove belly. Cooking over the chips was dirty as the fast burning cow-chips quickly burnt away, causing her to wash her hands every time she put more chips into the stove, rubbing them raw, wasting water, making trips to the well more frequent. How had that become her life? The thought still shocked her.

Breakfast was lively, leaving Jeanie feeling as though she'd known her guests for much longer than she had. After cleaning up, the Hunts decided it was the perfect time to introduce everyone to a Quaker meeting. Jeanie was fine with this as in Des Moines, Sunday was always a day of restful nothingness. And from what the Zurchenkos, Templeton, and the Moores said, Sunday was rarely marked by rest and contemplation of Jesus and his legacy.

So, they all sat and attempted to let the light within them—God—make an appearance and hopefully move one of them to speak with proper weight and depth. Jeanie supposed she could say that if Jesus had a robust interest in the role of fabric in pioneer life, then she was indeed visited by the Lord himself. But, the service was quiet and in the end, no one apparently was lit from within with enough of God to tell anyone about it.

The next order of business was to detail the various ways they could help each other make life as bearable as possible. Jeanie and Greta agreed to exchange a portion of the Zurchenko's vegetables and berries for Jeanie's graceful construction of work shirts for the men and dresses for the women and girls.

"I could teach the children, come fall, in exchange for a new dress and bonnet," Ruthie said, "I mean, if that's okay with everyone."

Everyone nodded. "Lutie and I can preserve our gooseberries and share our pumpkins, too."

"And Frank here," Templeton said, "Is going to build me a lounge and the Zurchenko's a bedstead. In between his commissions from Yankton, that is."

Despite the planning that took place, the Zurchenkos did very little talking. Except for Greta, the rest of them were nearly mute. A lot of nodding and serious expressions made their approval clear. They worked together as a single unit, knowing with a glance who was about to set off to plow more field and who was going to milk the cow.

Jeanie felt excitement grow inside her, the discussion, the idea of being useful, that it felt bigger than she imagined it would. And she watched the afternoon speed by with the creation of a web of interdependence that somehow gave Jeanie the feeling of freedom rather than dependence. Within the support system they were building, she thought she'd find time for reading, writing, thinking, inspiring her children to be more than people who could only see to the next chore that needed to be done. That was no way to live.

And so, when the Zurchenkos, Templeton, and the Moores set off for their homes around noon, Jeanie watched as they started as one big group and splintered apart as each took to the path that would lead them home. The sense of calm that told her the world was right and she was powerful in it lasted just long enough for her to walk into the dugout and find Abby Hunt, Quaker minister, nibbling grains of morphine from a box labeled "Dover Powders." The bell-shaped Mr. Hunt stood beside Abby, his hand on his head as he shook it, saying "Please dearest Abby, please, stop poisoning yourself, we need you here, not drugged or dead."

Jeanie slipped back out of the dugout, running back atop it, stunned at what she saw, shaken by the fact the scene wasn't unfamiliar to her. Though, in her case, it was her mother always begging her father to stop. Jeanie could imagine the exact conversation happening below her, as she ran dialogue through her mind. How could the Hunts have secured the Dovers?

There was no doctor in Yankton, and though it were possible for poppies to grow on the prairie, was it probable? Jeanie clenched her jaw. She hoped not, the sole positive in them being thrust into nothingness, was that there would be a lack of drugs and other mind-altering substances. Or so she'd hoped.

The Hunt children wrestled behind their wagon. Piercing screeches and a cloud of dust startled Jeanie out of her thoughts.

"Be careful, boys." Jeanie choked on her sympathies for them, knowing how behind the curtain of normalcy and religious façade, they must be living in an earthly hell. Or, their mother's addiction hadn't taken hold of her in any big way, yet. Her father, apparently, had been eating opium for well over a decade before the addiction drove him to lose his morals, values and ability to maintain at least a façade of an honest existence.

"Why don't you get into the wagon, Max? That way you'll be ready when your parents are ready. Hop up there, won't you?" Jeanie was struck by her desire to have the family ready to go, to ensure there was no turmoil to upset Mrs. Hunt, just as she'd always paved the way for her father's wishes to be met instantly. She'd never realized that she'd lived that way. That she'd worked so hard to keep normalcy that wasn't even really there.

She told herself opium use was terrible, but she remembered her father's doctor telling her, it was also common. Without offering names, the doctor had told her he had patients who were colleagues, housewives, farmers, and store owners. At the time Jeanie wasn't comforted by the information, she was repulsed that so many despicable people populated her life. Now, seeing the Hunt's family, the children, Jeanie felt sympathy slip into her body on the back of protectiveness for the family. Mostly she felt helpless that the lenient use of opium would only offer a soothing effect to the user's feelings for so long before it ripped the entire operation asunder.

Max nodded and tipped his hat at Jeanie. "Okay, Ma'am. Thanks." And with that, the Hunts came over the dugout, locked arm in arm, Mrs. Hunt giggling. Jeanie stared into her eyes, looking for foggy incomprehension, low muscle tone or anything that would indicate she had actually done what Jeanie saw with her own two eyes. Perhaps she'd been mistaken.

In the two months that passed since the Arthurs set up home in the dugout and filed the paperwork, the land transformed itself further into what resembled a jewelry box bursting with burnished gold, punctuated by precious colored gems. Sunflowers girded themselves, their faces toward the sun while pink prairie roses burst from greens in unexpected places.

Other bushes boasted fat berries of all shades of red and blue. Jeanie tried to remember what the grasses looked like when the land was jade and purple and yellow, but she couldn't quite put her mind around it. Had she imagined it?

The Darlington Township cooperative was in full swing. The men took turns making runs to Yankton to drop letters at the post, buy flour, coffee, and thread for Jeanie's sewing. When they were in a pinch, having too much work in the fields to warrant someone heading to the city, Jeanie used her coffee grinder to mill grain into flour and though it made for a bit lumpier flapjacks and pan bread, it was passable in taste and appearance. As long as no one allowed memories of servant-kneaded pastries, hotcakes, eggs, and bacon to enter their minds—that was the only way.

Fairly quickly Jeanie realized that their little Lutie offered nothing to the group but her beautiful face, slender waist, and a knack for weaving intricate wildflower crowns for herself and the young girls. Katherine was rarely without one of Lutie's designs and soon fashioned her own.

Katherine displayed them above the children's bedstead—much to the boys' dismay as they graced the space above their heads forming a giant crown over the bed—so Katherine could rise in the morning and fix one atop her head according to her hair-style of choice.

Jealousy, envy, obsession about beauty Jeanie lacked; these things had never been part of her personality. Even knowing her chin was a bit pointy, her nose a tad thin, and her dark eyes a pinch close-set, with the gold-flecked brown irises being less pools of mystery than pits of unspectacular earth—Jeanie had been confident. She moved her elegant, slim hips with accidental grace. Her shoulders naturally found a relaxed position, down and back. Her backside stood up, just a bit so that even as bustled behinds fell from fashion, Jeanie's body recalled the silhouette in just the right, subtle way. When she walked, normally lost in thoughts of books, sketches, her children, she was not always aware the image of her, was nothing short of mesmerizing—even with her plainer facial features.

She attributed her ease with her body as being due to the fact that in Des Moines, for the first twenty five years of her life, Jeanie was defined by her talents and family standing instead of mere, boring beauty. She felt fortunate to have been born with an intuitive inclination toward substance over style—even though she did adore style—but she knew it was her nonchalance that magnetized people.

The way she married fabrics, creating rooms that made one want to drop dead in them, just so their soul might hover there for eternity, and the manner in which she wove her prose into candid tomes that might be harsh if written by any other author, the way she conveyed the beauty of the small things in life, allowing other women, states away to create gracious homes. She'd built the life she wanted. Jeanie knew a woman of her standing, a married woman, to pursue a writing career while raising children was unusual, but she felt it was her birthright, even though it were unusual for society of the times.

Jeanie's doting father set Frank and her up in the house next door to him, even after they ran away and eloped, defying him. She stepped into a domesticated life so structured that, in Jeanie's opinion, only a truly lazy or inept woman could live it without also doing something constructive with her time. Had she not had fiery physical energy and the cool wits of an army general, she would have ignored her call to write for the benefit of housekeeping and Frank in an instant. She knew her job in the world was to coax the best out of Frank and help him be the best man he could possibly be. Luckily for her, she could do more.

But on the prairie, charged with creating work clothes, hardy shirts and utilitarian dresses, stripped of all the things that defined her as valuable, Jeanie saw herself in a warped reflection of Miss Lutie Moore, and what she saw was ugly and ordinary. This condition led her to irritation and spitefulness she hadn't felt since before she learned to be a lady. And it didn't help that every time Lutie and Ruthie were in their company that Lutie nearly crawled onto Frank's lap and offered herself as his lady in waiting. Perhaps if she didn't feel so dirty and ripe with smells that she'd only encountered on errant trips to the wrong side of Des Moine's railroad line on a friendly dare, she wouldn't have such jealous feelings.

A bathtub, what a luxury she'd enjoyed every day. Now, the image, the smell of cleanliness and soft relaxation was lost in her windblown memory, only asserting itself when something or someone stood in complete opposition to Jeanie's filthy appearance. Usually that was Lutie.

It was with this frame of mind that Jeanie was often confronted with Lutie's presence, appearing at first as though she'd come to help with this chore or that, but then before long, she'd settle onto the ground, the lounge, or just stand around, contemplating the beauty of her irresponsibility.

One Wednesday, Lutie showed up atop the dugout, and like a demon, her mere presence there, pulled Frank from behind the barn where he was building the Zurchenko's bedstead. It was particularly hot and though Jeanie hadn't cramped since they first arrived at their homestead, she wasn't feeling particularly vigorous that day.

The children had scattered over the land, knowing precisely how far Jeanie would let them wander and it was only as far as Jeanie could see in any direction. The one exception was when she would send them to the well for water. But she knew exactly how long they could take before worrying should begin.

Lutie planted herself at the naked table, settled in with a mug of water, clearly expecting to offer nothing in the way of help with the lunch.

"We just bought ourselves a new cook-stove," Lutie's lethargic movements were further underwhelming in contrast to her yammering which rolled forth like a train across the country.

"Hmm, you don't say," Jeanie said.

"It's a *beauty* at fifty-eight dollars," Lutie went on. "It was the one you recommended in the last column you wrote. Templeton, that dear, just brought the paper from town the other day. There was a line at the bottom of the article, stating that Mrs. Jeanie

Arthur, Maven of Domesticity had left her post for grander things. How about *that.*" Lutie chortled. "Grander things. Imagine that. I reckon they haven't been to a dugout on the Dakota Territory prairie lately, do you?" Lutie chortled again.

"A new cook-stove. Well, my oh my," Jeanie would not discuss the ruse she was living with Loopy Lutie. It was none of her business, but before she could stop herself she said what she was thinking. "I sure hope you won't disgrace it with your paltry cooking."

"Well, I won't if you would just help me, just show me a bit of that magic in your fingertips. Maybe that way I can catch a man as fine as your Frank. I do adore that man of yours."

Jeanie ignored the comment—the sarcastic way Lutie said it. "Lutie, is there any possibility on this earth that you're a leather-maker, a cobbler, a shoe-maker in disguise?"

Lutie squinted at Jeanie.

"Look at these wretched boots I'm wearing. Any chance you could fashion me a pair that look as delicate as these?" Jeanie pulled her bejeweled slippers from one of her trunks. Lutie's eye flew wide open and she took the shoes, running her finger over the sequins and jewels and satin.

"Those are the shoes a woman should be called to wear."

"Your boots aren't so bad," Lutie said. She kept massaging the silky shoe in her hands, but narrowed her eyes at Jeanie's boots. "Well, the boots are sort of…"

"Witchy," Jeanie said.

"Well, yes, I suppose, the way the toes are curling, the scars in the leather they are—"

"Oh tighten it up, Lutie. What's the point?" Jeanie ripped the shoe from Lutie's hands and stomped into the dugout, tossing the shoes under her bedstead. "Lutie, get your lazy bones into this dugout."

Lutie hopped to and skittered in, eyes widened again.

"Look at this place, Lutie. It's the size of my pantry and in the condition of an old outhouse back home. It's in the state of, well, nothing of my former life compares to this. It's a blasted cave for pity's sake. And somehow, even in its diminutive size I'm not managing to keep it as I think it should be. There's nothing here that defines me as an expert of domesticity, that says I know *anything* about keeping a home. I *can't* help *you*."

Lutie pulled at her slender fingers, shifting her weight, lowering her eyes, only stealing occasional glances at the woman she'd wanted to be her mentor. "Well, you do have all that beautiful material. Two trunks of it you said. The clothes you're making, it's all stunning. It's all everything you ever preached in those books you wrote. You were telling the truth, right? A man like Frank certainly wouldn't entertain a life with a woman not worthy."

Jeanie turned toward her blackened, second-hand, ten dollar cook-stove and shuffled the coffee pot and fry pan around. Jeanie was tired to pretending she was managing well. What was the point? She hadn't lied in those books, she'd simply been completely uneducated in the ways of the world she lived in now. Jeanie bit the inside of her cheek and poured chopped nuts, chicory, and the remaining "real" coffee grinds into the kettle of water and lit the fire.

There, she'd become functional in squalor. She should give herself credit, make a note of it on her barely used notebook, tuck the triumph away inside for later when she could write about it, and truly live it that way. In the sepia-toned dugout and the mood to match, Jeanie was suddenly protective of what was left of her, her world. Most especially Frank. No matter that Lutie knew nothing of his black moods, infantile needs, inability to follow through— Jeanie would not easily surrender the remaining shreds of the fabric of her life.

Jeanie turned to Lutie, trying to set aside the resentment that fueled her current thoughts. She forced confident relaxation into her limbs, as though she had nothing to lose to the numb-skulled beauty who busily haunted her home. "Heaven knows there is no greater misery on earth than when one's life fabric is embroidered by the hand of a caustic, clapper claw. I won't be that woman, Lutie. I won't let trouble fester, nor will I look for it, so let me say this clearly. I'm not sure what you're up to, but you have no rights to my husband or my life, in your mind or in reality.

"If you infringe beyond the limits set by me or society I will kill you. Like that jackrabbit I skewered the other day, the action that caused you to green at the gills and lose your breakfast over the prairie. *That's* the book I haven't written. The one I'm living. The other books weren't lies when I wrote them, but they aren't true anymore." Jeanie took a deep breath, let it out and smiled. Smiling always brought the necessary cheer to her spirit, even when it seemed as though nothing possibly could.

"So, let's work together and find a way to survive this hole that's hot as Hades on its worst day. How about that. Are we clear? I feel better. Excuse me please. I had to say that whether you are deserving of it or not."

Lutie stared at her nails, pushing back a cuticle. Finally she nodded. Jeanie ushered her back outside to light the fire for the laundry.

Jeanie splashed water over her face and filled her arms to over-flowing with table linens and dishes. Coming from the dugout Jeanie stopped at the sight of Lutie. She was seated at the table, back against it, arms stretched out resting on the top, head back, sun on her face making her the picture of an angel.

Jeanie set the linens beside Lutie, who didn't flinch, or pre-tend to notice. Jeanie held one end of the tablecloth and snapped it twice, airing it out. Lutie turned her head to Jeanie, irritation spread across her face.

"I'm bothering you," Jeanie said. "Why don't I bring you some hard-tac sweets and a swig of wine to assist you in your leisure. I know fires just start themselves on the prairie. I guess I just hadn't realized you could will one to start from behind closed eyelids. Perhaps I can simply imagine someone doing my laundry and it will be so?"

Lutie sat up and squinted at Jeanie. "Did I do something? I mean, in the last two minutes? I could have sworn you said you didn't want your next byline to read "clapper claw, extraordinaire."

"Light the fire. Don't make it hard for me to like you. I'm trying, I am."

Lutie groaned and lumbered to the firebox they'd built a bit away.

Jeanie snapped one of the tablecloths into the air, basking in the smell of a proper laundering, something Jeanie hadn't experienced since they left Des Moines. She smoothed the tablecloth over the pine table. Jeanie traced the pink flowered embroidery with her forefinger.

Lutie came beside Jeanie. "This is the tablecloth from the book, isn't it? The one you and your mother made before she passed. Right? That's so precious. I wish..."

"I thought it was time I brought it out. It's not doing any good sitting in an old trunk."

Lutie nodded, fingering the embroidery.

Just touching the fabric lifted Jeanie's spirits, making her realize that abandoning her beautiful things just because their home was ugly had been a mistake. She vowed to use at least one beautiful linen per day from that point on. Maybe she was being too hard on Lutie.

Jeanie sighed. "Look, I'm not angry. I look at you and see what everyone else does, a beautiful girl." Lutie batted her eyes at Jeanie who rolled hers back.

"Now stop that, Lutie Moore. If you could just see yourself. You look ridiculous. Don't you want people to take you seriously? If you learned to work at something. Perhaps you wouldn't have met with divorce."

"I know you think I'm lazy. I'm sure you must think the divorce was my doing."

"Think, nothing. I *know* you're lazy."

Jeanie drew back and whispered an apology.

"Way I see things," Lutie said, "you're some kind of other-worldly phenomenon, and you'd view anyone who worked any less than eighteen hours a day as slothful. And that's not fair. Everyone can't be like you. But, trust me on this, even you wouldn't have kept my husband in good cheer."

Jeanie ignored that comment thinking of course she'd have been able to achieve good cheer in that home. Her dull spirits and dull marriage at that moment in time was merely something to contend with, to look back on later as a blip in time, that did not define their marriage, but made it stronger. No, there was barely a circumstance Jeanie couldn't imagine remedying if she had her wits about her.

"You have to find a way to make yourself attractive to men, Lutie," Jeanie said.

Lutie threw her head back. "What, like learn to cobble shoes? Frankly, I think I've got the "attractiveness-hay" baled and stored for the winter."

"I didn't realize you knew how to bale hay since James and Tommy have done all of that for you."

"I knew you were angry about that. I just *knew* it." Lutie crossed her arms over herself and pursed her lips. Jeanie was getting sucked into a pointless conversation that would only result in her saying things that were truly mean or interpreted to be so.

"I merely think," Jeanie said, "you should have something more to offer than beauty."

"I have plenty to offer, I just need to discern the nature of my gentleman's desires and needs—the fields of his being if you will— before I commit the right crop to its earth."

"You're saying you'll wait to cultivate your interests until you understand those of the man to whom you'd like to marry? That will not be enticing to a man of any sort of substance." Jeanie stopped herself from going on. Hadn't she done this very thing back in the year leading to her elopement? Made herself as appealing to Frank as possible?

Lutie rolled her eyes. "Oh, sure, yes, I see that principle at work out here on the prairie. I can't believe you're saying that. Your books are all about making a pleasing home, working your fingers to the bone for the head of your domicile—in whatever way he expects. I like the decorative elements of your writings—the beauty you suggest for a home, but the women, their position?"

"Well, yes, partially a woman molds oneself to...yes, but one must cultivate her personhood to be attractive to a man who will then be head of her home. That goes beyond decorating a fine home."

"Pffflt," Lutie shook her head. "All that work so finally you can have the pleasure of the only aspect of marriage worth entertaining— the nightly duties. I certainly learned what I *don't* want in marriage from my former placement in one."

"Allow me to offer a secret I've never published though others have. Whatever success a man enjoys, it is only possible in the presence of a fully-realized woman." Jeanie couldn't believe Lutie just said intimate relations were first on her list of marital bliss.

"Templeton looks fully realized himself. And he's without a wife."

"Well, yes, that's true. But his home, it's disastrous without a woman's touch. Batching-it is not a friend to a pleasant home."

"Well, you're not the only one who could turn that outfit around. But, really I'm not sure I want that. I *had* that. I do have dreams, you know. Castles, kings, jewels..."

"That's it!" Jeanie said. "That's the kind of passion you need to find. I can teach you to sew, if you'd like. You're always saying how much you admire the advertisements in the newspapers, the women with intricate hats and perfectly appointed bodices."

Lutie shrugged and picked her cuticle. "Well, no, I'm not passionate about it. I can get excited about something—a funny story, the sight of a beautiful blouse or well made stool, but I can't *do* anything in those terms, I'm not a creator, I'm a partaker. That's just how it goes for me."

Jeanie had enough of her obstinate student. "Lutie," Jeanie said more harshly than she wanted. "Do you suppose you could summon the passion to finish setting the table?"

"Well, I'd be happy to, Jeanie. How about I set it according to the diagram on page three-seventy in the first book. Would that suit?"

"What would *suit*, would be if you never mentioned those books again." Jeanie ducked into the dugout without hearing Lutie's reply to that.

As the corn cakes finished cooking, Jeanie pulled one of her trunks of fabric from the dugout to begin the process of inventorying what she had left and which materials would go for what dress next. Lutie hummed as she set the table, commenting on how beautiful everything was.

"Perfect for a dress for a lady about my size and standing," Lutie said. Jeanie knew Lutie was hinting at the fact Jeanie hadn't yet fitted her or Ruthie for their new dresses. Jeanie was half-hoping just to remake one of Lutie's old ones rather than spare an entire bolt of her own material. Lutie finished the table and wandered to the trunk. They both ran their hands over the damasks, cottons, linens, lost in their beauty and exquisite cleanness. It couldn't have evoked a more powerful reaction had the trunk been bursting with gold. The fabric was treasure to Jeanie.

"Look at these buttons, Lutie. They're called paperweights."

Lutie held a pink glass ball up to the light, turning it back and forth. "Why it's like a little world in there. That little flower, there, it's a pasque flower, isn't it?"

Jeanie took it from her and examined it. "Why I suppose it is."

"Almost like the fates knew you'd someday live where they grew wild."

"My, my, my, aren't they exquisite. Not like pearls, but still." Jeanie had never loved the glass buttons. The pearl buttons were the ones that made her shudder with glee. She pulled another glass button from the box and held it up. Inside it was a teeny French house. France, oh to be there. Jeanie sighed and shook her head, feeling happy that Elizabeth had no idea of the value of the glass buttons, that she hadn't pointed to them when she was acquiring Jeanie's things. Jeanie stuffed the button into her pocket, loving the idea that another world lived inside the glass that sat beside her hip, that someday she'd be back in that world, out of the dirt and squalor. She took the button box into the dugout, planning to sort through them, to decide which should be used for which dresses and which should be never used, kept for Jeanie's fantasies.

"I could use these for your dress, Lutie."

"I haven't had a fitting yet, you're aware. Now that you bring it up. I don't presume to be forward in regard to the dress you promised to fashion, but that fabric in that first trunk…"

"Well, let me measure you. Two fittings is all I need."

"Two? I'm sure you'll need more than that. Greta is one thing, but I am a little more, shall we say, subtle in appearance."

"Two, Lutie. That's all I need."

"It'll fit like a thumbless man's wagon cover with but two fittings!"

"With the time you're wasting, it's already lunch. You'll be lucky if I get to two fittings at all with you. I'll fit you after we eat."

Lutie shrugged like a ten-year-old in response, but made Jeanie all the more sure that she was exactly what Lutie needed to further develop her personhood.

Chapter 8

Jeanie rang the lunch bell then rummaged through the materials in the trunk some more, with Lutie over her shoulder pointing to her favorites. They waited for the chirping of the kids that should have followed. But instead of happy voices, what she heard next was a great sound of crackling, whooshing, and wind so strong that she almost thought she could see it if she hopped above the dugout to look.

Jeanie looked at Lutie who had frozen in the middle of laying a fork next to a plate, head lifted, face paled as though a mask of fear had been placed over her.

"What?" Jeanie said. Lutie shook her head but didn't move.

Jeanie ran around to the top of the dugout and saw blackness sitting atop the brightest wall of orange and red and yellow that she'd ever have imagined before that time. "Frank! Fire! It's a fire! The children! Where are the children!"

Frank, atop the horse, galloped toward her, yelling that the fire had already swept past the Zurchenko homestead, the Moore's, and was obviously heading right for them.

"The gully? Did the fire jump the gully?"

Frank looked away, into the flames that were growling like a mythological beast, gorging itself, crackling. Frank had dismounted and yelled that Lutie and Jeanie should get on the horse and just ride as fast as they could to Templeton's. He'd prepared for times like this with firebreaks.

But as Lutie climbed atop the dugout, the horse spooked and bolted, dragging Frank with it. After a few yards, Frank let go of the reins and scrambled to his feet, running back to the women. The flames, behind Frank, rushed toward them, so thick that even though still one hundred yards away, Jeanie could feel the heat. She collapsed to the ground. Sobbing, head buried in her arms, she curled into a ball. Lutie yelled at Frank and though Jeanie couldn't hear the specific words, Lutie was clearly giving him instructions of some sort. And before Jeanie knew what was happening, Lutie had hauled her up and dragged her down the hillside, around the front of the dugout. It was then she heard Lutie's words, that the flames would leap over the dugout, that it shouldn't burn the sod barn, and that Frank should get the cow inside it. She was quite clear that their home wouldn't be destroyed and neither would they if they made it inside.

Jeanie didn't close the dugout door until Frank sprinted back after closing in the cow. The three of them stood, Jeanie near the front door, Frank by the lounge and Lutie by the cook-stove, in the dark dugout, no one moving to add candlelight or oil lamp glow. The sound of their scratchy breathing, occasional whimpers, and shrieks of disbelief didn't require light. Jeanie spread the curtains as far wide as possible and watched as orange flames ate past the window, keeping an odd ten-foot distance as though there was a reason to do so.

Watching those flames made Jeanie want to die, to find a way to harm herself if the fire itself didn't. She would not live without her children. Stunned, body shaking to its core, she turned from the window and fell back against the dirt wall. Frank pointed to the roof of the house and Lutie nodded. The roar of the flames running over the dugout, the realization that they were sitting inside the fire made Jeanie woozy, and before long, everything went black as night.

Jeanie came to, Frank squeezing her cheeks, moving her face back and forth. It took her a second to remember the flames, to be engulfed in the pain that accompanied knowing her children had just been swallowed up in the most painful death there could possibly be.

The fire that chomped at the land like a lion would gnaw its prey. Frank's face hung above Jeanie's and Lutie stood behind him, her chest heaving with deep, silent breath. The sound of the earth crisping had passed while Jeanie had been unconscious and in the dugout, a hush as loud as the flames had been, saturated the space.

Jeanie pushed Frank aside. He tried to keep her down, but she punched his shoulder, making him draw back and give her space to move and run to the window. Though mid-day, the earth and sky had gone black, choked with smoke that tumbled from the sky and hovered just over the ground, as though teasing it with descending then receding smoke streams.

It was only in seeing its blackness, the golds and yellows zapped from the earth, that visions of the original greens, purples, and blues rushed to Jeanie. Her teeth chattered as she scolded herself for noticing such things, for caring about the colors of the prairie when her children had been wiped from that same prairie, extinguishing their lives. She pulled at her hair, wanting to inflict pain on herself in a bodily sense to take away the pain of her spirit.

She ran to the cook-stove where a knife hung above it. She grabbed it and poised it across from her heart as though about to stab it into her body. It would end everything for her, the pain, the sight of her burnt children, or worse, not finding them at all. She could not live that way, with those images fried into her brain.

Frank nearly tackled her to wrench the knife from her hand.

"You give that back to me. You are not my father, you cannot control my life."

Frank ignored her and tucked the knife between the bedstead and the wall. Jeanie paced the floor, wishing she had thrown herself into the flames as they passed by.

Jeanie yanked on the hot door, ignoring the scalding handle. The door stuck then gave way, sending Jeanie backward onto her bottom. She scrambled to her feet.

Lutie and Frank implored her to stop, saying it was too smoky and searing hot to attempt to walk around.

"Those are my children! *Our* children!" Jeanie poked her finger accusingly at Frank's shocked face. She stepped outside where the charred heat bore right through her boots, making that tedious human instinct toward survival kick in, and so, she shut the door, and lay her forehead against it, trying to divine the spirits of her children as they must be circling the dugout, having come to bid goodbye before heading into Heaven, wishing the God she wasn't sure she believed in would perform a miracle and take her life right then.

Jeanie plastered her head and hands against the hot door, awaiting the smoke to clear so she could find their bodies, their little, innocent bodies. She squeezed her eyes at the thought of them crisp as smoked pheasant.

"Nonononononono! This can't be happening! This can't be happening!" She pounded slowly on the door. Running through one track of her mind was the conversation Lutie and Frank were having behind her—how Lutie had saved them by forcing them down the hill into the dugout—Frank's words tripping over one another as he repeated their children's names, pronouncing them dead.

Slamming down another track of her brain was the intellectual agreement that Frank was right. That Jeanie had been right in believing they were dead, how could they not be? But in hearing Frank wail and moan and tread in his pain while Lutie soothed at him, another track in Jeanie's mind took over saying there was no way they were dead.

That their family had suffered plenty and there was no way God would push pain further into their good souls. Simultaneously, she told herself, as she'd suspected there wasn't really a God at all. Not one like she'd learned about as a child. There was no God, not in places like that. She'd kill herself if even one of her children was dead. She'd have to.

And, it was all Frank's fault. His big dreams and flailing, wild energy that, this time, put them in a position they couldn't reverse or tackle or transform. Every bit of it, them being on the prairie in the first place, him convincing her to let the children roam like livestock. Jeanie ripped away from the door and began swinging at Frank. Anger broke loose from the recesses of her bones and flooded her bloodstream, took over her actions and sent her smacking and kicking and wailing at Frank. "Now, you stop your bawling! You help me send good thoughts to the kids! They're alive! They are not dead! So gather yourselves up and just...well, find some belief and make it real."

Jeanie stopped hitting and covered her mouth with her hand. She had never been the violent type. She shuddered and quivered as she replayed her actions in her mind. She'd never felt so out of control and hateful and empty. Frank stood, staring at her, crying without sobbing. Tears snaked through the black soot on his cheeks, the whites of his eyes flamed red, matching the flames that had driven by. Lutie's jaw slackened, her eyes shifted, showing fear.

Jeanie bit the inside of her cheek. "I'm sorry. I'm sorry. I'm so sorry." It was that moment that Jeanie found some clarity in what kind of character she possessed. She'd lived her life, prior to prairie life, moving from one special event to the next, aspects of them stilled and sealed in her mind to mull over after the fact.

Like paintings in a museum, or drawings in her publications, the actual scene at the time of the rendering didn't matter—the afterimage was paramount, the pictures that Jeanie revisited, enjoying more than the events themselves. It was then she realized the prairie would not afford her that kind of existence. It would be minute-to-minute experience that would leave afterimages she preferred to forget.

"You are cold and mercenary," Frank said, his voice as cold as he proclaimed her innards to be.

"I'm not cold, Frank. I'm just not..." Jeanie leaned her forehead against the door.

"Not *what*," Frank said.

Like her mind was suddenly as organized as the card catalog in the Des Moines public library, Jeanie sorted through scads of words she could use in the next exchange, but she was sure to be careful in her selection. "I'm not you."

A crack suddenly tore through the relative silence and settling smog. The three in the dugout jumped at the crisp, pointed noise. Jeanie and Frank looked around and went to the window. What could it be now?

"Thunder," Lutie said. "It's going to rain."

And, before Jeanie could wrench the door open, pellets of rain were pitting the land, cleansing it. The earth hissed as it accepted the water with the joy it would feel if it could. Although it was not cool enough to head into the plains yet, Jeanie shoved a water bucket and a water pail outside to gather the falling rain. It was a sign. Jeanie was surer than ever the children were somehow safe, even if she didn't know how they could possibly be.

Marble-sized raindrops pummeled the earth for some time. When she could stand it no longer, Jeanie risked her feet burning on the scorched ground, and tore out of the dugout and up the side. She stood there as thick drapes of wind and water plummeted and pushed and shifted direction, thrusting her body from side to side. Jeanie dug in and waited for it to slow enough that she would be able to start looking for the children. She raised her hands heaven-ward and closed her eyes to the barrage. She could feel her children, sense them breathing as sure as she was herself. They were alive.

When she managed to force her eyes open, she could see nee-dle straight bolts of lightning marching toward her then forming webs in the sky, nearly surrounding her in their flame. She wasn't afraid of dying, knowing that if she could stand in that storm and live, her kids would certainly have been saved a similar miracle. She would make it so, if only in her head it was true, that was okay.

Like the waves of cramps that often gripped her, the rain dumped over her then lessened before brutalizing her again, before totally fading away. She turned, looking around, stretching her hearing for voices, anything human. Frank and Lutie joined her atop the dugout. Lutie grasped Frank's arm as though he were her father, but her expression, the way she allowed him to hold her up and look at him in what was clearly an adoring fashion, made Jeanie think Lutie's motives were anything but childlike.

They headed out onto the land, not sure where they were going, but they followed Jeanie without a single question as to why. They walked for a time, plodding over the ebony dirt.

"There!" Frank pointed, pulled his arm free of Lutie and began to sprint toward the open land—the bee tree. From that dis-tance, Jeanie could see, three shapes that interrupted the expected straightness of a tree, as though it grew goiters during the storm. She got closer and her mind began chanting, *it's the children, the children, the children.*

Jeanie hoisted her dress and ran so hard she passed Frank. She grunted like an animal, bursting at the sight. If the children were in the tree, they must be alive, for if they'd died, they'd have fallen out. Surely they would have lost their grips.

Jeanie's feet pounded over the earth and her screams sliced through the now still air, becoming shrill as an animal caught in a trap. The children were motionless, non-responsive. Jeanie reached the tree, and grabbed its trunk trying to shake them out of it like fruit. They didn't flutter or show at all they were alive.

Jeanie stopped beating on the tree, settled her screaming and stepped away to get a better view of the three of them. Katherine was highest in the tree, then Tommy and James under him.

"James!" Jeanie's voice was tinny in her ears. She struggled to steady her voice, to make it reassuring to the children rather than alarming. "James. You three come down right now. This is no time for tree climbing." Jeanie's voice shook again. She could not wait to get her hands on them.

James finally made a move, looking over his shoulder as his arms were still gripped around the trunk. "Mama?"

At once Katherine and Tommy began repeating her name then shimmied down the tree so fast they landed atop one another as they reached the ground. The three of them heaped together, alive, clearly alive. Frank, Lutie and Jeanie cheered, pulling them apart, lying each on his or her back, eyes gaping, but blank. They shook their heads as though they'd never seen the adults before.

They tried to pull the children to sitting, but they were slack from their muscles having been tensed for an extended period of time. Jeanie suspected they felt as though they'd completed a full week's planting in just a few hours.

When it was clear her children might be struck dumb for some time, though able to walk, the six of them plodded back to the dugout, holding one another up, not speaking of the great exhilaration at gaining a perspective on life that hadn't been available until that very instant. By the time they reached home, Tommy had regained his voice and in his normal melodramatic manner, he retold the events that led them up the tree.

Soon after that, James engaged, explaining how they'd been lugging the water home when they heard the fire crackling toward them. Even before they saw the flames, James knew what was coming. In the oddest way, though he'd never been amid flames, he knew what was happening.

"Templeton and I had just logged the day's conditions— the dryness, the temperature, the winds, the pressure. Oh, Templeton—his frame house—where could he have hidden during the fire?" James' voice rose in pitch. Jeanie held him around the waist even tighter.

Jeanie wanted to tell him not to worry, that nothing could have happened to Templeton because he was too nice a person to have anything befall him. But as she inventoried her memory of the fire, its fierceness, she knew it couldn't have barreled through this dry land and not have killed someone.

Katherine sipped water and joined the retelling. Her face lit up, eyes wide and expressive as though intoxicated from having survived to tell it. "And I didn't want to get rid of the water, Mama. I just wanted to run home, but James said we'd never outrun the flames." Katherine spoke with her hands, illustrating her words.

"So we took the hand wagon with the rocks we'd filled for the wall around the property and laid them, circled them around the tree and doused the whole area with water. James just kept repeating that if the bee tree had lived fifty years on the plain so far, it wouldn't let them down then."

Tommy nodded enthusiastically while James picked at the mud on the bottom of his boot.

"And I just kept thinking of the light inside me," Katherine said. "Like the Quaker preacher Mrs. Hunt said. And I figured if the light was in me, it had to be in the tree. That God, in all of us, was more powerful than a great old fire. And the boy. He came and told me to hang on. He kept saying hang on, hang on, that if I lost my grip, I'd topple us all to the flames."

Jeanie nodded and pulled all three children into her body thinking Katherine's retelling a bit off.

"That boy," Katherine said. "We have to go back for him."

"What boy?" James said.

"The boy with the red hair, and the gold cross, glimmering so bright, I had to turn away from it at certain points. A cross like

Preacher Vail used to wear when he came for dinner. It was tied around the boy's neck with twine, but the cross shined like the light within, just like the Hunts said. He came to keep us—"

James and Tommy shook their heads, but wouldn't make eye contact with Katherine. Jeanie assumed they were too tired to discuss the matter or they weren't up to ribbing their sister for such thoughts after such a trying event.

"Katherine," Jeanie said. "You're exhausted. I'm sure it was just your mind, confused." Jeanie knelt in front of Katherine, kneading at her body to be sure she wasn't injured underneath her clothing. She did the same to James, then Tommy. She was utterly wracked with a hurricane of emotion, emotion that roiled her thoughts, sending them from areas of despair and sadness and joy and pride that her children had managed to save themselves as they did.

Jeanie knew there was more to the story, the reason the flames managed to just skirt the tree, and that scared her, made her think their days were being tabulated and scrutinized, checked off as being a gift that could be snatched back if the prairie needed to claim another soul and it made Jeanie think they should immediately leave the prairie.

It wouldn't matter what scandal they left behind if they had their lives. What were they doing there, pretending the land was theirs if only they wanted it? She wasn't sure she did, even if it meant Frank would lose his dream.

Jeanie left the children recovering in the dugout and went out to find Frank and Lutie. They were waiting for Jeanie to give them the okay to check on the others at their homes.

"Lutie," Jeanie said. "Why don't you and Frank head to your place, the Zurchenko's, everyone's, to be sure they're all okay. That their property survived. That the crops did." Lutie nodded like a child, seemingly less developed than Jeanie's children seven or more years younger than she.

It was that moment that Jeanie realized the degree to which prairie life altered their manner of living. She couldn't afford to hate Lutie and her luring charms and lazy approach to life. She didn't have the luxury. She had to access the part of her that trusted Frank implicitly, the part of her that built a bridge from her heart to his twelve years before. And Frank, whom she vowed to love and devote her life to, well, she simply had to trust him. To believe that God, whether he existed, with quiet illumination right inside Frank's wiry body or up above in the heavens, would guide him to a principled and monogamous life. Surely he wouldn't have the time to carry on with Lazy Lutie if Jeanie didn't have the time to contemplate it.

By the time two days had passed and they'd fully inventoried the fire's damages, the fear and want of what was lost, had passed. However, anxiety was in full throes of Jeanie's body, keeping her from sleeping, as even a few hours of rest left her dreaming of fire or her family, faceless, though behaving as though perfectly normal. She woke in a sweat every time and then would spend the next eighteen hours or so, sewing, cleaning, cooking, reading, or anything that she thought might finally release her to real, sound sleep.

At least Jeanie could say her longing for comfortable life in Des Moines was replaced by the want for simpler things like their dining table and her birthday tablecloth. Jeanie had pulled one trunk outside to sort through while she waited for the stew to cook. It had burned with most of her fabrics and her precious family linens. And also gone were Frank's commissioned work, Templeton's lounge, a chair, the Zurchenko's bedstead, and apparently, a slew of figurines Frank had fashioned while resting in between carving the larger items.

Frank moaned over on the bedstead and pushed the blankets off his legs. "Ah, Jeanie, my figurines, they're ruined, ruined. I've got to start over, but I feel good about it, like we can do anything now that we survived that fire. We are invincible."

Jeanie sighed deeply, lost in her thoughts only having to partially listen to the same tune Frank had been singing since the fire—that he'd found a oneness with the land, feeling as though he communed with the souls of those who tread there before, that the figurines, nearly shaped themselves right in the palm of his hand, that he only had to follow the knife around the wood more than tell it where to go. He was convinced that remaking everything that was lost would be no trouble and that the furniture and bedsteads would be even better than before. She sighed again, nearly taken by tears when she did.

"Don't sigh like that Jeanie. I hear your disapproval in every blasted one."

Jeanie didn't respond to this, but continued to stir the eggs. She'd been lost in thought of ways they might be able to make a go of it back in Des Moines. Who cared that they were scandalized, poor, dirty and had lost nearly everything? At least it was safe there.

But Jeanie knew they'd never go back, and really, she found comfort in that because part of her wanted to make it in the west, prove that she was made from the same hearty stock her Scottish ancestors were. She kept telling herself the same words Frank had repeated constantly; that they survived the fire, everyone was safe, and according to the Zurchenkos who really *did* seem one with the land, they'd never heard of or experienced more than one fire in a year. She sighed again, but cut it off halfway when she realized she was doing it.

"Jeanie, my sweetness and sugar, are you all right?"

She shrugged, stirring her eggs. The wood shifted as Frank got up from the bedstead. "Jeanie? Did you hear that? I'm sure more than ever that we'll make a successful go of this place, earn some money and then I'm thinking we can raise sheep or move to Texas where the cotton trade is shifting from the southeast to the southwest. I just have a really confident feeling about it all."

Jeanie gritted her teeth, not wanting to argue with Frank while the children slept. If he would just walk away and do his chores she could stifle her curdling anger.

"I need that milk, Frank. And the cow and horses, they need their water."

"I've had enough of the orders. You're always angry and that makes me angry."

Jeanie leaned forward, poking the spatula at him, keeping her voice controlled to a whisper. "You can't be mad at me for being mad at you. That's just life, that now that we live under such conditions that you need reminding what needs to be done. There's no hand or help to do it for you when you overlook it."

"Like that mess over there that you overlooked. Your books, and stacks of letters and journals and material and…I'm not the only one falling down on the job. And I never wrote the book on it!"

Jeanie ground her teeth together, afraid of what might come out of her mouth at that moment. She hated him, she shook with the feeling and she must have conveyed it silently because Frank, though not apologizing aloud, dropped his head in contrition.

"Okay." Frank's voice was limp and Jeanie was immediately swept with guilt. She stopped stirring the eggs and watched Frank disappear out the door, slow gait, shoulders slumping a bit. She felt like cracked china. Not the kind so compromised that it was unusable, but spidery lines creeping through it, foretold a future trip to the garbage. That cracking in her soul was loud in her ears, felt in every cell in her body.

"Blazes. Blame it."

"We heard that, Mama."

Jeanie jumped. "Oh, children, Katherine, you've always got your ear to the wall, don't you?" Jeanie tried to joke. She replayed the swears through her mind startling herself at the casualness with which they fell from her lips. Not that she'd never sworn before, but never with such flourish.

119

"What wall? We have no walls," James stood, went to the chamber room, winking at his mother.

"We sure don't, do we."

"I like it with no walls," Tommy said. "I like knowing every little thing everyone's doing and saying. And you're giving Father some real grief, Mama. This fire wasn't his doing. We're gonna be fine, just fine. The Zurchenkos survived worse than this. Aleksey actually pulled Anna from a fire two years back. He's the family hero." Tommy picked eggs from the pan and Jeanie swatted his hand with the wooden spoon.

"Ask Katherine, he's *her* hero," Tommy said.

"Is not," Katherine squealed as she pulled her bed covers up.

"Tommy, do like your sister and make your bed up," Jeanie said. "And leave Katherine alone. She's much too young to have any sort of hero worship for any sort of boy. Even those who yank siblings out of fires."

Tommy lumbered to the bed he shared with James. "Sure would be nice if my big brother could make his side of the bed. Oooh, Mama, smell that? James is doing his heavy business in the chamber pot. He knows to use the outhouse for the heavy business. That's grotesque."

Tommy yanked his covers up and stumbled from the dugout as though halfway to his death.

Katherine was too ladylike to wretch and make comment about anyone's bodily functions, but she left the dugout nearly as fast as Tommy, her prune-pinched face telling the tale her lips wouldn't.

James whipped the curtain aside and shook his head, his face pale, greenish. Jeanie stepped toward him. "I'm okay, I'm sorry to do that in here. I couldn't help it. Must have been something in that meal Ruthie Moore made us last night. I felt so great last night, nearly strong as I imagine an ox would, but this morning, my head feels heavy as an anvil. And I just, I'm sorry."

"Let me help, you lay down, I'll empty the pot," Jeanie said.

"No, I need the air," James said. He picked up the waste and gagged on his own stench as he carried it out of the house.

Of all the things that had gone wrong so far, the dugout instead of a real house, the fire, utter sense of disconnectedness from society, Jeanie hadn't contemplated illness much. Had they been in Des Moines, her conversations would have been peppered with references to the possible seasonal illnesses, who most likely would spread them, succumb to them, surmount them. But, on the prairie, the sense of immediacy didn't include the opportunity to wonder about whom was carrying what disease until it was upon them.

But, James bounced back fast, as though the emptying of the pot was all it took to rid his body of whatever toxin had taken him for a small time.

And in the same manner the earth followed suit. Just days after the fire—with the help of generous rains—the prairie shot back to green, and yellow and every color imaginable. What was lacking was the sight of beautiful corn, melons, wheat, and other garden items.

The balance of the damage their fellows incurred went as follows: Templeton's house and barn were devoured by the flames, though he was alive and well having been in Yankton to purchase food-stuffs and more wood for Frank's commissions and repairs on his own barn.

The Zurchenko's crops were devastated, their sod home still stood as the flames found it unappetizing as they did the Arthur's dugout. The Zurchenko's cows, horses and oxen weathered the flames in the sod barn, though Greta insisted that spiritually, the livestock was clearly harmed as their natural inclinations to eat and produce milk or waste had been suppressed since the flames cleared.

The Moore's frame home survived as resourceful Ruthie had learned from a book she read, to dig a trench about fifteen feet from her frame home. She had done so the prior year and then she watched as the fire fell into it and spread around her house like a miracle. Though, the Moore's garden, corn and wheat were partially obliterated, some of it remained.

The Hunts managed nicely. Their property stood out of the fire line, having none of their garden sacrificed, their property bore odd recognition of what had happened around it as smoke had merely blackened the windows. The biggest problem with the Hunt's property getting the least of the fire's rage was that they offered the least in way of useful foods and animals.

And so, as Jeanie couldn't have imagined before it happened, the fire didn't plow across the land in a high long wall, but serpentined, winding over the land as though directed by a demented artist orchestrating how he'd like to best see the land revealed and destroyed.

As the sun settled above them and as though there wasn't epic rebuilding to do, Jeanie's neighbors began appearing at their dugout to see the bee tree, to fuss over the children, to mull over the fiery events as a group.

James had spent the morning, after his bout with illness, with Templeton, recording weather conditions, predicting what might be on the weather horizon. Katherine sat by Jeanie, as though afraid to wander. Jeanie couldn't believe her luck, that she'd only dragged one hope chest outside the dugout, to show Lutie the fabrics. Though her most beautiful fabrics were destroyed, there was still much to choose from in her second chest.

Katherine insisted on Jeanie allowing her to sew Aleksey's work shirt. And though Katherine's stitches could be slow and uneven, Jeanie figured it was more important to finish the work and give Katherine the most opportunities to sew as possible. She'd tired of stitching napkins and practicing on samplers and embroidering wash towels that they rarely used any more due to how long the stretches between washes were going.

Jeanie washed a significant amount of clothing that morning and with her own hands, caught two prairie chickens and began cooking them for both dinner and soup for supper. And though that time, Jeanie didn't wretch with each pluck of brown feathers, she began to wonder again if coming to the prairie had been smarter than staying to deal with her family scandal. It wasn't as though *she* was the one who swindled friends, neighbors and strangers out of money leaving his daughter and her family to deal with it.

But that didn't matter to the people she saw every day and it would matter less to those she only saw a few times a year. She was the daughter of the man who stole from Mr. Wannamaker, Mr. May and Mrs. McCall. And their association with Jeanie didn't survive the acts of her father even if personally those powerful people knew Jeanie was as much a victim as they were. Scrubbing the filthy clothes over the metal washtub, Jeanie burst into tears as she admitted that to herself. She pushed and pulled the clothing, catching her knuckles from time to time, stopping to suck the blood off her skin.

She'd penned letters to the people who'd once clamored for her articles, awaiting her next book or column. She explained that she and Frank had been taken by prairie fever and wanted to try their hands at their own land. In her upbeat letter, she promised she'd communicate with them just as soon as she was established and fully inspired with a new perspective on homemaking.

And, even though she knew in her mind that when those old "friends" read the letters, they must have laughed hard, heads thrown back, mouths gaping at their ceilings, probably slobbering on their silk lapels, knowing how Jeanie lied, yet, in Jeanie's heart was the surety of truth, that her words were not lies. For, she'd never been the lying type before, so she made up her mind to weave the story into the truth she needed to survive and if that meant a solid demarcation between the knowledge of her mind and that of her heart, well she could live with that.

And so for the first time in months, instead of Jeanie fighting the anger and resentment that was foremost on her mind and in her body, she used the crippled anger to scrub their clothes cleaner than they'd been since she made them. She thrust back and forth, pushing and pulling the clothing over the washboard, skirts nearly swooshing into the fire that heated the wash-water from underneath.

She ignored her belly when cramping came. She gave into the rhythm of yanking the clothing back and forth. She squeezed her eyes tight, and behind her lids, images of a feed-sack, hanging over her head, splitting open dumping grain onto her head, flattening her, came to mind. With the imagined impact, came the realization that her life as it had been in Des Moines wasn't possible on the prairie. That she'd written books espousing "simple" ways to maintain gracious living even while doing charity, tending to children, that she believed women who lived anywhere under any circumstance could make use of her books, her thoughts, *that* ridiculousness hit her like a splayed feed-sack.

"How utterly, utter of me to not have understood my own idiocy." She spit out her words and finally gave into the cramps, resting on all fours. She tried to steady her breathing and recalculate how far she was in her pregnancy. She couldn't remember. She was nearly three months along, was that right? She counted back, then forward, unable to sort the dates in her head.

"Jeanie," Templeton said. He squatted next to her and put his arm around her shoulder.

Jeanie flinched at her unladylike position.

"You're exhausted. Here, let me help you inside. You need some water. Just by chance, in Yankton, I spoke with a doctor who happened to be caring for a woman like you and he said lack of water brought on early birth pains. All it will take is a little water and rest to bring you back to even keel."

Jeanie flinched away, at his candidness, inappropriateness, at the way his arm felt reassuring and strong across her back. When was the last time she felt Frank's arm this way? When had he last offered a supportive gesture? The warmth, the improper reaction, it all made Jeanie cry harder. She fell into Templeton's body and clung to him, digging at his shirt, pulling bunches in her balled fists.

"Here, let me help you."

Jeanie nodded into his chest and he stood, pulling her up and supporting her into the dugout where he lay her down and went to the kitchen for water. Jeanie knew it was wrong to be there like that, to have him fetch water like a servant, to have a man in her room while she reclined like, like a tramp or slovenly woman who had no boundaries or upbringing.

There was so much wrong with it, that she began to black out with the heaviness of it all. On top of the breaking of mores that humiliated her so, there was the appearance of her dugout. Having thought she'd put her material interests behind for simpler ideals, her shame at her home's appearance took over her thoughts.

She sniffled as Templeton poked around for a cup and ladle.

She turned away from the sight of him, looking at her ill-equipped kitchen. She closed her eyes, hand over her forehead. "You'd think it'd be no big concern to lose your money, your *things*." Jeanie spoke so quietly she didn't think he'd even hear her. "As long as you had family and health and mind, and determination. But then you lose it, the silk dresses, shiny gold, glittery gems, a household staff, and you realize all of those things are actually part of who you are. I was a fraud without even knowing it." Jeanie chortled, her throat scratchy. "How was I to know when I wrote those books, that my thoughts on keeping a home were entirely dependent on keeping my things. I really believed I was simply…"

"Shhh, shhh, shhh," Templeton sat on the edge of the bed. Jeanie kept her eyes closed, let him lift her up and put the cup to her lips, water running down her mouth, over her chin. She opened her eyes and looked into Templeton's face, his skin creased with his obvious concern. His grey eyes anchored his gaze into her soul, making her feel as though their private souls were slipping together, greeting one another in a way they couldn't verbally do.

"You have to go," Jeanie said. She searched his expression for evidence he'd heard what she said, that he didn't think she was awful. She was further shamed that she cared what he thought.

Templeton hesitated then nodded and stood. He pulled the chair across the room and set it beside the bed where he laid the water cup. "I'll find Frank. You shouldn't be alone."

Jeanie almost screamed for him to stay, to tell her she wasn't a fraud. Please, tell me, she thought. Someone, please tell me... please, she thought. She wanted him to put his hands back on her, to touch her face. She was swimming with the same feelings that Frank had once brought out in her just by standing nearby.

"I can't sleep," Jeanie said. "That's what's wrong. I haven't slept since the fire. If I sleep, I might wake and find out they died. I couldn't live, I couldn't."

Templeton came back to the bed and sat down heavy, as though this was exactly the invitation he'd been waiting for. "You don't have to be afraid to sleep. Everyone's fine. This is reality, you're alive, they're alive. And, I think you would do fine under any circumstance. Even if you can't imagine...it's what people like us do. We're pioneers, Jeanie, and it's what we do. We live no matter what."

Though convention demanded that she be humiliated at what had transpired in the room where she slept, with a man not her husband, Jeanie felt nothing at all. It was as though Templeton saw something in her that she didn't, and unlike Frank who might have said those very same words to her, Templeton saying them meant mountains, as he wanted and needed nothing from her. Frank's kind words were often the currency of manipulation to direct her actions down the path that would most benefit him.

Jeanie watched Templeton leave the dugout, put his hat on, straighten it before walking away. Jeanie's body felt as though she were trapped in mud, she had never felt such fatigue, yet her eyes wouldn't close, her mind wouldn't stop and let her sleep. And Frank finally arrived looking hot and sweaty. Jeanie didn't have a chance to inquire what he'd been up to because he began to tend to her as though she were his delicate angel, his greatest love, the way he used to treat her.

He mixed a drink and brought it to her. She looked at him, her heart beating with the surge of feelings Templeton had awakened, though now they were for her husband. She winced at the bite in the drink.

"Frank? What's in this?"

"Just some herbs. From the Moores. Nothing…"

Jeanie fell back on the pillows and almost immediately her mind lifted and her spirit ran with lightness that was nearly a miracle and her question, whatever it was faded from her mind. She reached up to Frank and felt his face, seeing two of him, but remembering every single reason she ever fell in love with him. And it could be whittled down to a list of three things—his good looks dwarfed hers and made her feel as though winning at poker to have him love her as though she didn't deserve to be with someone so handsome, but like any winner at poker, she could live with it once it happened. Two, his optimism that there wasn't anything in the world he couldn't do. And three, the way he loved their children, as though his life locked down in peace when they were born.

She finally coasted into sleep, feeling as though smothered in nothing but goodness, happy to be nothing more than Frank's wife.

Jeanie raised her head trying to wake, the room blurred, the fuzzy figures and furniture shifted and she dragged her thick tongue around her mouth, feeling as though dirty rags were jammed in it. Voices filled the dugout, Frank's strained while a woman's was pleading. Greta? Yes, it was Greta.

Jeanie must have fallen back asleep because when she finally woke for good, she could make out the people and objects in the room clearly. Frank and Greta were convened at the cook-stove,

Katherine sat on the floor with two-year-old Anzhela. It was the first time Jeanie could remember not seeing Anzhela attached to Greta's body with clasped arms and legs.

"Mama!" Katherine hopped up and tumbled into bed with Jeanie.

"Now, Kath, don't crowd your Mama, she's not up to speed yet."

Jeanie wrapped her arm around Katherine, squeezed her tight and kissed her forehead, smelling just washed hair. Roses.

"I got a bath at the Moore's, Mama," Katherine said, her eyes nearly dancing in her skull as the memory was clearly a decadent one for her. "They allowed me use of their big white porcelain tub, fit for queens, their shampoo—rose-scented, then a thick substance, apple smelling that they said would smooth the knots away after rinsing it, then they had me dry myself, put on a pinafore and they swabbed my arms and legs with the most wonderful rose-scented lotion."

Katherine thrust her arm under her mother's nose. "Isn't that fantastic?"

The intense smell caused Jeanie's stomach to tighten and shoot acid upward. She bolted up, covering her mouth. Greta dove toward Jeanie, shoving the water pail under her mouth where she vomited clear fluids, then nothing.

❦

Katherine's face crinkled with fear. She backed away, hiding in the corner where Anzhela was still playing with a doll. Greta climbed onto the bed, knelt beside Jeanie, ran her hand over the back of Jeanie's head and down her back.

Jeanie's breathing evened and she pulled her ankles in to sit cross-legged, handing the pail to Frank who appeared as horrified as Katherine.

"Come here Katherine," Jeanie said, "it's okay. With the baby my stomach is a little sensitive to smells. Those lotions and concoctions are something else. Why you're a veritable farmer's market with all the fruits and flowers emanating from your skin like that. It's just my being pregnant."

Frank flinched then snuck a glance at Greta who caught the gaze then looked away.

"What?" Jeanie said.

Greta and Frank stared at one another as though each was threatening to expose the other's worst secret. Jeanie'd seen the expressions, the tension that gripped a person's entire body.

Frank broke Greta's gaze and shrugged. "I just gave you a little—"

Greta cut her hand through the air. "Not with the kids in here. Katherine, could you make sure Anzhela is under the care of Anna and the boys. Aleksey's the most reliable, but see to it she doesn't wander."

Katherine nodded and pulled Anzhela to her feet and out the door. She took a final glance at Jeanie who nodded reassuringly before turning her attention back on Frank.

"What is it? Exactly how long have I been asleep? The baby?"

Frank shrugged. "Baby's fine as far as we can tell. You had so much trouble sleeping after the fire that I just helped you a little, I put a little elixir in your tea, that's all, just a little something to help you along to sleep. It wasn't good for the baby to have you living on two hours sleep."

Jeanie looked at her lap and let Frank's words wrap around memories of other elixirs. "No, no you didn't."

"I had to, I didn't know what else to do."

"The baby, he'll be slow or dead or—"

Greta grabbed Jeanie's biceps. "Now listen to me, I gave Frank, who I barely know, let alone know well to tell him his business, but I gave it to him good, Jeanie, I told him not to give you any more of that or your baby would be born limp or stupid or dead. I've seen people with just one swig of laudanum, marry it until death comes way too early and ugly and wasted."

"Okay, okay," Frank said. His words were hissing, his face disgusted at what Jeanie knew he would consider theatrics on Greta's part.

"Don't speak to her that way," Jeanie said. "Don't you dare."

Greta stood and ladled fresh water into a tin cup. She handed it to Jeanie and as the mug passed from her hands to Jeanie's, Greta patted Jeanie's offering comfort even though she knew she'd crossed the line into another's marital bounds.

Greta straightened and doing so, came eye to eye with Frank. She scowled at him then disappeared through the doorway. Jeanie downed the entire cup of water. She pushed from the bed, staggering. Frank caught her weight and they held each other until she recovered her balance. Once she did, they dropped their arms from each other and stood, staring at one another.

She shook her head, not saying what she thought. She didn't need to, she'd said the words to Frank once before, when he'd done this same thing when she suffered a late-term miscarriage. She'd said the words a million times about her father since she found out the truth about his lies. Frank knew better than to ever bring any form of opium into their home. And so they stared, silently posing arguments that if verbalized would have done even more damage than the act itself.

Jeanie pulled up her skirts and took the cup to the stove where she dunked it into the water, washed it and dried it. She hoped that Frank would have left the dugout, let her sort through her anger on her own. But there he was, behind her, making her hate him, *breathing*.

"Stop staring at my back," Jeanie said.

"I'm looking at the ceiling."

"I can feel your eyes burning a hole in my back. I'm not going to apologize or act like your regret is worth anything. I, right now, can barely stand the thought of you let alone the sight of you. So just go, Frank. Just give me some time to think."

Jeanie's verbal purge felt good while in the midst of it, but as soon as the words were out of her mouth she felt struck by her own venom. She hugged her midsection. This was not the time to make things worse, to push Frank away, to make him see her as weak and vixenish.

The image of the Moore sisters, indulging Katherine, popped to mind. The last thing she needed to do was spread her family out, she would lose them all, she needed to keep them close, and control them so to be sure they survived. Jeanie started to speak, to set things right with Frank when panicked voices wafted through the door. They both strained to hear then they looked at one another, questioning whether they really heard it.

Jeanie fled the dugout, shielding her eyes from bright sun as she did. The voices were coming from behind the dugout. She scaled the side of it, running toward the voices, behind the barn, then into clear land. She saw Greta lumbering over the land, wailing at the sky, her hands flailing, then tying her body up in her own arms before she ripped at her bonnet, her white blond hair that came loose from its bun and fell over her shoulders.

Whatever was happening to Greta, Jeanie could feel in her own bones. It had to be one of the children. Jeanie broke through her shock and ran toward Greta. She knelt beside Greta who had fallen to her knees, and pounded the ground, grunting at it. Jeanie unfolded Greta and pulled her into her arms repeatedly asking what was the matter. Greta choked on mucus and tears but then settled into a shuddering, quieter shock.

"Anzhela's gone! She's gone!"

By then the other Zurchenko children, Katherine, and Frank had circled the two women and were looking down on them.

"What do you mean? Let's find her, come on, the children were watching her, she can't have gone far, she's but two. Let's get up, we'll find her, let's go," Jeanie said. She stood attempting to pull Greta's six-foot frame from the prairie floor.

"She means Anzhela's dead, Mrs. Arthur. Not missing." Aleksey said.

Greta shuddered at Jeanie's feet, jerking at her shins as Jeanie tried to make sense of Aleksey's words.

"I don't understand. She was with Katherine then, you, I thought, it was only for a bit, five minutes, how could…That can't be right. It can't be."

But, Jeanie saw the Zurchenkos expressions fall, their eyes went to the ground as though in deference. Jeanie turned to see Nikolai standing behind her, holding Anzhela's limp body, in his arms, her head, lobbing at the neck, her legs dangling, her arm flopped loose.

"She fell into the gully. The one by the tree," Aleksey said.

Jeanie couldn't respond. She didn't believe her eyes, Anzhela's matted wet hair, her skin bluish, but her face placid, appearing simply sleepy. Jeanie shook her head. Katherine came beside Jeanie and Nikolai. Katherine lifted Anzhela's dangling arm up and laid it across her body, patting it so it would stay there.

Then she began to cry, apologizing for not watching Anzhela closer. She inhaled so fast and hard that her shoulders heaved and she fell to the ground, begging Mrs. Zurchenko's forgiveness for losing track of Anzhela.

Jeanie's heart stalled, she felt shaken as anger swelled her. How would Katherine be able to live with this? Jeanie bent down to her daughter and Greta. Jeanie pulled both of them into her body, rocking them. She looked up at Frank through her tears. How could he have been so stupid as to create a situation where the adults needed to talk privately? He was always trying to make things easier for him even if it made everyone else's life so much harder. How could they have come to live in such a place where the land swallowed little girls up in flooded gullies when fires didn't do it first?

Jeanie rocked Katherine for hours, leaving Frank to explain to James and Tommy what had happened. Somewhere between evening and night, Jeanie felt so out of control, so depressed that she almost asked Frank to mix laudanum for her, for the still trembling Katherine. Her body nearly begged for it and Jeanie began to understand why someone might use it, how easily the drug might become a reliable friend to charm one's sorrows away. She was so saddened by the death of a child. She knew she could not survive what was ahead for Greta. She only hoped she could help her new friend manage the loss. So, in that darkness she held Katherine even tighter, thinking if she didn't let go, she couldn't get up and request Frank bring her opium to make her life bearable once more.

The funeral service was short and quiet. Jeanie didn't make Katherine go and she charged James to care for her at home, to keep her still until she began to forget what she'd done. But, standing at the funeral, listening to Abby Hunt, Quaker opium-eater and by the looks of her poppy garden, opium-grower, Jeanie saw James slip into the circle of neighbors who'd come to say goodbye.

Jeanie couldn't listen to the words Abby spoke. Her eyes kept shifting to the red, beckoning flowers, the way they bent in the wind, making Jeanie wonder what it meant that the entirety of the Zurchenko's crops were overtaken in the fire, but the poppies were unharmed, as though they were saved by God. If there was a God. Jeanie reminded herself there wasn't.

James edged over to his mother and whispered that Aleksey hadn't been able to stay for the funeral, he couldn't handle it because it had been his job to watch Anzhela with Katherine. Aleksey promised to watch over Katherine at the dugout. The rest of the stoic Zurchenkos stood like sentries, faces showing none of the turmoil Jeanie felt inside. Greta stood, face red, bonnet blown off her head, her arms wrapped around herself, clutching Anzhela's blanket to her chest as she'd held Anzhela herself for the balance of her life.

After the service Jeanie was hesitant to go to Greta. She didn't know what to say, beyond adding to the pile of apologies she'd already dumped on her. Apologies that Greta didn't want, that didn't do anything but remind her that the Arthurs, in their short time on the prairie had changed the Zurchenkos existence for the worse.

So Jeanie became the friend she never wanted to be—a useless one, lost for words, unable to make someone's life better. Jeanie hated herself, hated the prairie, Frank, her father. The thoughts shot around her head, making her body fill with a mixture of anger and sadness that was new in its depths.

And, as Jeanie headed home, with Tommy unusually quiet, holding her hand, as though for the first time ever understanding Jeanie, she knew her children were all that mattered, that with every minute on the prairie that they all stayed safe, they were just that much closer to tragedy. She wondered whether this pain, the pain Katherine would have to bear for the lot of them, would be enough pain to stave off further bad tidings, death, paralysis, blindness, whatever was in the universe to make their existence even worse than before. And in what Jeanie deemed a sickness because who could think such things, she hoped that Katherine's pain would be enough to buy them all some freedom from more.

Chapter 9

1905
Des Moines, Iowa

Katherine laid a wet rag over Jeanie's forehead and she found herself offering words of comfort, the same ones she might have uttered to one of her children when ill. Jeanie stirred and groaned. Katherine shushed her and straightened the bedspread. Yale stood at the door, arms full of a pile of letters and some books.

"Yale? What are those? What are you..." Katherine went to Yale and relieved her of the stack, marveling at the sight of the yellowed envelopes mixed with blaze white stationary, tied with pink ribbon. "Where did you get these?"

Yale's eyes grew wide and her shoulders rose and fell in at the same time as though she wanted to disappear inside herself. Katherine laid her hand on Yale's arm.

"It's all right. You didn't do anything wrong." Katherine looked at her mother then back to Yale before paging through the envelopes. Most were from Howard Templeton, some dated as early as 1888 and some as late as 1905. There was a smattering from Tommy, return addresses from sites the world over. Then there were a few from Katherine's father—what must have been love letters between Jeanie and Frank, Katherine assumed.

"Mama said to. She needed them. She reads them every night. They're her salvation she said. No one else remembers. No one else cares."

Katherine took the books from Yale. The two Jeanie had written in 1885 as well as a collection of her newspaper columns.

"She wanted these?"

Yale nodded.

"But why, she can't even sit up to read."

"I read them to her." Yale's posture unfolded as she spoke the words.

"You can read?" Katherine shook her head, searching Yale's face for familiarity two sisters should have shared. She saw nothing, but felt it, the love, the sudden understanding that this woman, even with her limited mental ability knew things about her family that Katherine didn't. She was ashamed then angered that her mother had put Katherine in the position of having to be a less than perfect daughter and sister.

"Well then. Mother needs you, so go on and read. Give her the comfort she requires."

Yale nodded and settled into the chair beside Jeanie's bed. She held Jeanie's hand, kissed it, and told her how much she loved her. Jeanie stirred at Yale's voice. Next, Yale launched into the day's events as though Jeanie weren't comatose, was able to carry on her end of a conversation. Katherine's stomach caved in on itself as though she'd been struck with a flour sack.

Seeing Yale so fully intertwined with Jeanie as Katherine hadn't been in recent memory, sickened her. The sight of the two of them was so jarring that in Katherine's mind, a shift occurred. Her heart was impassable, she thought, but her mind, was another matter. She suddenly *wanted* to understand, wanted to let her mother know she at least tried to make sense of it all.

Jeanie's head rolled side to side as she clung to Yale's hand. "Yale," Jeanie's voice was thin. "Yale, I'm so sorry for your life. Where *are* you? Where did I leave you? Why can't I find you?"

Katherine stood immobilized. She watched Yale caress her mother's hair, calming her. What was her mother talking about? When was Yale lost? Was Jeanie remembering the other night when Yale got drunk at the bar? Katherine decided it was simply a mix of morphine and the steady fall into death that were confusing her mother.

She lingered there, watching Yale read the letters, remembering a time when *she'd* been the one to read letters to her mother, when her mother pored over them as though they held sacred answers to her dire circumstances. And Katherine knew. She had something to discover before it was too late and with that thought, she could finally move. The answers were in the letters. Not the ones Yale was reading. The answers were in the letters Jeanie had attempted to burn, the letters tucked away in the trunk in the attic, the one that hadn't been opened since 1888. That hideous year on the prairie.

Chapter 10

1887
Dakota Territory

The fire raped and exposed the prairie, land that then consumed baby Anzhela. But interspersed in the burnt, barren plains, almost immediately, certain sections of the land that had been narrowly missed or not completely ravaged, birthed vibrant grasses and sunflowers that shot from the ground like earthbound suns.

The Zurchenkos responded much like the earth. Like prairie plants, it was as though the family was made to survive such horrors. They tucked their charred emotions away in self-defense, ignored the reality that their daughter and sister was dead and that Katherine and Aleksey had been part of that terrible day, and simply started to bloom again.

They took Tommy and Katherine under their plowing tutelage, having them spend each day there, attempting to coax the land into yielding crops once again. Though they didn't have much hope for replanting the crops that had burned, they still turned the land as Nikolai had seen crops grow quickly when the right luck visited them in years past. Mostly the farmers focused on the gardens and crops that had survived the fire, tending them like newborn babies fresh from the womb.

James made trips to Yankton with Templeton to secure supplies and plan for Templeton's new home, discussing science and weather, making Jeanie sad that Frank seemed to have little connection to the prairie or her family. What was most sad was that he didn't seem to care or notice that it was so.

Just as the fire ripped open the land, exposing its guts and daring it to come back to its full strength, Jeanie felt the same challenge had been issued to her. She acquiesced to prairie life, allowing her children to traipse over the land from homestead to homestead, running errands, collecting cow chips on the way back from the Zurchenko's each day to be used as fuel.

Every chance she had, she sewed and tried to find the loving plains of her heart where her marriage used to live. Frank was moderately helpful to the other men, but he spent most of his time pretending to carve useful furniture as Templeton brought some wood back on loan.

The antipathy that strangled Jeanie in regard to Frank's laziness was numbing at times. The resentment would burst up, appearing at the sight of him lazing about, long after Jeanie and the children had done their chores. Then one day as the bitterness sat there inside Jeanie it became clear that it wasn't new to their prairie life. She recognized it as an emotional stowaway, only presenting itself when forced, that it had been a part of their marriage for some time.

It was simply that in Des Moines, she could cover up for any of his shortcomings, without even noticing she was doing it. She compensated for anything and everything that wasn't quite right. It was who she was. Or who she'd been, rather, as there was no time or materials for compensating for others on the prairie. She supposed it was only the depth of the resentment that still surprised her, the way she tried to charm it away, with sweet love speeches in his ear here and there. But nothing worked for either of them.

There in the dugout, she tried to counteract her anger by spending late hours when acid-stomach wakened her, culling the letters she'd written to Frank, and him to her, while they courted at the ripe age of fifteen. In her own letters, she tried to recognize the love that was there on the paper, to let it leap from the pages or pull her in, bringing back the love she once risked her entire life for. She shook the letters, wanting so badly to love Frank again, to believe in him as she had before.

Tommy, who worked like an ox, but seemed to have the same shallow reflection processes, barely noticed Jeanie reading her own letters as though they were written by Shakespeare or Beecher or any of the authors she once pored over. But Katherine and James noticed. Katherine often sat beside Jeanie reading along, smiling as her mother did, at the words. Jeanie would often fold a letter quickly, hiding portions of it from her daughter. Katherine would beg for more.

But James would sit, by the door, writing in his journal, or studying the science books he and Templeton had borrowed from a library in a town further east, watching Jeanie, not pushing for answers to his silent questions regarding Jeanie's study of her writings.

It was through the reading of these letters that Jeanie found some peace, that she was able to stave off the utter dread that her life had become like a massive, elephantine plain of drudgery that she had to traverse every single day. Once in a while she'd think of Lutie. Jeanie had also known a divorced woman in Des Moines and while Jeanie'd thought and said horrid things about the divorcee in the past, there was a part of Jeanie that envied the freer position, that the divorcee's time was her own and waiting on a man in front of her own needs was not a part of that life.

But, *that* divorcee woman had money, loads of it, and as Jeanie recognized, money changed everything. Sitting there in the dank, suffocating dugout, Jeanie felt her innards transforming, her mind entertaining thoughts that she had no businesses inviting.

Nothing Frank had ever done was grounds for divorce. Jeanie actually couldn't call up any circumstances that warranted it, but yet, there it was. The word swirled around her mouth. She let it dance in her head, create visions of independence in her heart, she knew at the end of things, she'd view a divorce as scathing failure, one that she wasn't sure she could overcome even if she still had her former riches and standing.

In her mind, the only way to have an independent life out-side of divorce would have been to have never married in the first place. And it was that thought that always ended her inner divorce machinations and left her with an ever growing sense of loss and disappointment that in a world where there were few choices, she'd had the ability to make some, and she may have chosen wrong.

In Des Moines, money had rarely been directly discussed. They, of a certain social order, understood who had what money and hold-ings and though often those matters were discussed behind one's back, one never sat in the parlor with mixed company discussing finances and how they impacted daily life.

But, as the Hunts, Zurchenkos, Moores, Templeton, and Arthurs sat down to dinner the day Templeton returned from Yankton, wagon nearly buckling with wood, food-stuffs and new clothing, the lot of them in fact disclosed the exact amount of money each of them had and or was willing to contribute to making their stay on the prairie profitable and worth the effort of pioneering.

Though no one asked directly, Templeton revealed he'd buried, behind his barn, a sum of money that was the stash that allowed him to buy more lumber in Yankton for a new frame house. He wrote a personal note to Frank, lending the amount it would cost for materials and labor to rebuild the commissions for furniture that had perished in the fire as well as to furnish Templeton's home, at least with a bedstead and lounge.

The information relating to Templeton's hidden wealth caused Lutie to flush and wiggle in between her sister and Templeton, to begin the process of flirtation. This satisfied Jeanie as she thought this would funnel any attention Lutie rained on her Frank onto Templeton instead.

But, it also galled Jeanie that Lutie so overtly shoved her own sister from Templeton's side, clearly staking her claim, without any thought for the dear Ruthie. Not that Templeton appeared to hold any interest for Ruthie beyond passing gentlemanly politeness, but still, if Lutie gave the pair some room, who knew what might develop?

Jeanie resisted the urge to shower the same amount of pity on Ruthie as her sister drizzled admiration over Frank. Jeanie despised her inclination to weigh attractiveness above all else for it was not as though she were a classic beauty herself.

Ruthie was quite gifted in the domestic arenas. She was strong, quiet, capable, smart and underneath her pocked skin, was the same stunning beauty of her sister. Ruthie just needed the right man to take notice of what lay slightly below the surface. Jeanie saw bits of her former self in Ruthie—the way she worked in ways that Jeanie could only think were attempts to lure Templeton into courting her.

But as happens when any woman feels her insecurities surface, Ruthie must have experienced just that when Lutie weaseled in between her and Templeton. Ruthie jumped to her feet, face crimson, eyes a bit wild as she ordered Lutie to bring some water, to stir the stew, to make herself useful in any manner of way that must have flashed to mind.

Jeanie stood and joined Ruthie by the fire where she cranked the spoon around the vat of stew as though it were the perpetrator of the slight instead of Lutie.

"Ruthie," Jeanie put her hand on Ruthie's arm.

Ruthie shrugged it off. She glared at Jeanie who backed off.

"I'm sorry. I was just trying to tell you what a wonderful stew you've made. That—"

"Oh, please, what does it matter? I'm a quilt-stitch from packing up and heading out of this hell on earth."

Jeanie looked around to see if anyone else heard Ruthie's outburst. The rest of them were chatting and greeting Greta as she came across the land, holding Anna's hand. Jeanie didn't want to cut Ruthie off in her time of need—some people lashed out when they were threatened and they could be diffused with a little tenderness and Jeanie felt protective of Ruthie, inclined to mother her a bit. But, Greta hadn't left her house in days, even though when Jeanie visited, she seemed overly cheerful, her face frozen in a grimacy smile, swearing she was fine, almost as though she couldn't remember what had happened to Anzhela.

And here she was, for the first time appearing her normal self, with the plain expression that only hinted at what was happening in her head rather than a crazy mask of grief that looked sideshowish more than real. Jeanie started toward Greta but Ruthie was already mid-sentence.

"Really, you have everything Jeanie Arthur, and I don't need pity or mothering or—"

Jeanie shook her head distracted by Greta, not willing to take the brunt of Ruthie's misplaced anger.

"You know, life is what you make it, Ruthie. You're a good woman, I can see that. And I think proving up your homestead is admirable, but maybe it's just too much for two women to handle on their own. Maybe the land wouldn't be your own if you were married, but you'd share in its riches and the riches of a husband's love."

Ruthie stopped stirring and smirked at Jeanie.

"You believe that line of you know what?"

"Of course, Ruthie, of course I do."

And with that intrusion into Jeanie's personal thoughts, she turned and stalked away. She was halfway to Greta when she realized Ruthie may not have been asking about herself. Jeanie turned back to Ruthie who was watching her. Jeanie lifted her hand in a wave and wondered if she did believe all that manure that surged from her mouth like lava from a great volcano. Jeanie rushed to Greta telling herself that it would be another long night with the love letters of her past.

Over a dinner of stew, oatcakes and coffee—real coffee not the seedy substitute they'd been forced to make until Templeton rose out of the land like a dream—the Darlington Township cooperative discussed their needs. They determined who could meet them and whether to address other families in the township who might have something to offer and needs to be met.

The Zurchenkos inquired with their immediate neighbors (those not part of their cooperative) and some had already packed up to leave while others were unwilling to risk sharing their plenty. So, the Arthurs, Hunts, Templeton, Moores, and Zurchenkos agreed to proceed in the manner they'd started.

The Zurchenkos would shoulder the bulk of re-plowing and replanting late summer corn and winter wheat as all they could do was take the chance that they would get 85 days for the corn in before the frost came. Even if the crop yielded a modicum of corn it would help the group throughout the winter.

Ruthie agreed to teach the children once the weather settled between the harvest and when it became too cold to venture out on a given day. Ruthie would tend her garden with Lutie's assistance as would Abby Hunt. Jeanie's tailoring would rest until Templeton's home was rebuilt as she and Mr. Hunt would assist him in rebuilding.

The next day all the men would frame Templeton's new home then disperse to do their other work while Jeanie and James assisted in lathing the home. Frank would turn back to his furniture construction as soon as the wood was up.

Jeanie couldn't stop thinking of the cooperative, the dangerousness of it—knowing Abby was an opium eater, how reliable could she be? Mr. Hunt and his pear-shaped body was nearly use-less beyond discussion of books and art, and the Moores were only semi-solidly invested as half of their family was taking more than she gave.

And Greta, the strongest of them all it seems was a bit too strong in the shadow of the loss of her daughter. Jeanie wondered if she was as all right as she projected, taking on her own share of plowing and planting as though her daughter never existed let alone spent her entire life with her little arms laced around Greta's neck.

Everyone but Templeton departed soon after dinner and the evening slowed to a lumbering pace brought on by oppressive heat and humidity that left them all tempted to drink their own sweat as it puddled and dripped from ears and noses and snaked down faces.

Jeanie felt the heat more so. Her body churned extra heat to grow the baby inside and by night, she couldn't wait to strip down to her petticoat and douse herself, cleansing her private areas as best she could. She tried to catch a whiff of her odor hoping that the fact that she couldn't smell herself anymore meant that she didn't smell at all.

As Frank and Templeton finished watering the horses, Templeton uncovered a special treat in his wagon. A surprise that James, Frank and he carried to the dugout. Jeanie had dried the final tin cup and turned to see the three of them grinning as though they'd created land and sea themselves.

"A tub?" Jeanie said. She covered her mouth. "Of all things…"

"Well," Templeton said. "We need it to mix the plaster for the lathe, but before we foul the tub with the earthy mud, I thought… I mean, James had said you'd been yearning for a well, I'm sorry if this is, I feel mighty impolite now that we're standing here like this."

"I told him not to," Frank mumbled. "Don't want no one going to trouble."

Jeanie ran her hand over the cool side of the tub. Of course he didn't because *he* wouldn't, Jeanie thought. She ignored Frank's grammar that had begun to lose its luster with the loss of the rest of his prairie manners. He crossed his arms and appeared bored—whistling at the ceiling—to have to attend to his wife in such a way.

"No, no. My James, sweet James is always considering his mother." Jeanie waved James to her, kissed him on the forehead and snuggled him into her side. He nestled his head on her shoulder, closed his eyes and his face instantly appeared as it had when he was a sleeping toddler.

Frank stomped out of the dugout.

"Well, I told Frank I'd help pull in the first batch of water, so..." Templeton said.

He hesitated then bowed into his hat, offering Jeanie a wink. Jeanie flushed.

"Wait, don't go...thank you," Jeanie held her hand palm up, not knowing how to express her gratitude for something that was a much too personal purchase, but the kindness behind it was evident. Templeton squeezed her hand then left to get the water.

Once the water was rising in the tub and Jeanie was salivating over it, Templeton bid goodbye so Jeanie could finally settle into a cool bath and get cleaner than she'd been in months. She settled into the water, nearly iced with the relative difference in water and air temperatures.

"Oh, that's good. Very good." She closed her eyes and lay back in ecstasy.

Katherine pulled the curtain of the necessary aside, holding a wooden bowl. Jeanie sat forward. In the bowl were Jeanie's love letters from Frank and a glass container.

"Here, Mama. Miss Lutie made this for you, thought you were looking a bit weary in your condition." Katherine opened the glass container and held it under Jeanie's nose.

"Almonds," Jeanie said, a smile pulling across her face.

"It's night cream. For ladies of a certain age, Miss Lutie said. She really slaved over this concoction. She even gave me the recipe...lanolin, cocoa butter, honey, and her famous rosewater."

"Ladies of a certain age she said? Well, that Lutie, she's always thinking isn't she?" Jeanie was too enamored with the possibility of smelling like a lady again, that she overlooked Lutie's characterization of her as old.

"What's wrong, Mama?"

"Oh, nothing, nothing at all. I'm utterly buoyed by our new neighbors, their inclination toward such kindness. I don't think..."

"Here's your letters, Mama."

"Oh, that's okay, I think this bath alone will soothe my soul enough tonight. Besides, I've read those letters so many times I think I could page through them in my mind without much trouble."

"Sure, Mama. I'm going to sleep. The boys are out like candles in a prairie gale already and I need strength for tomorrow."

"Well, okay, that's a good idea. Kiss."

Katherine draped her arms around Jeanie's neck and kissed her cheek. Jeanie dripped some water down Katherine's face. "Can I have the tub when I wake tomorrow?"

"Sure, better hurry though. Mr. Templeton needs it for the plaster."

"I'll rise bright and early and for once in a long time, shiny!"

Jeanie laid her head back, closing her eyes. She'd scrubbed her body upon entering the water and was enjoying its coolness, the way the water lifted the weight of her stomach. She was nearly asleep when a hand ran down her belly and between her legs. She shot forward holding her chest. Frank pulled back raising his hand in surrender.

"Sweet Jesus in Heaven if there is one!"

"*Jesus is right*," Frank said. "Why does the hand of your husband shock you?"

Jeanie wanted to tell him the truth, that for once she had a moment to relax and she would not spend her respite on Frank's base yearnings. For *once*, she needed something for herself.

"After all this work," Frank said, "old Templeton made for me, fetching your water like an errand boy, I think I should garner some reward."

Jeanie reclined in the tub and shut her eyes, turning away. "Frank. I'm exhausted. This is my first tub in months. I'm with child if you've forgotten."

She waited for him to whip the curtain aside, stomp away, showing his anger at her rebuff, but all she heard were his repeated sighs. She sighed back at him, refusing to open her eyes, or even turn her face toward him.

He dumped the last of the water into the tub. The water rose and splashed over the side. She kept her eyes closed even though she could very well hear the earthy floor turning to mud.

Leave. Leave. Leave.

She exhaled deeply again trying to find pleasure in her tubbing even if Frank was going to just stand there, watching, pouting.

A sour, male smell rose into Jeanie's nose. She opened her eyes. Frank was standing there, nude, foot up on the side of the tub. He was bent forward, rooting around his private areas, scratching, shuffling male body parts around like he was at the open-air market in Des Moines searching out the ripest plums and banana available.

"That's repulsive." Jeanie drew back against the far side of the tub as far as she could.

"Ah, Jeanie, sweetness, nothing new here."

She held her nose closed. "It's the gosh-blamed smell that has me recoiling. Not the mere sight of you ferreting around your body like a primate."

"What is *that*?" Frank pointed to slight redness under his left testicle.

Jeanie covered her eyes, fighting to relocate her repose, ignoring his question. She breathed through her mouth, listening to him splash water, presumably over his stinky skin. "There's rose water and lotion and potions and everything to relieve you of that stench over there," Jeanie said.

"If I go through that sort of operation, I expect some attention in return."

Jeanie paused. She surely didn't want her suggestion interpreted as an invitation for affection. "Suit yourself, then."

More splashing as Frank "washed."

You're ruining my tub. Ruining this wonderful moment. Get out, get out, get out.

Jeanie opened her eyes slightly, to see him sniffing his underarms. "See you in a minute," Frank slapped his stomach and waltzed into the main sleeping area, naked as a newborn. Jeanie waited, hoping for the sound of a child to interrupt a possible interlude, but there was silence.

How could he be so disgusting? How could he be the man she'd chosen? Jeanie pruned in the tub, nearly falling asleep again, hoping Frank was dead-away. When thoughts of Templeton repeatedly appeared in her mind, she finally rose from the water.

Focus on what is, not what never will be.

Jeanie circled her hands over her belly marveling at how much it had grown since she'd seen it nude, in the open like that. She slipped her cleanest nightgown over her head. The cool bath might lead to the first comfortable night's sleep she'd had since she could recall.

She lay on the edge of the bed as softly as possible, relieved at Frank's even breathing. She sighed, ready to slumber, then felt Frank push into the back of her. He wrapped her in his arm, pulling her toward him, angling her bottom into his hard body. She hated her reaction to him, but couldn't get rid of the nausea that accompanied his clumsy affection. Frank ignored her unnatural stiffness, played with the back of her hair at the nape of neck. He blew there then drew his fingers down her back rubbing in small circles then pushing into her again.

Jeanie wanted to hit him away, tell him that she was already asleep, that they had a long day ahead of them, that right then in that instant when he made such advances, a complete disgust toward him rose up inside her as though it'd been there forever. She wanted to say those things, but couldn't.

In the moments following his first pushings against her night-gown-clad body, his sad attempt to initiate intercourse, her mind whipped through various ways she could politely tell him no. She was his wife. It had been months since they'd had relations. Push, push, kiss on the neck. Jeanie moved away a smidge, poising further on the edge of the bed.

"Darling, Jeanie. Please, I just need something. Something, I won't take long, I promise. You don't have to do anything. My soul craves silent, loving sympathy."

Jeanie clenched her jaw, irritated at him, saddened at the state of her feelings for him. When had this happened? She rolled over and looked into his eyes, looking for the face that used to create such lust in her that there were times all she could think of was their next time alone. The confluence of rosewater and still unclean maleness made her stomach clench.

She thought back over the years when she'd been so taken with lust that she wondered if she'd inherited a male inclination toward the act of intercourse, but there on the prairie, it was as gone as the fire-eaten greens had been. Jeanie wanted the feeling back, but that in-loveness that accompanied the first years of their marriage didn't apparently send roots deep into the prairie of her heart, roots that would nourish flowers, waiting to send color and fragrance up into the world after the heat of fire had passed. Maybe the act of sex alone could bring it back.

Frank kissed her lips and pulled back. "I love you Jeanie Arthur. The kids are asleep. It's been so long for us. Please, my soul aches for this kind of communion."

"This alone will cheer your dull cares?" Jeanie asked.

"Only this, only you."

Jeanie nodded. That single motion was all Frank needed to move on, to set to working on the planes and hills of Jeanie's body and when he finally released whatever he'd built up inside him, Jeanie felt a mixed sense of relief herself—that he was done, that she still interested him, that although there was no reawakening for her, it was within the terrain of marriage that dry spells were withstood—that perhaps inside her, the roots were just not ready to bring life back. She was pregnant after all.

And so, as Frank got out of bed to use the outhouse, Jeanie fell asleep, her disagreeable feelings soothed by the act of giving Frank what he needed, knowing it was one thing she could still do well enough.

Jeanie woke to the first day of rebuilding Templeton's house with a racing heart and contented outlook. She thought that in thrusting forward, fixing what burned out with the fire, they would be layering their expertise on the prairie, adding to their innate heartiness in the same way the root systems of prairie grasses and flowers retained theirs to make use of later, after the worst of it—whatever *it* was at the time—passed by.

Jeanie felt optimistic even though Frank lay fitful, moved slower that day, needing several nudges to draw him from the bed. He pushed back the covers and sat up with his face greening over. His shoulders bent in, as though energy was being sucked right out of him and into the bed.

"You sick?" Jeanie sat beside him, holding his shoulders. No response. She brushed his hair back off his sweaty forehead. "You slept all right? I didn't even hear you come back to bed."

"Just tired is all, drained from everything. I'll be all right. Just give me a minute." Jeanie felt a tenderness in seeing his weakness and she realized how much she needed him to need her.

152

"Let me get you tea, something to settle your stomach. I have some—"

"Jeanie, no! Go on, let me be. Can't a man just be for a minute without being handled and prodded and managed all the God-blam'd day?"

"What's the matter with you? You were fine last night, you were surely fine then."

Frank rubbed his head, shaking it back and forth. "Just give me a minute. Can I use the necessary? This is just piss-proud, here." He pointed to his crotch—his morning hardness. "I need to push the blackness away, the—"

"Stop it right now. I'm feeling at sea with all this easy talk and such. We all have to find our manners again or we'll just puddle up and sink into the soil. Manners are everything, more than I ever pretended when we actually lived among them. Don't ever speak to me with such crassness again." Jeanie stopped but didn't face him.

"And there's no time for black and blue moods or anything else that comes with them. We'll die out here if you don't light a shuck out of here and do something useful."

"That's rich, Jeanie. That's very dramatic of you. I need some water."

Jeanie didn't move, back still to Frank. She felt abused and shocked. They weren't in Des Moines, they didn't have the luxury of Frank's black moods, his rushing to this doctor and that to give him a cure while he nursed on his own self-pity. They could not afford this kind of wallowing.

"Water? Please," he said to her back.

Thoughts of the night before, the way she let herself be used for his comfort and the way it meant nothing to him, stopped Jeanie from rushing to him, begging him to let her help him, to charm his sorrowful mood away the way only a wife can. She pushed her shoulders down and back and left the dugout without a word or deed toward his needs.

An hour later, Templeton, Frank, Mr. Hunt and Jeanie stood over the plans for Templeton's home. The paper, held down at each corner by scraggly rocks, lay across the table Frank had fashioned from old pine he'd discovered at the far end of the homestead. It was the first work Frank did after the fire.

The pine graveyard lay near the top of a dried creek bed that snaked through all of their properties. The pine was scattered as though piece by piece it had bounced off a wagon or perhaps it was split right there where live pines grew, when the spot was conducive to it.

Jeanie had been irritated that Frank went to the creek bed, the one they knew was dry, but once she saw the table the morning it held the plans, she felt proud of his work. She smiled at him and patted his shoulder, hoping he knew she did think his work was brilliant even if his attitude wasn't. The others slapped Frank on the back or shook his hand, all making Frank's face come to life with satisfaction that Jeanie hoped would lead to more hard work.

The men discussed who would do what in terms of raising the house as quickly as possible. Jeanie traced a pencil drawing next to the bigger drawing of the house Templeton was building.

"Mr. Templeton," Jeanie said. She dropped her hands to her side and balled and released her fists before running a hand over her hair, squeezing the bun that sat at the nape of her neck.

Templeton turned and raised his eyebrows.

"Looking at your plans—you've drawn the house to be 16x20, much the same as the original house."

Templeton nodded. Frank looked between the two, his body shifting away from the group, eyes rolling a bit. Mr. Hunt rubbed his scruffy chin, but listened.

Jeanie pointed to the squarish drawing. "Not to leap out of turn, but I can't hold my tongue and feel right about that either. But suppose we build it 12x24. And face it east instead of west, thereby drawing the daytime sun, and making it more rectangular in shape."

Jeanie tapped her finger on the drawing then smiled up at Templeton. He squinted at her in a suspicious smile. Jeanie wondered what she was doing, giving her ideas, and all of it really just an opportunity to flirt. Frank rolled his eyes at her which only made her rip open her wealth of smarts, dwarfing Frank's, embarrassing everyone but her.

"In the center would be the door which by and by may be ornamented by a porch and pretty flowers. On either side of the door could be a window. Inside, a tiny hall, with one side a boxy sitting room—12x10, with a window in front and on the side." Jeanie began to draw pictures in the air, showing Templeton where the rooms would be situated. Watching him watch her facile hands etch out a drawing in thin air made her shudder with excitement, that Templeton valued her thoughts.

"Let it be, Jeanie," Frank said, "he has his plans, he doesn't need to choke them up with new ones. Some of us have other work to do."

Frank nodded at Templeton, clearly waiting for him to agree, to put Jeanie back where she belonged. But Templeton circled his hand through the air, urging Jeanie to continue.

"On the opposite side of the hall, a door would open into the kitchen with two windows, also. The stairs, depending on your purse, could go up from the hall or up from the kitchen."

Jeanie turned back to the drawing and poked at it. Templeton drew near her, leaned over the table on his hands and followed Jeanie's finger with his gaze as she pointed to aspects of the map. His closeness, the smell of him, earthy, but clean, caused Jeanie to flush.

"Wait, let's make these changes," Templeton rested his pencil and looked at Jeanie, their faces so close they could have caught the nature of one another's breakfasts. Jeanie shuffled away, pointing to a part of the map in the far corner.

Frank snickered from behind Jeanie. Jeanie knew she was act-ing improperly, but what did it matter, her husband only saw her as a source of release. The days where his first order of business was to make her feel loved had dwindled long before the fall of the fam-ily in Des Moines.

She never had to notice it before, she never had to feel the absence of such attention because every other aspect of their exis-tence had been in place. Now, the simple gaze of Templeton, his interest in her thoughts was enough to make full resentment of Frank come forth. And though she'd drown in guilt for her behav-ior later, at that moment, all she felt was a warm embrace from a neighbor man who wasn't even touching her.

Damn Frank. Her flirtations were all his fault and so she indulged them. For the first time since she secretly eloped with Frank, Jeanie allowed ill-advised action to overcome sensibility. After all, if Frank was going to forget she was not a slop-house mammal subject to the whims of another or its owner, she was going to forget polite society.

She felt guilt that she was bringing to life the very condi-tion Frank had feared existed all along—she might not need him as he did her, she might see strengths in others that he lacked and in flirting she was telling him that she saw something in Templeton.

She hated for a second that she could be so mean, that she would flagrantly lead Frank to what would be bouts of emotional seclusion then when he couldn't pout one more second he'd wring his soul all over her.

"Mrs. Arthur?" Templeton said.

"Oh, yes, right here. Put the stairs between the two bedrooms and it will make the sitting room much cooler in summer. And because there is no door opening from the outside into it, it will be warmer in the winter. A real advantage, I think."

"Jeanie," Frank said butting in between the two. "Templeton here, doesn't need all that horseshit."

Jeanie recoiled. Templeton caught her gaze, but didn't intrude in the tension between the married couple. This only grew the tension between the spouses.

"Not to be ill-mannered, dear wife, but old Temp's batching-it. He can make adjustments as you suggest when he adds on in the future. He just needs a place to sleep."

Jeanie rubbed her belly as a contraction pulled. She ignored it. "It's more practical to add the second floor rooms now. It's still half the size it was before. But, it will offer the same—"

"Yeah, okay, okay," Frank said. "Let's just get building or I'll never get my commissions for any of us or the men in Yankton by fall. Now isn't the time for—"

"You're right, Frank. Let's get going on this." Templeton straightened and turned to face Frank, squeezing his shoulder, defusing Frank's anger as Jeanie had lost her patience to do so. "Your changes are well taken and I believe I'll have the funds to add the rooms come next year, but I'm going to keep things as simple as possible for now."

Templeton's hand flew over the paper, making the changes they'd discussed. Jeanie watched, feeling triumphant, that even though Templeton couldn't make her changes now, he valued them enough to note them on his plans.

By the end of the afternoon, Frank, Templeton, James, and Mr. Hunt had erected the small frame.

Jeanie prepared and served a small lunch of day-old bread, spread with the last of the butter and dried meat, and then settled into the space that would serve as Templeton's kitchen and began lathing the walls with James. This was something Jeanie could do that wouldn't tax her body too much. She would only do what she could, not push too hard. But she couldn't stand not to offer her hands where they could be useful.

They nailed the two-inch strips of wood horizontally up the frame, leaving a quarter inch space between each lathe so it would create a skeleton from which plaster would hang.

James stood at one end of the lathe and hammered his end into a stud and Jeanie did the same to hers. Templeton came into the room, puffing on a pipe. Jeanie squinted up at him.

"Mr. Templeton," she said.

He lay down more boards and squatted beside Jeanie where she knelt amid the nails. He lay more lathing beside her then puffed smoke away from her face before turning back to her with a smile. Jeanie felt rushed by excitement.

"While I will freely admit I'm ravenous with jealousy at building this frame home, clean, new, fresh," she took a deep breath and shut her eyes while letting out the smell of whatever she considered clean and fresh, "I can't quite grasp why you're insisting on rebuilding a home that is indeed so vulnerable."

Templeton tamped out his pipe, set it down beside him and lifted another lathe for Jeanie, putting it into her hands, covering hers with his for a moment. "For the same reason you'll build a frame home just as soon as you first can."

Jeanie opened her mouth as though about to reply, but pursed her lips instead and narrowed her eyes at Templeton. "Yes, well, I suppose that's correct. I suppose it is. But so soon after the fire. As much as the muck and animals who reside in my little hole in the earth set my stomach to nausea, I have to admit the fire has softened my hard stance against that abode."

"But still," Templeton said cocking his head toward the six strips of lathing Jeanie and James had completed so far.

Jeanie looked at the wall. "Right, *still.*"

Templeton patted Jeanie's shoulder and inquired how she was feeling in regard to the baby in her belly. Jeanie responded to the question by lifting a lathe to the stud and nailing it in. She hammered her thumb three times before plugging the nail in. She shook her hand then sucked the throbbing thumb.

"You're sure it's not too much for you? I could take over this before I start hauling the rest of the wood. Or James' side. I could do his and he could help on your side. I don't want you to strain, to hurt yourself."

Her breathing wavered as Templeton attempted to hold her gaze and offer his concern. He clearly wasn't going anywhere until he'd gotten his answer. She looked up at him and shook her hand again feeling as though she might crawl right out of her skin with this line of questioning.

"I'm fine. Things are as expected. Things are proceeding as expected." Jeanie trusted this baby would live, sitting around, thinking of it every moment of the day would do no good, she'd learned that hard lesson back in Des Moines. But, discussing it with Templeton, well she might as well, heave up her skirts and let him have a look between her legs if she were going to discuss these matters with him. It felt the same.

Templeton tipped his hat, stood, and lugged a tarp full of earth that would be used to make serviceable though not pretty plaster down the way until he reached James. Jeanie watched the two of them talk about strategy for building and finishing a home, and they entertained the topic of Templeton's passions—the weather.

She couldn't make sense of what she was feeling toward Templeton. She'd never felt any sort of attraction to any man besides Frank. Ever. And so within the confines of marriage, she felt quite safe entertaining her crush, knowing it meant nothing, would lead to nothing, that no one would ever know of its existence. She especially felt safe in its one-sidedness. Perhaps had she been approached by Templeton, the recipient of special advances, a different tone of voice than she'd seen him use with others, she'd have been scared. Scared of him and herself.

She banged another set of nails in and set another length of board against the wood. She waited for James to lift his end, but he had turned to look at something in the distance, some place Templeton pointed. Jeanie guessed it must be the weather flag station they were discussing—a station where flags could be flown to let residents know the weather that was on its way. Mostly it was for dangerous blizzard warnings, but as they all protested before, only a few homesteads were placed so its owners would see it.

To Jeanie, the weather was only important once it was overhead or under her skin. Though there was no way to determine what type of conditions would approach with any reliability and so discussing it, the subtle clues of what's coming seemed to provide some map of the atmospheric future. Frank dismissed such avenues of thought and made Jeanie pause, curious why he, a person who clung to what lived inside his brain, abstract ideas, art, music, all manner of things not normally leading to a materially abundant life, would not join Templeton in desirable, wide-minded thinking. But, even though Jeanie saw the usefulness in turning the invisible workings of the air into observable science, she thought discussing it with James, at that moment, was a waste of time.

A contraction pulled hard. Jeanie bent at the waist, feeling a wave of heat kick in with the muscle cramping. Templeton came beside Jeanie, sitting behind her, taking her weight while she recovered from the pain. He smoothed the loose tendrils of hair back from her face. When she opened her eyes, she realized Templeton was cradling her, that his chin rested on her head, and he soothed her with gentle words. She stiffened.

Templeton released her and slid around to see her eye to eye.

"That was a bad one," he said. "Why don't you lie down. James and I can lathe this—get the plaster in—in no time. The night's clear. As far as I can tell, there's no bad weather coming this way for some time. You go on home and rest for a time. For the baby."

Jeanie steadied her breathing and took his hand when he offered it to help her stand.

"I'm sorry Mr. Templeton. I suppose, I've had a hard time with several pregnancies since the twins. I don't mean to drag the operation to a stop like a body across the railway."

Templeton didn't laugh at her joke, but studied her instead. Her gaze darted from his, feeling self-conscious that he hadn't laughed with her. Finally Jeanie's gaze locked with his. Templeton's head dropped to one side slightly as though examining a rare gift, his gaze never broke hers as a small smile curved his mouth. He put his hand on her belly. "May I?"

"You already are." Jeanie's voice was hard though not cutting.

"It's just...it's so...it's divine." He stepped back, hand still on her belly.

Jeanie felt her nerves leap to life, she was instantly drawn into Templeton's awe of her. She knew she wasn't far enough along for him to feel the baby move, but she didn't tell him that and she didn't tell him to remove his hand. In the one touch, in his gaze, she was paralyzed by something wrong and wonderful. She couldn't say it aloud, but staring at Templeton as he marveled at her, she told him that his words, interest in her touched a hidden chord in her heart and caused it to send electric thrills, peculiar to love, through her whole body. It couldn't be possible that she felt that way—she must have mischaracterized it. The pregnancy must be getting the best of her senses.

"Mama?" James startled them. He stood there with the pail of water. He set it by his feet and went to his mother.

"I'm okay. Just a bad contraction." Jeanie took Templeton's hand from her belly and shook it with both her hands. "You and Mr. Templeton are going to work. I'm going to check on your father."

"And rest, Mrs. Arthur," Templeton said. "You'll need to rest."

"And rest. Yes, I'll try some of that," Jeanie said relishing in his attentions again. She should have been ashamed at James seeing such crudeness, seeing it perpetrated by his mother. But, she also knew she'd lived and taught a life where trust was utmost and as they weren't lying people, James would have no reason to see the situation as anything other than okay.

In the few seconds of connection she only felt satisfaction. The small touch and complete enchantment spurred by the act was as pleasing as anything she'd ever experienced.

At the horse, James threaded his fingers together and let Jeanie step into his hands as she mounted the one called Summer. Named for its color—yes to the Arthurs, the summer had a golden glow like the hair on their horse—and for Jeanie and Frank's love of the book *A Midsummer Night's Dream*. Jeanie rubbed her belly and straightened against a contraction. They called their other horse Night, inspired by the same literature.

"Mama?" James said. He had one hand on the neck of Summer and the other on Jeanie's leg. He squeezed it when she didn't reply. She looked down, her face somehow flushed and losing color simultaneously, taking on a deathly pallor.

"Mama?"

"I'm all right." She nodded and looked into the horizon. "I'll stop at the well for water and once I'm home, preparing dinner, I'll feel better. I'm fine. Don't you worry."

James bit his lip and squeezed his mother's leg again. "As long as you're sure. I won't stay long with Mr. Templeton. Just long enough to learn how knowing the pressure coming up and down through the air can tell us what the coming indications are." James shielded the sun with his hand as he looked up at his mother, his words tumbling out.

Jeanie reached down and cupped his chin with her hand. She smiled her close-lipped one that meant all was fine in her mind. My God, how had she and Frank created such a wonder as James? As she looked at her son's animated face, the way it was framed by his hand and hat, an image of him as a newborn popped into her mind. She startled then ran her hand over his shoulder marveling at the juxtaposition of his childlike enthusiasm and mature concern for her wellbeing.

"No, I have to go with you, Mama."

James tipped his hat then leapt onto Night, yelling out that he'd return once he saw his mother back to the dugout. Jeanie stopped protesting and took Summer to a trot, James beside her, looking as grown-up as he could be.

The motion of Summer trotting alleviated Jeanie's contractions—the ones coming much too early for the stage of pregnancy she enjoyed—and she relaxed, letting the horse go to a full gallop. She passed the well, as she'd felt good enough to carry on past and she hummed as she dismounted, tied Summer to the wooden stake outside the barn then watered and fed her as James headed back to Templeton.

Jeanie's clothes were still sopping with sweat and as she bent and stretched, tending to Summer, her own odors filled her nose making her cringe. She'd never been a woman who let circumstances dictate her cleanliness—the benefit of Templeton's bath all but wiped away with one day's work. She dismissed her desire for another bath. The prairie did indeed make use of a proper toilet difficult. Perhaps when the lathing and plastering were complete there'd be time for another bath. No, that would be...she growled at herself for entertaining frivolous thoughts.

She would have to settle for wiping her body down like a horse, as often as possible. Even inside the dugout, which was significantly cooler, it was not cool enough that she didn't break into a sweat while simply brewing coffee. Maybe she'd try a little of the rose water Katherine had made at the Moore's. Despite the scent that made Jeanie queasy, she thought it better than pure human stench.

Jeanie ticked off a mental list of things to do, accounting for where everyone was, what they were doing and when she'd need to have dinner ready. Cramps or not, meals needed to be cooked. And with everyone doing their part, she couldn't very well beg off. She kept reminding herself of the miscarriages, that they occurred when she lay corpse-like in bed. This child was meant to be and she could feel it as sure as she could the heat.

Chapter 11

Jeanie headed to the dugout. Frank's tapping of his hammer filled her ears. He would have constructed at least half of Templeton's bedstead that afternoon. Frank was always at his best when he had concrete work behind him and she was sure this was a good thing, that creating would release whatever mood he was taken by earlier.

Jeanie stood atop the dugout, leaned over the edge and was about to say hello to Frank when the sight before her stole any words that had formed in her mouth. There, in front of the dugout, below Jeanie, lay Frank, on his back. One foot was crossed over his knee, his eyes were closed as he chomped on an unlit pipe. His arms lay out from his body, his one hand's fingers lazily making circles in the dirt while the other held a hammer tapping a piece of wood beside him.

There wasn't a constructed piece of anything in sight. Jeanie bit the inside of her cheek, holding back the flurry of confused words—reprimands that swam in her mouth, wanting to flood out, drowning Frank in a scolding that ought to have put him in his place. She kicked dirt at him from above. It sprayed over the ground below, landing near him, but apparently not close enough to jar him from his respite. He shifted on his back and snored.

Jeanie backed from the edge of the dugout to settle her stuttered breathing to organize what she'd say to Frank to not encourage him to forge a path into a blue mood. This could not be happening. Frank could not be losing his drive to survive already. Not *there* on the prairie where laziness and dreams without the grounding of practical action would mean starvation, calamity, death. If a person stopped moving a person would die, Jeanie had come to believe.

She pushed these thoughts from her mind, smoothed her skirts and walked down and around the dugout clearing her throat. She hoped that announcing her presence would allow Frank the opportunity to save his face, so *she* could save their lives in the process. Jeanie rounded the side of the dugout and when Frank came into view he was still reclined, though his hands were now crossed over his chest like a dead man in a coffin.

"*Frank*," Jeanie said. Her voice was tight, hissing.

"Oh, hello." Frank rose to his elbows. "Oh, hey, you'll never believe what I've come up with."

Jeanie cocked her head. "I'd love to see."

"Uh, well, no." Frank tapped his temple with his forefinger. "It's all upstairs, tucked away with the riches, the *real* treasure."

Jeanie shifted her weight and ran her tongue over the roof of her dry mouth.

"Now," Frank said looking off into nothing, "don't set about fretting things that haven't come to pass."

Jeanie shook her head. "I don't even know what that means."

"It means sheep."

"Sheep? Sheep?" Holding back her anger had transformed it into frustration fueled tears. She began to cackle through them as it was clear he'd gone to his residence where air castles were built like a child's toy.

"I got a letter from Jack today. He's raising sheep in Tennessee."

"Where's Templeton's bedstead?" Her voice rose over the plains, screeching in a way she'd not done in two decades. She wiped her face with the back of her hand. She wasn't the crying type. Especially without even getting a full explanation, but she felt it in her bones that he'd been up to nothing of any promise or worth. While the rest of the cooperative broke their necks to survive, he'd been lounging like a brainless slug.

Frank stood, lifted and dropped his shoulders and wouldn't make eye contact.

A crash in the dugout made Jeanie jump. She covered her mouth wondering what creatures had infiltrated the dugout this time.

"Come on out ladies!" Frank intoned like a sideshow master. "Jeanie's home and I think she'll be satisfied to see her work's been halved at least."

Lutie and Ruthie appeared from the dugout, wiping their hands on their aprons. Jeanie looked at Frank's grin that swallowed his face as he seemed to admire the mere existence of the two single women. His eyes held and lost focus at the same time. Jeanie followed his gaze back to the women, to Lutie specifically.

Lutie's thick yellow hair hung in loose ringlets down her back, her dress, an empire-waisted silk, draped her body. A sharp wind burst through the air and pushed the material against Lutie's round breasts, displaying what was clearly an absence of proper undergarments.

The breeze lifted her hair and Jeanie's mind registered the scene as though it were equipped with a camera. The picture of Lutie, like a painting in the Louvre, or the illustrations in Jeanie's favorite book of fairytale princesses, seared into Jeanie's consciousness.

She gazed back at Frank who nearly licked his lips at the view and her gut clenched as the imprint of Lutie in the wind had clearly marked Frank's gray matter, too. Ruthie stepped from behind Lutie, clearing her throat. Ruthie's hair yanked back, bun strangling any attractiveness from her cratered face, dripped with sweat and her face expressed exasperation in the way Frank's did awe.

The two women stampeded toward Jeanie taking her by the hand, pulling her into the dugout, yammering about them having made dinner because they'd finished their work at home and couldn't allow poor Frank to complete his commissions and tend to women's work while Jeanie lathed Templeton's home.

"Templeton should just build a soddie at this stage," Ruthie said. "Money or not, building a frame home is simply foolish this summer."

Jeanie shrugged, holding back her comment that she admired Templeton's pursuit for finer things.

"Besides, he spent at least a month's time in our soddie due to the wind tearing through the plaster in the walls. A frame house may look sturdier, but it's not."

Jeanie stopped short, yanked her hands out of the two women's and did her best to apply a look of nonchalance to her face. "Mr. Templeton spent a month at your house over the winter?"

Ruthie nodded vigorously and stirred whatever was boiling in the pot.

"He did most of the cooking," Lutie said. "We were afforded the opportunity to read and reflect on the path of our lives."

Jeanie squinted as Lutie lowered herself onto her and Frank's bedstead. She leaned back and threw her hand over her forehead and closed her eyes, burning yet another image of startling beauty into Jeanie's mind.

Anger surged through Jeanie's veins. She wasn't sure exactly what she was more irritated by. "Well, I don't think it looks nice to see men washing dishes. In fact it is a decided infringement of woman's rights." Jeanie said before she gently, but firmly edged Ruthie away from her stove with her hip.

"And you two, here in my kitchen, that's similar, you know. An infringement."

Ruthie moved aside but didn't relinquish the spoon. "I quite agree with your assessment of the male position in the home, Jeanie, but I am, in a sense, your sister and in being that, it would mean my pride for you to allow me to honor you, a woman with child, with a meal. It's not as though you've been lounging about all day," Ruthie's eyes shifted then met Jeanie's again. She looked back into her stew and nudged Jeanie aside as had just been done to her.

"It's wild rabbit," Ruthie said. "I think you'll like this recipe." Jeanie suddenly felt grateful to Ruthie, exhausted and needing to rest. Jeanie glanced at Lutie and couldn't then decide where the balance between manners and necessity lay. She wanted to tell Lutie to get the hell up from her bedstead, to allow *her* to rest, to get the hell off her prairie, but that would be impolite.

Perhaps it didn't matter. "Please get up," Jeanie said.

Lutie didn't flinch, still sprawled as though being painted.

"Lutie Moore. I said get off my bed. Our marital bed. This abode is small and ugly and animal-like, but we have not fully abandoned—"

"Oh, oh, I'm sorry," Lutie got up then swept her arm to the side, inviting Jeanie to lie on her own bed. Jeanie did. She ground her backside into the bed, trying to find comfort as though it were not her familiar bed.

She closed her eyes and sighed. She could not simply laze about while others worked. "Oh, go ahead." Jeanie flew off the bed, smoothed it. She took Lutie by the arms and directed her right back onto the bedstead.

Lutie sat up on her elbows. "Well, I won't have you pushing me around like I'm some child. I'm just as—"

Ruthie spun around pointing the stew-covered spoon at Lutie. "Go for water. That would be a fine bit of help."

Lutie sighed and shrugged like ten-year-old Katherine might before tramping off, hair bouncing down her back, dress flowing like a princess.

Jeanie nodded to Ruthie who then turned back to the stew.

Jeanie sat on a small wooden, ladder-back chair and pulled her sewing onto her lap. It was a shirt she'd been fashioning out of the final spare wagon sheet for Nikolai.

Jeanie focused on her stitches, her fingers edging with machine-like accuracy and speed.

"Are you alright?"

Jeanie jumped at Ruthie's voice having forgotten she was there and looked up for an instant cracking a smile before plunging back into her work. "Yes, fine. Fine," Jeanie said.

"You look like you're in pain. It's not the baby, is it?" Ruthie walked to Jeanie and squatted in front of her. Jeanie stopped sewing and straightened away from Ruthie's presence.

"I know I've never been a mother," Ruthie said. She patted Jeanie's hand and squeezed it. "But, I've seen my share of women carry babies and you seem to be caught by more than your portion of pains."

Jeanie squeezed Ruthie's hand in response, touched by her consideration. She felt suddenly rich to have two women in the nearly empty prairie that cared so much for her. Who needed dozens of women like those she worked with on the Des Moines Welcoming Committee, symphony and hospital boards when she had two good friends like Ruthie and Greta to call her own?

Ruthie stood and Jeanie rested her hands on the sewing in her lap then rubbed her belly as another contraction pulled. "I suppose you're right," Jeanie said. "I've been so busy with everything, the fire, rebuilding, I don't have the time to muse about the state of my unborn. But you're right."

Ruthie glanced away from Jeanie's gaze then found it again. "Could I feel the baby?" Ruthie reached toward Jeanie's belly but pulled her hand back as though about to touch hot metal. She nearly tripped backward. "I'm sorry. That was ill-mannered to say the least."

Jeanie leaned forward and reached for Ruthie's hand. "No, it's fine. I hadn't realized how little I thought about this baby. How long it's been since I spoke of him or her." Jeanie pulled Ruthie's hand to her belly. "I haven't felt the baby move yet, but he's in there, I know that. My shape has gone to jelly faster than with the other pregnancies."

"I know how hard it's been for you. With the lost children, and your father," Ruthie said.

Jeanie stiffened. Ruthie pulled her hand back and rocked back on her heels, staring at Jeanie.

"It's hard for us women here on the prairie," Ruthie said. "Don't be angry at Frank for telling us. Well, he told Lutie who told me. I'm afraid she's as loose with her lips as she is with her thoughts and her...well, Lutie is Lutie, but this time, she was right in telling me. This way we can help you. You're better off me knowing the difficulties you've suffered than you are Lutie. Lutie can be, well, she can be Lutie, which is to say—"

"Oh, I think the picture of Lutie is quite clear," Jeanie said.

Jeanie jammed her needle through the material, tearing it back up, her pace choppier than before. "But, I'm afraid there's not much to say about the past. Hard as it might be, it's exactly that, past. And I'm not about to linger in thought or deed because things didn't progress as I'd expected back in Des Moines."

Ruthie stalked back to the stove where she stirred the pot, her back to Jeanie. Jeanie stopped stitching, slouched with a sigh and in the distance between them, she felt grateful for Ruthie. She'd obviously come that day to help because she recognized something in Frank that no one else did. As much as it embarrassed Jeanie that her family failures were known to anyone on the prairie—the place she'd hoped to be able to fully ignore the past—she felt comfort in knowing someone else cared. That she'd met this wonderful woman.

"Thank you Ruthie."

Ruthie didn't turn from the stew. "You're welcome."

Jeanie settled into her sewing again, satisfied with her new friendship. Ruthie turned and stared at Jeanie, still stirring the pot. Even in the poor light Jeanie could see Ruthie's eyes glisten with rising tears. She pushed a trickle from one eye away, and the other dripped onto the collar of her dress.

"Are you crying?" Jeanie said.

Ruthie turned away and shook her head.

"Good, because there's no room for tears on the prairie, in life, anywhere. So let today be the last of the tears for you and me." And with that, Jeanie rose from her chair, gave Ruthie a quick hug from behind then ordered her to set the table.

Dinner was pleasant with Ruthie and Lutie filling the evening with enough storytelling for ten times the number of people as themselves. Really, it was Lutie telling stories with Ruthie correcting nearly every word and detail, but the interaction allowed Jeanie the opportunity to sit quietly, eating, savoring the moment with her children.

James attempted several times to include what he'd learned about weather indications from Templeton, but Lutie stamped over his yarns with hers and Frank never stepped in to make room for James's thoughts. James, always respectful, kept his silence, but Jeanie didn't miss his intermittent, uncharacteristic eye rolls and crooked, sarcastic smiles as Lutie blathered about nothing.

Even realizing it was probably just James's verging on adolescent chemistry—still on the side of boyhood—that allowed him to put aside Lutie's charms, Jeanie hoped somehow this meant James would be immune to surface trappings. Perhaps one day he'd meet someone like Ruthie, whose beauty was trapped inside her—someone not stunning on the outside, but clearly sturdy and capable.

Katherine and Tommy sat on either side of Jeanie, gobbling their stew and cakes before rambling off to play atop the dugout. Frank had James feed and water the horses and head to the well for more while the adults savored coffee in the sun which was not yet low enough to classify as setting, but low enough that the burn of midday was gone.

The Moores helped clean up the dishes and for a moment Jeanie felt like a wealthy woman—the one she'd been before the fall of her family in Des Moines. Soon after that, Ruthie and Lutie mounted their horses and bolted into the horizon for home. Lutie's laughter rang over the plain as her hair bounced behind her.

It was not quite dark when Frank pulled back the bed covers and fell onto the bedstead for what looked to be the night.

"Frank. Could you check on the children? They can't wander about the prairie with the sun setting. You know once it hits a certain point, the light goes from adequate to gone in seconds." Jeanie stood with her hands on her hips, her body tense with anxiety, resentment that she had to remind Frank of these facts.

"Ah they're fine. What *I* want is one of our good old-fashioned discussions about life and love and dreams." Frank looked up from his recline, eyes nearly closed, his face slack—still looking like him but not exactly. And for a moment, seeing him like that, a flash of her father hit her—his face when he would be in the middle of his opiate high. But that would be impossible. For Frank knew what opium did to people, even the ones who weren't the eaters, and though Jeanie admitted more readily than ever to Frank's shortcomings, she knew he would never betray her with the very drug of her father's undoing.

"Frank. This is hardly the time or place for the building of air castles."

Frank leaned up on his elbow and extended his hand to Jeanie.

"You *used* to fully appreciate my dreams. I think an air castle or two would suit you at this point in time. We've had a hard time of it and I've decided that raising sheep, selling the fleece, having the yarn for you to make clothing and—"

"I think prairie fever has sapped your brains," Jeanie said. She slung the words hoping they stung him in his numbed state.

"Don't you think that'd be fantastic? To have that type of business to tend?"

"You want my advice about sheep-raising in this part of the state? This land is too flat, where it is not bottom land it is only gentle undulations and you know sheep are very subject to foot-rot—so in wet seasons they would be in great danger on land of this kind which is not sufficiently drained. So, no. Tending sheep would be fool-hearty."

Frank stared at Jeanie, his jaw slack, eyes lifeless. Jeanie knew she'd hurt him and in doing so she didn't feel the satisfaction she'd thought she would. She felt lethal, as rotten as he was lazy. Frank must have felt it too, and like she'd fatally wounded him, his eyes closed with the sound of air rushing in and out of his tight windpipes scratchy and loud, telling Jeanie he'd gone from hurt to asleep.

She finally headed out to corral the children. She wished she had an answer for what was happening between Frank and her. She'd felt this confusion before, but in Des Moines, she'd always occupied herself with a project or writing or the house, and in time, the angst between her and Frank would right itself.

Now, she kept wondering what it would be like if Frank were gone. But, there was no room for her to entertain the notion of leaving Frank. Or to entertain his shortcomings for she had to live with them no matter what. Yet there they were, her misgivings.

She was becoming surer that none of the work she did would infuse Frank with what was now missing from his soul—its color, its life, ambition. What was there now, on his good days, appeared full of plans and life and goodness, but it was mere covering for the pit that lay underneath.

These dark brooding moods never led to tangible progress. They yielded only trouble. Frank's energy was absorbed by thoughts alone with nothing left for solid action of any value. Yet there he was in Jeanie's life forever. She tried to envision their relationship as a mansion with many rooms and doors.

If their marriage was the entirety of the home, she could cordon off segments of who they were, shutting doors, enclosing his weaknesses inside so that the integrity of the house wasn't compromised, but nothing was left out, either. She could keep everything, good and bad and only open a particular door when necessary. She was strong enough for that, she was sure.

It was early September, two months since the fire and the point when the Darlington Township cooperative redefined its goals and responsibilities. Jeanie had become comfortable with her role on the prairie (not be confused with her *liking* her role on the prairie), with the way her family fit into its landscape, that almost without thought, she allowed James to go his way in the morning—to Templeton's, and Tommy to go his—to the Moore's, Hunt's, or Zurchenkos as each day determined.

That day Katherine would stay with Jeanie, learning the trades of womanhood. For Jeanie, that meant the obvious tasks—housekeeping and sewing, but she also charged each child with study of some sort. Even on the days Ruthie was not available to teach, the Arthurs were required to learn. Whether it was reading classic literature or studying the way the planets aligned above them, or the playing of an instrument, each child was charged with some aspect of learning.

On this particular day, Jeanie saw Frank off to Templeton's with James. The group had decided that storing the wood at Templeton's would ensure its safety. What they really meant was they felt more comfortable with Frank having to report somewhere to hold up his end of the cooperative as it didn't take long for the conglomeration of people to realize Frank needed to be held accountable by outside measures. Even the doughy Mr. Hunt could manage his end of the bargain (whatever odds and ends needed to be managed with an extra set of willing hands) without anyone having to prod or suggest he take to his work.

Frank had gone willingly about his work at Templeton's for two weeks before injuring his thumb. It was true that an infection flamed his nail with crimson pussy drainage. And it took two trips to Yankton to see a doctor to clear things up, but Jeanie couldn't help being impatient with the injury.

She felt a mixture of relief and sadness that other people noticed Frank's inclination toward air castles rather than solid objects, but boy when he finished a piece of furniture for someone, they swooned and soon forgot Frank's habits. He was that good when he did the work.

There wasn't a furniture maker in the land—machine or human who could top Frank's work. If only he'd had the gumption and follow-through of Jeanie, they'd have fewer worries. But when Jeanie stopped to consider the state of their lives, she nearly flew with joy that there were people in the world—the neighbors—that saw Frank's goodness amidst his unreliability and that they were there to help.

With everyone in his useful position that day, Jeanie felt particularly cheerful. She'd finally found some gratitude in the fact that she'd only pulled one trunk of fabric out of the dugout the day of the fire—that only one had perished. It was her favorite cache—the burned fabric—but still the fabric in the other trunk, wasn't terrible.

She'd completed two sets of shirts for each man of Darlington Township as well as one pair of wool nether-garments for each. For Ruthie, she'd sewn a tasteful gown in the richest, green wool she had. It actually was a mix of greens, but so subtle, that unless you were standing within inches of it, the material just appeared a captivating, tree-green.

For Greta, Jeanie needed to use extra material to allow for her height. Though, not needing to allow for decorative but useless crinoline, Jeanie didn't need to double the material used on the dress. So, Jeanie parted with one of her favorite bolts of materials—the red wool that, back in Des Moines, the use of it would take on the look of material that sat in the sun and grew tired and not suitable for city dress. But on the prairie, the mellow red looked appropriate and as though it might have sprung from the earth itself.

For Abby Hunt, the minister, Jeanie selected a deep blue fabric. Beautiful if one put the color in the context of the prairie sky as it turned to night in the summer moon, but plain, too. Something suitable for a woman of the cloth, though Jeanie did not claim to understand the inner workings of the Quaker life or the people who were deemed ministers in it. Jeanie hoped the gown wasn't at all too dowdy or insulting.

For Lutie, Jeanie had more trouble selecting material. Part of Jeanie wanted to give her the flimsiest, ugliest, material sewn to ill-fitted, imperfection. Another part of Jeanie wanted to fashion the most intricate dress, of lavender silk—Lutie didn't do anything to compromise such rich fabric after all—to display like a peacock Jeanie's skill to all who saw beautiful Lutie.

Jeanie's conscience—that light that according to the Hunts lived inside her in the form of Jesus himself—tried to ferret a third point of view out of Jeanie's soul. The kind part of her that would make Jeanie select something appropriate and pretty and practical for Lutie just as she had for all the others.

None of that inner struggle really mattered in the end because it was the collection of clothing Jeanie fashioned that thrilled her. She packed each family's new wardrobe, bound by plain tan ribbon, into the wagon. She and Katherine would spend the day delivering the clothes in exchange for weekly supply of vegetables, maybe a squash, and hopefully a melon of some sort.

Jeanie felt so good that day that not even the fact that she couldn't find the last pair of her silk shoes bothered her too much. She remembered throwing one pair under the bedstead just before the fire swept through. The other two pairs had been in the burnt material trunk.

She'd turned the small dirt house upside down—as much at that could be done in a space where really, nothing should be able to be lost for the size of the place said it was impossible. Perhaps she'd remembered wrong, that all three pairs of shoes had been in the trunk. What other explanation could there be?

Jeanie and Katherine, tucked into the wagon, a light breeze lifting the edges of their bonnets, made their way across their homestead to the Zurchenko's. The sun crept up Jeanie's back. The sky, a pale blue, lay overtop the green prairie. Jeanie had been shocked at the quickness with which much of the prairie shot back to green.

Nearly instant it seemed, were patches of tall grass tickling the knees again, yellow and purple blooms poked out of the edges of dead ground and danced in the wind. Pink roses that had escaped the fire, poked through their thorny, bundled stems. Even the once scorched, black land was sprouting greens again, the plants there having evolved to survive even the worst prairie fire, their seeds and roots deep below the plains, waiting to rise again.

Jeanie smiled and looked at Katherine, her little round face turned upward, a closed-mouth smile stretched her cheeks, and her eyes were closed as though she were gathering energy and life from merely sitting amidst nature's finest beauty.

Jeanie looked over the horses' heads, clicking her tongue at them then looked back at Katherine.

"Look at me, sweet Katherine." Jeanie cupped Katherine's chin then ran the back of her fingers over her daughter's cheek then her finger down her nose. Katherine giggled and pulled back playfully.

Jeanie grasped her hand, pulling her close again. With their hands clasped Jeanie gave Katherine three sharp squeezes.

"Remember that. Right? I. Love. You." Jeanie matched the words with three more clutches of the hand. "Nothing can ever change that."

"Silly goose. I know that." Katherine said, her eyes narrowing. She shrugged and suddenly appeared confused, her attention shifted off to where the sky danced with the land.

"I just wanted to remember this moment," Jeanie said. "Your eyes, they way the blue bursts, almost unbelievably with purples and golds, like the prairie itself. As though you and your father who shares your eye color were somehow born of this place. Just waiting to come back." Katherine nodded and squeezed her mother's leg and leaned into her shoulder. Jeanie slung her arm around her daughter's shoulder, contentment overshadowing anything else.

Though part of Jeanie still despised her prairie life and had to fight at times to entertain cheerful thoughts, she knew that without the prairie experience she wouldn't have had this moment with Katherine. She might not have slowed down enough to let the image of Katherine settle into her mind as it did right then.

Katherine had been generous with her love back in Des Moines, Jeanie realized. It was as though Katherine invented this incredibly close relationship between the two of them and then it became reality when they lit out for the prairie. It wasn't that Jeanie didn't adore Katherine before, she just didn't know how much more love for her children was possible until she stopped fretting over insubstantial matters of life like what hue of blue to paint the living room for the sixth time. Jeanie swelled with so much love at that moment that her heart seemed to warm inside her chest. She squeezed Katherine to her tighter. The great love scared her as much as it was fulfilling.

"It is sort of perfect, Mama." Katherine looked into the horizon in front of them. "Even with nearly nothing to our names. With the way we lit out of Des Moines—"

"We didn't run away. We ran to. Just like your father always wanted to. If I hadn't been so stubborn, so scared to leave our lot, we'd have a large frame home here on the prairie with a slew of cows, fields of corn, wheat, and rye. We'd have a well just outside the door and plans for indoor plumbing and, and...Well, we'd be settled but for my stubbornness in seeing the value of making the dreams I carried in my heart a reality."

Jeanie clenched her jaw at the gobbly-gook she spewed. She snapped the reins quickening the horse's pace.

"Even a little girl knows that isn't accurate, Mama." Katherine pulled away and turned sideways in the seat and stared at her mother. Jeanie kept her eyes over the horses pulling the wagon.

"Don't ever let me hear you say anything of the sort Katherine Arthur," Jeanie said.

"I don't mean disrespect, Mama. I was just looking at the facts and reporting them as I see them." Katherine turned back to face straight ahead.

"Things aren't always as you think you see them."

"So, Grampy *didn't* steal that money from his bank customers?" Katherine said, her hands flying through the air for emphasis. "Father *didn't* talk Grampy into investing in some sort of oil fiasco? Not that it didn't make sense on paper. After all, the Chinese first drilled for oil using bamboo shoots to funnel it up in 347 AD. The books we brought detail every bit of it. I see where Father got his logic what with the drilling nearly thirty years ago in California even Pennsy—"

"Enough." Jeanie snapped the reins. Her voice shot out hard and at hearing her own tone she shivered as her own blood turned frigid. She knew Katherine had overheard some of the details of the scandal, that Katherine was quite capable of reading the papers, but she didn't realize Katherine had taken the time to do so.

"But Mama, I'm studying like you said. Figuring out—"

"Study something else. We won't re-entertain our past failures and mull over, discuss—we have to move on." Jeanie's shoulders heaved with breath. Tears came to her eyes and she shook them off then found the serenity she counted on to keep her carrying on in the face of whatever had happened with her father. She'd thought she managed to hide her father's indiscretions—the fact that one of Frank's air castles had been part of the family's great fall as well as the three hundred other families who banked with her father— from Katherine, from all the children.

"All right, Mama, I know it hurts to talk. Oh looky! There's the Misses Moore headed to the Zurchenko's too!" Katherine sat high in her seat craning her neck and squinting into the horizon.

"Well, there's a bit of luck for us, Katherine. If we don't have to stop at the Moores' soddie on the way back home, we'll have enough time to finish the dress I've started for you. I think you'll love it." Jeanie was relieved Katherine hadn't pushed her further on their family scandal, that she would put her worries about their family aside.

"Oh, yes Mama. I can't wait to wear that lavender wool. And with a velvet collar. It's decadent for the prairie, but I can't say I'm sorry you've indulged me."

"You are a good daughter and a good dress you shall have. Even here in this primitive setting." Jeanie smiled at Katherine and smoothed a windblown hair behind her tiny, sea-shell ear. Jeanie nearly erupted with the love she felt for her daughter, the grace that had given Jeanie such a gem to bring to womanhood.

Katherine nodded so excitedly it looked as though her teeth might collide and crack into bits. She hopped from the wagon before they were even stopped and ran to the front door of the Zurchenko's soddie. Katherine pounded away as though summoning someone to save her life. Greta opened the door and wiped her hands on her apron.

Anna peeked around her mother's legs, more shy since her sister's death. Katherine's aggressive embrace was barely returned by Greta as her physical proximity to people was mostly practical more than it was driven by some emotional need to be close to others. At least it appeared that way to Jeanie. Greta's face folded into that strange smile that only made her appear more cross than usual. She watched Katherine hold her hand out to Anna and coax her over to the wagon to see what the Arthurs had brought. Jeanie was glad Katherine made such an overt gesture to Anna after being there when Anzhela disappeared. They all understood these things happened on the prairie, but still, Katherine carried these things deeply in her soul and Jeanie hoped it wouldn't color her life black as she grew up.

"Hi there," Greta said.

Jeanie stood in the wagon and accepted Greta's hand to help her climb down.

Jeanie looked Greta over. She'd lost weight, but seemed as cheerful as she ever had. "You've lost weight," Jeanie said.

"With the crop due in soon, I think I'll pick up some heft," Greta said.

Jeanie felt a surge of discomfort, as though Anzhela's ghost was sitting between them, reminding them both of the loss.

"Your Katherine. She is so sweet to care for Anna. She always indicates her concern for our family in such gentle ways. I want her to know I notice that, I am thankful for it."

Jeanie nearly fell over with Greta's generosity of friendship. How could she bear to be so understanding?

"I've missed you," Jeanie said.

"And I you." Greta smiled down on Jeanie and took her hand, squeezing it. "I'm fine. Really, life is life is death is pain and joy and back again. I find solace in my God Almighty. There, I feel no pain."

Jeanie held the opposite view, that God couldn't exist and inflict such pain, but she would never say that to Greta. Especially not now that she found the will to carry on with her Lord's help. That was something Jeanie wouldn't disturb.

Jeanie gestured to the back of the wagon, to discuss the cargo inside when Anton came around the side of the soddie. Greta had explained at an earlier time—so not to embarrass Anton—that Anton had the size to easily help the women load and unload the cargo, but he was still small enough that he wouldn't be terribly missed in the fields.

"Hello Mrs. Arthur," Anton said. He extended his hand to Jeanie and delivered one of his knee-buckling handshakes.

"My, my *my*! Anton, your grip is mighty!" He nearly floated away with pride when Jeanie exclaimed at his strength.

While exchanging pleasantries, the Moores dismounted their wagon and as usual, Lutie waltzed to the gathering and Ruthie nearly ran, asking what she could do to help make things easier for everyone involved in the exchange. While the women chattered about the state of the fields—the enormous growth that would allow a mid-October harvest even after the devastating fire—and the mysterious appearance of grapes on the Moore property as though the vines had been waiting for just the right time to pop back up from the earth and show themselves to the world.

The conversation dissolved and Jeanie took the silence as her opportunity to show her wares.

"I'm sorry to not have wrapped each garment in paper, but we are very short on supply and might need it for the dugout walls at some point, or perhaps, gasp, for the polite endeavor of actual writing."

Lutie bounced around like a spoiled child, her fists under her chin, face straining with anticipation. "Let us see the clothes."

Jeanie nodded and in wanting to delay this precious moment—the joy of having created something that would be beautiful and useful at the same time—she started with the simple utilitarian pieces—the men's shirts and pants.

Greta held up the shirt intended for Nikolai. "Oh, it's white. I don't believe I've seen this shade of white, I mean, simply clean, since we left Russia years ago. Nothing stays white out here for long. I almost want to hide it away just to take a look now and then at what it means to have something be white."

Jeanie cocked her head and let the kind words bathe her in pride and joy. She, too, was taken by the moment and nearly skipped to the pile that held Ruthie's and Lutie's dresses. She pulled Ruthie's green wool dress from the pile and held it up, peeking around the edge of it to be sure to see Ruthie's face when she realized it was for her.

Ruthie's mouth fell open then slammed shut. "That's not for me. It's beautiful."

"It's for you, of course it is." Jeanie stepped forward, turning the dress and holding it up to Ruthie's body. The other women gathered to see. "The green just lights up your hair and eyes. I knew it would be the perfect color for you."

"But, the color, it's *depraved*, to be sure!" Ruthie giggled. "Not for prairie wearing, that's for sure."

"Bish-bosh," Jeanie said. "Simply pair this blouse with the skirt for day to day work and then wear the fitted jacket for something special. These were the materials I was working with in Des Moines and there's no point in my tossing it all away just because I was heading into the Dakotas. I hope you'll all be pleased with what I've designed for each of you. I think we women have our strengths and weaknesses and drawing attention to the former is the first step in cultivating a pleasant self-perception. Oh, and though at the time we left Des Moines, the styles called for peacockish, elephantine bustles and mutton-leg sleeves, I've had time to reflect and found the style objectionable on numerous grounds."

The women cackled with delighted agreement. Except for Lutie who clucked her tongue and rolled her eyes. Silence draped over them and they stared at Lutie.

"Now Lutie," Ruthie said, "you know Jeanie will have designed the perfect dress for you, too. Why, how could she go wrong with all the strengths you possess?"

"Well, I suppose I could take a look." Lutie stuck her chin in the air and stalked behind Jeanie to the bundle from where Ruthie's dress came.

Jeanie cleared her throat searching for something diplomatic to say as all the things that filled her mind were either corrective or downright peevish in nature. None of which suited Jeanie's relationship to Lutie.

Greta nearly growled at Lutie. Ruthie allowed her face to soften and with a single disapproving expression, she told Greta and Jeanie she understood that Lutie's behavior was atrocious.

It struck Jeanie then, how much dealing with Lutie was like dealing with Frank. Their natures were such that they required gentle treading when moods were disagreeable. From afar, this type of gentle treatment would appear indulgent and unnecessary. But as Jeanie understood and clearly Ruthie must have too, the quiet handling of moods would ensure smooth movement forward in life rather than the tripping and falling through what could have been avoided if one were more facile in human relations. The environment of the prairie itself was hard enough to deal with without personalities coming into play.

The only thing Jeanie couldn't understand was what Lutie offered to Ruthie to make her want to keep Lutie around. Frank offered Jeanie love and support on his good days; beautiful craftsmanship, big ideas, enthusiasm, so much that was often so good. So far, Jeanie hadn't seen one thing that Lutie offered to her sister or anyone else on the prairie. Except for her good looks. That was clearly appreciated by all the men, even the reverent Mr. Hunt couldn't help but steal a glance or thirteen when in her presence. Perhaps that was her role—living art or something of the sort.

Jeanie held up Lutie's dress and handed it to her, awaiting approval.

Lutie pulled her dress against her body, its lilac wool—the counterpart to the silk material that was simply too fragile for the prairie. Though Jeanie went with the sturdier material, the design she selected was a bit impractical, an empire-waist that when bending and stretching over a fire would be more unwieldy than a tight-fitted type for it was the kind of dress Lutie favored.

Lutie smoothed the front of her dress, fingered the glass buttons with pasque flowers reaching out from inside the orbs. "The paperweight buttons." Lutie shook her head and her tense face seemed to be fighting back emotion. The women were silent, forcing Lutie to respond to the work Jeanie had done.

Lutie repeatedly ran her hand down the front of the dress then along the velvet ribbon that circled the waist. "It is spectacular," she barely said above a whisper.

"I'm glad it suits you, Lutie. I thought you would be partial to the paperweights. Appreciate them." Jeanie said.

"It does suit me. It does." Lutie hugged the dress to her, bowing her head into it as though there was a reason she couldn't make eye contact with Jeanie, as though there was something shameful that kept her from doing so. Perhaps the gift of a new dress shined a too bright a light on the degree to which she entertained her laziness?

A gust of hot wind struck the group of women like a two-by-four in the face and they scrambled to move the clothing inside. But, before they could gather any of the clothing up, the wind fell away as quickly as it rose.

"That's odd," Jeanie said.

"Odd is normal around here," Greta said.

"That much, I've learned in nearly four months. I suppose we enjoy the sunlight all the better for having a few shadows first." Jeanie said. She always liked when she could employ her favorite phrase, making her feel secure.

"Agreed." Greta held her dress up and petted it, grinning. "This is the finest dress I've ever seen. Even when we stopped in New York City and had a few days between trains, and the women seemed to spill through the streets in fine, nearly picture-perfect dress, I didn't see anything as well made or beautiful as these."

Jeanie looked at her feet, her face warming, so honored by such lavish praise from such a simple woman as Greta. The women began yammering over one another, clamoring for details regarding Jeanie's choices for each one of them.

Lutie cocked her head, squished up her face in phony disbelief and crossed her arms over her chest. "So, with all your talents, why're you here, on this prairie, fighting fire and dirt and—well, you never have really explained. Your dearest Frank has filled us in on a bit of it all, but you know men, they're always short on words when we need them most—"

"Because it's the way circumstances went, Lutie," Jeanie said.

Jeanie bent down and began sorting the already sorted clothing, hiding tears that welled in her eyes. Because, with the fall of her father's bank and his stealing of his customers' money, went the purses of three of the biggest designers in New York City. Jeanie was sure her likeness was posted far and near in New York, announcing a reward for the apprehension of her for doing nothing more than being the daughter of the man who destroyed the lives of many.

"Well, that doesn't explain anything," Lutie said.

"Well, we don't really—"

Jeanie's words were interrupted by the sound of a train roaring from the west. But the last of the railroad ended east of Darlington Township in Yankton. They covered their ears and spun around trying to match the sound with a sight of something, anything that could create such an auditory disturbance. At first, they saw nothing. Their voices rose over the escalating din.

A dark cloud appeared in the west, the rising drone accompanying the sight of dark storm clouds. Not storm clouds that developed slowly, darkening over the course of an hour or day, but instead, like the snapping shut of a window, the darkness was there, above, filling their ears, though dropping no rain or driving no wind. They all stood there gaping at the unnatural sight.

And, once the clouds blotted out the sun to a large degree, the black plumes began to descend upon the group. Jeanie instinctively covered her ears while running to the soddie to check on Katherine, to get her inside the house for cover. Katherine wasn't there.

Jeanie spun around, searched for the site of Katherine's home-spun flowered dress and white apron. Jeanie stood under the lip of the front of the soddie and in her mind it made sense that she wasn't getting wet. What didn't make sense was the sight of her friends, nearly running in circles, yelling for children and husbands over the storm, the perfectly dry storm.

Jeanie's chest heaved and she looked up into the sky. It was then she saw what was happening and what she saw was so unlikely that she was taken by laughter as chaotic as everyone else's panicked screams and flailing motions. What was happening?

Jeanie held her shaking hand out into the air waiting for rain to drench her skin, but instead of water, enormous insects landed there. What was she seeing? She let six of them sit there until they nibbled her skin. Grasshoppers! She'd heard about infestations over the years. The thought of the destruction that swarms of these miniature beasts could inflict took her from her laughter.

Still choking on laughter—that nervous laughter that always came at the wrong time, but somehow felt great when it did, she couldn't stop it, its inappropriateness, she choked on it as she spun around looking for Katherine. She stood with the others, hands moving across her face, covering her eyes, then mouth then ears as though she couldn't decide which orifice was best shrouded from the beasts.

Jeanie saw the world slow to nearly half motions as her mind watched the three-inch creatures, so large she could see their jaws work as they chomped on grasses. The freshly sprouted green that had seemed like such a miracle after the fire was consumed in front of her eyes.

She finally was able to stifle her laughter enough to run to the clump of women and Anton and begin pulling them into the soddie. She tried to step over the grasshoppers but every time she lifted her foot, the space below was filled with insects, piled three deep, fighting for anything remotely green. They crunched under her boot igniting chills in her body, nausea tore at her insides at the thought that she was killing living things. Except that stepping on them didn't actually kill anything, they merely readjusted themselves and began munching away.

"Everyone into the soddie!" Jeanie said. "We'll be safe in there!" She groped at Katherine and Lutie, pulling each by a dainty arm. Both of them crying, hid their faces with their free hands as they followed Jeanie to the home. She shoved them into the soddie and turned to pull the rest of them in, but Ruthie, Greta and Anton were still at the wagon. They were kicking and swatting at grasshoppers while they attempted to drag the clothing toward the house.

"Leave that stuff!" Jeanie stomped toward them. "They're looking for grass and vegetables! Come inside." None of them seemed to hear what Jeanie had said as they continued to hit and stomp and drag the clothing.

Jeanie pulled Ruthie's arm. "Come inside. They won't bother the clothes. It's greens they want."

Ruthie tore her arm from Jeanie's hand and bent down. When she stood up, holding the beautiful green dress to her chest, Jeanie gasped. She covered her mouth when she saw. She pulled the dress closer so she could touch it. Jagged holes covered the dress, as though they'd been cut into the design.

"What *is* that?" Jeanie said, not believing her eyes or the feel of the ransacked material. Another swarm of grasshoppers dropped and covered the dress, nearly eating it right out of Ruthie's hands. Finally Jeanie understood what was happening.

"Move! We'll lose everything!" Jeanie said. She was taken by insidious laughter as she bent down and scooped up the grasshopper-covered bundles of clothing. Greta and Anton were already half-way into the soddie, arms laden with all they could carry. Ruthie stood, statue-stiff, head bowed.

Jeanie threw her bundle into the soddie and turned back to Ruthie. "Ruthie! Come, now. You must come!"

Ruthie remained, her shoulders jumping with cries into the din of munching insects.

Jeanie ran to her, wrapped her up against her body and pulled her toward the soddie. Jeanie shoved her inside and slammed the door behind her, shutting out a bit of the drone of ravenous insects.

Katherine squealed, pointed to Ruthie and then buried her head into Lutie's breast. Jeanie turned and nearly fell over at the sight of clusters of grasshoppers, sitting on the flowered fabric of Ruthie's dress, jawing at it, too stupid to realize its lifelessness.

Jeanie and Greta batted at the insects, while Ruthie sobbed, face in her hands. Jeanie and Greta stomped them once the grasshoppers fell on the floor and then Anton swept them out of the soddie. Once this process was complete, the only grasshoppers they could hear were outside, gnawing away at anything they could.

With the buzzing of the grasshoppers beginning to sound like silence itself, the soddie became heavy with quiet.

They picked through the clothing Jeanie had so lovingly made, assessing the damage. Jeanie would intermittently rupture the silence with raspy cackles, laughter no one else seemed to be taken by.

The grasshoppers stayed for hours, twelve at least. Though no one could say how long they ravaged the land for sure, because even with all the worry about where the rest of their cooperative members were, even with the chilling sound of millions of insects eating the house that protected them, at some point, their bodies won the battle and each of them fell asleep. Except for Jeanie. She guarded the home against the occasional rodent seeking refuge. This allowed her to hover, watching over the rest of them.

She listened to their breath, holding the oil lamp over them, noticing the slack calm of their faces interrupted by a grimace here and a grunt there. She wondered if they dreamed of prairie horrors. When Jeanie finally grew so heavy with fatigue that she thought she could sleep, she lay down with Katherine. She closed her eyes and an oppressive fear settled inside her, shocking her with what felt like tangible weight, like she could have touched the black mass if she'd been able to open herself up and locate it.

Though she'd been met with fears like never before over the last few months, nothing had ever been as real as this, and she hoped her children felt nothing of the sort. She wasn't sure how she would protect them, not when things like grasshoppers descended like rain, but she knew she had to. And, somehow she would.

After the day of the grasshoppers Jeanie woke first. Katherine was folded into her body, both barely clinging to the edge of the bedstead as they shared it with Ruthie who slept like an irritated bull.

Jeanie stretched and crawled over Katherine. Upright, she crept into the bathroom and recoiled at the smell of six people having nearly overflowed two chamber pots.

She stifled her gag and even though scared of what she might see outside, she lumbered toward the front door, hand over mouth and barely made it outside before vomiting on the freshly shorn ground. She dry-heaved, feeling as though her insides might have been turning inside out, emptying its lining as much as anything else that had been in there. Her eyes watered and her head filled with fizz leaving her unbalanced. She steadied herself on the side of the soddie, her fingers digging into the earthen bricks, while her eyes squeezed shut, watered so forcefully that even though closed, tears soaked her cheeks.

Jeanie stopped heaving and the sensation of arms circling her from behind, made her jump. Greta helped Jeanie stand straight and together, their gazes slid across the land. As far as they could see, russet, naked land stretched. In the way that one would imagine bright, bold colors giving a person a jolt, the nothingness of bland earth tones, in the abrupt *absence* of the green, gold, and blues that had been present the day before made Jeanie's breath leave her. She leaned further into Greta's embrace.

Jeanie stole a look at Greta whose expression was blank except for the twitch at the side of her mouth, one that Jeanie thought was the precursor to tears, the sign of the frustration that they'd again lost everything. And this time, there wouldn't be a replanting and subsequent harvest. This time, it was completely lost for the year. Greta cleared her throat and clenched her eyes shut, but no tears came. Perhaps there was no point.

Jeanie made her way to the space behind the hill where the Zurchenkos had designated a necessary. The sound of horse hooves clopped over the land, growing louder, made her hurry to see who was coming.

Jeanie came from around the hill and in front of her stood the entirety of their Darlington Township cooperative. Everyone was safe and sound, but bearing the looks of people who've been pushed to the ground and trodden upon for the extent of their existences. Tommy and James ran to her and attacked her with hugs, hiding their faces in her chest and shoulder, forgetting their ages. She clutched them, making them choke on her desperate embrace.

Once the boys had sheepishly moved on to the other children, they began comparing notes on the events of the day past, re-enacting the unbelievable grasshopper descent.

Ruthie came out of the home and held the dress Jeanie had made her. Only some snarled fabric remained, dangling from the collar. She bowed her chin into her chest and sobbed. Jeanie went to Ruthie and wrapped her arms around her. Ruthie jerked away with a violent shrug of her shoulders.

Frank, his face stricken, watched his wife as she failed to soothe the anxious Ruthie. She snarled and ran back toward her home. Frank stepped forward then backed up, clearly understanding if Jeanie couldn't help her friend, he certainly couldn't either. He began to recount the state of their home, to describe how he had been working at Templeton's when the grasshoppers arrived. They had retrieved some of his tools, but many had remained on the plains, open to the gnawing insects. Their exploratory bites may not have rendered the tools completely unusable, but Frank, the scars from their little mouths, seemed enough to render him unusable, Jeanie feared.

Likewise, five of the chairs he'd begun to make were ruined. Some of the animals had been nipped at here and there, but mostly they were safe, though now, facing a shortage of food. Even Tommy and James looked sorrowful, their gazes drilling holes into the ravaged soil.

Frank's posture was sunken, his face gray. Jeanie's heart nearly shrunk to a pea at the thought of what this might do to him, that it would send him to that black place that handicapped his ability to function like a responsible husband and father. They did not have the luxury on the prairie, for Frank to fall into his darkness.

Standing there, clumped together like lost children, Nikolai methodically reported the inventory of crops they'd seen so far. The Moore's garden was decimated, the Hunt's vegetables were so badly destroyed that the ground itself looked as though large fist-sized rocks had fallen from the sky, pitting their land. The only thing they managed to save was hay stored in a shed that had survived the fire.

The Zurchenkos accepted this information with stiff posture and nods of the head, as though they were being told it was going to be sunny and breezy that day. The Hunts were quiet, but slouched in much the same way as Frank. Jeanie dismissed it as them possibly coming to realize that housing God inside one's skin, might not be the most useful place to keep him. Or maybe it was the realization that the poppy crop was annihilated. Jeanie knew all too well what an opium-eater faced when he was out of crop.

Jeanie was unable to read Templeton's expression—his stance was relaxed, leaning on one hip. He turned his hat by the brim, but something in his lounge made Jeanie want him to hold her. In Frank she only found disgust and the aversion was amplified by her adulterous mind. How could she seek even mental comfort in another man? Even if that man was unaware of her longings, even if she was always unaware of them too, until they sprang to mind, ceasing her heart in the process.

Jeanie was about to succumb to the despair she saw in Frank, to join the Moores in their pity party for no one beside the Zurchenkos had lost as much as she in the last months. If anyone should be blubbering, contemplating her suicide, it should be Jeanie. But a flutter in her belly reminded her that she wasn't just responsible for her own mood, but that her mood might flavor the personality of the baby inside.

She grabbed her belly and straightened as though she'd never been aware of the pregnancy until that instant. Her mind flashed to the near future, the way nurturing an infant could be precarious anywhere, and the way conditions needed to be at least adequate to ensure her baby's early health. A baby due to be born on the prairie in February would be dangerous in itself, let alone if they hadn't feasible housing and nourishment.

She edged closer to the men who had heads bowed in problem-solving discussion.

"We'll just have to go to the railroad until December at least," Nikolai said.

"The railroad?" Templeton nearly spit. "I can't yield to some mumble-mouth railroad superintendent and his henchmen. We aren't the kind of men who take orders and bow to others. We wouldn't have lit out for the prairie if we were. We'd already be at the railroad if that was who we were."

Frank nodded to Templeton. Nikolai rubbed his neck. "I will go to the railroad. If I don't, my family, this cooperative of Darlington Township, won't make it through the winter."

"Well, that's not entirely true, Nikolai. Why I have another stash—" Templeton said.

Nikolai raised his arthritic looking hand. "Now, I won't have you digging into your monetary stores to help us survive while we do nothing but sit around reading and dreaming about the land..."

"Nothing wrong with contemplating the beauties of nature," Frank said.

Nikolai turned his shoulders away from Frank, focusing fully on Templeton. "But, if there's a way for us to not borrow from Templeton, to build up stores for all of us, then we should do it," Nikolai said. "We never know what's next on the prairie and spending money when there's a way to save it, is foolish at best. And, I say that having never lifted a book in my life. But something tells me that within the pages of the tomes you folks inhale as though it were food itself, are the exact same sentiments I've expressed. We men need to do what's right for the group and we need to do it now."

"We can't just leave the women alone with the children. How will they survive?" Frank said.

194

Jeanie bit the inside of her cheek to hold in her thoughts—
the notion that she might survive just fine without Frank. The
men yammered on about how to ensure they had the necessary
provisions for winter and Jeanie mulled over that niggling thought
that had pounced into her consciousness—that she might not need
Frank, that she might feel relief if he were gone.

She stretched her heart, back to when she first met Frank and
he turned her foolish. There, in that memory was a strand of love
and generosity toward him. And she pulled that strand into the
present-time making her heart disagree with the idea she could
live without Frank. It was with that sliver of love that she battered
back her intellect and its pursuit of autonomy. It wasn't right to
house such thoughts and in doing so, only trouble could come.
"And trouble comes soon enough without courting it."

Abrupt silence startled Jeanie. The group stared at her. She
hadn't realized she'd spoken aloud. When conversation didn't take
up again, she pushed her shoulders down and back as she always
did when filled with confidence.

"Well, as I can see, the elements hold quite enough surprise
for us to go on ruminating and mulling over what might be or not
be or whatever. Let's just say," Jeanie spread her hands in front of
her, "we've lost nearly everything, so the answer to getting back
enough to subsist through the winter is the men going to the railroad until Thanksgiving.

"By then we'll have enough money—to purchase the items
we need to make it through winter. Do we even know if anything
survived the grasshoppers? Did they stay localized or is the entire
county wiped clean of greenery? Berries? Hay? Did the ugly creatures even eat the cow dung we use for fuel? These are the questions that need answered. Whether you men go to the railroad or
not is easy. Yes, you go. We'll be fine."

Jeanie's gaze shifted among the men. Though she wouldn't
be wounded emotionally if they brushed her off, she knew it was
a possibility they would and if so, she would be forced to forge

another path to solve the problem. She was growing ever more convinced that she'd been right about gender stations in America. It wasn't feasible for women to do everything men did. Though she was feeling at that time that it was she who could and would keep her family alive, not her very male husband.

"Well," Nikolai said. He put his hands in his pockets. "I think Jeanie is correct. We need to make a quick assessment at just what has survived, at what the women and children can do to preserve what's left. Then quick as night snaps to day, we need to head to the railroads. Much as I hate it."

The men grumbled agreement. Greta embraced her husband.

"Yes, you must go," Greta said. Nikolai laid his forehead on Greta's, closing his eyes as though in prayer in the first display of affection Jeanie'd ever seen between the two. Nikolai put his hands over top of Greta's then kissed them.

"I think one of us men should stay," Mr. Hunt said. He stepped closer to the center of the group. "Frank or I could stay. We need one man to tend to, well, whatever might be needed."

Jeanie burst with a spray of laughter then covered it with a cough, turning away. What was happening to her, her sense of manners and compassion for a man who may be lacking but was still her husband? An image of Mr. Hunt and Frank arm wrestling for the privilege of being superintendent of coffee boiling jumped to mind.

She swallowed another snort then coughed again. She turned to see Frank boring a hole into her with his gaze. She casually looked away, coughing again. She couldn't believe the thread of thoughts she'd been entertaining of late—divorce, infatuation of another man, the idea that she'd be pleased for Frank to take to the railway. The thoughts and desires seemed so familiar to her body, yet new to her mind. Where had all the impure desires been born?

She didn't want Frank to stay if the other men left. She wanted to be sure any money that was to be shared with the group was a direct result of Frank's work. Her mind ran quickly over how things might occur if Frank stayed, the lone man on the prairie. He might do the minimum while the others broke their backs at the railroad. Jeanie wouldn't be able to accept money from the others if Frank had spent the equal amount of time lounging about, tending to his violin and air castles built of sheep fleece.

"Why doesn't Templeton stay," Jeanie said. "The sisters Moore have no male in their home and the rest of us have young men, at least, to help us with some of the more difficult duties."

"Frank could help us," Ruthie said. "He's done a fine job… well I assume it's destroyed now, but he did a fine job tending our garden, weeding. Any way you divide up the men, leaving one in Darlington Township to attend to things here should be suitable enough. Lutie and I have done well so far without a man in our house. We've done just fine."

"I'm sorry, Ruthie. I didn't mean to suggest that, well, with winter coming, I just assumed that duties would be more strenuous in some ways. I didn't mean to overstep, to offend," Jeanie said. Poor Ruthie. She worked so hard to make her life successful, yet there was always a challenge for her that didn't seem quite fair. Jeanie went to her and squeezed her hand.

"There's no room for offense here," Greta said. "Think of Frank's injured hand. He's barely past infection. We can't send him off only to have him returned with greater infection or have him drop dead on the line." Anna climbed up her mother's body taking the place where Anzhela used to inhabit. "As I've said a million times, we can't afford to tenderfoot around one another. It could mean loss or death or great inconvenience."

"I agree," Mr. Hunt said. "So, where does this put us? Frank or me? Who stays behind?"

Nikolai shifted his stance, his wide frame absorbing even more space as he spread his legs and crossed his arms over his chest. "Frank. Frank stays behind."

Mr. Hunt began to protest, but Nikolai stalked away to his horse and mounted it. "Let's go. We need to find exactly what is left behind and what will be useful over the winter. We'll leave for the railroad morning after next. What's past is past."

And with that, the men followed suit, none of them revealing in words or expression what they thought of Nikolai making the final decision regarding who would leave and who would stay. But Frank's expression said it all for his part—his gaze slid into the horizon, face slack as though someone had written a death warrant with his name on it.

Jeanie thought it appeared as though tears were forming in Frank's eyes before he turned away. *We are not crying people, Frank Arthur*, she said in her mind. Jeanie hoped her face didn't bear the same look of unhappiness that Frank's had. That she might not have to explain her fear that he would be the sole, adult male left behind and that might be like having no man at all.

Chapter 12

1905
Des Moines

Katherine climbed into the dusty attic and ignored the feeling she was being watched by armies of mice and spiders. She wandered around the space, searching for the trunk—the book trunk—it was there she'd stashed the letters her mother had intended to burn. Katherine felt as though her mind had been stolen and transported back 17 years.

Images of her mother, pregnant with Yale, in the rocking chair, oil-lamp illuminating the letters she couldn't seem to put down. Katherine pulled the stack out of the trunk then smelled them. She plucked at the charred edges, half hoping they'd fall apart in her hands, only partly wanting to know what she was looking for.

Sitting there, letters in her lap, Katherine sobbed, not grasping what specifics brought such a surge of emotion. "We're not crying people," Katherine said to herself, wiping tears with the back of her hand, the scent of dust filling her nose.

She sneezed and lifted the first letter. A love letter from her mother to her father in the year before their elopement.

Dearest Frank,

You worry how we will contend once Father disowns me for our nearing elopement? It is not for a nice house that I am going to marry you but for LOVE and wherever you go, I will always gladly go with you. O darling! You don't know how much I wish to be your wife...

Though no longer sobbing, tears careened down Katherine's cheeks, as the words painted vibrant pictures of love—the kind only teenagers afflicted with first affection could with seriousness, appreciate. She found herself laughing at her parent's sugary words, their innocence, their hopefulness.

How could everything have gone so wrong? Katherine had never considered the *how* of the matter, only that it did go awry in the worst manner and in her eyes it was solely the responsibility of her mother. She'd admitted as much the day they left the prairie. And within weeks of leaving...Katherine squeezed her eyes shut on the memory. She couldn't bring herself to recall the events.

All she could do was feel the hate and resentment she'd carried all these years. She crumpled the letter in her hand before she realized she'd done it. She was so scared of what she'd forgotten. No! She wouldn't let her past rule her anymore. She smoothed the letter back out on her legs. It was time to move forward. And, so she sat. Reading for hours before falling asleep among the letters that spilled out of her lap, splashing over the floor, flooding the attic with her parent's crippled past.

Chapter 13

1887
Dakota Territory

Just days after the grasshoppers took the crops, every man but Frank lit out for the railroad and before long, money began arriving on the prairie. From Nikolai and Mr. Hunt there were letters dripping with yearning—the desire to come home, to sleep beside wives, hear children's laughter, and again, take control of one's life and property.

Templeton wrote to the Arthurs and the Moores. Jeanie read the letters, searching the straightforward prose for secret indications Templeton had come to think of Jeanie the way she entertained him in her mind.

Not that she had much time for such things. The assessment of the property revealed that, in the way God or whoever is responsible for orchestrating events such as the fire and the feasting grasshoppers, odd pockets of unaffected property presented themselves.

On the Arthur's land grew a substantial clump of undisturbed chokeberry bushes. Their green and red leaves, and clusters of rich red berries burst forth as though mocking nature, its apparent anger or nonchalance that people were attempting to tame this portion of the world. A tall, chubby hackberry tree stood nearby the chokeberry bushes and when Jeanie took the kids to pick the berries, they couldn't help but spend at least half an hour staring at the hackberry, wondering how its enormity was overlooked by the crazed, ravenous grasshoppers.

"Well, it's obvious, the light of God lives in that tree and these bushes for them to have survived the hoppers," James said. "I'm starting to buy into the Quaker way of thinking."

Jeanie put her arm around James and kissed his cheek. "It sure looks like God was present in this little patch of earth, doesn't it." She didn't believe in God, but she'd never been the type to stop talk of him. Just in case.

"He's in me, Mama, I can feel it," Katherine said, wiggling in between and wrapping her arms around Jeanie and James.

"The only God in you is Jesus, the one who knows the meaning of Psalm 23. Does that Quaker God understand what it is to walk in the valley of darkness? I ain't heard that." Tommy said. He dug in the dirt at their feet and looked up at them, peering from under the brim of his hat.

"I believe you've taken to being contrary for contrary's sake," Jeanie said. "I'm glad you've been reading. I'm glad you found something that feels important in the Bible. But I'd appreciate if you didn't lapse into the use of ain't or any other slang." Jeanie really didn't know what she thought about Tommy and his sudden Bible-beating ways, but it wasn't her problem to sort out. She'd taught her children to be thinkers, readers, designers of their own lives. If this was where it took Tommy, so be it.

"We've lapsed in just about every other way, why not language?" Tommy said. Jeanie cocked her head to glimpse Tommy's face to see if he was nudging her out of boredom or if he was genuinely curious at the collapse of their normal societal manners.

"What do you mean, Tommy?"

Jeanie kneeled down beside him. James took Katherine toward the crest of a hill to get a "feel" for the weather coming their way.

Jeanie could hear James explaining that if they stood with their backs to the wind they could determine low pressure on their left and high on their right. If the pressure is coming from their left, they could be assured a storm. Jeanie peered around the side of Tommy, watching James put his arm around Katherine's shoulder and she looking up at him with an admiring, curious gaze as their voices disappeared with their footfalls.

Though Templeton was gone to the railway, his influence on James's hobby of weather indications hadn't been dampened, and since he didn't have Templeton to prattle on about the state of moisture in the atmosphere, Katherine was more than happy to lend her ear to the task. And Jeanie fully realized how much she missed Templeton. Having him around had been comforting even though James spent far more time with him than she ever did.

Tommy lay back in the dirt, arms behind his head, closing his eyes to the sun. "I have to admit I sort of like the lapse in convention, when it's not unsettling me."

"*What?*" Jeanie didn't know what he meant, but she could feel it wasn't a good revelation he was coming to.

"Well, the way everyone does different jobs—the women plow when needed, the men do the dishes, and the way the sisters Moore live alone, forging their own way in life without the help of men. Except for those who want to stop by for hello. Like Father. In some ways, he seems happier than ever, helping the sisters, listening to them talk while he does the work they should be doing—"

"Tommy. What on earth are you talking about?"

He shrugged, not responding other than that.

Jeanie grasped Tommy's arms and pulled him to sitting. Jeanie's stomach clenched. Not fully knowing what Tommy was hinting at didn't stop her body from sensing it wasn't good. She'd felt like this before. But Frank had promised never again.

Tommy drew back and when his face registered pain, Jeanie let go and covered her mouth to gather her poise. She could hear Tommy's uneven breathing as she delved into her mind searching for what bothered her so much about Tommy's news. Was it that Frank was doing someone else's work when he should have been doing more around the house?

She felt dizzy with confusion. If he finished his daily assignments so easily then he should have made his way back home, and if he was going to help the women's right's fanatics, Lutie and Ruthie, to a life of finer, leisurely existences, then he had better, he had no right, absolutely...crazed thoughts of the women in Des Moines...the comforting attention they offered him over the years, interest he could explain away came to Jeanie. Could there have been more to it? She had forced herself to trust him, what choice had she? But now?

Jeanie's thoughts shot around her mind, visions of Lutie, on her lounge, dress draped against her undergarmentless bosom and hips and knees, and Ruthie, how could she allow such debauchery to occur under her roof? Jeanie covered her ears as though the thoughts were coming from outside of her head. She couldn't just allow this to happen.

"Get your wiggle on, Tommy," Jeanie said.

"What? What'd I say?"

"Let's go, full chisel." Jeanie dashed toward the horses and hoisted onto Summer and took her to a fast trot. She screamed up the hill at James and Katherine. They shot around, faces crinkled, questioning. They bolted from the top of the hill, their limbs churning over the land. Katherine's bonnet fell off her head while James held his hat on with his hand.

Jeanie didn't know exactly what she was so upset about, but she knew enough to shut her bazoo in the presence of her children and to go to the source of the problem rather than wallow in unknown possibilities.

The children hopped onto Night and every once in a while Jeanie looked back at them as she charged toward the homestead of Lutie and Ruthie Moore, but she didn't let up. Her legs gripped Summer's sides and the steady galloping motion soothed her jagged thoughts. She would find her answers. She would not be made a fool.

She reached the Moore's soddie and brought Summer to a short halt that stirred up a cloud of dirt. Jeanie grasped her chest, her breath catching faster than she wanted it to. From the chimney rose a thin snake of smoke, evoking a level of peace that seemed incongruous to what swept through Jeanie at that same moment. She swung her body off the horse, remembering she was pregnant only when the pressure from using her belly as a dismounting lever made pain radiate from her middle around her back.

She stopped and bent into the pain that seized her middle. She blew out her air and smoothed the front of her dress. She held her hands at her waist, pushed her shoulders down and proceeded as though dropping into the Moores for afternoon tea.

The only thing that escaped Jeanie's restraint was her knock, the way she wailed on the door like a person seeking refuge during a grasshopper invasion. The door flung open and Lutie and Ruthie stood there, masking what was inside, presumably Frank. Both women's faces reddened, mouths falling open as they looked around, trying to avoid eye contact with Jeanie.

"Frank's here, I gather." Jeanie's lips pursed and she tried to relax them, to dispel any evidence of tension or anger. She wouldn't play the stupid, weak woman, the one who crumbled at the feet of her husband's lover and she wouldn't be the wife who drifted into histrionics and hysteria in order to show her dominance.

"Why, yes. He's ill this morning," Lutie said. She stepped aside, sweeping her hand as though to make a path for Jeanie to follow into the house. Ruthie stood, still, her expression frozen in fear. Jeanie could see Ruthie's throat jump as she swallowed and Jeanie felt a surge of pity for Ruthie, for having to live with Lutie's indiscretions.

Jeanie crossed the threshold and in a motherly way, squeezed Ruthie's forearm to tell her she understood her plight at living with the woman Jeanie would forever think of as Loose Lutie.

Jeanie walked from one end of the house to the other even looking under the lounge as though Frank's body could fit between it and the floor. The place was dismal looking, not at all as Jeanie remembered it. The least of its squalor was a thick layer of dirt over every surface that wasn't equipped to support a sleeping body. The worst was refuse littering the place, a stench of poorly dried or rotting meat. Jeanie covered her mouth. She looked at both women, searching the faces for the reason their home would appear this way. Jeanie's eyes traced their bodies, searching for signs that they'd stopped keeping themselves up.

Jeanie turned then said over her shoulder on the way to the bedroom, "You might want to think about cleaning this place up. Before someone takes ill."

Lutie shrugged, her hair a bit greasy, but still fanned around her shoulders in sweet curls. Jeanie, repulsed by the slovenly appearance of the house, stood at the bedroom door and turned the knob. She pushed through the door.

Frank lay on the bed, flat out, sleeping harder than Jeanie'd ever seen him. Over his work shirt was a wide-knit cream-hued sweater. He was dressed but his pose lent the situation an air of familiarity that sickened Jeanie. How could he just lay there, take to another woman's bed even for a nap? She'd expected to see him hiding, climbing out the window, doing anything to help him get away from his affair with Lutie Moore. His slack face and the rag over his forehead made Jeanie forget the reason she'd stormed to the house and instead she just went to him, sat on the bed and put her face next to his. Did he smell like Lutie? Was something different?

"He's ill, Jeanie," Lutie said.

Jeanie nodded, moved the rag away and felt his forehead. "I'd imagine he'd be ill in this hot sweater. I'm sure I've never fashioned him any such thing."

"I made it. Pattern 311 from the back of...let me think...I can't, not your book—"

"*Definitely* not my book. I don't recall designing fisherman couture or suggesting it for anyone who wasn't within walking distance of an ocean and a bucket of fish."

Lutie pursed her lips. "Well, I'm not very skilled you know, but I took your advice and tried something. Something I thought might be impressive because it was different."

"Help me get it off of him. He's soaked to the bone."

Lutie got beside Jeanie and helped her wrestle the sweater off his limbs. "He was shivering not ten minutes before. He was working so hard for all of us. I just, well, I won't say a word more." Lutie said, her eyes conveying fright.

When wasn't Frank ill? He was more fragile than the Limoges china Jeanie parted with in Des Moines. "Don't want to incriminate yourself, eh?" Jeanie pushed out a phony cackle to cover her true fear—that Frank had indeed left her, at least mentally for this younger beauty, divorced or not, apparently, none of it mattered to Frank. Jeanie wished she'd been more inclined toward religion, that she'd forced it on Frank. Even if she didn't believe, she should have respected its power to make people behave appropriately out of fear of going to hell. She should have been smarter.

Ruthie's voice startled Jeanie. "He stopped by as he always does, milked the cows, emptied the chamber pots, and accompanied me to the well for water and then without any warning at all, he just took to the bed."

"I'm sorry, Ruthie. He should have gone home," Jeanie was embarrassed by the supreme inconvenience of Frank, that it was now something the neighbors had to experience firsthand.

"Frank." Jeanie shook him about the arms, squeezing his biceps. She looked around the room searching for evidence of what he'd been up to.

"What the devil are you doing sleeping like this? Like a... Blame-it, Frank Arthur." Jeanie shook the mattress, trying to stir him. Suddenly, images of her own father slammed into her mind. She remembered his daytime naps. How she'd always stopped at his house to make him tea for when he was ready to rise. She leaned on the mattress mid-push, chest heaving for air as she put it all together.

It wasn't until her father was dead that she realized what had caused his need to nap during the day. Opium. But Frank wasn't that stupid. Mrs. Hunt might be a user, but certainly Frank knew better, he'd seen the damage such use could do to people and their families. She shoved his shoulder again, attempting to stir him. Nothing. Fueled by anger, Jeanie slammed the mattress one more time then tore around the room, opening drawers, trudging into the necessary, back to the kitchen, tossing bottles aside, searching for laudanum, opium seeds, Dover's, anything that would explain his behavior.

Jeanie broke a bottle then finally realized she'd lost control, that she was humiliating herself. Falling apart in front of Ruthie and Lutie would only send out the scent of a wounded animal, a boon for predatory women like Lutie clearly was. Jeanie couldn't believe she had tried to help her, given her the benefit of the doubt. And Frank. How could he?

She realized her anger was lost on him and rather than debase herself further she would leave him there like the slug he was. She stomped to the front door.

Frank's voice, thin, limp, pained, came from behind Jeanie. She turned slowly. Frank stood in the doorway, gripping the door-jambs, his head lolling forward. His eyes were unfocused. "Jeanie? I just, I am, I'm..."

Jeanie stalked across the floor, hands balled at her sides, mind twisting around different tracks of thought. She wanted to rail on him, tell him she hated him, while another track was aware they were being watched, she couldn't just fall into hysterics.

"I'm sorry...just sick. Can't swallow. Need some laudanum."

Jeanie clenched her jaw, stunned that he would breathe those words to her.

She slapped his shoulder so hard her hand stung. Then without even realizing what she was doing, she immediately slapped his cheek, causing his head to bounce over and up, his jaw moving in slow motion.

The noise echoed off the bare, wood walls. She drew back, covering her mouth with her stinging hand. She'd rarely raised her voice at anyone, certainly didn't go about hitting people.

She whispered, her throat tightening around the words. "Look what you've done. You've turned me into a horrible woman. I'll never forgive you." Frank backed into the bedroom and closed the door on Jeanie's face, quietly, but sending a signal that the feeling was shared.

Jeanie turned to see Ruthie wringing her apron, nearly tearing if from her waist. Jeanie avoided her gaze and felt the weight of her utter collapse of manners.

Jeanie drew deep breaths, staving off the anger that crushed her insides as she decided what sort of illness would cause her to take to her bed. No! What event would cause her to take to an unmarried man's bed while her husband broke his backside to run their household? The only illness she could name was death itself. She plastered a mask of nonchalance on her face before meeting the gaze of the sisters.

"Well. I'm sorry for Frank's taking to your bed. But I hope that's the only impropriety happening here. I trust that Frank is not contemplating the nature of your beauty, Lutie."

Lutie's jaw dropped and her eyes narrowed.

"Why no. No, of course not." She cowered back from Jeanie.

"Because I think I said before, and I want to emphasize, I won't tolerate such things, I married that man and sloth-like or not, he is the head of our family and I will not—"

"I think we understand," Ruthie said. She stuck her chin in the air a bit, sticking up for her sister. It's not that there was any real proof of an affair, but something made Jeanie understand there was one. A feeling under one's skin wouldn't really suffice as reason enough to accuse a woman of sexually gratifying herself with another's husband. But, she couldn't stop herself.

Jeanie lifted her chin and looked down her nose, infusing her expression with all the snobbery that'd coursed through her blood since birth, the sneer that she'd checked and restrained since the first time her innocent wielding of smugness left a peer weeping in a heap. Jeanie never used her former position as a tool of derision and she was surprised at how easily she did it then. She left the Moore home having shamed Lutie so greatly that her sister grimaced with a sour look of anger on Lutie's behalf. Jeanie understood. She would have probably done the same if she had a sister to defend.

Outside, her calm restored, Jeanie mounted Summer without so much as a fingertip lift from her children who were scattered, playing in the Moore's vacuous garden. She took off for home without even looking back for them. What was she doing? What was happening to her? How could she have hit her husband?

Mentally, as hard as it was to know he wasn't the man she'd married, not recognizing her own self was harder. How could she have reacted that way? What was next? Hitting her children? Would the Moores talk? Why did that matter? Talk or not, it didn't change the fact she'd hit another human in a fit of anger she'd never felt before.

She tried to sort through the events she'd experienced. Was it just that Frank might be using opium or was there an affair? She couldn't imagine that Lutie could look at Jeanie in the eye, so matter-of-fact if she were bedding Frank. Ruthie seemed more unsettled by the situation than Lutie was and perhaps that said it all. Knowing that Lutie could carry on with Jeanie as though simply borrowing her damask napkins instead of her lazy husband had clearly taken its toll on Ruthie.

At that thought Jeanie let a grunt into the prairie. Blinded by tears and groaning frustration, she beat across the naked land wondering how she could have agreed to come to the prairie. She'd had no choice. Her husband made the decision and she was duty-bound to live up to his decisions.

In addition, living naked—with her former society knowing the details of her economic and social downfall—in the town of Des Moines would have meant stark, shame. Unlike on the prairie where barrenness was the norm for all who lived there, Jeanie had not thought she could live with being the one to strip her children of all they knew while still living in the place they once had everything. But still, she should have known Frank's weaknesses would be exploited in a place where nothing could be depended upon.

The land atop the dugout came into view. Jeanie clasped her chest with one hand. She was trapped. She had to find a way to live with her life as it was, not as she wanted it to be. She tried to call up the feelings she once had for Frank, the love that had been sparked by what at times was his goodness, his passion for her when he was in the mood to feel it. She wanted to pretend her life had not taken this turn it had into the home of the Lutie Moore.

And, as Summer trotted up to the stake where Jeanie would tie her, she knew that it was that original attachment to Frank—the nearly childish one that tethered their foolish hearts—*it* was the trust that wouldn't allow her to push him away. Underneath all his shortcomings was a man with untouched strengths. No! She told herself to wise up, to grow up.

Oh my, she thought. The prairie had ripped the shroud off that lie! She had to face facts. Frank was not the man she'd thought he was when they married, no matter what his talents and gifts. And living where every inch of the day was a struggle, where Jeanie couldn't cover up his shortcomings, finally made that clear. Trouble was, no matter how inept Frank was, he was her husband, owner of everything hers, and she couldn't live without him—socially or otherwise. It wasn't done, wasn't permitted, not really, not for a woman with children.

Jeanie dismounted Summer and patted her side as she surrendered and recommitted to her life and her plan to make it as she desired. She had no choice. She stared into the horizon, seeing her future as one with the prairie as much as the line of sky that met the earth was. She had no choice but to force herself back into love with Frank, to at the very least, search for the goodness that was once there in him. She'd make herself see it. She could do it. "If a woman is unhappy in her marriage, she has only herself to blame," Jeanie said aloud. "If I want life to be a certain way, I have to make it so. I can do this. I can do this."

"Jeanie?" Templeton's voice came from below the dugout, startling her.

She dabbed at her sodden hairline with her sleeve then with shaking hands, smoothed back the tendrils that escaped her hat. Had he heard? Jeanie's heart clenched then released leaving her lightheaded.

"Mr. Templeton?" Jeanie removed Summer's bridle and put the feedbag to her face before refilling the trough with water. By then Templeton was behind her.

"It's me," Templeton said.

Jeanie turned.

"Well, yes, it is. Aren't you early? You're due from the rails in two days."

Templeton removed his hat and looked down at it in his hands. "Yes, yes, well the opportunity presented itself and that's not important. What's important is that I've made it here with money in hand, and then I saw you lighting out over the plain and I thought, well, I overheard you, but, well, I know what's polite in terms of society, but I, I just."

"Spit it out, Templeton. I've come to agree with Greta that the prairie holds no sentiment for manners beyond the most basic." Jeanie brushed Summer hard, using the action as a means for not having to look Templeton in the eye.

"Yes, yes, I suppose but it's that I can't discern whether this observation fits into that category of base or basic—"

"Out with it Templeton. I'm not in the mood for discretion," Jeanie said. She knelt beside Summer and ran her hand down her leg, causing her to lift her hoof so she could dig the pebbles from her shoe. She only felt comfortable having something to do while they had this conversation. She wasn't sure she could stand still, looking Templeton in the eye and discussing such matters. She stole a glance at him then couldn't look away. She stopped brushing.

"I suppose I'm asking this to make sure you have what you need. That Frank's able to...well, I've noticed that he sometimes... Now don't look away, Jeanie. You deserve to have certain aspects of your marriage upheld, no matter the circumstances or where you hang your hat—in the bustling city or dead prairie—"

Jeanie felt the rest of her strength leave and had no choice but to balance with her hands on the ground, the dirt, under her nails. Templeton latched his forearms under her arms and lifted her to standing. He leaned her against the post and grabbed the brush from the ground and put it in its holder. Jeanie straightened and wiped her hands over her skirt.

"Templeton, if it's our small purse or lack of production in the area of plowing or carpentry or, well, whatever may be at hand for Frank and what he can provide, let me put your mind to rest by saying if it were only wealth I wanted why I would prefer working for it myself than to be indebted to any man merely for financing."

Templeton grabbed for Jeanie's hand. She pulled it away.

"We get what we deserve, don't we, really? And what use is money without love? I am sure it cannot be enjoyed. And, Frank and I love each other as though still poppy-minded fifteen-year-old lovers we were twelve years ago. Templeton, you do not know what a woman can do for the man she loves, nor do you know of the greatness and worth of her love." Jeanie's throat caught on her words. She stared at her feet. Templeton cleared his throat and began to speak, but Jeanie cut him off, meeting his hard gaze with hers.

"Frank is not like other men, I grant you. But he will find his path, his success and when he does, I'll be standing there with him, basking in the fact we found it *our* way." Jeanie didn't believe one word she said, but for her, each utterance built an invisible wall between Templeton and that kept her from jumping into his arms, begging him to take her away, to hide them all from Frank and this awful land.

Templeton threw his hand into the air. "Stop talking."

Jeanie glanced away then fell back into Templeton's mesmerizing gaze. In that visual embrace, she felt a tide of emotion push through her, surprising her so much that it couldn't be followed by anything but tears.

Clearly, Templeton hadn't believed her speech. The thought that her loyalty was built of fine dirt that dissolved in the wind made her bury her face in her hands. She tried to suck back her sobs. When she couldn't stop them, she shuddered and shook, wanting to curl up on the ground and be absorbed right into it, disappearing like the healthy crops had done. Where was the unexpected prairie fire to eat her alive, or the grasshoppers to munch her clean, taking her out of existence?

Bawling like a child, she felt released from tension that had gripped her for months. "I hit Frank, just now at the Moores, I'm falling apart, beating people. This is *not* who I am!" She felt Templeton's arms around her as he pulled her into his chest. She could smell his clean shirt mixed with fresh perspiration as he smoothed the back of her hair like she would have done for someone who needed it. His fingers released her hair from her bun and she felt the length of it drop down her back. Templeton pulled it gently making her turn her face up to him.

Her hands moved from her face to his shirt, where she dug into it, kneading the cotton, she opened her eyes only enough to see his face lower onto hers, his eyes finding her soul, making her feel the way she had when she'd written sugary letters to Frank. His lips met hers. The soft kiss grew harder, as their bodies seemed to coax one another into perfect symmetry.

Templeton nipped Jeanie's lip. She dug her fingers through his hair, pulling him as close as was humanly possible. She wanted to feel his body on hers, as she had lain with Frank so many times before. She ignored every thought that told her to stop as the thrill was too great to resist. Then as quickly as it started, her unwilling subconscious took hold of her body even as her mind readily surrendered it.

She gasped and stopped kissing. She stiffened in Templeton's embrace. He responded in kind, taking his lips from hers. Neither pulled away fully, gazes still locked, chests still meshed as Jeanie wiped her mouth with her palm then the back of her hand.

"Jeanie, please..." Templeton said.

She shook her head then raced down the slope of the dugout, rounded the side of the hill and tramped into the bleak tunnel she called home. Templeton screamed her name from above as she stood at her cook-stove, hovering over it, hair falling around her shoulders, brushing the cook area. She whipped it back, liking the way it felt for her hair to move as she did.

"*Go away, Templeton!*" She yelled at the earthen ceiling. She wished to die for allowing her body free reign of its wants, especially after harboring and wielding anger at the Moores. She had no evidence Frank was anything more than the lazy man she'd known for over a decade, yet *she* behaved in the same way she had judged to be so wrong.

She gripped the cook-stove with both hands. Was she even breathing? Minutes passed before Jeanie shrugged and moved the coffee pot onto the cook-stove. She did not have time to fool with such things. That much she knew. She glanced over her shoulder. What was she looking for? The children? Templeton?

She refused to answer her own question, to mull over the great mash of emotion inside her. She wanted so much to enjoy Templeton's gifts and comfort he would clearly offer her, but it could never be. She swallowed hard, willing the desire for something other than her marriage to Frank to go away.

Soon she heard the chatter of the children and Templeton outside the dugout. He was still there after what happened? Had it happened? She would make it so it never did. She started toward the door to tell him to go then thought again, that perhaps the best way for the kiss to go away was for them to pretend it never existed.

"Mama, what's for—" Katherine stopped short then drew back. "Supper? Your hair."

Jeanie waved her off. "The ride back on the horse, the wind, it blew it all to hell." Jeanie slapped her hand over her mouth. "To pieces, I mean…" Katherine nodded, but her expression was as confused as it should have been given what had transpired over the past hour.

Katherine walked toward her mother then patted the bedstead for Jeanie to sit. Jeanie stared at Katherine's hand.

"I'll do your hair back up, Mama. I know you're so tired with the baby sapping your strength. I know you must be so…well, just sit, Mama." Katherine sat and held her open arms to Jeanie.

Jeanie's head dipped with shame and contentment that her daughter was not only kind and loving, but she was observant enough to notice when another needed a moment to be loved with gentle hands and soothing touches.

Jeanie collapsed onto the bedstead beside Katherine and let her preening begin. Jeanie's hair pulled her scalp giving her chills as Katherine worked the brown strands into braids then into a bun.

"The braids should keep it in the bun while we entertain this wind, Mama. I told Mr. Templeton that Father's sick. I can help you make supper. That Mr. Templeton is *really* something else. Early back from the rails, he is." Katherine said as though *she* were the one with the crush on Templeton.

"I'll make sure everything's ready for our meal." Jeanie reached for Katherine's hand and pulled it to her lips then nestled into her lap. "You've been so helpful already. I don't know how I would live without you." She kissed Katherine's hand again.

"Just make sure the animals have water then go play." Jeanie didn't wait for a reply but pulled Katherine to standing as she heard Templeton and James nearing the dugout door again. She shuffled Katherine out and stood by the door, unseen, listening to her son and Templeton prattle on about warm air rising from the south, accompanied by wispy clouds, meant a rainstorm was coming. Jeanie couldn't help but see them as father and son. When was the last time Frank and James spoke of anything other than who would go to the well and who would muck the horses' waste or settle them under the falling down structure they called a barn?

Back at her cook-stove Jeanie ground chicory, seeds, and a touch of cocoa, using it as a barely tolerable replacement for coffee as the grounds from Yankton had long been used. James brought a load of buffalo chips into the house and Jeanie began the process of loading them into the stove, lighting them, washing her hands, making the buckwheat cakes, and then repeating the process. She knew it didn't make sense that Templeton was here in their home while her husband lay in another woman's bed across the plain.

She wiped her mouth with her sleeve again, removing any trace of Templeton. She had no hard evidence Frank gave or even offered his heart or body to Lutie. Yet, Jeanie had plenty that she'd done so to Templeton. Frank was simply in his blackness, the shroud that paralyzed him as much as a disease or accident might. It was simply who he was when he wasn't the man she married. For better or worse. For better or worse. Perhaps it wasn't opium, just his moods, perhaps the cause of his actions didn't really matter.

Jeanie told herself *her* strength was creating beauty from nothing, joining fabrics in surprising or delicate ways to create clothing that made people lose their breath upon seeing them. Or writing, communicating the beauty of homemaking to millions of other housewives. And with her marriage it was the same, she was the tailor of it, adding and removing details, coaxing unusual components together and in the end reaping beauty and function from nothing. Knowing this made her happy, settled her, gave her the peace with which she could carry on her duties as woman, mother and wife.

And with that final thought she wiped out every bit of Templeton, as anything but a neighbor, from her heart and mind. She couldn't afford to let romantic thoughts of him inside her. It was that simple. Or so she would will it to be. She would have to consent to visions of Templeton, the feel of his arms around her, the sensation his mere gaze incited in her and she was strong enough to resist the temptation of all those memories.

As the brown of fall months collapsed grey into November, the rest of the men returned from the railroad and brought with them frigid weather and mounds of snow that often layered so high, the Arthurs couldn't leave their dugout without tunneling out. The first of this weather brought another influx of vermin and creatures that Jeanie never felt comfortable killing, but always did because living with them seemed worse.

Frank had drawn a visible sigh of relief when the men returned with the Darlington Township cooperative funds in hand, when they divvied up the resources and planned for each family, to some degree, to withdraw into their own units during the winter months. Ruthie continued to offer her expertise, teaching, when the weather permitted the children to trek over the plains.

And, on the days when the children were studying with Ruthie and the chores were done early, Frank would crawl back into bed and pull the covers over his head or disappear into the horizon, returning with an emaciated pheasant or tiny prairie chicken for dinner. He rarely spoke to Jeanie, his nightly "Good Night Sweet Friend" being his sole verbal offering on many days. The scant words were always splashed with sarcasm and made Jeanie ache all the more for what she lacked in marriage.

Seeing him, his lost expressions and quiet whir of repetitive carving, reminded Jeanie so much of her father's opium use that she pushed Frank on the topic. This line of questioning was the only thing that brought his face to life and animated him at all as he cursed her for not trusting him, for thinking he could have such a problem.

When Jeanie reminded him that even Quaker ministers fell prey to the substance, that knowing Abby Hunt had her own supply, would make obtaining it easy, understandable even when a person felt taken by hopelessness, Frank recognized the ploy for what it was—an attempted seduction for information.

This seduction would incite anger. Frank would throw anything fist-sized around the dugout, sending the children into the necessary where they sat out the storm, waiting to come out, ready to pretend nothing was going wrong in their lives. Jeanie was paralyzed by what she suspected, as though broaching it would only make life worse. Besides, due to the weather, he was around more. She could watch him and she'd seen no signs of him sneaking off to ply himself with drugs. Just his typical, ever-shifting moods.

The cramped lifestyle—tucked within the walls of the earth— was suffocating to Jeanie. From cooking with buffalo chips to the way dirt fell through the ceiling, stuffing the wagon sheet so full Jeanie had to empty and hang it twice in the fall. The stuffy quarters, in combination with Jeanie's growing belly and the sluggishness pregnancy brought on, made bathing harder. Jeanie, daily, drew a whiff of herself, and her stomach would turn, that her body was so unclean. Though Jeanie accepted her former habits of cleanliness were in stark contrast to what could be achieved on the prairie, the desire for a fresh-smelling home, clean linens, hair, and body was fully present in Jeanie, making her fight back her own depression each day.

Jeanie worked hard to find some cheer inside the home, laughing and reading with the children, playing all manner of childish games to please the bored youngsters. At night when silence came she scooted to the edge of the bed as far from Frank as possible. She teetered there recalling her intimate moment with Templeton. She hugged herself and evoked the sensation of his lips on hers, the way her hair felt as he released it from its bun and it swooped down her back, his fingertips dancing down her spine as he worked his hand through the long brown strands.

That single collection of moments would have shamed her if she ever entertained any aspect of the fantasy during the day. For Jeanie the act never happened, it was merely a dream and therefore could be repeatedly explored in deep, private nighttime.

It had been decided that the five families of the Darlington Township cooperative would gather for Thanksgiving at Templeton's home. When that day arrived, Jeanie's spirits rose with the mere thought of seeing her sturdy Greta and reliable Ruthie. Jeanie hummed as she boiled water and prepared her stove for stew and cakes and squash pie as her contributions to Thanksgiving dinner. Every once in a while her mood would dampen with the sight of Frank, out of the corner of her eye, lying in bed so still he could be deemed a corpse.

If the dugout itself was undesirable for Jeanie, for its filth and lack of privacy, the sheer snugness of it threatened her mood as much as anything. If they had another bedroom, Frank could burrow into his nest and at least be out of sight and out of Jeanie's mind.

It was times like this—when the thought of Thanksgiving, the gathering of her new friends, surrounded by warmth and food and hope and what should be joy—that little bits of hate for Frank, for his character flaws, threatened Jeanie's soul. She couldn't afford to hate him, to see him as only lazy or a failure or selfish for when she did see him that way she found her only recourse was to take to the bed herself.

So, in the presence of such kernels of discontent, Jeanie dug deeper into her mind, her heart and past to call up exactly what she felt for Frank when she fell in love with him twelve years before. And, each time she was able to access that place inside her, to see Frank through the compassionate eyes of love, she grew in strength and hope. From nothing came these things and that made her powerful.

And in the condition of strength grown from weakness, she felt content. She could care for her family, give them what they needed and in the process give Frank the space to finally find his path to satisfaction and wholeness.

James removed his wet boots and peeled off the rest of his outer clothing revealing his red long johns. Jeanie stopped stirring and turned to see James stand over his father, hands on hips, as though determining whether Frank was alive or dead or silently daring Frank to wake and interact with his family. He shook his head and without looking at Jeanie sat in front of the fire and pulled his legs to his chest, staring into the red and orange jumping flames. Jeanie turned back to her stew then began to grind the coffee.

"I know you hate this dugout, Mama," James said.

"Oh, James. I didn't know you were there." She didn't want to discuss gloomy topics in front of Frank.

"I know that every time one of us kids or a cow or horse runs overtop, causing the roof to shudder like a salt shaker, releasing dirt onto your scalp, settling in like some sort of perverse fairy dust, that your stomach turns in disgust." James paused. He removed his hat and hung it on a hook inside the door.

"But really, I just left Templeton's and his place is frigid. He's excited to host Thanksgiving and all, but I couldn't help but notice that even with the thick layers of plaster we set, there are spots where the air sails through like wind off the ocean. For as hard as this winter will be, I think we have the prize home, the smallest, most insulated, being that we are basically one with the earth and thus one with God and how could we go wrong? We're essentially living in the womb of God. If he had a womb, I mean."

Jeanie turned from the coffee she was grinding. James shivered so hard his body jerked. Jeanie pulled a blanket from the chair and set it around his back, smoothing it over his shoulders several times. James grabbed her hand.

"We're going to be all right, Mama. I have this feeling in my gut. I don't know where it comes from—maybe the Hunts are right about the Lord living right inside each of us, because I feel it, that sort of Grace they talk about. All the talk of sin we heard at church in Des Moines, that never struck me as pertaining to me at all. I never felt particularly sinful but never holy either. Now, out here, on the prairie, it's as though I was born here."

"James, my sweet, you are profound this morning. Is it simply thoughts of Thanksgiving on this special day that has you so full of this Grace?"

James shook his head and shrugged before turning his face up at his mother. "I don't know, Mama. This swell of hope and near glee has been building in me. Every time Templeton teaches me a new way of thinking about weather, patterns, stuff that barely exists in terms of schooling but is so obviously true in this environment, I feel powerful, like I can do anything. And with each problem we encounter and surmount, I feel as though we are imbued with strength that can't lead to anything but success."

"Well, then all I can imagine is that you will indeed find nothing but success because in your hopes and dreams is purposeful action, James. And that is what matters."

When James didn't respond, Jeanie turned. James had stood and now towered over his father, peering down on him as though he were the parent, awaiting his lazy child's wakening.

"That is the difference," James said not moving. "I see that as clear as the wind blusters right through the seemingly sturdy walls of Templeton's frame house. Sometimes, what things look like is not at all what they are."

Jeanie watched as James's posture straightened with each word as though saying them, their full weight, was realized in his bones and made him into the man his father would never be. Jeanie buckled at the picture of the two of them, grasped her chest, surprised at the pain she felt and in the next breath she took, felt the grip of contractions.

Chapter 14

Jeanie had fought through Thanksgiving morning's contractions by sipping tea and sitting quietly whenever her duties would allow.

The weather was odd for November. In the morning it had been frigid, the ground blanketed with snow. But by noon it had warmed enough to obliterate the whiteness and create a pleasurable day. James, Tommy and Katherine rode to the Zurchenko's to see what they needed in terms of hauling food or preparing it for Thanksgiving.

And, as though the mild weather seeped into Frank's blood, he rose at noon and with no more than six words reported that he would stop by the Moore's to see what they needed in terms of chores and hauling food and supplies to Templeton's. Jeanie, who had been resting for a moment on the edge of the bed rose at this pronouncement.

"No," Jeanie said.

Frank turned his hands palm up and smirked.

"I mean it."

"I heard you."

Jeanie shifted her weight not knowing what he meant. He buttoned his work shirt, a dirty one.

"Wear this one." Jeanie held up a clean shirt.

"I'm working, I don't need a clean shirt."

"You're going to the well?"

"Yep." He raised his hand over his head in that way he always did to signify he was moving on. He headed to the door.

"You're going to the well for *us*, right?" Jeanie hated that her statement came out as a question.

"After I tend to the neighbors. You're always saying to be neighborly, manners and such, so I'm doing that. Just for you."

Jeanie nearly doubled over from the pain that sentiment caused, the way he used her words against her, made her into a vixenish woman, deserving to be resented. As though *her* actions pushed them into a prairie life.

She ran after him. "Frank. We need you here. We need you to laugh in the house, talk with us, help us, to be the man you used to be."

Frank's eyes widened then a cold smile came over his face. "I'm not sure I'm the one who needs fixing. You've been riding me since we arrived on this great land. Nothing I do is good enough for you. And instead of giving me a few seconds to catch my breath and scratch my ass, you do my work for me then you seethe over the cook-stove, angry because you're doing everyone's work. Well, my sweet Jeanie, if you don't want to do everyone's work, then just stop doing it. Simple as that."

Jeanie processed his words and realized she'd folded into herself, pushing back at the contractions that wracked her, taking the verbal blows, partly feeling like he was right, but knowing he was wrong.

"And you *hit* me," Frank said. Jeanie thought she saw his lip quiver.

"I will never forgive myself for hitting you, Frank. When I thought you were using opium, I lost all sense. That's no excuse, but *we* are your family, Frank." Jeanie shouted. She took deep, fast breaths to bring her voice back to normal, so her words wouldn't careen into the air, carry over the plains into their neighbor's ears.

Jeanie bent into another contraction. "Like it or not. You are stuck with us and you better ride tall and satisfied from now on. We are your *life*." Jeanie's voice was thin, barely full of the zeal enough to get them out of her mouth let alone convey strength. Frank sauntered to his horse, Night, and mounted it with the ease of a teenager. Nothing in his body communicated the blackness that clearly lived in his soul and nothing seemed to show he cared for his wife in the least.

She watched him disappear, dragging her soul behind him, pitting her heart with his callousness, leaving what was already a hobbled marriage, further crippled. She cleared her throat. There were mouths to feed and chores to be done. She returned to the stew. For some time she fussed with the dishes she was to prepare. Her anger grew though she didn't want it to. She stirred the stew, nearly punishing it. The spoon flew from her hand and clanked against the pot, spewing meaty broth against the wagon sheet. "Blame-it!" Jeanie said. She spun around looking for a rag. She dipped it into the water and rubbed at the stain as though her life depended upon its removal.

Frank came back into the house, stood beside her, trying to look busy, searching for something. Jeanie huffed and puffed, hoping he'd just do what she needed him to. But instead of him agreeing to do what was his responsibility anyway, he began picking his nose. Jeanie tried not to watch out of the corner of her eye, to give him the space to do what he needed to without embarrassing him, by telling him it was grotesque and she'd had enough of such things. The act of plowing through his nose with one finger then the other would be, she was sure, the thing that would in the end make her hate him. She shuddered and turned her back fully toward him.

"It's okay, Jeanie. I love you and everything will be okay. I just need to get out of this mood. You know how these moods take me and I can't, I just, well, I love you and I promised the Moores, you know, Ruthie especially, she's been a big help to us and I just want to repay…"

Jeanie *wanted* to soften into his arms, to understand how one minute he was hard and the next he was loving. She searched his face for an answer. Nothing was telling. She called up portions of his letters to her, the way they made her feel. Nothing came. She tried to love him right. He was right, she told herself, Ruthie had done a lot for their family, even if Lutie had done nearly nothing for them and the cooperative.

"Ruthie said she'd understand if I couldn't help them load up their wagon, if you needed me. She knows…"

"No, go." Jeanie shrugged his hand off her shoulder. "Ruthie doesn't deserve to carry the weight of two people with nothing in return. James already loaded the wagon with our knapsacks and linens and—" Jeanie wiggled away from Frank and disappeared behind the necessary curtain to use the chamber pot. The only thing Jeanie could figure was that Frank was indeed using opium. How else could she account for such sweeping moods?

She'd yanked her skirts up and pulled down her netherthings. Squatting there, Frank pulled the curtain aside. Jeanie should have been swept by humility and embarrassment that her husband was watching her relieve herself, but none of that came. And as she finished up her business, she stood, resituated her clothes and washed her hands while Frank watched every move she made. Jeanie couldn't decide what it all meant, that neither of them flamed red as they would have, as they'd done, just months before.

Back at the stew that didn't need stirring, Jeanie bit the inside of her cheek. "Just go on, Frank. It's fine. We're all set. We'll see you at Templeton's."

Frank pulled on his outer clothes and boots and hesitated at the door as though wanting to say something.

"You're not eating that opium, are you Frank?" Jeanie cringed away at her words as they floated off into the air. He snorted and shrugged his shoulders and in the end he roughly yanked open the door and disappeared into the blinding sun leaving Jeanie to consider how she'd allowed her feelings to tangle as they had.

How had they come to this point where circumstances dictated their feelings for each other, making her daydream of how it might make things easier if he were dead, if they were divorced, if that kind of thing were possible to do and continue to live. Yes, she wanted him gone, but there could be no divorce, no way of making him disappear, to stop him from influencing their lives one way or another. They would die without him, it was impossible for a woman to keep a family once she'd been divorced.

So, it was clear that she needed to harden herself to anything sweet or sentimental because there was nothing more wasteful of energy than the constant rumination of one's feelings. She would be the one to hold their family together. She'd known that for some time, yet every time she thought it, the realization felt stunningly new.

At Templeton's Jeanie and Greta laid the pheasant in the middle of the Thanksgiving table and draped their arms around one another. Anna held her mother's hand, clearly having regressed to role of baby since Anzhela died.

Jeanie's children had always been independent, never latching on past the point when they could walk themselves. They had been curious to the point of dangerous, but in Des Moines, between Jeanie, her mother and the nurses Jeanie's mother always provided, the children never wandered too far into trouble. Jeanie squeezed Greta's waist and smoothed Anna's yellow hair down her back, cooing at her, hoping that the baby in her belly might be like Anzhela, clingy.

"Well, the table is perfect. The linens, the pumpkin color, it's stunning and the perfect complement to the real thing," Greta said.

Jeanie dropped her embrace and looked at the table. "All that's missing are Katherine's candles. She worked days creating what she deems a masterpiece—or several masterpieces. My little artist."

"She is talented," Greta said. "Not that I really know, I mean, formally I have no education in the arts, I have no education period, but I know what looks pretty and that Katherine has a way of seeing the world that's beyond her years."

"She does," Jeanie said. "I agree."

"Maybe she'll be famous, painting's hanging all over the best walls in the world someday."

"Oh, I don't know." Jeanie flushed, not wanting to boast about her daughter. She walked to Templeton's front window.

"Greta, is it me or is it impossible to keep a window clean around here? Have you noticed?"

Greta raised her eyebrows.

"I washed Mr. Templeton's windows just minutes past. I scrubbed and scraped. And as soon as I thought they must certainly be clean, I stepped back and all I saw was the other side, the dirt on the inside of the pane stood out like a beacon in the sea. I'd never noticed such a thing."

Greta shook her head, face blank.

"I mean," Jeanie said. "I suppose it's sort of like people. There're all these layers of trouble and angst and when you finally think you've cleared away some aspect of the muck, when you stand back to take a deep breath, you see the other side of the person, the rest of the dirt. And you never can get it all clean, can you?"

"Well, not on the prairie, anyhow," Greta said, her voice gentle.

"I must have alternated between the outside and inside panes five times. Both sides only gleamed together, for mere minutes and then the other was dirty."

Greta nodded at Jeanie's ramblings as though she understood Jeanie's need to express her thoughts. They worked side by side, as though they'd been friends, working a kitchen in tandem, for decades. Jeanie had never been so grateful to be in the company of a friend as she was that Thanksgiving morning, after the weather had kept them hibernating for weeks.

"I think my Aleksey notices Katherine's artistry, too."

"Oh, Aleksey is a sweetheart, but you're not suggesting they're whispering sweet love speeches to one another are you? Katherine barely mentions him."

"Well, have you watched her when he comes into her presence? Her eyes nearly cross with glee."

"Oh my. My, my. You're right. I'll have to pay more attention, I suppose." Jeanie said hoping Greta was wrong. Aleksey may have been a sweet boy, clearly hardworking, but his lack of culture would be a big obstacle for partnering as far as Jeanie could tell.

"All I know is," Greta said, "I realize this is coming from the mother of a stable of work horses and you've given birth to the breeders, the stable masters. We need all kinds to make the world work and I think Aleksey and Katherine may have already matched themselves up like a set of those candles she so carefully crafted."

"Well, your boys are getting an education with Miss Ruthie. She is a fine teacher," Jeanie said.

"Well, teaching is only a quarter of what needs to be done around here. I don't know how Ruthie deals with Lutie's laziness. How she gets up every morning to do the day's work while Lutie lays about, thinking." Greta said.

Jeanie's shoulders rose at Greta's words as they invoked images of Frank.

"I'm sorry," Greta said, "I know you Arthurs are thinkers, too. I don't mean to disparage the act of contemplation, but sometimes,

I just think busting a hard trail to the next chore is the only way, the *only* way to live."

Jeanie shook her head. "Oh, no, Greta, you didn't offend me. I think you're right, it takes all kinds. And it's hard to know what a family is living with, what they know about each other, the allowances that are given for reasons the family members themselves might not even be aware of. That's probably why Ruthie can withstand her sister. Ruthie is a special woman who has many burdens and I can only hope that she finds a man who matches her in abilities and love."

"It's just you all are so different than Nikolai and I. Sometimes we actually sit there, heads thrown back, taken so hard by laughter at the thought of all of you out here, without the likes of us. Other times we're stilled by worry. You're all so, well..."

"Soft?"

Greta tilted her head to the side and then righted it before nodding, smiling shyly.

"If it's any consolation, I've thought the exact same thing about us. We, or at least me, I know how much your family means for the existence of the rest of us. We depend on your kindness and skill. I know that to my core."

Jeanie shifted her pot of stew from one side of Templeton's cook-stove to the other. She spun around to Greta when an idea came to mind.

"Why don't you let me to repay you?" Jeanie clapped her hands.

"But, the sewing. You've done your share."

"No, no. I can lend you my library. Or part of it. Oh, *Greta*, much of what I brought is instructive and would appeal to your sensibilities. *Farm Ballads* and *Farm Legends!* You would love these—the piece, *Over the Hills to the Poorhouse*, is very touching and shows how cruel it is to send a poor old mother to the poorhouse.

The sequel is nice when the black sheep of the family came home. And there's a funny piece where the girl hid one of her lovers in the churn and the other one in the garret. Just think of having the cream poured all over him! Oh dear, it makes me laugh to think it." Jeanie gripped Greta's arm and Greta grinned.

"Another good one is *Betsy and I Are Out*. One line attracted my attention, 'And she kissed me for the first time in over twenty years.' Imagine husband and wife living together without *once* kissing each other in twenty years!" Jeanie was invigorated by the thought of sharing literary conversation even with someone who'd clearly only had scant opportunities over her life.

"That *is* a variety of reading." Greta pulled her arm away from Jeanie.

"I'm sorry to go on like that," Jeanie said. "I don't mean to imply those issues are funny in themselves, it's just the way they're presented."

"I can't read, Jeanie."

"But I've seen you."

"No, I simply get by."

Jeanie flicked her hands over the skirt of her apron then grasped for her invisible pearls. "Allow me to teach you."

Greta shook her head. "There's no time for that. And I don't suffer for not being able to oblige my literary sensibilities—if one could possess them without having fully entertained them."

"Why yes, I think that's possible. What if I simply entertain your literary sensibilities for you, with you, when we're together."

Greta nodded. "I would consent to that."

The two women made light work as Jeanie regaled Greta with tales from Shakespeare, Carlton, Beecher, and Taylor. Greta became bent with laughter and quieted by the awe of some of the most famous literature in the world, further engaging the two women in a friendship that filled both their souls with contentment.

But, their friendship was cemented when Greta inquired about Jeanie's own published books and insisted upon hearing about them. Jeanie recited some of what was in them and admitted as only a true friend might, that she had never been a true housewife until they moved to the prairie. Greta laughed heavy at the idea Jeanie had only *overseen* the skinning of a rabbit or plucking of a pheasant before she lost everything and took to the prairie.

At one point Jeanie's storytelling slowed, her voice lost its gusto and it was Greta's turn to take Jeanie by the arms, to offer reassurance.

"I would never have suspected you were a fraud if you did not tell me yourself." Greta's face was stoic, but her gaze was warm and she seemed almost pretty that way. The delivery of the sentiment inspired great laughter in Jeanie who knew Greta was sweetly lying through her serious expression. Jeanie pulled her arms from Greta's grip and took the big, wonderful woman into a full hug. She patted her back and squeezed tight.

"You are a true, perfect friend, Greta and I've enjoyed this laughter over the ridiculousness that was my former life."

"Well, this has been nice. Since Anzhela, I have not laughed. I'm shocked I forgot about her for a moment, here with you." They clung to one another, Jeanie wishing she could remove Greta's pain. "And, I enjoy a woman who can laugh at herself."

"That, I've learned to do," Jeanie said as she released her friend and greeted a swarm of hungry children looking for their Thanksgiving meal.

By mid-afternoon, the entirety of the Darlington Township cooperative was seated at Templeton's table, the one Frank apparently crafted in secret, without even Jeanie knowing it was in production. It was both elaborate and simple—using primitive pine, but carving intricate floral patterns into the apron and legs. The guests couldn't help but fondle it, running their fingers into the grooves, feeling the magic in something so remarkable—one who isn't skilled in such things can't begin to imagine how it has come to exist.

Several times over the course of the meal Jeanie closed her eyes, sometimes to will away the contractions that had been pulling more consistently than ever and sometimes to carving the sight of them—what felt like a miracle of mild weather, the gathering of people who she's come to depend on in so many ways—into her brain.

And while the children squealed intermittently, laughed a lot, bickered about who could do more work in twenty minutes, and even broke into a wrestling match or two, the dinner remained somehow calm, the noise being absorbed into the big sky, the air whisking it away, creating a calm and peace that Jeanie was positive could not exist anywhere else in the world.

Each woman, with the exception of Lutie, made several pies to share for dessert. Lutie, did however manage to work milk into cream and by some feat of God or whomever, she created a whipped delicacy that nearly disappeared in their mouths before realizing it was even there, making every person partaking in the feast to gorge him or herself, the pies acting as vehicles for the otherworldly cream.

By the time dessert was finished and everyone had agreed to coffee, the kids had gone to play and Greta seemed irritable, angry that Anna wouldn't stay by her side, that she wanted to play with the others as she always had before Anzhela's death. Clearly Greta's lighter moments from earlier that day had passed and she could no longer shake Anzhela's ghost.

Every once in a while, Greta would wince as though in pain. After removing her own plate, Greta stood at the doorway to the kitchen. Jeanie gathered her plate and Frank's and joined Greta in the doorway. Greta stared into the space where everyone sat.

"Are you all right?" Jeanie asked.

Greta closed her eyes.

"It must be so hard for you." Jeanie said. *I couldn't go on*, Jeanie thought. *I would be of no use to anyone if I were you.*

Greta didn't respond, but began to sort the dishes and scrape the scraps into a slop bowl.

"Greta, I'm your friend. You can share your sadness with me. I'm amazed at how you're doing, managing it all with what must be impossible pain."

"I'm simply not sleeping enough. That's when grief comes for me most." Greta's voice was nearly inaudible, but she dug at the plate so hard with the spatula that both flew from her hands, hitting into the wall, splattering gravy and grease into blob-like designs.

Jeanie looked toward the door. Ruthie stood there watching both of them.

"Oh, my hands are so greasy," Jeanie said, "the plate just flew from my grip like a pig from…well, not that I've ever handled a greasy pig myself, but I'm sure—"

Jeanie heard a pop that sounded as if it came from far away and seconds later a gush of water hit the ground under her skirts. She lifted her dress to be sure.

"Well, Jeanie Arthur, don't tell me you've lost your bladder, you're not that old," Lutie said coming up behind her.

"No, you fool," Ruthie said, "her water broke. And early. This baby will not last the night."

Jeanie's consciousness heard Ruthie's words but she wasn't able to fully grasp what she meant or why Ruthie's tone would be so harsh when in the past, Ruthie had been only kind.

Jeanie wrapped one arm around her belly and folded over. Greta supported her, moving her toward the bedstead.

"This is too early. I'm only…I think…maybe I'm off…I think, this baby is too early…maybe I'm wrong."

"Shh, shh, shh," Greta smoothed Jeanie's hair back then settled two pillows under her back. "It's all right. Just let it happen. It's possible it will stop. This same thing happened with Anzhela, then she waited three more months. A little water doesn't mean the baby's coming for sure. Let me have a look."

Frank rushed into the room as Greta was lifting Jeanie's skirts and Jeanie reached out to him, unable to speak. She saw him tapping his leg, nervous, before he ducked his head, recoiling out the door. Jeanie couldn't speak. She didn't have time to consider Frank's weakness.

Greta was wrong. Jeanie may not have emptied all her water, but she was contracting, the cramps quickly progressing to purposeful, cascades of pain that meant nothing but Jeanie's baby was on the way. She tried not to be afraid, to fear the loss of her baby. She'd never gone this far in a pregnancy and then delivered still born. If this baby was coming, Jeanie was sure it would be alive and sure it would be healthy.

James stuck his head in the door. Luckily Jeanie was between contractions, and her skirts were lowered.

"James, honey, I'm fine. Go on, take care of everyone. I'm fine."

"Sure? I can help. I know I can."

"I'm sure, baby, go on, the others will need you." Jeanie doubled over into a contraction, vomiting her pheasant dinner onto the floor. Greta ran to Jeanie, propping her up so she wouldn't choke. James ran to the stove where he took a cloth from a shelf.

"Here, I'll clean that up, Mama." Jeanie wretched again, with mostly clear liquid coming up after the last heave. She watched James clean up her vomit. When he'd gotten most of it by way of the cloth, he looked at his mother and wiped sweat from her hairline with the back of his hand. "I'll get some water and a fresh cloth. See, if we were in our little dugout, all I'd have to do is take a shovel and carry the soiled part of the floor away. Clean, licketysplit, good as new."

Jeanie chortled. "Well, I guess our definition of clean has changed a bit, hasn't it?"

James kissed his mother's forehead and left the house, shouting for Frank to fetch some water. He stuck his head back in the door. "Don't worry Mama, the baby will be fine. She's strong like you, I can feel it."

"She?"

"I know it's a girl, you'll see."

Jeanie squinted at him then fell back onto the mattress. They'd been so overwhelmed with the move, settling in, suffering the constant breaking of disastrous environmental waves over their community that the Arthurs had scarcely spoken of the baby inside Jeanie. She'd barely thought of it herself. Yet, in the moments since her contractions began, Jeanie couldn't have felt closer to the baby or sadder at the possibility of it not living. She needed that baby, someone to care for, to need her.

Another wave of contractions came, then another on top of it and before long, she was bearing down to push. She pushed so hard that the baby flew out of her, landing in between her legs, shocking both Jeanie and Greta. But the crash of the landing made the baby begin to wail immediately.

"It's a girl," Greta said. She handed the baby to Jeanie. "Let me get the scissors."

"A girl?" Jeanie watched the baby's face curl into any number of angry faces, crying so hard that Jeanie was afraid she'd cut off her own airway. She cooed at the baby, pulling the bed covers over top of them both. She was so small, legs twig-like, skin transparent, sounding more animal than child. This baby was definitely early, at least two months, yet she was mighty and seeing the baby fight, angered by her rude entrance into the world, reassured Jeanie.

Jeanie leaned forward, looking past her knees to Greta.

"What's wrong?" Pain shot through her belly. Greta looked up from between Jeanie's legs, eyes wide, and though Jeanie could feel her lips moving, she knew she was forming words, she couldn't hear her words leaving her mouth. Jeanie thought she was begging for Greta to help her, but Greta faded to an outline of a person and then darkness shut over Jeanie's consciousness, blacking out her world.

Jeanie woke and the room was moody with candles from the Thanksgiving table flickering from various spots in Templeton's house. Jeanie shot up in the bed. Her hand flew to her stomach to find it remarkably flat.

"Greta? My baby? I need to hold her. My head's foggy, what did you give me?"

Greta sat in the chair next to Jeanie, still as stone. "It's early hours of the day after Thanksgiving. Three a.m., around about, I imagine."

Jeanie looked around the room. "Where's my baby?"

"She's over there in the cradle. We've wrapped her tight. There's just a matter of time, now."

Jeanie felt Greta's words settle into her skin, chilling her. Jeanie would not allow her daughter to die simply because she was born too early. "Bring her to me," Jeanie said.

Greta held her position.

"Get her," Jeanie said.

Greta rose slowly and plodded to the center of the room where the baby had been nestled into a wooden box near the stove, to keep warm.

Greta turned with the baby in her arms. In the darkness, her clear-blue eyes were bathed in wetness and silent tears saturated her entire face as though Jeanie were supplying the sobs and Greta the tears.

Greta sat on the bed beside Jeanie, settling the baby into Jeanie's body. Jeanie stilled.

Greta stood and slid back onto the wood chair beside the lounge where Jeanie lay, examining her miniature baby. In Jeanie's mind, she calculated her weight, the size of a healthy hen. Three pounds or so. Her perfectly formed face, legs with no fat to speak of, each blue vein visible. Jeanie traced them, causing the infant to flinch. The cold air from being uncovered wakened her. She nearly growled at Jeanie, squalling like a bird of prey, angry to have been roused.

237

Jeanie smiled down on her. Good, be mad. And live. Better to live, fueled by anger, than to not live at all. Jeanie shifted the blankets to the side and put the baby to her breast. She sucked for a moment then her eyes flew open and she stopped as though choking.

"Well, you *are* a fighter. An early bird. A woman with a plan," Jeanie said. "You'll fit in just fine."

Jeanie wrapped her back up knowing that it could take a day for her milk to come in, that the baby would be fine. She looked up at Greta whose brow was wrinkled, more so than usual.

"Don't doubt her, Greta. She's going to live. I know it might sound crazy but she will."

"I didn't say anything about crazy," Greta said. She rocked back and forth.

"I'll make her live. I can do that, you know. I am that strong. I have enough will for both of us, all of us."

Greta nodded then looked into her lap.

Jeanie knew it wasn't fair to say things like that, to somehow imply that Greta hadn't been in the position of forcing her child to live.

"I'm sorry. I just need, this baby has to—"

Greta put the palm of her hand over Jeanie's forehead, then the back of her hand. "Shhh, now you just rest. You've been fitful, you should rest, that's your only concern."

Jeanie nodded, feeling fevered. "I know. But I can't lose one, Greta. I'm strong, I believe I can make my children live, but I know *I* can't live without one of them. That much I know." Jeanie kicked off her covers, drenched in sweat.

Greta nodded and went to the stove. There, she took several rocks that she had warmed over the cook-stove and wrapped them in a woolen blanket. She tucked the blanketed rocks beside the baby.

"Here, for when the sweats force you to throw the blankets, the rocks should keep her body temperature stable. And you'll need some laudanum for just one night, for the pain," Greta added.

Jeanie hesitated, then nodded. She knew she would have to, as she had with her other births.

"Just half the dose. I don't want to sleep for long. Just enough to get my strength back."

Her teeth chattered. Greta gave her the medicine. She wiped Jeanie's brow and smiled down on her as Jeanie imagined she must have done so lovingly to all her children. And that was the final image Jeanie saw before falling into a deep sleep, grateful to her bones that she had met Greta Zurchenko.

Jeanie awoke to sunlight bathing her so fully she was sweating from its directness. Where was she? She jerked up to her elbow then fell back on the bedstead, dizzy. She was still tucked inside Templeton's home. She looked down to see she was wearing her nightgown. Frank must have gone for it at some point. The baby! The thought startled her. She realized only then that her daughter had been nestled beside her, under the nightgown, against her skin.

One breath caught on the next as Jeanie skinned the blanket off by kicking her feet. She wrestled with the buttons of her nightgown and she felt lightheaded, fearing she would find her baby stiff having had her last breath stolen by the very nest Greta thought might have helped with the baby's body temperature.

Jeanie gripped the baby under her arms, her body so small Jeanie's fingers knitted together across her back. "Breathe, breathe," she said. The baby was warm and pliable, though Jeanie could see no visible signs she was inhaling. Her egg-shaped head, bowed slightly at her neck, bore none of its weight no matter how small, her face as tranquil as a mother could want her baby to be. Jeanie held her face to her ear to hear her breathe. Nothing. Jeanie's staccato panting was all she could hear. She laid the baby across her legs and as still as wood, she sat, waiting to see a tiny rise in her chest.

And there it was, a small rise in the chest and an accompanying wail.

"Is that what *I* sounded like, Mama?" Katherine came into the room, watching the series of events that led to the baby's bellowing.

Jeanie felt her breasts tighten, fill with pain, making her want to feed the baby. She would try again. She settled her onto her breast and she took a few sucks before choking and turning from Jeanie with an expression of pure piss and salt and the angst of a cantankerous old man.

"You sounded much different," Jeanie said. She smiled at Katherine while shushing the baby and rubbing her back. "This little girl wasn't quite ready to be born. I suspect her insides aren't fully grown or she wouldn't sound so funny, like a puppy that lost its mother."

Katherine nodded at her mother but didn't go closer to her.

"Could you get me the cleanest cup you can find, Katherine? We're going to have to be creative because it appears something's not right with her eating from the breast."

Katherine rocked on her feet as though about to follow her mother's directions then she stopped.

"Katherine?" Jeanie said.

"Father and Ruthie and everyone, really, said we're to just make the baby as comfortable as possible. That there's no way a girl born, they suspect, two months early could survive such an inauspicious start. There's simply no way."

Jeanie rolled those words in her mind, waited for anger to swell because of them, but all she felt was calm certainty, like she had when the children survived the fire. Sometimes a mother just knows.

Jeanie jerked her head toward the kitchen. "You go on and bring me that clean cup. It has to be absolutely clean so there's no chance of passing infection, and bring it to me and you'll sit with me and learn to care for your sister because I'm going to need your help and as sure as I'd enlist an army to ensure your health, we'll do the same for your sister. She won't die, you needn't worry. There'll be no dying here, we're not dying people."

Katherine's lips split into a quick smile then she darted into the kitchen and came back with a stack of tin cups. "Here, Mr. Templeton bought these in Yankton. He didn't need to use them yesterday, they're brand new, but I rinsed this one to be extra sure. They're pristine, Mama, in the prairie sense, anyway. He asks about you every fifteen minutes or so. He and James take turns reporting to Father." Katherine handed Jeanie the cleanest looking one.

"Now, that's my girl," Jeanie said, wrapping the baby in a blanket. When the infant was curled inside the bundle, Jeanie held her up toward Katherine.

"Hold your sister. I need to expel some milk into this cup and we'll feed her. What *should* we call her? We'll drip the milk into her mouth with our fingers. When I was a girl there was a piglet, a teeny bugger, and Mr. Samuels fed that creature with his finger, dripping the milk from his finger right into the piglet's mouth. I think that's exactly what we'll do with this one. What *should* we call her?"

Katherine recoiled at the sight of her mother squeezing her breast like a cow's udder then she patted her sister's head, smoothing the thin hair back from her forehead like Jeanie would have done.

"Mama?"

Jeanie yanked at her breast. "Yes, dear Katherine."

"Last night, while you were tossing, pained, under the laudanum, you said your life was a pie—"

"A pie!"

"Yes, you said the pie was cut so that merely a sliver, a hair's breath contained joy and contentment, that the rest of it was utterly awful. No part of the pie offered any sort of thing you wanted in your belly."

Jeanie squinted. "That's gibberish, Katherine. Don't tell me you're worried."

"It's just so different than anything I'd ever heard you say, you don't look for trouble. You see good in all things, solutions to all problems, yet in the midst of your delirium, you sounded so articulate, with this metaphor, as though you'd contemplated it before."

Jeanie looked at the ceiling, trying to remember, knowing she could have very well said those things, because she had felt that her life had shifted to represent those exact proportions of happiness and displeasure. Jeanie shook her head, not wanting to show her daughter weakness, to allow anything but positive thoughts into her daughter's mind, because although Jeanie was suffering from a sudden shift of mind-set, she didn't want her daughter feeling the same.

"Katherine, a pie? That's too utterly, utter. Really, that's juvenile even for a lowly writer of everything domestic, wouldn't you say? I was pained, crazy with fear. This baby will live and we will live, together, full of pleasures and hopes and happiness. Even if things are hard for a while. We will live and we will live together."

"Well, you did start talking about dreaming that Father had no face, that you couldn't see him even though he was standing right there. I suppose that is as fantastical as anything." Katherine broke into a smile and lay down beside her mother.

"See that, dreams, delirium, none of it means anything in the real world."

Jeanie reveled in the warmth of Katherine's body, her sweet demeanor.

"Oh, *galoshes*. I worried myself for nothing."

Katherine and Jeanie sighed at the same time in the same way, both satisfied that the other was okay, that the world had reset itself in their eyes, that they could push on.

"I feel better, Mama. Thank you."

Jeanie did, too. She studied her daughter, smoothing her light hair back from her face. Yes, Katherine's expression had relaxed and her shoulders released the tension she had clearly been holding. Jeanie savored the moment, Katherine laying on her side, molded into her body, while she dripped milk into the baby's mouth, hoping if the infant couldn't swallow correctly, that at least her throat would allow the milk to dribble into her belly without choking her to death in the process.

And so, the next month went. The baby girl was named Yale by her siblings who researched names in literature, the Bible, and by polling every person who walked into and through Darlington Township. They chose Yale because the original Yale in Greek mythology possessed remarkable strength that surprised all who said he was weak.

She wasn't an easy baby, as Yale seemed to carry her strength into every area of her being. She did not give in easily to sleep, or happiness or anything that would be pleasing for other infants. She seemed to be miserable, as though an adult stuffed into a small skin with all sorts of ideas to tell and plans to enact but without any means to express them except for conveying her disgust with being in that very position.

But, for Jeanie, it didn't matter. This miracle allowed her to funnel every bit of energy into her, knowing it would result in something good and great.

Frank was slow to warm to Yale. And that hurt Jeanie for a time, remembering the way they used to playfully fight over who would do what for which child. Jeanie smiled at the image of Frank changing a diaper, with his face reflecting the mutual joy he and the children took in one another's presence. He never generated or reflected that emotion with Yale. That thought would trip Jeanie up, causing her to stop whatever she was doing and be grateful that she was the only living person who knew Frank's behavior had transformed. For all the children knew, this was exactly how Frank had been with them.

Templeton had been kind enough to share his home with the Arthurs as they weren't prepared to move Jeanie and the baby to the dugout until they were sure Jeanie was recovered from the birth. The days in Templeton's house were emotionally warm even when it physically was cold. James enjoyed Templeton's continuous companionship as they challenged one another in predicting the weather and they even went so far as to feel out a spot—near the bee tree where they claimed the best indications of weather could be garnered.

Frank enjoyed the month at Templeton's because he could putz with his woodwork—creating useless though beautiful, intricate designs and then disappear to contemplate the beauties of nature for half the day. And Jeanie, in the swell of new motherhood, felt no interest toward Templeton beyond simple gratitude that he allowed them to stay on.

Katherine and Tommy enjoyed the use of Templeton's horse so each could have their own to visit friends, even getting caught at the Zurchenko's for six days when a snow storm blew through while they were warming up there after a ride.

Templeton and Frank had waited out the initial snowfall then made their way across the plain, plowing through the snow in order to discern the safety of the children. James fed the fire while Jeanie fed Yale, and in their silence, both were alone with their thoughts, sharing gentle laughs and stories of the past or reading books that the children had brought from home.

Every once in a while Jeanie would start at the thought that she wasn't worried about Katherine and Tommy, that again she felt in her soul they were okay, that there was no way they weren't. She wondered once for five minutes what this said about her. Did she really know in her bones that her children were safe or had she merely accepted that some day on that prairie one of them wouldn't be? No, no, that definitely wasn't right. She was not Greta, she could not mourn for a day and carry on as though a life stomped out was meant to be. She shook her head at herself.

"Mama?" James said squatting near the fire.

"I'm fine. Everything is fine, sweet James."

James squinted at her and stood. "I've got to twist the hanks and I'm going to try to follow Father's path, see if there are any buffalo chips there. I won't go far, but we can't let the fire go too low."

"Are we out of cow chips and wood? Those hanks burn so fast they're not always worth using." Jeanie rocked the baby who had, after two hours of angry thrashing and screeching, finally dropped off to sleep.

James pulled on his boots, coat, overpants, and hat. "That's all we have until the snow breaks a bit."

"Be safe, my darling. I can't have you not here," Jeanie said.

"Are you talking to me or Yale, Mama?" James grinned.

Jeanie looked up from the baby. "I suppose I'm talking to you both."

"Nothing will happen to me, Mama. That much I do know." James knelt in front of Jeanie and snuggled his cheek against Yale's. Jeanie inhaled the scent of both of them. Her babies.

James rose and strode across the floor, his swagger having transformed from boy to man at some point on the prairie. This was a person who could take care of himself. Someday Jeanie would have to let him go, let him marry, start his own home, but she didn't need to think of that.

James yanked open the door and snow blew in, giving the wind eerie shape and weight. James raised his hand above his head in a wave goodbye, but didn't look back to see Jeanie return it.

Jeanie nodded as the chill rushed through the room, over her skin, and she noticed her hairline was drenched. James finally got the door shut and snapped off the howling wind as though it never existed.

"I love you James. Keep safe, my son." Jeanie said to the door, to herself more than anything.

Chapter 15

1905
Des Moines, Iowa

"**K**atherine." Aleksey shook his wife's shoulder. "It's nearly six o'clock. Come down. I've made dinner."

Katherine's dry eyes burned as she rubbed them, her nose stuffed with old tears gave her voice a nasal quality. "Oh, my. I'm so sorry. Almost dinner? Tell me you're teasing."

"Don't worry." Aleksey started making new piles of the scattered letters. "I've made sandwiches and the boys made potato salad."

Katherine covered her mouth laughing out loud at the thought. "No, please, tell me you're not serious."

"I am very serious. And, everyone is requesting the pleasure of your company." Aleksey dusted off his hands, slapping them together. He pulled Katherine to her feet and wiped the back of her dress, pulling her body into his. Katherine curled into his embrace, her head nestled against his warm chest, his presence forever calming, loving and permanent.

"Why don't you ask what I'm doing?" Katherine said.

"I know what you're doing."

"What?"

"Giving your past a funeral."

Katherine sucked in her breath. "That's ghoulish."

"Sometimes the truth is."

Katherine took Aleksey's hand and studied it, the lines she memorized long ago.

"My mother was delirious, asking for Yale, saying she'd lost her, put her somewhere or something. But, until the other night she never let Yale out of her sight, ever. I don't know what she's talking about."

"It's probably nothing." Aleksey started toward the steps, pulling Katherine's hand.

Katherine looked back at the letters. One, in a dark envelope, the only one not pale yellow or creamy white, caught her eye. "Let me get that one." Katherine picked it up and turned it over in her hand. It was addressed to Ruthie Moore.

"The sisters Moore. Remember them? They were so...the letter's from Texas. Why would we have a letter written to her from someone in Texas? Just days before..."

Katherine didn't have a chance to complete her thought or words as their son, Asher, flew up the attic stairs bearing news of a bloody sibling who was most definitely in need of stitches.

Katherine tossed the letter back on the floor relieved she wouldn't have to read it until she was fully ready to absorb all it had to say.

Chapter 16

1887
Dakota Territory

Christmas came and went with sparse decoration, gift and commotion. But Jeanie and her family hadn't felt as though those things were missing. To have had the dugout burst with crimson wrapped boxes, pine dripping from every surface, and the constant flow of exquisitely dressed gifts would have felt obscene on the prairie after the demise of their crops.

Six months before, Jeanie would have thought it were a disgrace not to somehow work all those brilliant holiday elements into their prairie Christmas, or recreate them symbolically. But, instead, the Arthurs celebrated under three feet of snow. Inside their dugout wearing their ugliest clothing, they reenacted the scene with the three wise men at Bethlehem and in between the time the one bearing myrrh (Jeanie) and one bearing Frankincense (Tommy) came on scene, baby Jesus (Yale, of course) had to have her dirty pants tended to three times. This actually gave Jeanie great feelings of joy as for the first few weeks of Yale's life, she didn't make much water and barely expelled any solid waste at all.

The little things thrilled Jeanie at that point—the rock candy she'd made after Templeton surprised them with sugar from Yankton, stringing popcorn with the children while singing carols. In those moments, she felt contentment and optimism that all that had gone wrong had merely been a dream, like the one she always had of Frank where she couldn't see his face.

Christmas had renewed Jeanie's determination to meet the spring thaw with her entire family intact, but to do so happily, warmly, with hope shading every contented moment—the kind that would allow their later years to be filled with fond memories of their first year on the prairie. She wouldn't let the base elements of such an existence be what she remembered, not without the conquest of such nothingness being attached to the memories.

Once the wise men fulfilled their obligations and baby Jesus began to squawk for the food she didn't seem to really want and the sleep she always seemed to push away, it was time to do the afternoon chores. After dinner they would settle in to enjoy their gifts.

As he always did, James would open the door and determine the degree of bite in the frigid air, determining whether Katherine and Tommy were too young or just old enough to help with a given series of chores at a given time of day and the corresponding coldness. Frank was remarkably cheered during this time as though his lack of choices in activity—he couldn't light out over the prairie to do who knew what when the snow tumbled from the sky as though God were standing above, shaking it down himself. Frank was a lot of things, but ready to risk his life wasn't one of them.

And in his capture, he seemed happier than he'd been in months. Seeing Frank jailed nearly gave Jeanie the opportunity to feel pity instead of resentment for him. It became clear in her mind that his dreams, the way his mind worked, was actually a burden. That, having a narrow vision of the world, like Nikolai Zurchenko, might be an easier brain to have to house.

A narrow man's thoughts would never travel to exotic, alluring locales, betraying the body that had no means to travel even a mile for whatever the reason. And in that dugout, watching Frank yank on each piece of outerwear, she deemed him a frustrated genius who needed but the opportunity to add the real-life lathe and plaster to his air castles. And Jeanie would be there to help him do so. She knew she could achieve her goals—to create gowns so ethereal the wearer had to stop herself from taking a bite of it to be sure it wasn't made of sugar and flour—and to create an existence on the prairie that spoke of larger ideas and a life filled with joy, not duties and manners that did nothing but frustrate and separate.

James read the thermometer that Templeton gave him as an early Christmas gift. Negative four degrees.

"Well, with the way the wind is blowing, I suspect it feels like twenty below out there, so I think it's best Katherine and Tommy tend to duties inside the house, Mama," James said. "Father and I will empty the chamber and slop pots, feed the livestock, and bring in the last of the buffalo chips and finished hanks."

By the time James and Frank blew back into the dugout, their faces were frozen. It took a moment for Jeanie to grasp just how cold it had been outside. James burst through the door first, with an armload of hay for Katherine and Tommy to tie hanks to burn. Frank came behind him, arms piled high with chips that would need to dry a bit before burning.

Jeanie checked the water on the stove for coffee and when she didn't hear laughter or conversation she turned and saw just how stiff the two Arthurs were. She and the twins helped peel off clothes, then decided to pull them back on to hold in any heat there was inside them. Frank and James's faces were gleaming white as they'd never seen. They couldn't even open their mouths to form words. Jeanie grabbed some snow from outside the door and she and Katherine rubbed it on their faces to ensure minimal damage.

The rubbing with snow erased the whiteness, but the image of red streaks where their faces weren't frozen created a ghoulish picture more fitting Halloween than Christmas.

"Get the kerosene," Jeanie said.

Tommy brought the lamp to her.

She pushed away her emotions spiking from the sight of dark red streaks alongside deathlike pallor, the skin as hard as wood. Jeanie laid kerosene-drenched rags over their faces as she'd seen done countless times when a person was exposed to the cold for too long.

The smell of the oil caught in their noses and throats and choked them. Tommy opened the door from time to time to let a whip of fresh air into the dugout. Once they were sure the kerosene had done its work, Frank and James inched toward the fire as to sit in front of it before they'd thawed enough, brought on scorching pain as though fire were burning from underneath the skin rather than happily bouncing in the belly of the stove across the room.

Finally James and Frank, returned to less severe condition, were shivering in front of the fire—a sign they would be fine. Jeanie collapsed into her chair, her arms flopped over the sides, body wanting to shut off and sleep. But, the gurgles then wails of Yale told her there was a different plan in store and instead of her body resting, her mind did as she breastfed the baby. Right there in the dugout was everything she could ever need or want and that was, for her, the meaning of Christmas.

When Jeanie woke to feed Yale on the morning of January 12, she knew something was different. She used the chamber pot and latched Yale onto her breast but was drawn to the front door. She knew better than to open it before James had gone to get the morning buffalo chips, to let the warmth escape, but she opened it anyway, and in from the outside sailed the most surprising warmth, like a blanket it fell over her.

Frank came up behind her and patted Yale's head over Jeanie's shoulder. The sky was still black, peppered with starlight.

"That's amazing," Frank said. "I think we're in the midst of a winter thaw. I feel like my head is opening up and my body is coming alive."

"Just like that," Jeanie said. She looked at Frank, waiting for a surge of anger to hit her, but all she felt was indifference. As long as she didn't think of Templeton or remember the way she used to feel about Frank, she thought she could handle forty more years of indifference. At least it was even-keeled. She watched Frank poke around the bowl that held the leftover sugar Templeton had brought and she nearly leapt toward him when she thought he had hidden opium in there. She'd been watching him, never seeing him eat opium, or drink laudanum. But, he hadn't gone through withdrawal, shown any signs that he was either on the drug or off of it. Maybe she had overreacted, maybe he hadn't been lying, perhaps the prairie and all its drama had gotten the best of her. She shook her head at herself, she'd never been so incapable.

"Like a miracle," Frank said.

"Hmm?" Jeanie said.

"The weather."

"Well, I wouldn't be inclined to call five minutes of new air a warming trend, but I have to agree, it does feel good. Trouble is, we're going to have to deal with the roof of the dugout thawing. I'm afraid we might be drowning in slush by late evening. Do you think you could clear the snow off the roof after the chores?"

Frank didn't respond, but his body still pressed up against Jeanie's. She turned to see his face.

"Frank? Could you do that? You have to or we'll be staying at Templeton's for the rest of the winter while everything we own is molding and disintegrating. Maybe we should move our books over there no matter the weather. But then what would we do in the evenings? No, we'll make the best of it."

Frank still gazed over the top of Jeanie's head, his eyes shifting every once in a while as though he were reading the sky, as though it offered him wisdom and a plan. "I'm thinking today would be a good one to finish that bedstead over at Templeton's. The one Smith from Yankton paid me for before the fire. He's been plenty patient and I have to bet he'd want to see it at first sight of spring."

"So, that means what?"

"Well, it means what I said," Frank said. He kissed Jeanie's forehead and disappeared into the darkness where the black sky was tinged with hints of navy blue, the sign of what would definitely be a beautiful day.

"I'll do it, Mama," James said.

Jeanie jumped. "James, I didn't know you were awake."

"How could I sleep when the earth shattering plans of Frank Arthur are being dispersed into the atmosphere."

"James, why would you talk about your Father that way, with that tone? He is who he is and I trust his mind, his plans, that he will rise to create the world for us he says he will. He's simply creative and—"

"Mama, stop. Stop. I understand we have to plow the land we've decided to settle, but we don't have to look at its infertility and claim it rich and productive, do we?"

"Sometimes barren land is just resting and its next turn will yield what we expected all along. But leaving the land, in any way, cursing it will yield nothing in the end except for bitter memories of what didn't work out. We make things work out, James. We are intractable, prolific people who find a way to ferret success out of failure and for us there's no other choice."

James shook his head and yanked on his boots, clearly having something to say, but holding it inside either out of respect for his mother or out of kindness. "Don't send Tommy and Katherine to Ruthie's for lessons."

"Well if the weather is this mild, they should go," Jeanie said. "They have the final round of that spelling bee to contend with and if I have to hear the second half of the dictionary one more time..."

"Mama, please. I know it doesn't make sense, but I've learned a lot with Mr. Templeton about the indications. Katherine and Tommy can help me with the morning chores and then I'll head to Templeton's to discuss the weather indications. I'll send Father back to help with the roof and we should go to the well. We should take advantage of this weather because unlike my father, I don't see this as a warming trend, but rather a teaser, a lure of sorts that if taken too lightly will end in disaster."

"What are you talking about, James?"

"Nothing, everything will be fine, I just don't think we should view this as the end of winter. And I think for today Katherine and Tommy should stay close. If I'm wrong then tomorrow they can go to Ruthie's and you can say you told me so. But, it couldn't be, statistically speaking, that winter's over. And this pleasing, dead air, hot, and thick compared to yesterday, it portends something other than tranquility."

Jeanie switched Yale to her other breast and waved James over to her. "Okay. I love you James, but I don't want you old beyond your years. You can trust your father to handle things. He won't hurt us or let us see harm. As hard as it is to understand his dreams and hopes and dispiritedness, he is...well, I know you're growing up, James, that you see things, but remember, things aren't always so simple. He simply isn't capable of certain things and I've come to expect that and therefore can stomach it."

"I sure hope I find a woman to love me past all my shortcomings, someday, Mama."

"Well, let's not sell you to the highest bidder yet," Jeanie cupped James' cheek and he looked at her. With his hat covering his forehead to his eyebrows, he looked every bit like the infant that Yale did. Jeanie moved her thumb over the scar that had formed from frostbite on his cheek. Just a half an inch long or so, but still there, a reminder of the harsh conditions under which they lived.

"Do you know what weather is, Mama?"

"The temperature, moisture?"

"It's simply the atmosphere trying to balance itself out, but it swings one direction—harsh and stunning in its form and then it tries to right itself and swings too far the other way. It's never-ending. And sometimes I feel like this is the way we live with Father. We're forever, *you* are forever trying to bring to center his disparate thoughts and ideas—"

"Shshshsh, my James." Jeanie slid her hand around the back of James' head and pulled him into her, his head on her shoulder above Yale's. "You worry too much."

"I just have a bad feeling. I had it since last night, like the air was shifting, and I woke up this morning and it had. I just think today isn't what it seems."

"We'll take care and we'll be fine," Jeanie said. "I'll start the roof when Yale goes to sleep. I'd like the benefit of that fresh warm air, myself."

"Okay. I won't stay at Templeton's more than a few minutes."

"You deserve a half an hour doing something you enjoy. And don't worry about your father so much."

"Don't let Katherine and Tommy wander too far today."

"Okay, okay, gramps, you head on out or you won't enjoy two seconds of this gentle weather."

James cocked his head to the side and squinted at Jeanie. He looked away and then nodded before heading into what was now blazing sunlight. He propped open the door without Jeanie having to ask him to and he walked away, toward the well, in a straight line from the doorway. Jeanie could see him shrink to a black dot, wondering what he was thinking of, wishing he hadn't taken on grown-up worries at such a young age.

Around nine a.m. Jeanie tucked Yale into her cradle, swiped her nose and pulled on her coat and hat. She stepped outside and began to sweat within three strides around the side of the dugout. She went back to the dugout, dropped her coat down her arms and laid it across the chair where she spent so much of her daily life since November.

Suddenly curious at the temperature, she stopped outside the door to peer at the thermometer. Twenty-three degrees. A full forty warmer than it had been the day before. In her mind she knew twenty-three wasn't warm, but her body disagreed as it took to the southern warm wind like a sunny summer day. She hadn't realized the degree of lift she would get from being outside, enjoying a lull in the cold. It didn't matter that most likely the next day would be much colder, that the Arthurs would be holed up like prairie dogs again, their senses having to readjust to limited visual stimuli and stiff odors.

Tommy and Katherine were busy clearing the snow from above the dugout. They took turns, one using a makeshift shovel and the other using their feet to push it away. Jeanie wrapped them both in her arms, nuzzling their faces with kisses.

"Mama, this weather is stupendous, don't you think? And when James said we didn't have to go to lessons today, I thought that was simply a gift. I think I'm going to draw and write and study today, right here in front of the dugout." Katherine bounced, her cheeks lit red, mouth wide with a smile as though the change in wind had brought good cheer on its back rather than just a change in temperature.

"I'm going to the Zurchenko's," Tommy said. "Aleksey said I could fire his gun and I'll bring back some melons or a pumpkin."

"No Tommy. Don't go there. Going there for work is one thing, but I want you close by today, not shooting guns and taking food we don't need."

Tommy dug his shovel into the ground with a grunt.

"Close by, why? Because know-it-all James said so? He's not my father."

Jeanie took his face in her hands and pecked his forehead. She understood his need to wander. He wasn't like James, intellectual as much as he was gifted in more physical ways, like a Zurchenko might be.

"Well, maybe," Jeanie said, "I'll prepare some cakes and grind some coffee—real coffee—for you to offer Mr. and Mrs. Zurchenko. But don't stay long. I don't trust this weather. And, there are some matters about which your brother holds considerable knowledge."

Tommy grinned and stepped away from Jeanie. "Yes, well, I'm not sure anyone has any knowledge regarding the weather before it's upon him. The Lord shall keep us all, Mama." He dug into the snow double time, humming Marie Antoinette's song, upbeat. "Where's Father's violin. I feel the mighty Lord calling me to pluck a tune on his behalf. I can only surmise he'd enjoy a turn or two around Marie Antoinette's song."

Jeanie drew back at Tommy's reference but decided that wasn't the time to wonder about God. "I guess none of us will ever get that song out of our heads, will we? Not even sweet Jesus himself." Jeanie said.

"I don't ever want to Mama. That song lives in me." Katherine said. "I'll help you milk the cow if you'd like. Then if you'll allow it, I'd like to do some of that painting—I don't want to miss the light."

"I agree. Let's get the cow handled and then you're free to get some air and create some art. I miss seeing you do that, seeing you find joy in the environment."

Jeanie and Katherine were trudging toward the horses when animal-like squalling made them turn northwest. Coming over the land were the Zurchenko's horses attached to the wagon, bearing down like a train.

"What is she *doing*?" Katherine said. She grabbed Jeanie's hand and moved into her side. Jeanie squeezed her tight.

"Oh, my, oh my. I've never seen anything like that," Jeanie said.

Tommy stopped shoveling and after staring at the oncoming wagon he dove off the top of the dugout, out of the way in time for the horses to turn sharply left, saving themselves from falling over the edge of the dugout. The wagon spun around, the back right wheel nearly dangling off the edge.

Jeanie raced to the wagon. There, buckled over in the front seat, reigns tangled in her hands and draped up her forearms was Greta. Naked. Or nearly so. Her skin shouted wildly as its ruddy flush tore off the mask of this faux warm day. It may have been forty degrees warmer than the day before, but it was still only in the high twenties. Greta had stripped down to scant underthings, even her bloomers had been tossed aside before or during perhaps, her tear across the land.

"Get my coat Katherine, check to make sure Tommy is all right."

Jeanie bounded to the wagon and climbed into it, her breath catching at the sight of Greta's eyes, bloodshot, her hair braided but out of its bun. Her skin shivered on her bones as though no connective tissue joined the two systems. Jeanie smoothed her hair back from her face.

"Greta, Greta, what, oh how can I, oh Greta, What's wrong? Where are your clothes?" Jeanie said. She scrunched in beside Greta and pulled her upper body onto her lap.

"Anzhela. I can't...I'm looking for her. She has to be here. I hear her calling to me. She needs her Ma, that's what she says every time." Greta grasped the sides of her head as though trying to keep voices or objects from entering her ears.

Jeanie rocked her. Every time she opened her mouth to say something that might be remotely reassuring she shut it because she knew there was nothing to say to salve the wounds caused by a lost child.

"I've been looking. The first break in the weather. Not one day let up snow until today and this weather bestowed upon us told me to take every corner of our cooperative's property searching for Anzhela. I just know she's burrowed into a drift and is just waiting for me, my arrival. Children don't give up hope for their parents. I can *hear* her, Jeanie."

Jeanie closed her grip around Greta, trying to cradle her, to give her the comfort she wanted for Anzhela but would never be able to give. They'd buried Anzhela. Greta had lost her senses and no talk of facts would be comforting, Jeanie could see.

"Greta, why didn't you send word? I didn't realize. You're so stalwart, so strong, I knew I'd be incapacitated, but you seemed... your clothes, where are your clothes?"

Greta moaned into Jeanie's body, slobbering as she sobbed for what Jeanie thought was the first time. Jeanie had heard of people lost in the cold, disrobing just before dying as their bodies tricked them into thinking they're hot instead of nearly iced to the bone.

Maybe that's what's happening to Greta. But she wasn't that cold. Could grief have done this? Knowing there was no way to comfort Greta or elicit a response, Jeanie dug around the wagon, under a blanket, for signs of Greta's clothing. She yanked the wool blanket up and drew it around her throat, tucking it around her legs.

Jeanie rocked Greta and hummed to her as though a baby. Feelings of grief swept through Jeanie, as though they were leaching from Greta's heart into her own. But, Jeanie pushed them away. The surge of pain frightened her and she didn't have to feel those feelings and it wouldn't help for both of them to puddle to tears. She'd find a way to help Greta. There must be some way to help her find comfort.

Tommy huffed to the top of the wagon and held the coat up in triumph.

They stuffed Greta into it, taking turns holding her bobbing head and liquid-like neck. Her eyes were glassy. Jeanie leaned in to smell Greta's breath, thinking she looked drunk as much as grieved. But there were no signs of drink. Tommy and Jeanie dragged Greta into the back of the wagon and knifed the edges of Greta's blanket around her body and added a pair of Frank's wool socks to her exposed feet. Jeanie should have known Greta couldn't be dealing with the death of her daughter as well as she'd appeared to be—that grief could make one stupid, transform them into someone unrecognizable.

"Now Tommy," Jeanie said. "This isn't a game. You've got a woman in the back of this wagon, you're not the best driver, I've seen, so be careful. The ground will be disjointed with a mix of frozen earth, melted sections, possibly rutty where the wagon trails are melting—"

"Mama, I can do this. I'm a man like James. I won't let you down. For once trust *me*."

Jeanie felt her chest thump, hearing Tommy's words but not being able to take the time to argue. "Just be careful. I love you."

Tommy nodded, his eyes shining with the pride of responsibility. It was ten a.m. and Jeanie hadn't accomplished any of what she'd set out to and Yale was screeching for her mid-morning snack.

"And hurry back, Tommy. I don't trust this weather. It's too fine a day to be true." Jeanie hugged Tommy hard, kissed his forehead and hopped from the wagon.

"I'm riding with the Lord, Mama. I'm safe." Tommy shook the reigns and clicked his tongue at the horses before sloshing onto the prairie, Greta splayed in the back.

Riding with the Lord? Well, that's better than riding alone, Jeanie suspected. She bound around the front of the dugout, sweating from the heat spurred from distress as well as from her body having not adjusted back to thinking twenty-three degrees is cold.

Katherine had already picked up Yale and was comforting her as best she could a hungry baby who wanted nothing more than her mother. Katherine hummed a down tempo version of Marie Antoinette's song, waltzing around the dugout, gaze locked with Yale's, both of them enjoying their closeness, their dance.

Jeanie unbuttoned her blouse and watched the two of them from the wooden chair. "You will be a wonderful mother someday," Jeanie said.

"You think so?" Katherine said.

"My, yes, look at you. She calms at your touch. That's unusual for grumpy Yale, you know that."

Katherine did a deep plié forward and then in every direction after that. "I don't know if I will ever be a mother," Katherine said.

"Of course—"

"No, I'm not sure I *want* to be a mother. To feel what Mrs. Zurchenko feels. I think I'd die. I know I would."

Jeanie put her hand to her throat, then waved to Katherine to hand her Yale. Jeanie pulled back Yale's blanket to let some air circulate inside her wrap.

"Motherhood is not about loss. It's about greatness. Even in the small things, there is greatness."

"Oh, shuckles. That presents a problem."

"What?"

"Besides the pain I see in Mrs. Zurchenko. Even knowing mamas love their babies more than themselves, there's the matter of marriage."

"You find marriage problematic?" Jeanie said.

"Very." Katherine began to pace the space, her hands going up and down for emphasis. "You brought a book with us by Catherine Beecher. She essentially says women find equality in society by being *given* the opportunity to select her own master—her husband. That's freedom? That wrings my gut just thinking of it. I can't imagine if I ever got to meet her. Even the sisters Moore have a copy of the text that grew from the Women's Rights Convention of 1848."

"How fascinating of them. I believe Beecher is deceased. But then again, I'm not sure. You do realize I formulated many of *my* ideas at the pages of Catherine Beecher."

Katherine sighed and gave Jeanie a look that indicated her thinking was errant whether supported by Beecher or not.

"I'll start the water for lunchtime coffee, Mama," Katherine pirouetted to the stove. "Then, if it's okay, can I steal that minute for my painting? I can't rid the sight of Mrs. Zurchenko from my head. I have to put it on paper to get it out of the sight of my mind."

"You think that will do it?"

"I think it will."

Katherine clanged the water jug against the coffee pot. "Mama, why do you have that Beecher woman's writings, anyway?"

"Well, though you are of a younger, more liberated mind, I see, your mother is more traditional, I suppose. I guess I see the organization Beecher's thoughts lend to marital relationships. If a couple spent all their time grappling over who makes the decisions and has the power, well, that would be entirely disagreeable. As a lifestyle, I can't subscribe to that for the benefit of just saying 'we are equal.'" Jeanie said the words as though rehearsed for a play. Did she actually believe them? She shook her head at herself.

"Well," Katherine ground the seeds in the grinder, "I think you and Father have things reversed a bit. You are definitely his mas—"

"Bite your tongue, young miss." Jeanie leaned forward causing Yale to unlatch and prepare herself to belt out a cry. Jeanie settled back in the chair and Yale reorganized herself.

Katherine turned away and shrugged, pouring the grounds into the filter. "Well, I can say for sure that I want my own land. Like the Moores. Imagine them, they are so contented simply to be alive, to enjoy life in their own skins without tending to anyone but themselves."

Jeanie stiffened at Katherine's observations, clearly those of a girl whose eyes were half closed and brain half off when she was around the Moores. This stiffening caused Yale to unlatch again. Jeanie bit her tongue to stop herself from telling Katherine that although the Moores claimed themselves independent, they in fact, depended on everyone in their vicinity, in ways that weren't appropriate.

But, then she'd have to explain Frank's weaknesses, his part in their dependence and though part of Jeanie would love to do just that, she knew what it was like to have the image of one's father smashed—that it destroyed part of the daughter as much as the memory of the father. She wouldn't do that to any of her children.

If Jeanie didn't finish with Yale there would be no time to get some laundry done and head to the well. She ignored the fact that the water would be frigid, not subjected to the relativity of warmth that they all were.

"Thanks for putting the water on, Katherine. Why don't you paint now? Then you can help me with the laundry. Just a few things while the weather's broken."

"You're welcome, Mama." Katherine bound to the chest that held their books, paper, and her art supplies. "But just to set to verification, Mama, you are a women's rights supporter. You just don't know it."

"Well, I don't like that phrase a bit. And I fear I'm not that at all. I simply make do with what I'm given—circumstances and material-wise—and that does not pronounce one a women's advocate in any circle."

"Hmph." Katherine embraced her paints and canvas across her chest, leaned on one hip and raised her eyebrows as her lips folded into her mouth and she bit on the side of her mouth. "Well, I think my lady doth protest too much."

"No, I'm insistent, not full of defensive assertion as you suggest and you're treading mighty close to disrespect. In some homes you'd have been banished to the outhouse for just the first exchange."

Katherine playfully bugged out her eyes and headed toward the door. "Well, lucky me, I'm in the home of progressive, indulgent parents."

Jeanie laid her head back against the wood and smiled at their playfulness. "Keep the door open," Jeanie said, "we want to absorb every bit of outside before we're forced to close back up."

"Righto, Mama," Katherine said in an English accent for some unknown reason as she opened the dugout door and let a gust of warm fresh air blow in bringing the scents of lovely, teasing spring.

As much as something inside Jeanie told her not to let the weather inject her with too much lightness—the mild weather would last, probably just two days before the air crept back into negative numbers, snapping the lightness out before they knew it—she couldn't help but move faster, see the best in their small abode and revel in the progress Yale had made over the past six weeks. While holed up inside the side of the earth, one's thoughts either went to global, philosophical things, or to the second to minute to hourly duties that were required just to live to the next morning. The angry winter and the resulting mole-like existence didn't allow for much reflection regarding how far they've gone in any manner of speaking.

But as Jeanie scraped her underthings over the ridged metal, she now hummed Marie Antoinette's song and without even realizing it, her eyes would go into the dugout, searching out the cradle, seeing its stillness knowing Yale had passed the worst of her young existence. Things would be easy for her after such a plodding start. Though she tried not to bestow any sort of idolatry upon the baby or see any special grace inside her, she couldn't help thinking Yale was intended for great things. How could she not be after her nearly fatal, early life? She was *special*.

Katherine squatted beside Jeanie, having painted for the past two hours, as though the canvas sucked her essence right from her body and onto the canvas.

"Do you like it?" Katherine held the canvas up for Jeanie to see.

Jeanie stopped scrubbing and drew back. She started to grab it to get a closer look then stopped. Her wet hands would ruin it. She craned her neck.

"Katherine," Jeanie said. She wiped her hands on her apron.

"Is it all right? It's not finished, but I need it to sit a while before I really finish it. Sort of a first draft, like the writings you do. I miss you writing. The way you look when you frantically scribble over your paper. When you look into thin air, thinking."

Jeanie shook her head and took the painting into her lap. "I miss it too. But your painting is remarkable," Jeanie pointed to various parts of the painting, not touching it. "All the women in the cooperative. There isn't a person I can't pick out. You've really captured every one of us, doing the things we love."

"Well, no, I was thinking I captured what you *had* to do more than what you loved," Katherine said.

"Is that how you see us?"

"Not completely, but—"

Jeanie and Katherine stopped talking as the quiet day grew somehow even more so and in an instant, the atmosphere released itself with the sound of earth detonating, crushing them with pressure Jeanie had never felt before. She and Katherine hunched away from the sound, waiting for a physical blow to follow, like the earth moving, or rock falling on top of them from nowhere, but none of that happened.

The rumbling noise filled their bodies, shaking their insides. They grabbed hands and looked north where the sky seemed to peel from itself, falling, blacking out the atmosphere, until, in front of their eyes, ice and snow burst from nothing, blowing them so hard they doubled over and nearly didn't make it the ten feet from the wash to the dugout door.

Jeanie pushed Katherine the entire ten feet and with a heave that caused her to fall to the ground, she jammed Katherine into the dugout. Jeanie crawled the final two feet inside, slammed the door with her entire body before falling to the floor, sitting against it for fear the great wind might blow it open.

Katherine stood over the cradle and put her finger to her lips to signal Yale hadn't wakened at all. Then the two of them stared at each other, ears taking in the sound of a storm that had shown no sign of coming until the air exploded on itself, shooting ice so fine Jeanie's face felt as though she'd been pricked by thousands of pins at once.

Jeanie waved Katherine over to the door. She made a funnel with her hands so, though she had to shout, she could more quietly than if they weren't so close. "This can't last. It must be a freak storm, like summer hail, it'll be gone in a few minutes." Katherine nodded and sat with her back against the door too, her head on her mother's shoulder, wrapped up in her arms, shaking so hard that Jeanie couldn't tell if it was Katherine or her own body quivering.

Jeanie thought there was no way something like this could last, but she also knew she'd never experienced or heard of such a thing happening in the first place. As though someone had pulled the weather off the earth and replaced it with its polar opposite. Things like this didn't just happen. Yet, there it was, crushing, unbearable weather, trapping them inside the earth, making Jeanie further consider the existence of God. And it did seem possible in those moments that if there was one, he was a surly fellow with some sort of score to settle.

Two hours passed. Jeanie and Katherine attempted to move from the door, but the wind, stiffer than any that had plagued the dugout so far, kept blowing open the door. They hesitantly moved the chest with the books in front of it, afraid that if Frank, James or Tommy were attempting to come in, they wouldn't be able to hear them knocking. The wind was so loud, unimaginably deafening that every so often Jeanie would attempt to talk in a normal voice just to remind her that the wind was blowing as hard as she thought it was.

"This isn't ending. The horses must be spooked. We can't lose the animals. And buffalo chips or hanks, we need something to burn until the boys get back," Jeanie said.

Katherine nodded, her eyes glassy as though she felt what Jeanie did—that something about this storm was different, that its stark inception—crashing out of nowhere was the least of what would set it apart from others.

Yale began to wail, stopping Jeanie from putting on Frank's coat and hat. "I'll feed her, Katherine, then I'll tend to the animals and...well, I don't know." Jeanie rubbed her forehead and smoothed back the bangs that had popped from her bun and tickled her forehead.

She ripped down her blouse and tried to relax, but knew her stiffness would keep the demanding Yale from settling in for a good meal. She was petulant as usual and until that moment, Jeanie had viewed that as just part of who Yale was. Now she viewed it as a big problem.

Finally, the babe latched on to her breast and ate about half her normal take. After it was clear Yale was finished eating, Jeanie handed her to Katherine and ordered her to nuzzle the baby until she was back to sleep, hopefully, somehow unaware that she hadn't eaten her normal fill.

Jeanie buttoned up her blouse, pulled on long johns, extra socks, Frank's coat, his hat, and even stuffed an extra set of socks into her coat just in case. For the first time on the prairie, Jeanie was grateful for her too big shoes. She drew another pair of socks over the first and jammed her feet into the ugly clodhoppers.

Jeanie tended the fire, checked the water level in the barrel, and took a swig of coffee then water. She faced the stove, lifted her skirts and let the warmth travel up, hoping to trap extra. She took several deep breaths as though readying herself for what was waiting outside, but instead of tearing out of the house, she removed all of Frank's outerwear and unbuttoned her blouse again.

"Mama?" Katherine rocked Yale.

"I'm going to dispense as much of this milk as I can. We have one more of those cups from Templeton that we didn't use after Christmas. Then I'll cover the milk with clean material, tie it on and set it right inside this bowl. We'll fill the bowl with snow and every once in a while you'll have to open the door and take a handful of snow to replenish the bowl. It'll stay cool there for when you need it.

"You'll have to use this spoon or your finger to drip it into Yale's mouth. But, don't use your finger unless you're absolutely sure it's clean or she'll get sick. Um," Jeanie yanked on her breast as though milking a cow. "If the milk runs out, remember the most important thing is that she gets some liquid. Don't give her lots of water, but if the milk is gone and I'm nowhere in sight, give her drips of water, just enough so that she keeps her pants wet. She *has* to keep making water. That's how you'll know she's all right."

Katherine's eyes grew wider then narrowed on her mother. "You sound like you're not coming back."

Jeanie looked up from her breast. "Of course I'm coming back. But I just want to be sure the horses are tied and safe and I need to get fuel. I don't trust this storm's pattern. It started too strange. But if we don't get something to burn and if I don't attach this red cloth to the top of that shack we call a barn, if your brothers and father are out in the storm...they'll never find this pit we call a home. They'll walk right over it never to be seen again. And I can't have that."

Katherine laid her cheek against her sister's forehead and closed her eyes.

"They're safe, right? You can feel it like you did when we were caught in the fire, right?"

Jeanie tucked her breast into her dress and buttoned up. "I don't feel anything particular, right now. Except that the next thing I need to do, is to get something for fire and make our home noticeable from a distance. I won't be long. Ten minutes is all it will take me."

Jeanie leaned over Katherine, kissed her cheek and inhaled the scent of both of them before standing and heading toward the door. Katherine grabbed Jeanie's hand, pulling her back. She squeezed her mother's fingers three times for I love you.

"Come back quick. I'm not the mothering kind, you know."

"You are. We're mothering people, we Arthurs."

"Still," Katherine said.

"I'll return in five minutes." Jeanie gave Katherine three squeezes of the hand.

Katherine nodded and Jeanie turned from her, hiding the tears that rimmed her eyelids, telling Jeanie that despite all her willing the world to be the way she wanted, she wasn't so sure she had the kind of power that this type of willing would require.

Chapter 17

Jeanie touched every item she needed. Frank's hat, his coat, extra socks in his pockets, the red cloth to tie to the stick above the barn. Then she mentally drew a map of where she needed to go, knowing that as soon as she committed to the storm, the only way she would find her way to the barn and back would be to count every step, inventory every turn she took and follow the exact path back. Jeanie knew that the very short distance between the house and the barn would take exponentially longer to navigate than it did on a typical day.

She took a deep breath at the door, slid the chest to the side and bent toward the wind, pushing through the doorway as though plowing through mud rather than thin air. She hung on the door knob until she was sure Katherine had slid the chest back and finally turned into the wind, focusing her mind on every step, and how the earth felt as it sloped up. She counted each step she took.

Jeanie'd been caught in snow storms before, not been able to see, had to turn away from punishing winds, full of snow that pelted her like knives, but nothing she'd experienced prepared her for the current storm. She held her hand up, touched her face and drew it back a bit, just to be sure, sure that she hadn't gone crazy, that in fact it was true that she couldn't see two inches in front of her nose. Whatever storm had befallen them, it was not typical in any sense. And by the time Jeanie decided checking on the horses, gathering fuel, and tying a cloth to the barn was not a profitable idea, she'd wandered too far not to finish her task.

Jeanie didn't know how much time had passed when she realized she'd expended her mental energy just telling her body how to stay upright, she'd no idea at which point the land sloped which way or how many steps she took. She bent at the knees, chin tucked to her chest, heaving for breath, but only taking in searing granules of ice. She righted herself, trying to find a glimmer of the sun, to locate the ghoulish outline that often came with cloudy stormy weather.

But, every time she raised her face to look, ice pierced her eyeballs and when she'd look away, shutting her eyes, the ice would crust across her lashes, sealing her lids until she warmed the lashes enough with her glove to open her eyes. The only sense she could apply to actions seemed to be the mantra she began to say keepyoureyesopenkeepyoureyesopenkeepyoureyesopen.

The wind ripped in several directions at once and in an odd instance, it stilled, the particles of ice and snow hanging there long enough for Jeanie to realize she could see. She turned her head, and caught the sight of a clump of brown. The olive trees! Jeanie knew if she could rest against one of them for a moment she could reorient herself and head directly northwest to the barn from there. So quickly, Jeanie had to pray the lull had actually happened, the winds tangled up from all directions, again. Dropping her head and shoulder into the wind, she ruptured a seam in the wind and pushed ahead.

She'd gathered her wits enough, focused on the barn ahead, forcing the thoughts associated with cold from her mind. If she didn't acknowledge the cold air—so icy it felt three-dimensional, as though if stilled and turned on its side it could hold a cup of water—the way it froze in her nose, making her swipe at it cutting the skin, feeling blood seep warm, then beginning the reclogging again.

Jeanie trudged, pushing her legs forward, losing time, though sure she would reach the barn any second. Her lungs felt as though they were cementing in her chest as they grew used to the searing cold and she adapted a more shallow breath pattern. She bowed into the wind, and as she did, it let up again, the swirling snow and exploding particles of ice stopping mid-air. As the atmosphere stilled, Jeanie raised her head, seeing the outline of the olive trees again.

She plodded faster at that thought, giving up on the idea that she would find the animals, and finally letting her mind go to Katherine and Yale. The storm kicked up again and the lull had given enough space in the air for Jeanie to note that it had turned from day to night. Sunset, maybe a little after five o'clock. When that happened, Jeanie couldn't have said; she didn't notice in the blackout caused by the avalanche of white.

Jeanie finally reached the trees. And it was at the first tree in the bunch that Jeanie began to hear the sounds of Frank's violin, the dark, slow version of Marie Antoinette's song that he fancied. Another boost to her confidence. Frank was in the home, with the kids, keeping their minds off their missing mother by playing the violin. Thank you, Lord, for dear Frank. Jeanie knew he would have managed to make things right when they needed him most.

So, holding onto one tree then the next, and so on, she finally reached the front door where she pounded with her gloved hand, hoping they would hear her over the storm and violin.

Jeanie leaned against the door, her forehead there, eyes shut, the ice finding its way in between her and the door, freezing her eyes closed as she banged on it with her frozen fist. Finally the door groaned open and Jeanie fell inside, feeling immediately a hard wood floor, knowing even with her eyes iced shut that she had stumbled off course and into the home of someone else.

Jeanie rolled to her back, her thoughts tangling among them-selves...where was she? The babythebabythebabymyKatherine-myKatherineJamesTommyFrank.

She felt hands on her shoulders propping her up, someone rub-bing her back, pulling at her. She realized ice had formed in her ears and it muffled the voices of the people who were handling her. She couldn't even hear her own words as she repeatedly said she needed to get back out to go home to find her children, that if she thawed she'd never make it back home, but the hands kept rubbing her back, the voices, though muddled were clearly tension filled, as though bickering. Maybe about how to approach the pro-cess of thawing her out.

How long had she been out? How frozen was she? Her lashes melted first and as water worked its way under her lids, she could feel again, she opened her eyes and looked around, then twisted her body to see who it was caring for her.

And there, behind her, kneeling with expressions of horror on their faces were Frank and Ruthie.

Frank? Ruthie? Where am I? Your house? How did I get all the way here? I was only outside for twenty minutes, thirty at the most. To check the animals and get some fuel. Jeanie covered her mouth and stared at the two of them. It sunk into her mind hard that all four of her children were separated from their parents and two of them were without adults at all.

Frank grabbed Jeanie by the shoulders and started to pull her up.

"Yes, yes, get me up. I have to go back to the house. Northeast will take us home to Yale and Katherine and James and Tommy. Where are they? Oh my God. I can't have nursed that miniscule baby to health to have her die because I lost my bearings in a storm."

"No," Ruthie said, "don't have her stand yet. She probably saved herself by not stopping in the storm, but her blood is cold and if she stands up before her body temperature warms, it'll freeze her heart. She'll die."

Jeanie stopped struggling, the words of Ruthie and Frank sounded garbled to her, as though they were slurring, though making sense at the same time. Jeanie's own words felt like solid masses inside her frozen mouth. She wondered if any of them were understandable. "That's right. That happened to Pete Carroll last year when…you go, Frank. Go to the house and, and, I'll expel some milk into a cup and you take it to Yale and drip it into her mouth like we did…"

"No one's going anywhere. It's seven o' clock—"

"Seven o'clock?" Jeanie said. "I couldn't have been out for three hours. That's not possible and if it is then Yale will starve, she'll starve! Katherine will freeze. They don't have enough fuel! Tommy had to take Greta back before getting buffalo chips and the hanks will only last an hour or so. You have to go, Frank. They're your children."

"That storm will have me into the next township if I attempt to go out," Frank said.

"Then I'll go," Jeanie struggled to get her feet under her, but they were thick as though actual ice blocks were tied underneath them, the pain that suddenly pulsed through them felt as though it were fire surging through her veins.

"You'll die and then what will we do?" Frank said.

Jeanie closed her eyes and struggled to breathe. The children! She couldn't stop thinking of them. She knew she couldn't walk, that she'd never make it ten feet from Ruthie's house with her body already staggered from the temperature change, she'd die for sure either freezing or her heart giving out. She closed her eyes, willing herself to calm down, to find some strength and with it a solution.

She tried to open her eyes yet exhaustion overcame her still, while she ran the facts of the situation through her mind. Frank and Ruthie had clearly been in the house since the storm started or long enough that each sustained normal body temperature. One of them could go. That was the way it was on the prairie, one of them would just have to risk their lives for the children.

Jeanie tried to form the words, ready to tell Frank to do exactly what his fatherly gut should have already told him to do. She mumbled and lifted her head toward the voices of Ruthie and Frank. *Why aren't they helping me?*

Jeanie forced her eyes open. Across the room in the kitchen, she watched Ruthie, wearing a night-robe, pour tea, as Frank, in his long johns, shoveled buffalo chips into the stove. Jeanie reached out. They didn't notice her hand extended toward them.

They stopped their chores to gaze at one another as though lovers.

Jeanie dropped her head back down to the floor. She was hallucinating. She'd heard of the great damage cold could do. She must have lost her mind along with the numbing of the rest of her senses. She looked back again. Ruthie, still embraced in Frank's gaze, reached up and traced his lips with her finger.

Jeanie's mouth fell open.

Frank parted his lips and took Ruthie's finger into his mouth, smiling around it as though they'd just discovered the secret to happiness and long life.

Jeanie closed her mouth and ground her teeth so hard she nearly cracked a tooth. She breathed heavily as her mind seemed to lift itself from her body, filling her with grief she'd never imagined anymore than she'd ever entertained the notion that Frank could possibly be interested in Ruthie of all people. Ruthie.

"Ruuuuuuuthhhhhhhieeeee," Jeanie bellowed across the room. The lovers flew apart. Ruthie jumped back into the stove setting the sleeve of her robe on fire.

The fire sizzled up her sleeve so quickly it burnt off some of her mousy hair before Frank was able to tackle Ruthie to the floor and roll the flames out.

Jeanie sobbed, watching them from across the room, on her knees, body pulsing, understanding what her mind didn't. How could this have happened? How could she come to be sitting in a friend's home during a blizzard while her children were unattended and her husband was well-tended by another woman? The dowdy friend.

Jeanie's ears were useless, feeling as clogged as they had when they'd been ice filled, as though her confused thoughts were so real they took up space in her head, blocking out noise. She could see them talking, heads together, comforting one another, but she had no idea what their exact words were.

Jeanie knew she was sobbing loudly, she could feel it as her shoulders rose and fell and she watched Frank look back at Jeanie from atop Ruthie after extinguishing the fire on her robe. His face scrunched up as though he were crying. He was crying, though she couldn't hear him. Ruthie's body heaved also, crying, but not looking toward Jeanie.

"You are not allowed to cry, Frank Arthur! You are not allowed to feel anything but despicable shame. Our children are lost in this storm, *I* was lost in this storm and you're here playing the violin, making love to another woman. Where's Lutie? I thought. I was *sure*..."

Jeanie lurched up to her feet and then forward, lumbering toward the lovers. Ruthie and Frank's faces were aghast, as though Jeanie were a spirit that had risen from the dead, as though she'd been a danger to them instead of them being a danger to everything Jeanie valued in life.

Jeanie fell into Ruthie and steadied herself, gripping Ruthie's arms, feeling as though her nails were digging through Ruthie's flesh. Ruthie's face looked like it were made of clay, remolding itself into untold faces of shame for what she'd done.

"You're hurting me," Ruthie cried. "My arms. You're hurting my arms."

Jeanie relaxed her grip and smoothed the sleeves of Ruthie's robe, feeling as though she wasn't breathing, yet didn't need to.

"You are the worst kind of woman, Ruthie Moore. A traitor. A worthless thief of the heart."

Ruthie's chin dropped to her chest as she sobbed.

"Look at me," Jeanie said.

"Come on, Jeanie, let's just get through the night," Frank said.

"You look at me," Jeanie said. When Ruthie didn't look up, Jeanie grabbed Ruthie's pocked cheeks, digging her nails into the flesh, pulling Ruthie's face up to eye-level.

"Open your eyes, weak woman."

Ruthie opened them, tears barreled down her cheeks. "I'm so sorry, Jeanie. I don't know why I did it. I just felt loved for once, for…forgive me, please forgive me. Please, I never…"

Jeanie watched Ruthie's wracked face, dug into her cheeks, and listened to her pleas and attempts to explain away such evil behavior, but all Jeanie could feel was equal amounts of hate to Ruthie's shame. When Jeanie drew blood from Ruthie's cheek, she startled at her own aggression, quiet at it was. Her hate didn't diminish, but her desire to rip Ruthie's face from its bones scared Jeanie into reality, forcing her to remember the most important thing of the moment. The safety of her children. Nothing else compared.

When she'd spewed all her boiling hate, when her throat was too raw to speak, when she'd realized the only solution to her predicament was to wait out the storm, Jeanie crawled into a corner of the room, tucked her legs under her skirts and up against her chest, creating a ball of warmth. She wanted to exist as far from Frank and Ruthie as possible. And there, lodged where two walls met, she set her mind to finding a way to save her family even when it seemed impossible that she might.

The three captives of the storm sat still as wooden carvings of themselves. Jeanie wouldn't speak or move for fear of what she might do to the two of them. They probably sat still for the same reason.

Jeanie was able to focus her attention away from Frank and Ruthie and what they'd done for some time, due to the intense thawing of her limbs. It took all her might, eyes squeezed shut, watering, nose running, to get through the experience of blood re-infiltrating starved layers of cells and muscle and skin. She thought she could feel her bones actually releasing the fiery blood from inside them, could feel minute drips of blood meet the tips of her toes and fingers, searing them.

Once the acute pain passed, Jeanie was left with thumping, more dulled pain that she thought might last forever, and that was fine with her because at that point she could at least turn her attention to how to save her children. It was also at that point that she realized Lutie was missing, that she'd always thought it were Lutie Frank was interested in, that if he were to have found another woman's flesh under his, it would have been her pristine, creamy skin.

Jeanie lifted her head from atop her knees to see Ruthie heading into her bedroom, probably to the chamber pot.

"Where's Lutie?" Jeanie asked.

"She went out just as the storm crashed in. I'd given her a note to give to James. He was hanging the flag at the stupid weather station he and Templeton built and I knew, I knew this storm wasn't a normal one the minute the sky went to ash. So Lutie—"

"*Why didn't you go?*"

Frank opened his mouth to speak, but nothing came out but a cracked squeak. He looked into his lap.

"Don't look into your lap like a shamed little boy. You are a man who acts as a ten-year-old. Don't you dare go do that now, not under these circumstances. You have their lives on your hands. All of the children's, and now Lutie's life." Jeanie shivered, her teeth chattered.

"Why would Lutie agree to such a thing?"

"She went to the Hunts. I sent her. She made it to James, gave him the note, but then I sent her to the Hunts."

Jeanie realized why and instead of the pure anger that normally swam through her when she realized someone was destroying his life with opium, she merely felt numb. "You sent her to the Hunts for opium?"

Frank crossed the room to Jeanie. "Sit by the fire."

He crouched beside her. Jeanie jerked away from him, as far into the corner as she could. Frank put his hand against the wall where she sat. "There's a breeze firing through there like a locomotive. It'll suck the heat, what's left of your heat, out of you in two hours time and then who'll be there to care for the children in the morning?"

Jeanie glared at him, could feel her cheeks shuddering with her clicking teeth. She wanted to spit at him, tell him he would care for them like an adult, that their entire lives shouldn't have to depend solely on her. She felt a stubborn mass in her belly, telling her not to go to the stove, to make them suffer in seeing her freeze to death, to have to explain to the children that she'd died because Frank was a piss-poor person full of nothing but dirty pig shit. But, he wouldn't do that. He'd somehow sell the story as brimming with heroism, his, of some sort.

Jeanie shoved him away, making him stumble backward. He caught himself with his hands, behind him, but rolled onto his back flipping over doing a somersault. Ruthie came into the keeping room and stopped at the sight of them having actually moved. She stared down at her hands then whisked into the kitchen to load the buffalo chips into the stove.

Jeanie pulled a heavy carved, mahogany chair near the stove. She sat it in, disgusted because she knew without anyone telling her, that this stunning, expensive chair had been carved by Frank. His stupidity, that he thought she might never notice this chair on a call to the Moores, that his signature, thick carvings would elude her. Though this chair was different in the content of the carvings—fruits and trees and a violin graced this one, it was unmistakably Frank's work.

Frank took the modest pine chair beside Jeanie, and Ruthie pulled a decrepit chair that had been wrangled out of raw tree branches from the kitchen. Ruthie tossed the last bunch of buffalo chips in and sat on the chair. It eeked with her body weight, until she shifted and finally settled into silence.

A few minutes passed. "We're out of buffalo chips. That's the last load," Ruthie said, her voice thin and empty of emotion.

"Hanks?" Frank said.

Jeanie bent forward to see past Frank. Ruthie shook her head so slightly Jeanie wasn't sure she answered at first. Jeanie noted the dried blood on Ruthie's cheek then looked at her hands, now getting their feeling back, the numbness and pain finally fading.

Jeanie leaned back and cursed them to herself. What kind of fools would play with their lives like that. Even if the unexpected blizzard hadn't dropped upon them, they still should have managed to collect a few bushels of extra buffalo chips. Stupidstupidstupid people.

"We'll be all right," Frank said. He squeezed her shoulder and Jeanie threw his hand off with a growl.

"I'm not upset for us you stupid ass. It's your daughters. They're alone in the dugout, that horse-shit hole in the earth, alone, with nothing to heat themselves with. They're probably dead. They're probably dead already."

Jeanie bounced in the chair and pulled her knees up to her chest again, hoping if she physically latched herself together she might not fall apart inside. Her sobs settled, her head was stuffed and it felt as though her brain had swelled and was pulsing against her skull.

"You don't believe that, Jeanie. They're alive and you know it. Like with the fire, you felt it in your bones that they were safe. I know you know they're safe."

Jeanie used her knees to knead her brow bone, hoping the rubbing would release the pain. She tried to find that place in her that would divine the safety of her children. She couldn't find that place, she was filled with numbness and all she knew was she knew nothing about her children's conditions. She wasn't panicked, but she wasn't calmed either.

She silently traced the various scenarios that could have befallen each child. Tommy could be warm at the Zurchenko's or he could have left their homestead at just the time the storm broke. James could be hidden inside the bottom of the flag station, at Templeton's, or, or, well, no she wouldn't think of the other scenario, that she couldn't bear. Katherine, dear Katherine with another child's life in her hands. Jeanie knew she was smart enough to carry out the directions Jeanie had given her.

The problems would be what was beyond Katherine's control—the end of the fuel, the end of the milk and a reliable way to feed the baby. Jeanie felt the most dire about Katherine and Yale because she knew the exact limitations under which they would be living. She knew they didn't gather more fuel, or enough for the night before the storm broke.

Stupidstupidstupid people.

She knew how hard it would be to keep Yale alive. And Lutie. Stupid Lutie. Either so dumb that she didn't notice her sister's affair, or so dumb that she would give them sanctuary to carry it out. Stupid, stupid Lutie.

She stared at Frank's profile as the fire lit his face with dancing light. And she knew it was all Frank's fault. Because he had to have an affair.

A weakweakweak man.

She stared at Frank, and as the flames began to cast less light on his face, the accompanying chill was immediate. They were out of fuel. Ruthie began a squealy sob. Frank turned to her. "Ruthie, don't cry. We'll be all right."

Jeanie shot to her feet. "Of course we'll be all right, you dumb jackasses. We have plenty to burn in the house, don't we?" Jeanie twisted at the waist, looking around the house for just the right thing to burn. She saw it. She waltzed across the room to the lounge. On it, laid Frank's violin.

"This is first to go. The perfect size for the stove."

Frank started to get up, but her gaze leveled him, pushing him back into his seat. Jeanie sauntered to the stove and ceremoniously laid it on top of the remaining chips and ashes.

"Oh, well, yes, that burns very well. Slow, it looks like," Jeanie said. She turned to Frank and Ruthie. "Well, let's get to the next stage of making fuel. She tapped the mahogany, carved chair. "This will do well."

"Now, Jeanie, there's plenty of other things to burn before that chair," Frank said. Jeanie spun around and grabbed the rifle from its spot leaning against the wall. She pushed the center of it back and it expelled a casing, cocked and ready to go. The sound it made as it was readied seemed to hang in the air. "We'll start with that chair Frank and I'll take no arguments from either of you. And mark my words. If we're trapped in this place for a week or so, I'll eat you for dinner Frank, and you for breakfast the next day Ruthie Moore. So you better just do what I tell you."

Ruthie and Frank pushed to their feet and then the two of them began to dismantle the chair while Jeanie made coffee. Every once in a while she'd turn to watch them, as the two of them seemed so dour about the process as though the dismantling of their secret little life was embedded in the process of saving all of their lives. Jeanie felt a surge of pity for them, and a sense that she should tell them she was sorry for threatening them. But she'd earned the right to threaten them at the very least.

Thoughts of what to do next, how to deal with a cheating husband came to Jeanie. Ruthie could oblige them by leaving the prairie, killing herself, whatever. But due to the circumstances of life and society, Jeanie had no choice but to keep Frank. As much as she wished he were dead or gone. Divorce. No, that was impossible. They'd starve. She couldn't keep four children without a husband, even a lazy sloth like Frank.

There would be plenty of time for that. They had to get through the night and she was sure, that feeling had come over her at that moment, that everyone was safe. She knew it in the bones that had been nearly frozen down to the marrow, that her children were safe.

Jeanie expelled breast milk into the cleanest cup she could find. That process turned her stomach. This was so wrong, to be so separate from her baby. She ignored the thought and tugged at her breast as though it weren't hers and it was the natural thing to do. If only she'd stayed at the house. She never should have left, been so damn sure she could take care of things. She imagined herself in the dugout, with Katherine and Yale in her arms, James, stoking the fire and Tommy claiming his boredom as lethal. She ached with the emptiness, the sensation, that she'd never have the four of them together in her home again.

As the night grew deeper and they were down to zero chairs, they sat in their assumed spots, staring into the fire. Frank leaned forward to shift some wood from the front of the stove with a poker. When he did, thin strands of light leapt down the length of the poker and off his hand. He flew back across the room. The women turned to see his hair standing on end, dancing in the air like seaweed in a fish tank she'd seen once in Des Moines. His breathing steadied but his face grew horrified as he looked back and forth from one woman to the other.

"What?" Jeanie asked. Frank pointed and the women looked at one another to see each other's loose tendrils waving above their heads as well. It was then that sparks of electricity would appear out of nowhere, running across the top of the stove, down a mirror, and at times, right off the ends of their fingertips. The storm had indeed gone completely the way of bizarre and if it hadn't wrought such turmoil, Jeanie would have merely been impressed by its atypical power.

Jeanie balled up again, trying to make sense of such an occurrence. She tried to believe this was simply another component to a normal storm, that it wasn't unprecedented, that what everyone knew about surviving wouldn't be challenged by such great complexity, that it actually made sense that fire snapped right out of thin air.

Though none of the three pioneers taking cover in Ruthie Moore's home ever slept that night, they did fall into exhausted stupors characterized by blank stares into the fire, only coming to consciousness to break furniture into pieces and toss them into the fire.

Every once in while, Ruthie would sob, apologize to Jeanie and beg for forgiveness. Jeanie didn't respond, nor did she feel anything at all.

In the midst of one of these trance-like silences, pounding on the front door, like bullets from several guns at once, signaled that day had broken, perhaps the storm as well. Jeanie got to the door first and wrenched it open. A blast of air threw her back and its frigid force in combination with sun so bright turned her vision to black. She spun away from the door before she could even see who was there.

As she turned back, shielding her eyes, the sounds of Tommy filled her ears. His squeaky voice chirping about the time he'd spent overnight at the Zurchenko's poked through the relative silence. Jeanie's eyes finally adjusted as Tommy's arms collapsed around his mother, squeezing. "Oh, my Tommy, I'm so glad you're well." She rubbed his body, making sure he was actually standing there. His unusual affection made clear the weight of the night before.

She kissed him over nearly his entire body, not able to formulate thoughts or words regarding her relief at seeing him. Tommy reddened. "Ah, Mama, I'm fine. You knew I was at the Zurchenko's. It's Artem, Aleksey, and Anton we need to find..."

Tommy rattled off thirty-three ways—God this and God that—all the ways God would help them locate the Zurchenko boys while Nikolai hung back at the door, holding his hat. Ruthie disappeared into her bedroom. Frank was already pulling on layers of clothing, as was Jeanie.

"Mama, Father. Where is everyone? It's mighty cold outside. Mr. Zurchenko said we should all just stay put today...hey, where's everyone else?"

"We don't know," Jeanie said. "And I'm afraid this day is not so sumptuous as to allow our staying put."

"We'll need to check your place," Nikolai said. "Aleksey set off yesterday for your place with a load of buffalo chips. He was probably half way there, when the storm came up. As for Artem and Anton. I cannot guess." Nikolai nodded. Jeanie knew the panic he must have felt inside.

"I'll go," Frank said. He shoved his arms through his coat.

"Oh no you won't," Jeanie said. "You give me that coat right now. It's not my dilemma that you chose to so foolishly spend your day yesterday, without a thought for your heavy coat. I'll take that and you can—"

"Here," Nikolai stripped out of his outer coat to reveal another underneath. "It's got to be fifty below outside with the chill quite raining down from north. We've got to make everyone safe, not bicker about who was where yesterday."

"You're right, Nikolai," Jeanie said. "Let's go." She pulled on the coat he offered her then hiked up the hem that dragged by a foot or so on the floor. "We'll check the house first. They've got to all be there safe, they just have to."

Tommy was ordered into the wagon by Jeanie. She didn't care a whit that Frank suggested Tommy stay to help Ruthie with her chores, that she might need human companionship while she awaited news of her sister. Ruthie buckled at her door as she watched the wagon leave and Jeanie, who couldn't take her eyes from the sight of Ruthie sobbing there, puddled onto the floor, couldn't decide whether the nausea she felt at that moment was because she hated Ruthie so much she could have killed her or because of the happiness she'd felt, the power that surged at the sight of Ruthie's world coming unraveled. The pride and hate tasted good to Jeanie and she knew that with such feelings came the end of who she'd been for the first 27 years of her life.

Chapter 18

1905
Des Moines, Iowa

Katherine stood in the doorway to the guestroom. She listened to Yale and Jeanie's breathing, a rhythmic match, each of their breaths paralleling the other, as Katherine imagined it had been for seventeen years. She waited for anger and resentment to come on the heels of jealousy that someone other than she shared that relationship with her mother. But nothing came. Nothing. Indifference sat there in her heart feeling as though it was approaching contentment, that maybe she'd gotten past her mother's horrid decisions.

Katherine crept to the bed and scooped the envelopes from Yale's belly and set them on the bedside table. Howard Templeton. Katherine vaguely remembered her mother mentioning Howard's continued correspondence, but what she remembered most about Mr. Templeton was an argument he had with Jeanie at the dugout and then again once they'd left the prairie. She stretched her memory back to those days. What had they been arguing about?

Templeton had been a big part of their life on the prairie and there had been a lot stress for all the families. But now, looking back, Katherine recalled her discomfort in overhearing snatches of heated words. What could there have been for them to argue about? Katherine lifted the triangle flap open and pulled out the letter.

She opened it and though her gaze fell over the words, her mind didn't see any of them. She was too preoccupied with the letters in the attic. She folded it again and slipped it back into the envelope. She looked at the ceiling. The letters from her mother to her father. *Those* she wanted to read—those she needed to read.

Katherine folded the flap back over and the sharp paper sliced her skin. She stuck her bleeding finger into her mouth. The sudden pain pushed her back in time. A flash of her parents arguing came to her then was pushed aside by more images of pained arguments between Jeanie and Templeton. That's it. The argument. The last time she saw Templeton. That day at the hotel was the beginning of the end of everything Katherine had loved about her life.

Katherine turned toward the bed and saw her mother's eyes open, staring at her. She jumped and dropped the letter back onto the bed.

"Go ahead. They're yours as much as mine."

Katherine's mouth fell open at the sound of her mother's voice, her suddenly coherent words. She felt a rush of excitement at the prospect that perhaps her mother wasn't dying. That she could... well, she didn't know what she wanted from her mother, but she had to sit there.

She didn't know what to say. She didn't feel forgiveness inside her, she wanted to, but couldn't and so she sat there and after a bit, finally reached across the bed and held her mother's hand, tracing each crevice and bump in it, remembering the hands that used to flash over fabric like lightning, used to soothe, used to create heavenly everything out of nothing. Those hands. She did remember those and in looking at them she could feel what she used to—utter and complete love.

Chapter 19

1888
Dakota Territory

Of all the days Jeanie spent on the prairie so far, that morning, Friday, January 13th was the most beautiful of all. The blinding blue sky draped deep azure and cloudless over the snow, so stark was the contrast that if she'd seen a painting depicting it, she'd have thought the artist left his senses at the door of his studio and created from only his imagination. The yolk rising in the east cast such bright light that she had to squint when looking at the snow itself. The deep-freeze had crystallized the top layer of white so perfectly that it lost its whiteness to diamond clarity and reminded Jeanie of her grandmother's blue velvet jewelry box that burst with diamonds and sapphires.

Jeanie choked on the goodness that the scene brought to her because until each child was within six feet of her, Jeanie would not further appreciate God's work. Not far from the point where Jeanie decided to put aside the beauty at the end of her nose, Jeanie glimpsed black lumpy splotches about fifty yards to the east, but fifty yards that would take them off course to their home. They squinted at it. Was it merely a bush that somehow escaped the snow?

"We have to check to see what that is," Jeanie said.

"It can't be nothing. Someone lost a mitten is all," Frank said.

"That would be a lot of mittens. Go, it could be...just go, go, go," Jeanie rose from her seat in the wagon and gripped Nikolai's shoulders so hard he actually grunted and pulled away.

"I'm sorry, but we can't just..."

Nikolai nodded and guided the horses off course.

They arrived at the black spot and saw it was nothing more than a woolen coat. They dug under it and around it and it yielded nothing but sore fingers for the men. The body heat they generated in such action wasn't even enough to melt the snow when it touched their bodies.

While the men were climbing back into the wagon, Jeanie looked from one end of the prairie to the next. As far as her eyes could see there were people, like black ants against the white, moving over the snow, plodding, bending, and wailing into the thin air, cries of discoveries that none of them wanted to make.

"It can't be that bad," Jeanie said. "It can't." Her companions didn't respond.

The horses lost their footing a few times, but scrambled back to right themselves before tossing anyone from the wagon. And after some time, much longer than it would normally take, Jeanie saw the stick where she had intended to tie the red cloth when she first set out the day before.

"We're close. There's the bee tree. Stop here or you'll take the horses off the end of the dugout." Jeanie hopped from the wagon. She held up the coat and wouldn't let the thought that there was no smoke rising from the stack dampen her excitement at seeing her children. She slid down the side of the dugout like an otter down the bank of a stream. The cold air shrunk her lungs as she forced them to work hard as she moved like an ox.

She banged on the door while Frank and Nikolai began digging snow from below. Once enough snow was cleared, they shoved the door three times before it gave way. At least the trunk had held tight, Jeanie thought.

Three more pushes and the door opened far enough for them to enter. The sun filled the space and Jeanie pushed by the men. Jeanie tripped over a large mass before her eyes had a chance to adjust. When they did, she found herself draped over the side of a cow. The dugout was warmer than outside, but there was no noise or movement.

"Katherine!" Jeanie shrieked as though there were miles for her voice to carry. The men behind her shifted and let more sun inside and the picture of what had happened over the course of time became clear. There was not only one cow, but two inside lying side by side. Between them was a brown woolen blanket. Poking out of the top of it was a hand, grayish, unmoving. Katherine's.

Jeanie ripped back the blanket. Underneath lay Katherine and Aleksey, facing one another, each with an arm over the other's midsection, their feet intertwined. Yale? Jeanie spun around looking for a sign of her.

She bent down and shook Katherine and Aleksey. They stirred then sat up, eyes squinting at the sunlight. Jeanie took Katherine by her shoulders kissed her all over her cheeks and forehead then realized that Yale had been there all along. Katherine had tucked her into her dress and there she was, just as pink as she'd been when Jeanie left her.

Jeanie gasped, hugged them both then tore off the coat, unbuttoned her dress and let Yale eat. They all cried and hung onto each other—Aleksey, Katherine, and Jeanie. When the dugout door closed, Jeanie turned to see Frank and Nikolai standing there, watching all of them.

Nikolai's lips quivered and provided the only evidence other than a single tear down his cheek that he was crying. Aleksey struggled to his feet and shuffled slowly past Frank who helped him move to his father where he fell into his arms and cried the sobs his father didn't.

Frank took the spot that Aleksey had abandoned near Katherine and rocked her as though a baby.

"I'm going to finish with Yale and then we have to set out for James," Jeanie said.

"He's not with you? Father?" Katherine pulled away and crinkled her nose at Frank.

"He wanted to hang the flag, the blizzard flag—"

"No, *after* that," Katherine said. "He and Templeton did that much. And then they stopped here, but refused to stay, said they needed to find you, Father." Katherine lifted her hand and pointed at Frank. "That you were making a mistake of some kind. He needed to find Mama, to warn her. I told him Mama didn't need a warning, that was very clear on the weather dangers! I told him to stay, but he said he had to do something before Father…"

Jeanie felt her face freeze with fear as she patted Katherine and turned her mind from her husband's stupidity. There was no time for that. Where was her James?

As though taking a cue to cover up the weight of what Katherine had reported, Nikolai set Aleksey on the lounge then went to the wagon for buffalo chips. Jeanie shook her head. If she hadn't been feeding Yale she would not have been able to capsize the urge to strangle Frank's thin neck. She knew what Katherine meant by James wanting to warn Jeanie, even if her daughter didn't. James *knew*. He'd known that Frank was having an affair and when he found her not in the dugout, thought it more important to save Frank's reputation than his own life.

"We have to hurry," Jeanie said. "Katherine, are you okay to care for Yale, just a bit longer?"

Katherine's face paled and she shook her head. Jeanie pulled her into her chest. "There's no wind, no clouds in the sky, no sign of anything to change the weather—"

"But there wasn't yesterday, either," Katherine cried into Jeanie's shoulder.

"That can't happen again. Ever. That's not normal, even here in this wicked, weathered place."

Aleksey squatted near them and took Katherine's hand that lay across her mother's back. "Katherine. Your hand was exposed while you slept. Let me tend you. We can care for Yale until they bring back James. It won't be long. He's probably in the haystack by the Moores. He's not dumb."

Jeanie nodded and kissed Katherine's hand. The gentle pressure of a kiss made Katherine yelp as the frozen limb had begun to thaw. Jeanie knew it would be an excruciating time while the blood began to snake its way through Katherine's hand again. She shouldn't leave her.

Jeanie looked at Aleksey, then at the cows that were barely alive themselves. Aleksey recounted the pure luck that had occurred when the errant cows appeared at the door, bumping it with their heads, making Aleksey and Katherine finally pull them into their space. They had felt bad for the freezing cows and couldn't turn them out and didn't realize until Nikolai told them that in saving the cows, the cows saved their lives by sharing their considerable warmth. Jeanie listened, gulped back a cry then peeled a contented Yale from her breast. *Pure dumb luck*, Jeanie thought.

"There's plenty of fuel now," Jeanie said. "Tommy will stay with both of you and I won't stay longer than a few hours no matter what the status of our rescue expedition." Jeanie pulled from Katherine and stood. Frank did too and Aleksey sat where Jeanie had been and took over caring for Katherine.

Back in the wagon with Nikolai on one side of her and Frank on the other, Jeanie was sure her anger and fear were all she needed to fuel her body. Though the sun raged hard, none of its rays could be felt, as though it weren't working at all, but just part of their memories, sparked by the idea that the sun should be there, that it should produce heat.

They crunched across the prairie, headed, in their best estimation, in the direction James would have taken. No one seemed to know if Templeton had made the trip with him or gone toward his own house. And they just repeated the facts as they knew them, over and again to one another as though mechanical representations of themselves rather than fleshy humans.

Their gazes scanned the prairie for odd shoots of color in the crystal-encrusted white. And they wound up back at Ruthie's house, heading toward the haystack that stood fifty feet from the house.

In daylight, they could see a distinct hole had been cut into it, that there was movement.

They screamed for James.

More movement in the shadow. Perhaps the light wind lifting loose hay?

Jeanie grabbed her chest hoping to calm her erratic heartbeat.

They drew closer.

The movement was deliberate.

From inside the hole came two hands gripping the sides of the haystack that created the archway to the inside. A head emerged, then a body straightened.

Jeanie sprung to her feet in the wagon and dove out of it, charging through the snow. Nikolai held up the horses as Jeanie ran directly through their path.

"JamesJamesJamesJames!" Jeanie said. Her body filled with such pleasure at the sight of James walking toward her that she thought she might explode. She'd known he was alive all along, but had been too afraid to admit it, to believe in it. She was afraid a family wouldn't be permitted such luck as to survive yet another catastrophe intact.

James held his arms open and from fifteen yards away Jeanie could see his mouth part into his quiet smile.

"Mama."

Jeanie couldn't hear her name leave James' lips, but she saw him form the word sure as she knew her name.

"James!" Jeanie lifted her skirts and ran harder.

"Stay there! I'm coming, James. You're safe! You're alive! I love you!" she screamed.

James stopped. "I love you..." his lips formed the silent words then his eyebrows knitted into worry and he touched his face, which had drooped into a frown before he dropped straight forward into the snow like a stiff board.

He looked like an actor in a play who'd been directed to play dead.

Jeanie reached him and pushed him over onto his back shaking him. "James, Jamie, James, don't you do this to me after the night I've had. Do *not* treat your dear mother like this!"

Her voice rose, pitchy screeches sliced through the frigid air. Tumbling through her brain at once were the thoughts that he'd sought to protect her, his father, that he'd embodied such loyalty even if his father shared none of it.

She put her cheek on his. "All right, James, that's enough. Enough play-acting for now, don't you suppose?"

He didn't respond.

Jeanie pulled back and looked at him, watching peace creep across his face which was more grey than pink and she realized that whatever allowed him to stand and walk toward her had extinguished like fire doused by water.

She felt his throat for a heartbeat. Nothing. She shook him up and down at the shoulders. Nothing. She pinched his cheeks, slapped his arms and embraced his lifeless body. And though she couldn't hear any of it, she cried into the air, her insides turning out, as her body realized what her mind couldn't make sense of. Her son was dead and she'd never see him quietly exude life as he had for the past twelve years.

As Jeanie's mind unwound into insanity, holding her son, noticing everything about him that she hadn't really paid attention to before—the scar near his ear, the way one nostril was slightly larger. Her fingers quaked as she brushed every exposed part of him.

She could hear Frank, Nikolai, and Tommy rushing to the haystack, pulling Lutie from it. She looked up, pulled James onto her lap like a baby and bolted her arms so tight around him that they went numb. She watched Nikolai hoist Lutie's stiff, curled-up body and bring her into the sunlight. Her yellow ringlets, the only thing still alive on her body, danced with every step her rescuer took. Nikolai laid her in the snow and attempted to make her body go flat.

Jeanie began to hum, rocking James, watching the dead beauty, the one whose beauty had no prairie peer. When Jeanie was sure they would not be able to straighten Lutie's body, nausea swept in. She buried her face in James, telling him he'd live, that he couldn't die, that there was no way he should or could be the dead one in this scenario.

Rockrockrockrock. She said the words to herself as her body went back and forth, replaying James' entire, short lifetime in her mind, stealing her existence with every second that told her she'd never see her son alive again.

The day the members of the Darlington Township cooperative buried their dead was the third that yielded warm enough temperatures that the men could bust through the frozen earth, to dig black holes, from which steam rose as they reached warmer soil that mixed with the still cold air.

The weeks following the blizzard, the inventorying of frozen carnage, living with Frank's infidelity, addiction, and nearly complete isolation inside their hovel left Jeanie hardened, and each day, she dug further into numbness. She'd sat with James' body until Mr. Zurchenko dragged both her and James' dead body to the barn.

There, Jeanie had hunkered in to let the cold take her as it had James. But Katherine appeared in front of her, holding the wailing Yale. This crying and the sight of two of her live children was enough to make her milk come in and with it the core sense to go on with life, even if inside, she was as dead as James.

Katherine's finger, somehow escaped the warmth of the cows and Aleksey and it had to be amputated. Frank took Katherine into Yankton where a doctor happened to be visiting his sister and was able to perform the surgery. Jeanie had been surprised at Katherine's nonchalance at removing the finger, her pinky finger, but Katherine's thought was losing it was better than poisoning her entire body and dying. She thought it better to cut off the memories of the blizzard.

Yet, it was clear to Jeanie that Katherine wasn't going to cut off everything that reminded her of the storm. Aleksey and Katherine were nearly joined at the bone when not doing chores or studying with Ruthie—they were certainly joined at the heart. Not in a romantic way, but in the same way soldiers found common ground even if not good friends.

Jeanie felt grateful Aleksey was keeping watch over Katherine, to help her through her grief, because Jeanie couldn't do it herself. She couldn't discuss James even though images of him, words they'd shared, phrases that characterized him, were locked in her mind as though if she was to converse, the topic of James would be all that she could produce. Her language was reduced to a grunt and a hand wave when she needed something. She was blind in every way a person could be, and to her, there was no way to address it. She sobbed, either quietly, or madly, loudly, gasping at air, choking on mucus that she hoped would infect her lungs with pneumonia and kill her fast.

Tommy had grown sullen at the death of his brother, poring over the Bible, muttering and memorizing passages. He sang praises to God, especially upon the reappearance of Summer and Night who had ambled away in the storm, but had been returned by a merchant from Yankton.

Jeanie never told Tommy, Katherine, or anyone the circumstances of their father and Ruthie. Jeanie couldn't bare the humiliation of disclosure or the notion she'd poison the kids toward their father, or the failure she'd have to deal with if her children knew she couldn't keep a man or that the man in question was the cause of James' death.

Still, Tommy picked up on something. Perhaps he knew more than Jeanie thought, as James clearly had. But at the sight of his father, droopy-eyed, all sense of his self swept away with opium grains, made Tommy flare with the anger that, inside Jeanie, sat as hard resentment rather than volcanic anger.

Katherine didn't show any sense of knowing anything in regard to what part Frank had in James' death. She wore a neutral expression, talked little, but seemed at peace with the fact some of them had lived. That she was alive and she'd kept Yale alive, too. Katherine was empowered by her ability to care for someone weaker, Jeanie thought and thank God, one of them was.

Jeanie felt the only glimmer of peace in herself at the sight of Katherine, competent, lucky, whatever was the truth about her surviving and keeping Yale alive, it was good, and Jeanie worried less and less about Katherine as time went by. Katherine's age made her nearly a woman, but her experience made her fully adult.

At the bee tree, the Zurchenkos stood in staggered rows, faces hardened, no one touching except for Anna who was draped around her mother's neck. The Hunts wrapped themselves in each other's arms, Ruthie stood near Templeton, and the Arthurs felt the cold weight of grief standing with them, between them, inside them, leaving no room for any of them to hold one another in any sense.

Frank stood behind Jeanie, hiding from Ruthie. Every few minutes Frank would lean on Jeanie or pull her body into his. She would stiffen, shrug or step away as she couldn't have found any more concern for her husband and his weaknesses if her own life depended upon it. All she wanted was to be dead herself. Jeanie could sense Ruthie staring at her, but she didn't return the gaze.

She didn't offer an understanding nod for the pain Ruthie must be feeling at the loss of Lutie—Ruthie's only family member except for aunts and uncles in Canada.

Jeanie stared at her feet, the scarred black boots that were too big, that curled up like a witch shoes Jeanie'd seen in illustrations of evil women. Though she felt nothing for Frank—she'd have to deal with him for the rest of her life and numbness would be a better state than constant anger—she felt rage against Ruthie.

She just couldn't square the notion that a woman like Ruthie would betray Jeanie the way she had. Luckily, James stole most of Jeanie's thoughts. Like an artesian well that provided a constant swell of water, seeping in from hardened rock many feet below the surface of the earth, from an unseen though consistent source, Jeanie's pain did the same inside her skin. With its force, Jeanie had decided it would be her life companion, if there was nothing else she could rely on, it would be the constant replenishment of pain at James' passing.

They would bury four that day. James, Lutie, Anton, and Artem.

Jeanie sobbed inside, but no tears fell, no shudders visibly wracked her body, though inside torrents of grief ravaged, punctuated by tremors of shock and disbelief.

Greta coughed and Jeanie looked at her. She remembered the day they searched for loved ones, stumbling on friends and strangers, standing upright, frozen hard, mid-step, their faces grimaced, so lifelike in their pose, yet so dead that Jeanie and Greta found themselves laughing through tears. It couldn't be real, these iced humans, people they knew or at least had seen from time to time.

The sights were utterly impossible, yet there they were, people hard as marble, mid-stride. The storm had turned out to be of historic interest, nothing like the United States had experienced before. The newspapers Frank brought from Yankton delineated the way the atmosphere had shifted—low and high pressure fronts, the kind James always spoke of—with angry force, more characteristic of an explosion than a winter storm—the sound and fury Jeanie and Katherine had heard when the storm tore open the sky.

The scathing reports showed how the information that could have warned people to stay in their homes on that alluring warm January 12th day had been in the hands of experts, yet there'd been no system in place to warn people of the impending disaster.

Frank put his arm on Jeanie's shoulder. She shook it off and leveled him with a death glare before turning back to stare at the caskets then her ugly boots.

Jeanie was startled as Greta's sharp wails took to the air. She remembered finding Anton and Artem just behind the Zurchenko's barn, the brothers' arms laced, gripping one another, frozen in sibling comfort. Jeanie and Greta dragged the human sculpture into the Zurchenko's house, then lay it in front of the fire, Anton's leg oddly to one side, making it impossible for them to stay righted, as they had been leaning against the hay. Jeanie and Greta cried and odd laughter ripped through the tears making the rest of the children and Nikolai recoil at the sound.

But they couldn't stop themselves. Insanity had fully gripped them and with insanity there was no room for manners, upholding social expectation and the cackle of their laughter, Jeanie would never forget the sound of it, though she wondered if she'd ever be able to find it odd that they laughed; given the circumstances, anything could have been deemed a normal reaction.

They'd determined that it would be days before the bodies thawed enough to be buried flat or to dig the graves. Jeanie found it grotesquely comforting that she could visit James' frosty body in the barn. She knew intellectually that it was gruesome, that she sat beside him, hand over his heart, trying to will his soul into hers, half-hoping it was still present in his chest, free to enter hers, half-hoping there was a God who led James into sweet Heaven to look down upon her for the rest of her life.

So, it was there at the funeral in the glaring sun that spilled from the sky, then sprung off the diamond-blinding snow, that

Jeanie came to understand she felt as frozen inside as the bodies of those left to die on the prairie. Perhaps it was Jeanie herself who recognized in herself, her detachment from the death that lay statuesque on the prairie.

A minister from Yankton came to perform the service, and Jeanie heard none of it. At unwarned intervals, Jeanie's numbness would give way and pain like a scalpel over unanesthestitized skin left her mind as loose and wild as a rabid animal. In the wake of that pain, she found a new standard for emotion, one that had risen to unimaginable heights only to maintain its bite until the bite became the norm.

Before she knew it, the wooden boxes were lowered into the gaping earth and she suddenly was awakened by the last time James' body would be on topsoil. The silence was thick. Greta finally broke the silence as the sound of dirt hitting wood brought tears over Jeanie's lids. Katherine gripped her around the waist, squeezing her tight.

"We'll be strong, Mama," Katherine's voice floated up into Jeanie's ears. She looked down to see Katherine's eyes overflowing with silent tears, but her face conveyed all the strength Jeanie wished she felt herself.

"I'll take care of you Mama. Yale, Father, Tommy, everyone. I can do it. We are Arthurs. We're not crying people."

Jeanie ran her finger down the path of Katherine's tears that dried in the cold nearly as fast as they fell. She wanted to tell Katherine she was right, that they weren't crying people, that they were strong, that she just needed time to think, to heal, to get through the next minute, day, week and they'd be fine. But, all Jeanie could do was stare at Katherine's falling tears, wishing they were indeed, not crying people.

Murmurs from the other mourners grew louder as everyone turned their backs from the tree, the thud of dirt hitting wood. Jeanie heard snippets of conversation—plans to trek to the Missouri River for wood in spring, who would take milk to New Holland to have cheese made, recapping all the places they would be able to locate wild grapes, buffalo berries, cherry trees and gooseberry bushes that summer. And the weather. The way the air felt so calm, what that meant, how to tell what was coming next, the ways the government would create a system to warn about the weather.

Jeanie clasped her ears to shut out the chatter, but she couldn't shut off her own mind or mouth. "How can you people talk about weather?" Jeanie stalked over to the group, her voice tightening as it rose. She swung her arms for emphasis. "Weatherweatherweather? I never want to hear the word again! I never want to notice it, to *understand* it. I don't care what's happening in the atmosphere and damn you Templeton for making James give a damn about the blasted weather. Do you understand? *Do you understand?*"

Jeanie stalked over to Templeton and beat his chest with her fists. "How am I supposed to live when the weather is central to our existence and every time someone mentions it, I think of James, I feel James, I feel him missing." Jeanie screeched and pounded on Templeton. "How am I supposed to get over something that is as present as the weather? Howhowhow?" Jeanie wrapped her arms around Templeton and then crumbled to the ground, sliding down his body like it were a pole. She balled up on the ground, her face buried in the snow, hoping it would suffocate her.

Templeton squatted down, trying to pull Jeanie up, soothing her with quiet reassurances he didn't mean to hurt James, and that he was sorry, that…it didn't matter what he said, Jeanie couldn't hear him. Other hands fell over her, pulling at her.

"I'm sorry, Jeanie," Ruthie's voice infiltrated Jeanie's ears over all the rest. She looked up from her ball, seeing Ruthie's face near hers.

"You. Get. Out. Get out! I'll never forgive you."

"I'm so sorry, Jeanie. Please accept my apology," Ruthie said.

Jeanie spit at her, feeling her teeth grind, knowing she looked like a rabid animal. Jeanie watched as Mrs. Hunt pulled Ruthie away, comforting her, telling her that Jeanie's reaction was typical for a grief-stricken mother, that Jeanie couldn't have meant what she said.

Jeanie watched as Frank tried to comfort Ruthie, the way Ruthie told Frank to tend his wife, that there was no place for him near her when his wife hurt so. Frank looked down at Jeanie, his face covered in angst, that Jeanie thought was greater at Ruthie's rejection than at the death of his son. Jeanie hated them all, every one of them. And no one more than herself.

How could she have agreed to go to Dakota Territory? How could her shame at her father's actions been so great, humiliating, that she gave up everything and only got a dead son in return, the destruction of the only thing that mattered. As angry as she was at Frank, Ruthie and unfairly, Templeton, she was utterly destroyed by her own part in James' death. No one could be blamed beyond herself.

"This is too utterly, utterly, utterly..." Jeanie shot to her feet, knocking Templeton back. She took off running for the dugout. She thought momentarily of Yale, that Katherine held her, that she'd need to be fed, then she tore off, knowing Katherine wouldn't be far behind, that she wouldn't let anything happen to Yale.

Jeanie burst through the dugout door. Katherine was ten minutes behind.

"Mama?" Katherine put her hand on Jeanie's back. Jeanie's posture softened at the touch. She turned from the stove.

"Katherine. I'm sorry. Does Yale need to be fed?" Jeanie ran her hand over Katherine's bonnet, pulling it off her hair, running her hand down her daughter's back. Katherine's face was drawn, sunken with lack of hearty food and sadness for her lost brother and crumbling family.

"You sit, Katherine." She kissed Katherine's forehead and cupped her chin, forcing a smile. "Let me take Yale." Jeanie pulled some pillows from the other bed and built a nest for Katherine to nestle into while Jeanie settled into the rocker to feed Yale. Katherine's eyes drooped as she watched her mother. Once Yale latched onto Jeanie, Katherine's eyes shut fully, falling into a snoring sleep.

Jeanie drew back some of Yale's coverings. The storm had taken its toll on her, too. She seemed as slight as she had when she was born two months premature. Jeanie knew that couldn't be right, that she had to be at least ten pounds by then, but her legs had grown spindly again, her skin sallow. A swell of fear came over Jeanie, but the feelings dissipated when Jeanie remembered James, that he'd never come back. That was all she could experience at the time, his loss. The loss of James.

"Jeanie?" Frank knelt in front of Jeanie. She shot up straight, she'd fallen asleep while nursing Yale. "Could we make some coffee?"

Jeanie's eyes were hot and dry, blurred from the aridness. She stared at Frank, not sure if he was seriously waking her up after weeks of sleeplessness to make him coffee.

"You want coffee, Frank?" Jeanie said through clenched teeth. He rocked back on his heels and stood, hands spread.

"I can make it," he said.

"Oh, no, My,my,my, no. No thank you." Jeanie rose and put Yale into her cradle. "Is there anything else you could use?"

Frank glanced sideways before locking Jeanie's gaze. "Well, I uh, my pants are split, and the one pocket's come apart. Um, that might be nice. I know how you like to feel useful and all."

Jeanie spilled water into the kettle, dumped in a mix of coffee grinds, herbs and chicory, and lit the stove.

"Is there something else?"

"Well, I'd like for us to make a go—"

"A go? Really? That's what you'd like?"

"I mean, I love you and I made a mistake, Ruthie made a mistake. She's so sorry. It wasn't her fault."

"Don't you dare apologize for her, smooth things out for her. I hate that woman and she will burn in hell with you."

Frank's eyes drooped at the outer edges.

"Why don't you tend the animals, while I do this. That would be fine," Jeanie said, slamming a spoon into its proper storage place.

Chapter 20

Jeanie didn't hear Frank go out the door, but when she turned he was gone. His absence brought extra air into the dugout and Jeanie realized how much she hated Frank, how much she wanted him dead or just gone. She didn't know how they'd carry on, together, pretending to craft a life, to carry on with roles and expectations, and hopes and dreams. He was the cause of her baby's death, he betrayed her in every way imaginable, yet she was tethered to him for life.

Divorce was not an option. If she divorced him, there would be no way she could support the children. She'd lose everything—everything that the act of homesteading was supposed to save was now in jeopardy because they taken the risk of running away. Her father, his acts put them on this path, but it was Frank who sealed things up.

Jeanie was enraged again. She paced back and forth. Every so often she stopped pacing to gaze at Katherine or Yale, sleeping peacefully, not aware of the extra layer of pain that sat under the death of James, she tried to find comfort in the sight of them, but couldn't.

She grabbed three pairs of Frank's pants and her sewing basket. She started by mending the pocket of one pair of pants, then hours later had mended anything that even hinted it would be a hole in the next year. Frank entered the house, red-faced from his work in the barn.

"Take those off. I'm mending everything now."

Frank did as he was told then lay next to Katherine. Jeanie sewed in a trance-like state, her hands flying like a machine. Every now and then she'd glance at Katherine and Frank, and the only thing that stopped Jeanie's sewing was the startling resemblance between Katherine and her father. They could have been twins rather than father and daughter.

The day bled into night and Katherine and Frank slept right through dinner. Jeanie didn't disturb them, but when Tommy came back from wandering in the land of the Lord as he put it, Jeanie and he slipped into the children's bedstead for the night. Jeanie hadn't realized how numb she'd become until they pulled the blanket up over them and the scent of James wafted off the blanket, the smell breaking through the nothingness she'd grown accustomed to, causing her fresh pain she didn't think possible until it was smothering her.

At daybreak following the funeral, Frank shook Jeanie awake. "Baby's cryin.'"

Jeanie oriented herself to where they all were, who was in which bed, and in the midst of the fresh realization that James was dead, Jeanie began her morning chores.

Frank slipped back into bed and Katherine rose, a half-smile over her face. Jeanie's raised her eyebrows, questioning.

"I feel better, Mama, for this one instant, I felt good enough that a smile popped to my lips. It surprised me, but it was there for a second."

Jeanie hugged Katherine with one arm and flipped oatcakes over the fire with the other. "Why don't you brush the horses and then take some of these cakes to the Zurchenko's," Jeanie said.

"Okay. That's good, that's good." Katherine sighed as though she'd been waiting for that exact instruction.

Tommy rose within minutes of Katherine leaving. Wordlessly, he shoveled down oatcakes and then pushed out the door, never even looking back at Jeanie. She yelled for him but he was gone so fast that Jeanie wasn't sure if he didn't hear her or if he was ignoring her on purpose.

Frank stirred in the bed then reached under it for a small tin of opium that he nibbled on then fell back, his face, ecstatic as far as Jeanie could see. She began to slam her pots and spoons around.

"Blast-it, Jeanie. Could you keep it down a bit?"

"I'm sorry," Jeanie cocked her head to the side. "Am I disturbing your sleep?"

"I was thinking about that cotton idea we had."

"*We* had?"

"Yes, we are a we. Like it or not. We are. You need me whether you know it or like it or not."

"Well, I'm not sure about that."

"Sure about what? I told you the cotton industry is shifting from the southeast to the southwest. We could get in front of the wave and—"

"Listen to me Frank. I can't handle this or you or your schemes or air castles or air-cotton-plantations. Nothing that you suggest exists in reality unless I have a hand in making it so. So, forget it. I'm not pulling up stakes."

"You hate it here."

"I do."

"So?"

"So what? I'm not leaving James ever."

"That's just…"

Jeanie stood over the still reclining Frank. "Do you care a whit for your son?"

"Don't harry me."

"Harry you? You're lucky I don't pluck you like a prairie chicken then twist off your toes and fingers and feed them to the rattle snakes before I kill you."

Frank opened his eyes. "I can see this isn't going to work. I'm leaving, Jeanie. I didn't hurt our son on purpose, or you. I didn't. It was simply circumstances. Hundreds, *hundreds* of people died that day and that *has* to be forgiven. You're my wife and any living you made from your books before is gone so I'm going to leave and give you a moment to consider the intelligence of your recent mind-set. Can't you feel the bitterness I see in your whole being? Greta has lost too, yet she still has an eye for household cares, yearns for the comfort of Nikolai—"

"You don't see the difference in our *circumstances?*"

Frank looked away, shrugging.

"Go ahead Frank. Make a go of it alone."

"*We* are still alive, Jeanie."

Jeanie's mouth pulled. She realized that in many ways, to her, Frank and their marriage, anything they meant to one another was as dead as poor cold, rotting James. All she cared about, all she could understand was the loss of her son; she didn't want to or think her capable of soothing her childish husband's spirit. She quaked with anger.

"You make a go of it, Frank. Go ahead."

Frank, facing away from her, buckled at the words.

Jeanie held the spit in her mouth that she'd wanted to release all over his face, picked up Yale and headed to the Zurchenko's. She cared so little for the outcome of Frank's threat that she decided to walk to the Zurchenko's, to leave Frank the wagon so he couldn't use his not having transportation against her. Why couldn't he have been the man she thought she married so long before? Because she was a child at the time, subject to infatuation that she read to be love and compatibility.

Jeanie wasn't half way to the bee tree when she heard Frank caterwauling atop the dugout. She turned to see him in his under-garments, waving all four of his pairs of pants above his head, his face twisted with insult.

"Oh, I guess I did do that," Jeanie said out loud. She shrugged then walked on. She snickered as the memory flooded back, her sewing madly, when the mending of one pocket turned into her sewing all Frank's pockets shut, the button flies shut, and on two pairs of the pants, she'd madly sewn the leg holes shut. Jeanie snickered again. It was like a dream. Had she really done that? Well, she had, and to her, at that moment, it seemed fitting.

Frank was gone. To where, Jeanie didn't know. She'd spent many spring days, trekking to the bee tree with the baby hoping to find solace. No one else ever went there and that suited Jeanie fine. She wandered as though she were the opium-eater, and from certain perspectives she didn't appear any different than one.

All she could manage to do was feed the children and accept charity from Greta who was much stronger than she. And Greta had a decent husband after all. No wonder she could function.

Jeanie had told Tommy and Katherine that their father left the prairie, spurred by the crushing loss of James. Both kids nod-ded, accepting that statement. Katherine pushed Jeanie on it a few times, inquiring where she could write, what exactly Frank said when he left. And Jeanie, who hated Frank in the depths of her body and soul, couldn't tell Katherine the truth. So, she stitched a shirt-waist of lies, depicting how Frank cried when he left, that he could barely spit out his grief-laden words, but that he was clear that he loved them all down to his toes, that he couldn't stand the pain, that he'd be back just as soon as he could breathe again.

Still, Jeanie couldn't press herself to be productive in her nor-mal sense, she did note from time to time how comfortable she'd become living in squalor, doing nothing, expecting nothing from anyone or anything, how that condition was somehow comforting. She'd even burned one of the books she wrote when she ran out of fuel. And page by page, she cackled at the disappearance of Jeanie as the print certainly exemplified who'd she'd been at one time, not a bit like the woman she was at that moment.

A few days after Frank disappeared into the horizon and Katherine took off to the Zurchenko's with Tommy, Jeanie trudged off to the tree with Yale. Yale had been lethargic, still just barely the size of a newborn. Being born two months premature then having been stunted by the blizzard catastrophe, there were times Jeanie wondered if Yale would ever grow.

The sun swamped the pair and as they sat under the blooming bee tree where Jeanie spent over an hour talking to James, Lutie and the Zurchenko boys as though they were alive and well, though unusually mute. Yale whimpered and when her breath became even more choppy, Jeanie held her to her breast, but Yale turned away. It sounded as though Yale was swallowing her tonsils, hacking so hard her limbs tensed then finally she went limp.

Jeanie hadn't even realized what happened right away, that Yale had stopped drawing breath, and that she had stopped moving, looking so angry and upset to have been born. She guessed it had been an hour before she fully processed the death of Yale, the death of her second child in just months. Jeanie felt her insides rip open like a hot anvil had been dragged through her soul. She was being torn in two, wanting her body to take its own life in the same way Yale's had, by simply giving up on itself. Jeanie rocked the baby, crying into her neck, begging her to start breathing again. In between sobs, Jeanie would hold her own breath to see if in fact, Yale would start to breathe again.

Jeanie screamed, cursing herself for not being more careful with the baby, for not noticing how weak she'd gotten, for writing it all off as a consequence of prematurity and the stress of barely eating anything during the blizzard. But mostly, she admitted to herself, that she'd let her pain of losing James control every aspect of her life and in doing so she'd lost another child. Jeanie ripped at her clothes, scratching her chest, her face, her body, trying the scrape the life out of her from the outside in.

Still clutching Yale's lifeless body, Jeanie had made the decision to kill herself, then abandoned the idea, going back and forth several times, finding strength in the moments she'd made the solid decision to end it all. Either way she had to get back to the dugout or go to the Zurchenko's and inform the children of Yale's death. They would want to say goodbye. But as she began in the direction of the dugout, she heard someone calling her name.

In the blaze of the sun Jeanie couldn't see who was coming toward her at first, but shielding her eyes and listening to the voice as it came closer she realized it was Ruthie. Jeanie turned to walk away, cradling Yale like she were still alive, but something in Ruthie's screeching voice made Jeanie wait. Ruthie stumbled, rested on all fours then rose again, careening toward Jeanie.

It wasn't until Ruthie fell into Jeanie that she realized Ruthie was wearing her silk shoes, the ones that went missing in the fall.

"*You*." Jeanie ripped her body out of Ruthie's grip. "My shoes. You. How could you steal my shoes? My beautiful, little tokens of my life before. *My shoes!*" Jeanie clenched her teeth. Back in September she had allowed her mind to let go of the shoes, to take their absence as a sign that she'd embraced her prairie life, that she didn't need such ridiculous reminders of her past, because her future was going to be fulfilling.

But in the end, her missing shoes only signified the life that had been stolen from Jeanie. She could have cared less about the actual, beautiful, but now well-worn, dirty, shoes.

Ruthie groaned, hugging herself, face contorted with the look of pain that Jeanie knew only too well. Ruthie was having contractions that were wracking her body. Her legs began to give way. With her one free arm, Jeanie caught Ruthie under her armpit as blood gushed, splashing over the ground, the shoes, Jeanie's hem.

Not only was Ruthie pregnant, but she was in the middle of what appeared to be a labor going very bad. Ruthie's hands were bloody and her skirt was dripping with fluid and blood as well. Ruthie slurred her words, unable to make eye contact. But she clung to Jeanie begging her for help. Jeanie stiffened and pulled away though Ruthie's grip was surprisingly tight and Jeanie stumbled under Ruthie's weight. She lowered Ruthie to the ground.

Jeanie nuzzled Yale's dead body. "You think I should help you, Ruthie Moore? I have another dead child to bury!"

Ruthie nodded, her eyes rolling back in her head. "Please, please, forgive me. I'm begging you. I can't go on if I know you won't help me."

"I'd rather slit my wrists." Jeanie started to stalk away, to leave Ruthie to have what she suspected was Frank's child on her own. God knew he was not really there for Jeanie and now he was definitely not there for his mistress.

Ruthie reached up to Jeanie, opening and closing her fingers. "I'm sorry. I'm so sorry. I won't stay here. I'll go to my aunt's home in Vancouver. I won't make trouble. All I want is the baby. Someone to love me." Ruthie's words were scratchy, barely audible.

Jeanie shook her head. "I don't forgive you. I hate you, you weak woman." Jeanie didn't trust Ruthie, that she would leave on her own with a baby. Ruthie would end up living near Jeanie forever and if that was to be the case, Jeanie would not grant her forgiveness. Jeanie wanted to walk away, to pack her bags and head to Des Moines where at that point, to live in shame there would not feel as bad as living inside such bad memories with people she couldn't look in the eye for reasons that dwarfed those that originally sent her to the prairie.

Stupidstupidstupid.

Ruthie grabbed Jeanie's wrist. "I need your forgiveness. I didn't mean...I never had anyone love me...ever...no one, my parents, no one. Frank loved me. I had no choice...I will take this baby and go. I realize now, that's the only love that matters. I'm so, so sorry to have been a part—"

"Shut up Ruthie. *Shut. Up.*"

"To understand...I wouldn't...I didn't mean harm..." Ruthie curled up in pain. She choked, spitting out mucus tinged with red. This got Jeanie's attention.

She rubbed her temples and looked down at Ruthie again, finally feeling Ruthie's pain as her own, knowing how frightened she must be in that position and Jeanie decided right then her life would be a series of decisions based on what was right rather than what didn't scare her. Right then, she decided fear, in fact, was everything, the only thing she could count on.

Jeanie lay baby Yale's lifeless body under the bee tree. She brushed back Yale's wispy hair, signed a cross over her body as she'd seen the Zurchenkos do, and kissed Yale's lips before tending to Ruthie. She got between Ruthie's legs, pushed them up and tried to discern exactly what was happening. Ruthie was nearly silent but for shallow breaths. And the baby crowned then slid out as though Ruthie'd had several children before.

The baby, a girl, had black hair, but round, blue eyes. Though she'd just come out of Ruthie's body, the baby was all Frank G. Arthur, the rebirth of Katherine.

Jeanie was so enthralled with the resemblance to Frank that it took a moment to realize the baby wasn't breathing. Jeanie thwapped her on the bottom and back and gave her a good shake, but only a whimper came from the baby. She was months younger than Yale, but due to Yale's inauspicious start, Ruthie's baby was nearly the same size, but plumper, pinker, even in whatever distress she was experiencing.

Jeanie looked around the ground and picked up the sharpest rock near the bee tree. Without thinking too much about what she was about to do, she pounded the sharp edge against the throbbing umbilical cord until it finally severed.

Ruthie reached up and Jeanie handed her the baby. "It's a girl. She's beautiful. She is."

"Oh," Ruthie said.

Jeanie massaged Ruthie's belly to speed the dispelling of placenta.

"Please, my pocket, get my medicine. My medicine. It hurts. I hurt so much."

Jeanie stopped kneading and looked at Ruthie. "Still? You're still using that drug after all that happened?"

"My pocket, please, I need to stop the pain."

Jeanie squinted at Ruthie wondering how Ruthie could even have medicine as they all would have known if a doctor had made a trip to the Moore's. Jeanie pulled the glass bottle and a piece of paper from Ruthie's pocket. She lay the paper aside and read the bottle's embossing: Laudanum. Jeanie tipped the bottle into Ruthie's lips and let her take a swig.

The baby was curled against Ruthie, still pink, but not displaying the normal cries or jerky motions or grimaced faces that most newborns did, just thin wails and a loll of the head here or there. Perhaps the laudanum had reached the baby, Jeanie wondered, making the baby as sluggish as her mother.

Jeanie returned to Ruthie's nether-regions to check on the placenta delivery. Not only had the placenta come out, but Ruthie was bleeding so much, thick clotted blackish blood, that Jeanie nearly threw up. She had no idea how much blood was normal as she'd never tended to her own afterbirth, but the amount saturating the ground seemed excessive.

It didn't take long. Ruthie bled to death with Jeanie talking to her, telling her to hang on, that it would stop. Jeanie felt as though a bad joke was upon her, the amount of death was astonishing, even though she'd heard of prairie deaths, and deaths in childbirth were not uncommon, but still, so much at one time, it strangled her. She lay on Ruthie, her fingers in Ruthie's neck, feeling for her pulse. She felt a thud of pressure and Jeanie felt swept by forgiveness. She couldn't believe she was party to so many deaths—just being in the presence of death again made her feel responsible.

Jeanie found a patch of softness in her heart and told Ruthie she forgave her, but Ruthie didn't respond.

"I forgive you Ruthie, I forgive you, I forgive you." Jeanie shook Ruthie, pushing her face side to side. "Please hear me. Do something to show me you hear me." Jeanie sat back on her knees, face upturned to the sky, crying, feeling a different kind of grief, the sort that only comes from one inflicting pain instead of absorbing it. She'd not been an awful person until the time on the prairie. There, she'd been transformed into a person she didn't recognize nor did she want to.

Jeanie was sorry Ruthie died, that Yale had too, in that instant of death, Jeanie's heart yielded toward Ruthie then hardened again that it took death for Jeanie to realize her own stubbornness.

Once Jeanie went dry, the paper that had been in Ruthie's pocket fluttered in a gentle wind. Jeanie picked it up and noticed Frank's handwriting hidden by the folded crease.

"I'm sorry, Ruthie, but I have to read this."

Dearest Ruthie,
My love, my soul—both live with you even when I don't.

Jeanie covered her mouth, her hands shook as she read what she knew she didn't want to know.

I'll be gone for a short time, to set about making a life for us in Texas. I'm heartbroken that you can't travel, but that baby inside of you—our sweet gift from God—is too precious to risk. I will forsake my family for you, as it can only damage them all to live a lie right in their presence. It will be better this way. For everyone. I'll be back for both of you and we will spend our days contemplating the beauties of nature—the kind that

sprouts white and puffy out of Texas dirt, the kind that lives within the
two of us, holding hearts over many lonely miles.
    Love, dearly,
    Your Frank

Jeanie couldn't feel the final loss of her marriage. She was dry,
empty, singed inside, with nothing but a mind whose sole quest
was to figure out how to keep the rest of her family together, so
they wouldn't all perish in squalor.

Ruthie's baby let out a cry, startling Jeanie. She shushed the
child, petting her head. Jeanie didn't think Ruthie's infant would
last more than a few minutes, with the way she laid there, limp.

Jeanie pulled Ruthie's pocket out, to put the letter back inside.
She noticed a round glass button—the pasque flower paperweight
button, and another paper—a train ticket to Seattle with a transfer
to Vancouver, British Columbia. Jeanie covered her mouth, tasted
blood that spackled her hand. Ruthie *hadn't* been lying.

She was on her way out of the country, to Canada. Jeanie buckled at the thought. It was her fault. If Jeanie had accepted Ruthie's
apology, she might have had the strength to survive. The button.
Lutie's lavender dress had been missing its buttons when they
found her the morning of her death. All but one. Jeanie couldn't
fathom why Ruthie felt it important to keep, but Jeanie stashed it
in her pocket, knowing she wouldn't part with it.

Jeanie hadn't thought another exposure to grief could actually add pain. But there it was, building. How could she live with
Ruthie's death on her hands? She could have gotten help. Done
something besides let the woman die, in pain, emotionally alone.
She had begged Jeanie for forgiveness and she'd denied it, felt
power in denying it. The shame Jeanie felt stopped her breath. She
wretched, vomiting amid the red soil.

The letter. Frank was coming back for Ruthie. How could she
explain this? Jeanie felt as though she'd killed Ruthie and though
she knew she hadn't she wasn't sure that guilt wouldn't be draped

upon her, pointing to her as murderer, negligent at the very least. She was a murderer.

She said the word aloud to see if it fit.

Jeanie dragged Ruthie's body into the shade of the tree. She wanted to clean her body, to make her body presentable. But there was no way to do that. Next, Jeanie lay Ruthie's baby in the crook of her dead arm. Then she lay Yale in the crook of Ruthie's other arm, hoping that eternity might be a little easier in the arms of a mother, even if Jeanie had so recently despised that mother's very being.

She ran back to the dugout and retrieved a shovel and a wet cloth. Jeanie was glad Katherine and Tommy were still at the Zurchenko's. She didn't want them to be part of another burial, she didn't want to explain how she was the cause of Yale's death, Ruthie's death and soon, Ruthie's baby. And if they knew Ruthie died, well, she didn't want to deal with that or the baby she'd born on behalf of their father. Jeanie despised the man, but she wouldn't let her children know that. She would not let them feel the disappointment and rejection she had felt when she learned the truth about her own father.

By the time she returned with the shovel and began poking at the stony ground, Jeanie was sobbing, wondering how to tell her children she'd let them down as much as their father. How could she claim herself a mother if she allowed her baby to starve to death or didn't help her fight a sickness she hadn't even realized was there?

The shovel bounced up with every throw-down, but Jeanie found the digging came easy because of the spring thaw. Jeanie heard a cry, but wrote it off as her mind playing tricks. Then she heard it again, coming from behind. She turned and her mouth fell open at the sight of stone-dead Ruthie and Yale, while Ruthie's baby jerked and pulled in her limbs, scrunching her face in disdain. Jeanie crept to the baby, unbelieving of what she saw and heard.

She bent down and poked Ruthie's baby. It scolded Jeanie with another wail.

"Oh my," Jeanie said. "You're alive."

Jeanie cocked her head and stared at the naked, blood-encrusted baby and marveled at her. Jeanie slid her hands under the baby and picked her up, holding her in the air, turning her back and forth, looking for defects.

"You are alive," Jeanie said again. She unbuttoned her blouse and put the baby to her breast to nurse. The strong suck that Yale never quite achieved pulled at every inch of Jeanie's being, the sensation on her breast spread throughout her body. This child would live and she'd be motherless because of Jeanie.

After nursing the baby, she settled her back in Ruthie's arm and continued to dig, trying to discern what she was to do with a dead mother and a live baby. After digging as deep as she could, partly running into one of the caskets they'd laid there earlier that year, Jeanie still had no answer.

She settled Ruthie's body into the grave, making her look as though she was comfortable in her death. She positioned Yale inside Ruthie's arm and then closing her eyes she threw the dirt over the bodies, promising Ruthie that she would find a home for her baby if Ruthie would find a home in the afterlife for Yale. "Take care of my girl. I'll take care of yours."

As Jeanie filled the hole, the repetitive spattering of dirt over Ruthie and Yale's skin was sickening. In just several months, Jeanie had buried her first born and last daughter. How had her life arrived at such circumstances? How could it be?

Chapter 21

1905
Des Moines, Iowa

Though Katherine didn't read any of Templeton's letters during the time she sat at her mother's bedside holding her hand, swimming in confusing memories, she knew she would eventually. Jeanie was lucid for only minutes before she fell back into oblivion. Katherine sat for hours, hoping she might come back to tell her what she needed to know. But it became clear for the time being, she was either going further into death or resting up for another moment of clarity.

While she sat with her mother, Katherine tried to piece the events of the prairie back together. She couldn't do it though, and it became clear that she first had to read the attic letters, needed to try to understand why her mother had decided to burn them, why Katherine herself would have been compelled to lift them out of the fire and tuck them away where her mother would never see them again. And why would her father write to Ruthie Moore, why would her mother have that letter?

Jeanie stared at her mother's relatively smooth face. She should have been more wrinkled to have death courting her so hard.

Katherine touched her mother's cheek, its softness made a smile flit to her mouth.

Eventually, Katherine trudged up the attic steps and settled back into the spot she'd vacated the day before. Aleksey had made three stacks of letters, not in any order. On top was the one that didn't fit with the rest. From an address in Texas to Ruthie Moore. Katherine's hand shook while holding it, as though she knew what was written inside was something she didn't want to know. But the feeling that she *had* to know won out and Katherine opened the letter.

Katherine's eyes fell over the words and then she reread and reread. *What* was she seeing? She traced the words with her finger.

"Baby." Katherine's hands shook and she dropped the letter, curling into a ball. "Baby." She bounced her forehead off her knees as though doing so would make her thoughts untangle. Nothing complete or coherent would come to her mind. She read the letter from her father again. *Dearest Ruthie. Our baby. Texas. I forsake my family for you...* Other words flew through her mind, too.

The words that she'd flung at her mother in hateful ways over the years. Divorce, Mama's fault. Selfish. Baby. Yale. Ruthie Moore. What happened to Ruthie? Katherine was numb with the disparate thoughts, but amidst it all, she couldn't stop remembering one thing. The argument with her mother in the dugout, the time she realized her mother was a liar, but wasn't able to understand why. Images slammed through her mind. Katherine touched her face, the hollow under her cheekbone, where her mother had slapped her, the one and only time she'd ever done such a thing. Katherine had known something was wrong. Baby. Baby. The baby. Yale.

Katherine shot to her feet and tore down the steps into her mother's room, where Yale peacefully read to Jeanie. Katherine crept into the room, staring at her sister, studying her black wavy hair, thin lips, and prairie blue eyes. Suddenly with the lucidity that should have been there for seventeen years, but went by the wayside with a stinging slap, Katherine admitted what she'd known to be true all along.

Chapter 22

When Jeanie headed back to the house with Ruthie's baby, her mind had sorted through every scenario under which plans for Ruthie's baby could be made. She could have Templeton drive her to Yankton and drop the baby at the nearest orphanage—they would find a fine home for her. Jeanie would keep her promise to Ruthie for if she didn't she feared her Yale would wander eternity alone. She couldn't have that.

But Jeanie didn't want an attachment to this baby. She wasn't the right woman to raise her. So, even when she breastfed the baby and changed her diaper, she averted her gaze from the child's, treating her as though she were an object—a fine, delicate one—rather than human. Or, she could confess to everyone how Ruthie had died at nearly the same time Yale had and that Jeanie would care for Ruthie's baby. But, it all seemed wrong.

There'd have to be an explanation about Ruthie's baby. Jeanie's children would know the story, everyone would know and the humiliation would be too great. Jeanie had a moment when she thought about fear, about how she seemed to be ruled by it yet again, but she told herself there was a difference between doing what was right for one's children and being scared of one's own humiliation. It was the children's lives she was concerned with now, not her own.

Jeanie had been washing up in the dugout after Ruthie's burial when she got word from the Hunts that Katherine and Tommy were quarantined at the Zurchenko's with the flu. They'd driven up above the dugout, wagon groaning with all the belongings they could fit as they were leaving the prairie, heading back to Vermont. They bid each other goodbye, offering platitudes that meant nothing to Jeanie and probably the same amount to the Hunts.

In the absence of everyone, Jeanie had the time and space to fall in love with Ruthie's child. It was only a day before she'd slipped into calling the baby Yale. Two days passed when Jeanie actually felt as though her Yale and Ruthie's Yale were actually the same soul, when she felt her own soul commune with her dead Yale who somehow meshed with Ruthie's baby as one and the same.

Templeton stopped by to drop off mail from Yankton. He and Jeanie barely said a word, just their gaze holding one another, wordlessly agreeing they were both too lost without James to talk about him, but understanding full well their loss.

"I stopped by for two reasons. One, I have news regarding Ruthie Moore. Her aunt and uncle were expecting her in Canada. She never showed up and the train she was to take jumped the track. Casualties everywhere. They couldn't say for sure who was who. But, she's gone from her home and so is the train ticket her uncle sent."

Jeanie covered her mouth. Her hand shook. She swallowed hard, pushing down the truth that was trying to force its way out. Jeanie couldn't allow it out. She'd dealt with too much already. There would be no way to explain her actions.

Templeton shifted his feet. "I know how much you liked Ruthie, before all that happened. I knew you'd want to know."

Jeanie nodded and looked at her feet.

"Second, I'd like to take you and the children berry picking in the next week or so. The bushes in the far corner of my homestead are full as though last year's fire had served to revitalize them."

"Berries at the end of March? That can't be right."

"It's true."

"Well, then, berries it is." Her voice was flat even though she was happy for the invite.

"Let me know when you're available."

Jeanie nodded. Templeton leaned forward, his hand cradling Jeanie's elbow while he kissed her forehead. Her stomach flipped, igniting her nerves, sending excited chills over her skin. They stood there like that, for a minute. His lips on her head, her leaning into him, wanting so much to fall onto the bedstead with him, to be taken care of, held, loved.

When she didn't move, he finally backed off, placing his hat back on his head. They nodded at one another, saying their silent, "I'm so sorry for the loss of James," before he left the dugout. How Jeanie wished she could alter her reality, have somehow met Templeton twelve years before rather than Frank. It was only at *that* point, before Frank and she existed as one, that it would be possible to alter her reality, make Templeton her love, to allow him into her life in the way she wanted him.

She shut the door behind Templeton and leaned against it. "My tired heart never found rest until you, Templeton. My heart rests on your love alone." Jeanie said that aloud to hear it herself, to gauge whether she'd ever utter the words to Templeton so he could hear them. There was no point entertaining the impossible.

Jeanie went to the letter Templeton brought from Yankton. From Frank, somewhere in Texas. It contained a note—five words long—saying he would be returning to the prairie. Jeanie snorted at the words. Had she not found Ruthie's letter from Frank, the words would have indicated to Jeanie that he was returning to her.

But, she knew better and though she felt nothing in terms of loss for their love anymore, she did feel scared about how she'd survive with the children. Was there a way she could divorce Frank? If he would send her money, yes. But she couldn't count on that. She did think she could count on Frank's love for his children, possibly his guilt for his part in James' death. Perhaps he would send her money. She no longer cared about the societal forces that would shove her out of important circles of friendship, but eating, surviving with pride was another consideration.

Could she stomach Frank in her home? As useless as he was, he was dependable in some ways—at least periodically. Could she bear to look at him? Really, it didn't matter, what she felt about their marital circumstances paled against the loss of James. That loss prevailed over everything else, but with the death of her Yale, she'd woken up a bit, ready to at the very least care for her children so to not experience another loss and worse, be the cause of it. There was so much she'd never forgive herself for and she would do her best to be sure she never hurt another one of her children and never allowed anyone else to hurt them either. She'd failed at that enough for one lifetime.

"Mama?" Katherine stood in the doorway of the dugout and even with her body completely outlined by the sun, Jeanie could see that Katherine had lost weight with the illness.

"Oh, Katherine," Jeanie lay Yale in the crib and ran to her daughter, holding her so tight, that Katherine choked. Tommy came in behind her. Jeanie pulled him by the coat, into their hug and she smattered them with kisses until they were pushing away from her, tired from the walk from the Zurchenko's.

"Here, let me put you to bed. You're doing well? I mean to have the quarantine lifted, but you're still both frail. You're thin as sunflower stalks." Jeanie felt both of them over their bodies and tucked them into bed.

"Can I hold Yale?" Katherine asked.

"Well, she's sleeping."

"I'm not contagious, I swear. They wouldn't have let us leave."

"Well, okay," Jeanie said. She held her breath and lay Yale beside Katherine. She watched as Katherine studied her sister's face, cooing at her like a little mother.

Katherine's eyebrows knitted. She looked up at Jeanie and back at Yale. Jeanie said a silent prayer.

"What's going on, Mama?"

"What do you mean?"

Katherine sat up and lay Yale on her legs, unwrapped her and played with her legs.

Katherine shook her head, opened her mouth and closed it again.

"It's all right, Katherine. We're going to all be all right. I promise. Your father will get well, we'll move to the city, maybe Yankton, maybe...we'll all be okay."

"But Yale's face."

"Yes?" Jeanie groped her neck then wiped the front of her apron.

"It's round."

"Yes, well, she's finally gaining weight after well, you know, the blizzard, her early start, there wasn't much luck on this girl's side at first, was there? Now she has your face, a real cherub. Like you, wouldn't you say?" Jeanie's voice cracked.

"Something's different. I just...I don't know. Maybe it's the fever, but I swear this baby *isn't* Yale."

Jeanie turned and went to the cook-stove, trying to remain calm. "You're right, it's the fever, it must have made you silly," Jeanie forced a laugh into her words, as though teasing.

Katherine appeared beside Jeanie who was stirring an empty pot. She held Yale out for her mother to see.

"Her flat spot on the crown of her head, it's gone."

"Well, a baby's head changes, Katherine. It's the way of the world. Change. Heads change. That's what they do."

"But, her little mole. Right there, that wasn't there before."

"What are you *saying*, Katherine? That I traded our Yale in for another? Just where would I find another baby in this Godforsaken dung-hole?" Spit flew out of Jeanie's mouth as she became enraged with unfamiliar feelings. "Is that what you're saying?"

"I don't know, Mama, it's just—"

Jeanie took deep uneven breaths and before she realized what she was doing, she slapped Katherine. Tommy ran to their sides, his mouth gaping.

"I should have taught you a long time ago to respect your elders. Hasn't your mother been through enough this year not to have her daughter tell her she's a baby switcher. Of all things, *of all things*. As if it were *possible*. As if it were so."

Jeanie's rage vibrated inside her skin, so hard she could hear it. And before she said or did another thing that would forever haunt her, she ran from the dugout and didn't stop until she reached the tree. The tree that held half of what had been dearest to her in the world. How could she not have known they were more important than escaping scandal in Des Moines?

How could she have ever agreed to leave, to follow Frank into a wasteland he had no business in? How could she have been so utterly stupid? There'd be no answer for Jeanie in that vein and all she could do was take the next right step, even if it felt wrong, even if just a year before that next step would have been unfathomable. All that was left for her to do was to burn the letter, get rid of the last trace of evidence that there was a baby born to Ruthie Moore and Frank G. Arthur.

Jeanie had been interrupted by Greta when she was attempting to burn not only Frank's letter to Ruthie, but the letters that she'd written in the year leading up to her elopement. She'd managed to torch half of the letters, but then Greta pulled her away, in a panic because Anna had gone missing. They found her in the garden, napping without a care.

By the time Jeanie returned to the hole she'd dug to burn and bury the letters, she found them all gone. The wind had obviously had its way with the correspondence and she thought it fitting that her relationship with Frank should have blown into the atmosphere, scattered like tree pollen.

Back at the dugout Jeanie found Katherine asleep, her body curled around Yale's. Jeanie had buried the truth of Yale so deep that looking at them there, knowing they shared the same father, that they had the same round, blue eyes, the same tiny noses, that even though the baby had Ruthie's jaw-line, thin lips and black hair, as clear as fresh scrubbed windows, it didn't matter because no one but Jeanie knew the truth. And she could live with it if it meant keeping them together.

Over long open patches of prairie Jeanie felt Templeton's eyes rest on her as she gazed down at Yale, fussing with her blankets. She knew he was attempting to pry into her soul and discern what she'd done to turn her playful toughness into bitter resentment.

They arrived at the berry bushes, laden with plump, crimson orbs. She tucked the sleeping Yale into the back of the wagon. Katherine and Tommy ran over the land, stretching their legs, running so far away that finally Jeanie was alone with Templeton while he helped her pluck the berries into her baskets. She dodged every gaze, every question until Templeton grabbed her by the arms so tight her fingertips momentarily went numb. She dropped the basket.

"I'm going to live in Yankton for a bit, Jeanie. I want you to come with me. But I know that's impossible right now. But maybe it won't be impossible forever."

"It's impossible forever."

"I'd like to write to you if that's okay. I've already penned a book of poems, words of yearning for James, what he meant to me, what *you* meant to me, mean to me. I didn't realize I'd constructed my very own Frank G. Arthur style air castle in my own mind. But mine isn't full of business propositions or stately homes, it was built of you and the kids."

"I *can't* Mr. Templeton. This entire line of conversation is impolite at the very least."

"Do you deny the way we're connected in some unspoken way, the ease with which I befriended James as though he were my own, the fact that you reside in my heart?"

"I *can't*. I simply can't. Frank is coming back and this is no time to—"

"He wrote? When's he coming?"

"Well, I don't know for sure." Jeanie was positive that Templeton was aware of Frank's infidelity, but she wouldn't fill him in further, to confirm for him that she was going back to a man who had treated her so shabbily when Templeton thought so highly of her. She shouldn't have cared, as though it were possible to really hide something, but she had bigger secrets to protect. Yale. Ruthie. Everything.

She felt a surge of shame. Ruthie was a lot of things, but she deserved a proper burial and Jeanie had denied her that. She did a sign of the cross over her, made a cross out of bended sticks and horsehair, prayed over her body, with every shovelful of dirt, she did her best and promised Ruthie, hoping her soul was there to hear it, that she would do her best to care for her baby, in the fashion she would her own, that she forgave her.

Templeton's face drooped, no trace of the half-smile that had always been present just a short time before. Jeanie stared at her curled black boots, remembering the way she'd sworn to herself that she'd be back in silk slippers by this time.

"You're remarkable. You understand that, right?" Templeton drew Jeanie's chin up, electrifying her body.

"You're mad."

"That may be. But it doesn't change your magnificence. Who you are. Everything you are, what you think you were is still inside you. You weren't wrong when you told me that true riches were held in the heart and entertained in the mind."

"You've been reading your Shakespeare? I don't recall commiserating over literature."

"I do."

"Well, then. Good. I thank you for your time."

Templeton dropped his hand and stepped back from Jeanie, turning to the bushes. The sound of a wagon coming over the land startled Jeanie and Templeton. They both turned, hands shielding the sun from their eyes.

Frank. There he was. Back on the plains.

Jeanie whimpered and reached for her neck, for the first time in a long time, searching for those missing pearls.

"Well, well, well," Frank said. He leapt down from the wagon and spun Jeanie around. She stiffened in his arms, nausea filling her. Templeton looked away from them both, Jeanie thought she saw a tear glimmer in the corner of his eyes. "My wife and good friend, out berry picking. Looks like my arrival isn't a moment too soon. I hope you weren't attempting to cheer Jeanie's dull feelings away." He set Jeanie down.

Jeanie scowled. "Not at all. We were simply engaging in your favorite practice—contemplating the beauties of nature—this early batch of berries is quite the prairie miracle isn't it darling husband?"

"Well, I'm back and I thank Templeton for looking in on you."

"It was nothing," Templeton said. He stuck his hand out to Frank. They both smiled at one another, as though they'd just put the order of the world back together again. Never in Jeanie's life had she felt so insignificant. Not when she'd been left out of decision making once they lost their money in Des Moines, not when she'd sold her belongings to Elizabeth, or when she realized her family name was now linked to scandal forever.

Now, watching Frank assert his power over her, their lives, as though he was God himself, Jeanie felt blackness shut her away, realizing she'd never be happy again. Thomas Jefferson. Jeanie thought. She'd never have guessed the depths of unhappiness that was possible when she first heard of Jefferson's idea that happiness lived in the pursuit of it, not in the achievement thereof.

"Mrs. Arthur. If you'll take baby Yale out of the wagon," Templeton said, dipping his hat, "I'll be sure to let Katherine and Tommy know their father has returned. Frank. Is. Back."

"You do that!" Frank said. A grin swallowed up his face, as though he wasn't cognizant of the entire year's worth of sad events.

Jeanie lifted Yale from the wagon without the baby making a stir in the least. She waited for Frank to ask to see Yale, the baby he would have thought was his with Jeanie, but he never did.

She hooked the two half-filled berry buckets in the crook of one arm and headed to the wagon where she waited for Frank to greet Katherine and Tommy. In the wagon seat she was rigid with anger, catatonic with paralyzing rage that Frank would return, acting as though he loved her when she knew for sure he'd planned to return and reunite with Ruthie. He must not have stopped there to find her missing yet. But why would he come to Jeanie first?

Jeanie didn't know how to play this hand so she didn't. She sat silently, feeling a fresh wash of pain splash over her spirit, drenching her with the same bluish-blackness that Frank seemed to have battled his entire life. And she pulled Yale closer to her chest, feeling comfort in the baby that was not of her flesh one bit.

Two weeks passed, then three. Jeanie had tried to get along with Frank, but she couldn't bear the sight of him. He grew increasingly irritated as the time passed. Had Jeanie not known the secret he shared with Ruthie, she might have just supposed it was his ordinary mood swing. But she knew what it was. His loss of Ruthie, his one true love.

"Frank, I need some water. The kids didn't even wash up this morning and they're going to get sick from filth." Jeanie said at the stove.

"Well, I can't get it." He rolled over in bed, facing the wall.

"You know what Frank? You have a family to support. You love strutting your maleness all over the prairie when it suits you, when you want to lay your claim over me, yet you do none of the work associated with the claim. If you're my master, then do your end of the work, my king."

Frank flew from the bed, his eyes circling in their sockets. "I can't help it Jeanie. There's nothing I can do that pleases you. I'm never good enough, fast enough, smart enough, follow-through enough. You are impossible to please."

"Oh, so that's it? That explains it."

"Explains what?"

"Why you selected Ruthie of all people."

"I'm having a hard enough time."

"Hard enough time with what?"

"Nothing."

"Could it be that you selected Ruthie because she was so much less than me and thereby you could be her king? She would forever be indebted to the mesmerizing Frank G. Arthur and therefore sing your praises and yank your, your..." Jeanie flung her hand in the direction of Frank's crotch.

"You can't even say the word and you certainly wouldn't suck on it either. Ruthie understood everything there is to know about a man, how to be a woman, how to chase away my dull feelings, to allow her man the room to take care of her. You have no idea how to be a woman. She was nothing compared to you in many ways, but in other ways she was *everything* compared to you."

Frank curled up and began to weep, his body jerking with sobs he never cried for James.

Jeanie stalked over to the bed, hands on hips, screaming at him. "You never cried for the son you lost, the one whose death you caused! You're womanizing and opium eating. *You're* the reason our son is gone forever, yet you never cried for that. It's the loss of precious, ugly Ruthie that brings you to tears. You are Satan!"

Frank rolled over and sat up. "You don't even believe in God, never mind Satan himself."

"Yet. Here. He. Lies." Jeanie threw her hand in his direction with each word.

"You can't live without me. Like it or not."

"You watch me." Jeanie felt as though she was melting inside, as though she wasn't sure she should say the words because she wouldn't take them back once they were out there flying around.

"You think you'd be better off without me? The children, too?"

Jeanie swallowed, her throat swelling around the word. She thought she shouldn't say it because she wasn't so sure the world would let her be better off if she let Frank go.

"Yes."

"Well, then I'm out of here. I'll stop in Yankton before heading to Seattle, and file papers. You can sign them there at your leisure. This marriage is over, Jeanie Arthur. You now, officially, have nothing. You are nothing. Just like me."

Frank left the dugout, yanking his coat from the first carved chair he'd made when they arrived, overturning it. Without a glance back he swiped his hat from a peg and strode to the wagon. Jeanie shuddered, the iron weight of what she'd just done crushing her. She felt panic swell and ran out of the dugout. She watched him head to the ramshackle barn, looking for his tell-tale sign that he wasn't sure of his actions—the way he tapped his leg when he was nervous. But it wasn't there, nothing. He was sure of his decision to leave, he had just needed Jeanie's guts to make it happen.

Like everything else in their lives, she had to make it happen or it didn't.

"Mama?" Katherine and Templeton came over the side of the hill.

Jeanie wiped her eyes and righted her breathing. "Yes, Katherine, Mr. Templeton. I uh, I'm just making a little...tea, I'm having tea. Would you like some?"

Katherine shook her head, eyes vacant of expression. Jeanie didn't know if they heard the argument. What could they know?

"Katherine what is it?"

"Father left. He just said you divorced him. That you chose pride over your family. Over us. That we could now count our address as six Hell's half-acre. All because he wasn't good enough for you, that he could never be what you wanted him to be."

Jeanie covered her mouth. "He is mistaken. He doesn't..."

"Mama, you didn't send him away. Did you? He says we won't survive."

Jeanie walked toward the dugout, headed to the cook-stove and busied herself preparing tea.

Katherine stood beside her, Templeton inside the door. "I didn't do anything wrong, Katherine. I'm preserving our family, not destroying it."

"If you made Father leave, allowed him to divorce you, then it was you. All you. You can't support us. Even with the Zurchenko's help. They can't keep giving us stuff."

"I thought you were a women's rights devotee, my darling Katherine. We'll live in Yankton. I can write, sew, do whatever it takes, but we won't suffer because your father left. You were right what you said that day of the storm. I've been doing it all along as it is."

"You've lost your mind, Mother, just like the Hunts said, you've crossed the line from grieving mother to insane."

Jeanie spun around. "Is *that* what the Hunts said? The drug addicted minister and her family who fled when things got tough?

337

Those Hunts? Well, let's just say their opinion counts for nothing in this house."

"Well, mine isn't nothing and we can't do this, Mama, I want to stay here and we need Father. I'm going to get him. I am!" Katherine flew from the dugout, leapt into Templeton's wagon and tore into the horizon.

"Well, it appears I have nothing, Templeton, and now my daughter stole your wagon, so how about some tea?"

Templeton's face dragged about down to his boots. He sat in the rocker and Jeanie handed him a cup of tea. He sipped it, not speaking.

"I have to leave the prairie, Jeanie. Just for five months or so."

Jeanie felt a stab in her chest. She hadn't realized how much she'd built a dependency on the idea that Templeton would be around to help her with her husbandless family—her very own air castle.

"My mother is ill, my brother and father, too," Templeton said, "I'm stopping in Yankton first for provisions, and then I'm going to Boston to help my family."

Jeanie straightened in her chair, suddenly finding the backbone that had been hers for most of her life. "Do you love me, Mr. Templeton?"

"Yes."

"Then stay."

"I have to go to my family. It'll only be for five months, I will return as soon—"

"Don't bother." Jeanie stood and crossed her arms over her chest.

Templeton stood, his gaze barely meeting Jeanie's.

Jeanie shook her finger at him. "You see, you simply adored the opportunity to dream of me as your love. The reality of me as your love is not so precious is it?"

"That's not it."

"Yes, well, we both know it is. So go on. I'll have Katherine drop the wagon over your way and have a good trip. Good thoughts and luck to your loved ones."

"I'm coming back." Templeton stood and yanked Jeanie into his body, smashing the air out of her. *"I'm coming back for you."*

Jeanie sniffled in his arms, letting the smell of him sit with her one last time.

He let her go, his eyes filled with the tears she'd thought she'd seen a few weeks earlier.

Jeanie smoothed back her hair then her skirts. "Well, go on."

"I love you. You are in my heart."

"Well, I'm tired. I have no room inside my heart for you. There was a time when my weary heart would have liked to rest on the love you claim to want to give me. But now, it's full of ugliness and in the little loving spot that's left, there is vacancy only for my children. You are with me, I won't deny that, but I hold you outside my heart. And that is no place for love to grow."

"I don't believe it. It's just circumstances."

"Isn't it always."

Templeton shook his head.

"Go on," Jeanie said raising her chin toward the door. She silently begged him to stay. She knew if he left he'd never return. She could never risk leaving for a man who wouldn't stay for her. Not after what she'd learned from being married to Frank.

Jeanie didn't move, wanting with all her being for him to stay, to give her a plan of action, to show he wanted her for real, that a divorce meant nothing to him, that he loved her in a way that mattered, the kind that meant follow-through and support, the kind that would be there sixty years later. But she wouldn't beg him, tell him what to say or how to say it, what to do or how to show that he meant what he said.

Templeton backed out of the dugout, his eyes finally smiling a bit, finally his mouth lifted in that way that charmed her so much a year before. "I'll be back."

"I dare you."

And finally Templeton did disappear. Jeanie fought the urge to rush out the door and chase him, yell for him, fall to his feet, begging for his love. She would never do that again. She did, however crumble to the floor, wracked with renewed loss, wondering what she'd done in life to deserve so much pain in such a short amount of time.

Jeanie had been impulsive in love. Once in her life, back when she eloped with Frank G. Arthur. Perhaps had she not had the year in Darlington Township, Dakota Territory, she might have retained some of that impetuousness. But with the loss of so much materially and emotionally on that land of gritty, inhospitable sandy plains, she had nothing left to give to impulse.

She loved Templeton, in a quiet, calm way she'd never felt for Frank, yet she couldn't risk anything for Templeton. Besides, legally she was still married. It would be some feat to secure a divorce, certainly not an endeavor manageable in one short month.

Jeanie told herself that if after he settled his ailing family, if he returned to join her back in Yankton or perhaps Des Moines she would consider keeping his company. But she would not allow him to show up to claim her like 160 acres of land, to be used up and plowed over, like Frank had seen fit to do.

What was left of the Arthur family deserted the prairie in early summer of 1888. They went to Yankton where they met with relative prosperity as Jeanie sewed for a prominent widow, offering the lady of the house decorating and homemaking advice much to her delight. The widow also employed Tommy and Katherine and allowed them all to stay on their third floor, including baby Yale, who was quiet, almost too quiet. Jeanie often wondered if Ruthie's use of opium with Frank left the baby "not right."

Templeton had a room in the Regency Hotel as he delayed his trip to Boston to fight a bout with pneumonia. Jeanie and the kids saw him at the library as he grew stronger and Jeanie quietly hoped he might never make his trip to Boston.

She felt periodic flurries of contentment at having steady work in a good woman's home with intermittent contact with Mr. Templeton. But that was short-lived. Templeton was finally putting together his supplies to leave as Jeanie's employer died just months after the Arthur's arrival. She and the children were left destitute as the widow had been the only one in the small town capable of hiring the entire family. It was just days after the widow died that the Arthurs were told to evacuate the home. A week later they had run out of money and the only choice left to Jeanie, in order to save her family, was to board Tommy and Katherine out to strangers.

Amputating limbs wouldn't have been more painful, but there was no other choice for Jeanie. With thoughts of James never far from mind, she could only trust that putting each child into what seemed like respectable homes to earn their keep was the best thing to do for her family until Jeanie could construct a plan to bring them all back together. Jeanie figured it would only be a month of separation. Just a month to find another city, maybe even Des Moines, where they could all live together while Jeanie worked and the children attended school. That was the plan and for Jeanie that should have been enough to make it happen.

Jeanie vowed to make her children's lives good. She took a private oath not to sully Frank's reputation in the eyes of her children. She knew how damaging it was to discover one's father was weak and lacked integrity. She would protect them from the knowledge that their father had chosen Ruthie and her unborn baby over them. Even if it meant a few weeks of discomfort, a short time apart, Jeanie thought in the end it would be best for them to strike out on their own.

That last time she saw Templeton at the hotel she had almost given in. Their explosive argument had slammed into heavy silence, the quiet daring each to make the next move.

Had Templeton stood in front of her one more second, begging her to join him in Boston, Jeanie thought she might have weakened enough to leave with him. But she couldn't get rid of the certainty that had *he* looked deeper into her soul, to where the truth of what she felt for him lived, *he* would have not been able to leave her. She could not gamble on another man. Not ever. Not after choosing so poorly the first time. A man would have to gamble on her. And as Templeton left that day, she knew in the thinning marrow of her bones that he had declined the bet.

Her future had been mapped and she had no choice but to follow its path.

1888
Yankton

Katherine squeezed her eyes shut, trying to block out the argument she was overhearing. She was hidden away, under the bed in the hotel room. Her mother and Templeton shouted over one another. Finally over his pneumonia, he was on his way to Boston. He seemed so excited with the news, to return to his maternal home.

But Katherine's mother was not pleased. From under the bed, Katherine watched Jeanie's feet pace across the floor, stopping at the window then turning, traipsing back to Mr. Templeton. Their boots nose to nose.

"I will not allow myself to be treated like cattle, not *ever* again. My heart is through resting on the love of another as there is no lasting trust in the world except that which lives between mother and child."

"I can provide. I want you in Boston. Or wait for me here. I will return." Templeton said.

"I've heard that song and dance, Mr. Templeton. And all I've got to show for the exercise is bloodied, blistered feet. Frank is gone, but that does not mean I'm free to leave."

Silence fell. Katherine edged under the bed, moving to where she could see what was taking up all the quiet.

Katherine could hear her pulse in her ears. She began to sweat as she dug her fingers into the braided rug under her body. What was Templeton suggesting? They had a father to provide for them. One who Jeanie had promised would return. She had told them, he was only grieving for his first-born, their wonderful James, that Frank would return. But, Katherine could hear the cold strength in Jeanie's words. Heavy gloom fell over Katherine and she began to shudder, afraid her mother would discover her hiding spot.

As Jeanie and Templeton stood face to face, Katherine felt the realization that her father would never return, settle in. It didn't matter that she didn't fully grasp this discussion between her mother and Templeton, what mattered was that she knew from the depths of her being that her father was not coming back and they were on their own.

"I promise to return," Templeton said.

I want my father to return! Katherine thought.

Katherine watched Jeanie's feet shift to the opposite wall then move across the floor.

"Time will be the judge of that," Jeanie said, barely above a whisper. "I am loyal to my children. We are safer here than anywhere and I won't simply gallivant around the country to please a man. I will stay right here and craft the life that was meant for me. I will make this work."

Katherine almost crawled from under the bed to comfort her mother, but as the conversation went on, her mind had turned off, knowing one thing—her mother swore she would take care of her children. She couldn't listen to any more talk. She covered her ears and tried to convince herself that her mother would not let any harm come to them. That her mother, the Jeanie she'd known and loved for her entire life, was much too strong to let anything else come between them.

Katherine stood outside the hotel, her clothing wrapped in a blanket, sitting at her feet. Tommy paced back and forth, muttering Bible verses and Jeanie cooed at baby Yale, trying to get her to smile.

Katherine's mouth felt dry like dirt without enough saliva to moisten the grainy earthy sensation. Her stomach ached. She wrapped herself up in her arms.

"Please, Mama, we'll be good, we'll do anything to earn money, anything, but please don't send me with strangers. I can't do it. I need you, I need you. Please, Mama."

"Just read the Word," Tommy said as he paced by. "The Lord is here for you if you let Him into your empty soul."

Jeanie smacked the back of Tommy's head as he paced by, "That's enough young man. That kind of talk is hurtful not helpful."

"As though boarding us out is helpful?" Katherine's mouth was wide and misshapen with her pain. "You will kill me Mama. Please, you are strong, there is nothing you can't do, I know you don't want to do this. I know how much you love your children. I know you want us with you." Katherine had heard her mother swear she loved her children more than anything in the world. Hadn't she said that to Templeton?

Jeanie pulled Katherine into her side, kissing the top of her head. "That is all true. It will only be for two weeks. I promise. Until I can find a benefactor to take us all. You're right. I'm strong. Don't ever forget that. I will do right by you. I promise. But more important than that is that *you* are strong. There is nothing you can't do. You are indomitable. You are Katherine the Great. Simply follow the woman of the house's rules and you'll do well and within no time, a flash of time, I'll be on your doorstep, bringing us back together. Tommy will be two doors down from you."

"Where will you and Yale be?" Katherine sobbed. She coughed in between sobs, staring up into her mother's upturned face.

"I don't know that yet, but we'll be okay. I promise." Katherine saw her mother's eyes fill with tears as she looked up and looked beyond them. Katherine turned her head then latched onto her mother's waist at the sight of a proper, but stern, pinched woman coming their way. She was attended by a burly man with wiry hair that shot out from under his hat and a glint in his eye when he made eye contact with Katherine that made her turn and vomit.

"She's not a sickly child is she?" the woman said once she reached them.

"Oh, no, no, just a little nervous is all. She's well schooled, mannerly, strong, has common sense."

Katherine wiped her mouth and re-latched onto her mother's side. Jeanie looked down at her. "Now Katherine, it's time for you to go, be grown up. You can do this."

Jeanie tried to pry Katherine's hands away, but Katherine gripped harder, ripping some of her buttons off her blouse, begging her mother to stop. Spit flew from Katherine's mouth as she thought at that moment, she felt what her mother had when James had died, that a piece of her was being torn away.

Katherine thought for sure her mother would see how much she loved her and needed her, that she would break down and stop this transaction from occurring. She knew how much her mother loved her children, how she ached for James, how she'd do anything to keep them together.

The woman tried to pry Katherine from her savoir.

"Her finger?" The woman yanked her hand away from Katherine as though on fire. "Is she malformed in other ways? Retarded?"

"Yes!" Katherine screeched. "I'm malformed in every way. You must find another girl who suits your needs. I cannot possibly attend you properly with a hand like this!" Katherine shoved her hand into the woman's face. The woman drew back, causing her hat to fly off. She ran for it as the wind took it away.

Katherine grasped her mother around the waist, her fingers laced together like vice-grips, hoping the woman might be disgusted with her.

"She'll do just fine. She's more than pleasing to the eye everywhere else." The master of the house stood over Jeanie and Katherine. Katherine saw fear take her mother's expression and she knew Jeanie would never let her go. Never.

"If you harm one hair on her body," Jeanie said through gritted teeth. "I will kill you with my own hands." Jeanie nodded. The man grimaced. Katherine felt a flicker of relief. Her mother would keep them together. Always.

So, Katherine couldn't form coherent thoughts when her mother nodded at the master of the home to which Katherine would be employed, satisfied she wouldn't be harmed. Katherine's heart folded in on itself, her blood racing through her head, blocking out the words the adults were saying, making her dizzy. Katherine would not go. She held her mother so tight her nails dug into her own skin, little knives making it perfectly clear what was happening.

The man gripped Katherine's wrists, tearing her off her mother. Katherine pulled backward, digging her heels into the dirt. Finally he simply lifted her like a sack of feed and flung her over his shoulder, carrying her away. Katherine lifted her torso off the man's shoulder, reaching out for her mother, screaming.

The chilling screams finally caused Tommy to stop pacing and praying. Everyone in hearing distance stopped. They watched, mouths dropped open as Katherine's world was ripped apart. And the one person who could have stopped it stood there and did nothing. Katherine saw her mother's face, quivering, as she bowed her head into her hands and her cries met Katherine's over the muddy street. Katherine was sure, seeing her mother's pain, that she would rescue her after just hours. She would just have to survive for the shortest time as Jeanie Arthur was not the type to let a child go.

"Katherine the Great!" Jeanie suddenly lifted her face from her hands and yelled, her voice lilting over the space that was growing between them.

"You did this Mama, you buried our family on the prairie with James. You murdered our family when you sent Father away! Muuurrrrderrrr!"

It was there that a two-week plan morphed into years, never seeing the Arthurs reunited under the same roof. Again and again, Jeanie stopped by the home in which Katherine worked, promising the next week they would be together. That Yale was sick and Jeanie couldn't find work. That the woman she was working for shorted her. There was an excuse every time. But, it only took a few more disappointments for Katherine to stop feeling anything but resentment for her mother. How could the woman who could do anything as far as Katherine was concerned choose to do nothing? That was unforgivable.

And for Katherine, the only spot in her heart softened to the world at all was inhabited by Aleksey Zurchenko and it didn't take long before it was he who rescued her from her lonely life, filling her with all the love her mother couldn't.

Chapter 23

1905
Des Moines

Dearest brother Tommy,

You must come now. I hope the swamps of Texas haven't swallowed
you, that you are pieced whole and able to make this trip. No one
understands more than I that our mother isn't wonderful. I know you
think she did not marry for love—she spoiled one man's life and the other
left her…what a dreadful thing it must be to marry without love, what
a life of misery must surely follow. It did follow for Mother and Father,
but circumstances may have been different than we suspected as children.
It is clear that death is less objectionable than marital separation, but it
is with this letter I say that Mama is at death's door. Her cancer is real
and I'm left to care for her and find a proper home for Yale thereafter.
Though being in the same room with Mama turns my blood acrid, I can't
deny I hate to see her pained this way. You must find it in your minister's
heart and come or you will never forgive yourself. Please.

Your adoring sister,
Katherine

Katherine sat cross-legged on her mother's sick bed with yellowed letters littered over her lap, crisp recently written ones from Templeton over those. Yale was stretched long against Jeanie. Both were sleeping on their backs, heads cocked to the same side at the same angle.

So much had changed for Katherine, she had learned so much, but she still felt agonizing grit was lodged in her heart, like there was no way to fully carve it out and forgive the way she wanted to. She dropped her face into her hands. There was much she still wanted to know. Their Yale? How had the babies been switched? Why?

"I couldn't let your father stay."

Katherine's head snapped toward Jeanie who was now staring at her.

"What?" Katherine said. She straightened her posture when her mother's papery hand wrapped around her wrist with a weakened grip.

"You must be wondering why," Jeanie whispered. The tendons in her neck strained with every word.

Katherine couldn't move.

"It was because of James. Frank sent him into the blizzard to lie for him. James was trying to protect *me* and cover for his Father when he died...I never wanted you to know that. I thought a fate of knowing your father failed in so many ways was the worst kind of blow for a child."

"And Yale?" Katherine's voice was thin as spring wind.

Jeanie's eyes widened. "I..." Her voice cracked, breaking into a cough, choking her.

Katherine flew off the bed and poured fresh water into a glass. She rushed back to Jeanie and held her up from behind, slowly dripping water into her mouth a sip at a time, practically the same way they had fed baby Yale when she was too small to nurse.

Katherine slid onto the bed, behind her mother, cradling her between life and death, between their former roles of mother and daughter. Her mother's bird-like bones against Katherine's chest filled her with sadness, the bitterness crumbling away.

"This bun must give you a headache," Katherine said to her mother, who had fallen asleep. She loosened Jeanie's hair and fluffed it at her scalp as the rest of it fell in a wave. Yale stirred and woke, and reached for a brush. She took sections of her mother's soft locks and brushed tenderly, gently laying each finished section around her shoulders while Katherine put herself in her mother's shoes—those curled black boots.

She imagined one of her daughters or sons dying, she pictured it being Aleksey's fault. Could she live with him? She didn't have that answer. Nor did she have every answer she wanted about that year on the prairie. Though, she thought, perhaps she was finding that she had every answer she needed.

Yale finished brushing her mother's hair, picked up one of Templeton's letters and began to read. One by one, she read them starting back from 1888. Although Katherine knew she had chores to attend, listening to the letters riveted her, made it impossible to do anything but absorb Yale's sweet voice as the letters answered many of the questions Jeanie couldn't.

"This is cozy," a voice came from the hall.

Katherine jumped and turned to the doorway. Tommy stood there, tapping his leg, shifting his weight. Katherine lifted a photo from under one of the letters still sprawled over the bed, holding it up in the air. "My God, you are Father, standing there, the exact image of him seventeen years ago."

"You call that a greeting? How about a hug for your old brother?"

Katherine nodded and slipped out from under the stacks of letters, trying not to disturb her mother. She laid her back on the pillows and nestled the quilt around her chin to keep her warm.

Katherine stretched her arms out to her Tommy and they collapsed into a hug that felt as good as anything Katherine ever experienced. As though the presence of Tommy took her home. They pulled apart.

"Now don't cry, dearest Katherine. I'm here aren't I?"

Katherine wiped her tears away with her ring finger, nodding. Tommy's gaze went to her missing pinky-finger then back to Katherine. She shrugged. "Oh, I've put that worry to rest, Tommy. Who really uses their pinky-finger anyhow, right?" She gave him a playful nudge in the shoulder.

"Well, as a matter of fact, I certainly did employ my pinky-finger just the other day when I lost my toe-hold on a cold mountainside and—"

"Tommy. Don't you think you should say hello to your Mama?"

Katherine and Tommy were startled at their mother's voice. Katherine hadn't heard it so strong in weeks. Tommy hadn't heard it in years.

Tommy stepped forward, removed his hat and finally moved toward Yale and Jeanie. Yale was stretching, smiling at her brother. He grinned and went to Yale, hugged her then kissed his mother's cheek.

"That's it? I'm dying and all I get is a little peck on the cheek? My darling son." Jeanie's lips curled up, but never broke into a full smile.

Katherine felt tension between her brother and mother as though it were fast drying plaster that adhered to her skin pulling at it while sinking into her pores. She hadn't had the opportunity to fill her brother in on what she'd remembered and found out about her parents and Yale nor had she had the chance to ask her mother more questions, to ask her why she lied to her about Yale, why she didn't come back for her, ever?

Still, Katherine found pity for her mother, seeing her weakened, reading those letters. And seeing Tommy treat Jeanie coldly, she'd finally found some warmth for the mother she'd grown to hate.

"Now, Mama, now, I'm sure Tommy is simply spent from climbing down off his mountain and finding you in this condition. Allow me to feed him and then you can have him back in better humor."

"Pfft," Jeanie said. "I could be still and cold by then, you know."

"Just a few minutes, Mama. That's it."

"I'm hungry, too," Yale said.

"Oh fine, there, everyone go on ahead, enjoy your meals." Jeanie sunk into the bed, turning toward the window, pulling the quilts over her head.

"Mama, just a minute and we'll be back. We won't throw a party in there. I'll send in the children to sit with you while we get Tommy settled. If you're up to it, we can bring you to the kitchen. Aleksey can carry you."

"Pfft. See what bearing and raising children gets you," Jeanie said.

Tommy chortled at the ceiling.

Katherine felt the hardened tension crack, flying from her skin in great chunks. She couldn't hold her temper.

She balled her fists at her sides. "I won't have this argument in my home. My home. I'm in charge and we won't entertain incivility, especially at a time like this. Tommy, you find some respect and *Mama*, we're not dying people. I can see from your rising spirit that we'll have you for many a week, month or year."

"Pfft," Jeanie said.

"Bathroom. I need the bathroom," Yale said. Katherine led her from the room and Tommy followed, pulling the door shut.

In the white tiled kitchen, Tommy sat at the pine table, digging his thumbnail through a worn groove while his nieces, nephews, and Yale gathered to hear tales of his adventures—bona fide air castle building—he called it. Katherine wiped the final dish dry and shooed them out of the kitchen to sit with their grandmother and get ready for bed.

Katherine sat at the table across from her brother. The silence was thick and scratchy, as until that moment, Tommy hadn't stopped talking. His yammering had been soothing to Katherine's prickly worries.

"You're so much like Father," Katherine said.

"Is that an insult?"

"Should it be an insult?"

Tommy pulled a knife from his pocket and used it to push his cuticles.

"Well, I don't know. I've done my best not to contemplate our family life as I plow through my own and tend my flock."

"Don't talk like that. You sound affected."

"Let's not get judgmental about one's life."

Katherine nodded.

"What *aren't* you telling me?"

Katherine's mouth dried like batting in an old blanket. She didn't know where to start.

"It seems that perhaps we misjudged our mother and what she had to deal with that year."

Tommy stopped with the knife, closed it, and tossed it on the tabletop. "Meaning what? That driving our father from our lives and then turning down the proposal of the one man who might be able to overlook her inability to soothe a man's constitution properly, that boarding us out like farm animals, is forgivable, that there might be a solid reason for such choices?"

"Think of all the changes she went through that year. In Des Moines she was a *writer*, wealthy, pampered...and then we lost it all...how hard that must have been for her. That was just the beginning. Yet she took it all on and did a good job until..."

"Right. *Until*," Tommy said.

"Where's all that Lord and Bible stuff you were so fond of *until* apparently today? It didn't happen like *that*."

"Like what?"

Katherine took his pocketknife, opening and closing it. He watched her, but Katherine had no idea what thoughts he entertained.

She leaned forward. "Listen, every time I think of the Millers, the years I spent in that house with the pitiful weak wife and subhuman husband…the desperation I felt trying to service each of them in utterly different ways, the utter loss at knowing our mother was down the street, protecting Yale, who should have been institutionalized by the age of three, all of that…I *know* what anger and blame are, what they do to people. But she's dying. Strong as she appears at this moment…" Katherine rubbed her face with both hands.

"My sweet sister. There's a difference between respecting and loving your parents. You've done the former and done it well. I couldn't have lived in the same town with her, inviting her to functions, acting as though what happened to us was proper. You don't have to beat yourself with her pending death. We don't have to say we forgive her. Well, maybe I should say it, but you've already said as much with your actions over the years."

"No, I haven't. I hate that woman. I hate her and that's wrong. Even now, making a case for her, I can feel the hate, less of it, but it's still there, mixed with crusty old love. In my head I know the story—"

"What story?"

Katherine took a deep breath and then pieced together most of what she'd learned over the last weeks regarding their family for Tommy, who listened intently.

"It's the letters from Templeton that really…"

"What letters from Templeton? I thought the only letters she cared for were those she burned—the engagement letters between her and father."

"I rescued half those letters before we left the prairie. She started to burn them, some from Father, and then got distracted and I pulled the others off. But Templeton wrote to her for the last seventeen years. If not for those letters, I might not know everything that I do."

"Katherine," Tommy said, "it's easy to love from afar. Notice Templeton didn't call our mother to him in Boston or come back once she said no. He knew better than to wrap his life in her cold arms."

"Stop it! You are a Presbyterian minister, for Pete's sakes."

"Irrelevant to my experience with my mother. You saw how she treated Father. No wonder he sought warmth—"

"Stop it, Tommy! Father is not the hero you make him out to be. I can only hope that you don't see your marriage—"

"My marriage is just fine, thank you. My wife understands her role in the world. And our mother should have done better by us. Maybe Father was weak, but that doesn't give her the right to—"

"Tommy. It wasn't the cheating that did their marriage in, it was the fact that he put opium and his lover over his family and the result was James' death."

"Sweet James. Doesn't the cloud of James remain forever over our heads?"

"Stop it. Imagine that. Imagine your firstborn taken from you in that gruesome way, due to the ridiculousness of your husband. The father of that boy. Imagine that! He was our brother. How can you claim the Lord and all his trappings but have nothing in generosity for your family?"

"Well, it sounds as if you've more than forgiven our mother, Katherine. I hear it in your voice, your words, your defense of her."

Katherine stood. She shook with fear, sadness, knowing he was right. In some way she'd forgiven her mother, though Tommy was wrong about her actions over the years being proof. She operated with resentment, not love.

Tommy shook his head, smirking. Clearly he hadn't bought into what Katherine had presented so far. He was not ready to find compassion for his mother. Katherine felt the need to be more convincing.

"You're right, I have begun to see her differently," she said. "It was the letters. If I hadn't read Templeton's letters. If I hadn't read that *last* letter, I might never have forgiven her."

Tommy narrowed his eyes at Katherine. "What? What *last* letter?"

Katherine sat back down took his hand in hers, his calluses pricking her fingers. She shrugged. How much should she reveal?

"Just spill it," Tommy said. "After all this time, just say it."

"Father left us. He intended to replace Mama with Ruthie. He wrote it in a letter to her. Templeton's letters confirm the information as well. Templeton's letters verify Father was partly responsible for James' death. But that last one *from* Father. It was clear. He gave us up for Ruthie and all the while we thought Mama gave us away. It wasn't her. She tried to hide his weakness from us and in turn made herself into the rotten one. It wasn't her fault. She loved us more than anything. She did her best. I believe that now."

Tommy pulled his hand from Katherine's and pushed it through his hair. "Wait. Ruthie died on the way to her aunt and uncle's. That had nothing to do with Father. If anything I'd say he had an interest in Lutie, not Ruthie, if I recall correctly."

Katherine's eyes began to sting. She wiped away a tear. She was about to tell Tommy that she thought Yale, that she *knew* Yale, the one in the bedroom with their mother was the daughter of Frank and Ruthie. But, she hadn't had a chance to thread together how that could have happened.

Ruthie *was* supposedly on that train to Canada. Perhaps she boarded it. None of them ever knew she was pregnant. But Frank's letter was so clear. Her father stated firmly, he was leaving Jeanie and the kids for Ruthie and her unborn baby.

"Well?" Tommy threw his hands in the air, his face folded in angry creases. And in that moment Katherine decided it was better to keep Jeanie's final secret like a precious heirloom. She would not humiliate their mother by allowing Tommy to accuse Jeanie of somehow raising a child that was not hers—to question her actions further. She would honor her mother that way. And in doing so Katherine hoped it might serve to mend the broken fence of their once stalwart relationship.

Katherine stiffened, her jaw clenched as she turned away from her brother, unable to look him in the eye anymore. Tommy did not want to know the whole truth. He had too much invested in his anger. So when he still refused to believe their mother had entertained goodness in all her bad decisions, Katherine reiterated everything she knew, face in hands, peering through her web of fingers at the table. She made her case, but left out that one small sliver of information. Yale. Tommy remained unconvinced.

In his opposition, Katherine was suddenly struck by a sensation of Grace. Her posture softened and she lowered her hands and looked into her brother's face again. She imagined he preached about Grace on a regular basis, but clearly did not know it by experience.

"Listen Tommy," she cupped his cheek. He drew back then relaxed into her gesture, putting his hand over hers. "Father's letter was clear, but that's just half the matter. Still, stung by our mother's actions as I am, I understand how James' death left her beaten, unable to act as she would have before then. The way she was before the storm. That changed everything. If only he hadn't died, I believe she might have been totally different. And, when she dies I'm going to take in Yale."

"After what she did to us?"

Katherine took her hand from Tommy's face and put it in her lap.

"Because of all that, actually. I've been cruel. My upset over Mama. It colored everything, all my interactions with Yale. I've been unfair. I can't shake the ugly feeling still inside me for Mama. Even though I understand intellectually. But, I've been…What she did for us, up until she boarded us. It's just, well, I can't judge her anymore." A loud crash from upstairs made Katherine get up from the table and run toward the commotion.

Yale was in her mother's room, pulling her up and down in the bed, crying.

Katherine went to the other side of the bed. "What is it?"

"She threw up," Yale said. "She says her heart hurts."

Katherine put her head on her mother's chest listening for heartbeats. She felt Jeanie's neck. Nothing.

"No! No! Mama! Please, let me tell you I'm sorry. I'm sorry. I forgive you. I, I, I see how you were left without choices, all that you had and in one year to lose it all. I'm so sorry."

Katherine yanked on her mother's body. She groaned with fresh pain, intermingled with the old. "Please don't die, Mama, please let me say I forgive you."

Katherine bent over her mother, sobbing, begging her to stay alive, to give them the time they needed to forgive each other. Yale simply lay beside Jeanie, nestled up to her, holding her hand.

"Now shush, my sister Katherine." Yale's voice was small. "Now you know we're not crying people. Mama always said, you know."

And as Yale spoke those words, Jeanie moved. Her frail hand flailed upward. Katherine grabbed it and clutched it to her chest. She kissed her mother's fingers, begging her to stay strong.

And then there it was.

Katherine felt it.

Clear as a summer prairie sky on a rare windless day. The pressure was delicate, but distinct.

Three squeezes.

Katherine's gaze jerked to their clenched hands, to her mother's face then back to their hands.

She held her breath and returned the silent I love you to her mother.

She closed her eyes, hoping for more.

Nothing came except Jeanie's labored breath that seemed to grasp for the last of her life.

Katherine had felt her mother squeeze her hand as sure as she felt her own dizzying heartbeat rail against her ribcage. Her mother was aware. She had let Katherine know that.

Now Katherine needed to tell Jeanie, to help her find the quiet she needed—the kind of stillness that came with forgiveness, the sort that arrived upon knowing you were understood.

"Mama," Katherine put her lips to Jeanie's ear. "I know you did your best. You were my everything. I will hold your secret with me forever."

Katherine pulled back from Jeanie. She wished so much she could ask how it was one Yale was exchanged for another. She wanted years back, more time to talk with her mother like they had so long ago. But, right then, all Katherine needed was to discern whether Jeanie heard anything she said at all.

"Mama? Did you hear?"

Jeanie turned her face up to Katherine and, though her eyes were closed, her mouth turned up in what looked like a small smile. She seemed to nod. Katherine swore she did and that was her only comfort—knowing her mother heard her forgiveness, that Jeanie felt the redemption in her fragile soul as it left her body bound for final, deserved peace.

Katherine couldn't offer Yale much comfort as she sobbed on into the night, wracked with mashed emotions, wishing everything about their lives could have been reversed seventeen years, just so she could redo it all for her mother. To save her mother the way she always trusted Jeanie could save her.

Aleksey rubbed Katherine's back, sitting with her through the night. Tommy stood in the doorway, mumbling prayers, but unable to let the crusty resentment soften in his heart. Katherine stared at her brother—so removed from feeling, from Yale, Aleksey, Katherine and his mother.

Katherine would deal with him later. For those moments, she allowed herself to feel her mother's spirit, she was sure it was still in the room, accepting her forgiveness, pardoning her own stubbornness. She was grateful that somehow, she was not as hardened as her brother. She could grow and forgive.

And, as the sun peeked over the horizon, glowing around the edges of the shades, Katherine realized the pain that built up over the years would not completely pass, but that she was absolutely sure Jeanie had heard Katherine's pleas. And though Katherine didn't have the chance to tell Jeanie of her plan, she was sure Jeanie would be looking down on her, watching as she took in Yale and gave her a home, keeping them together in a way that Jeanie never could.

For that opportunity, Katherine felt lighter, as though darkness had lifted from her soul, selfishness that she'd never really admitted was even there was gone, leaving her with wide open acreage in her heart to devote to a sister she had only begun to get to know. Finally, she could look at her sister and understand her mother a little more. Her mama. Mama. Jeanie Arthur.

The End

Acknowledgments

This book is pure fiction, but was inspired by the long gone lives of my great-great grandparents. As was typical of the time, they logged endless hours writing letters. What's unusual is that so many of them survived. The letters depict the simplicity, love, worries, successes and failures, and hardscrabble lives of a family who lived together well over 100 years ago.

Sadly the real Jeanie and Frank did not live happily ever after, but they left a legacy that still matters to those who know their story.

Besides using family correspondence to inspire the plot and characters in *The Last Letter*, the letters were full of details regarding every day prairie and pioneer life and did much to inform the story happenings.

In addition to my stash of letters, I tapped countless resources that shaped the novel. Most prominent was the nonfiction book "The Children's Blizzard," by David Laskin. His meticulous and beautifully written account of the deadly blizzard allowed for me to time the blizzard in my story and helped shape what the characters might have experienced in such a storm. I did my best to keep my blizzard timeline in line with the real one and if I didn't succeed, it isn't because he didn't give me enough to work with.

Thanks to my dad for ensuring that the desire to write was inescapable.

Thanks to my mother who passed the letters to me and kept bothering me to pay attention to them—without you this story would not exist.

To Lisa Mcshea, without you the novel would not have been written. You read every revision and helped solve every major problem in it. You are my muse. Not in a weird way, though.

To Beth, Jamie, John, their spouses, and my sisters and brothers in-law on Bill's side. You're always good for support and a laugh when I need it most.

To Catherine—it's tremendous to have a writing partner in town! Your feedback is insightful and much needed. To Michelle and Gwen. Thanks for reading drafts of books you don't normally buy! Mary Kay—especially thanks to you for your multiple reads, love of everything historic, and the title!

To my summer friends—being stuck at the pool has an upside—a captive audience who gossip about my characters as though they are real people who just might wander into the grill for a salmon salad at any moment. For your never-ending title suggestions—thank you ladies!

To Critique Group North, Fat Plum, Pennwriters, and Sisters in Crime. The endless stream of enthusiastic support for my work that I find in those groups makes writing easier.

Many thanks to my in-laws who raised a son who sees the value in what I do!

To Jake and Beth—two great kids who think I'm a New York Times bestselling author. It's all the same to you.

Thanks to Jen Bonaroti Condron-Gold and Mike Marlette at MumboJumboLaya. You are both so creative and fun.

For all the work Crystal Patriarche has done to bring attention to *The Last Letter*, thank you!

To Stephanie Elliot, copyeditor extraordinaire! One more read through?

To all those who have shown interest in my work over the years. Thanks to Madhu Wangu, Lisa Ryan, Isabel Beck, Cheryl Sandora, Jeanne Truchel, Kate Shorter, Dave Fleager, Cindy Closkey, Judy Burnett Schneider, Julie Long and many others. Your name may not be here, but I appreciate your support and you know who you are.

Finally, to Bill, my husband, the best.

Resources

I'm forever indebted to the people and organizations responsible for the following sources. Any errors in factual information were my doing and not that of the authors or websites below.

- northern.edu/natsource
- state.sd.us/state/sdsym.htm
- netstate.com/states/symb/flowers
- nature.org
- homepages.dsu.edu
- theflowerexpert.com
- nebraskastudies.org
- sdgfp.info
- persi.heritagequestonline.com
- *Grasshopper Summer, Turner, Ann*. Macmillan Publishing Company, 1989.
- Museumoftheamericanwest.org
- Rootsweb.com
- Shawnature.org
- Plattesd.org
- Members.cox.net/awise130/plains.htm

- Nps.gov
- *History of Charles Mix County*, Peterson & Peterson—Opening and Closing the Lands to Settlement, 1906.
- Geoimages.berkeley.edu
- Plainsfolk.com
- *South Dakota*, Griffith, T.D., Compass American Guides, 2004.
- Infoplease.com
- Frontiers.loc.gov
- *The Prairie Girl's Guide to Life*, Worick, Jennifer. The Taunton Press, 2007

Book Club Guide

1. Why does Kathleen Shoop tell the story from Jeanie's point of view in 1887-1888 and Katherine's point of view in 1905?

2. How does Jeanie's upbringing seem to prepare her for prairie life?

3. What role does James play in the book in terms of decisions Jeanie makes? Do you agree with her response to his death?

4. Consider the decisions Jeanie made throughout the book. How did the era in which she lived influence the path she took?

5. To what degree were Katherine and Jeanie able to find peace in life and in death?

6. How might Katherine and Tommy's lives change now that they know more about their mother's difficult life?

7. To what do you attribute Frank's biggest character flaws? How was he a good man?

8. Why would Jeanie think that her children knowing their father was "a weak man who failed at so much," was worse than them believing she was responsible for the family's struggles?

9. Under what circumstances is it appropriate to board out children? How does your modern perspective on parenting shape your response to the question?

10. How has this book changed your view of pioneer life? How might Lutie and Ruthie fit into your new prairie view?